RICK MOFINA

vengeance road

Published in Great Britain 2011
MIRA Books, Eton House, 18-24 Paradise Road,
Richmond, Surrey, TW9 1SR

ISBN 978 0 7783 0444 9

60-0611

Printed in Great Britain
by Clays Ltd, St Ives plc

This book is for Barbara

I am the man that hath seen affliction
by the rod of his wrath.
He hath led me, and brought me into
darkness, but not into light.
Surely against me is he turned; he turneth
his hand against me all the day.

—*Lamentations 3:1–3*

The evil that men do lives after them;
The good is oft interred with their bones.

—William Shakespeare
Julius Caesar, Act III, Scene ii

1

The taxi crawled along a road that knifed into the night at Buffalo's eastern edge.

Its brakes squeaked as it halted at the fringe of a vast park.

Jolene Peller gazed toward the woods then paid the driver.

"This is where you want to be dropped off?" he asked.

"Yes. Can you kill the meter and wait for me, please?"

"I can't, you're my last fare. Gotta get the cab back."

"Please, I just have to find my friend."

The driver handed her a five in change, nodding to the pathway that twisted into darkness beyond the reach of his headlights.

"You're sure your friend's down there?"

"Yes, I need to get her home. She's going through a rough time."

"It's a beautiful park, but you know what some people do down there at night?"

Jolene knew.

But she was living another life then. If you could call it living.

"Can't you wait a bit?" Jolene asked.

"Not on my time. Gotta get the cab back then start my vacation."

"Please."

"Look, miss, you seem nice. I'll take you back now. I'll give you a break on the fare because it's on my way. But I ain't waitin' while you wander around looking for your problem. Stay or go? What's it going to be?"

Tonight was all Jolene had to do the right thing.

"I have to stay," she said.

The driver gave her a suit-yourself shrug and Jolene got out. The taxi lumbered off, its red taillights disappearing, leaving her alone.

She had to do this.

As she walked along the path, she looked at the familiar twinkle of lights from the big suburban homes on the ridge that ringed the parkland half a mile off. When she found Bernice, they'd walk to a corner store then get a cab to Bernice's apartment. Then Jolene could take another one to the terminal, claim her bags and catch a later bus.

But not before she found Bernice.

Not before she saved her.

And tonight, for one brief moment, she thought she had.

Less than an hour ago they were together in a downtown diner where Jolene had pleaded with her.

"Honey, you've got to stop beating yourself up for things that were never your fault."

Tears rolled down Bernice's face.

"You've got to get yourself clean and finish college."

"It's hard, Jo. So hard."

"I know, but you've got to pull yourself out of the life. If I can do it, you can do it. Promise me, right here, right now, that you won't go out tonight."

"It hurts. I ache. I need something to get me through one more day. I need the money. I'll start after tomorrow."

"No!"

A few people cast sleepy glances at them. Jolene lowered her voice.

"That's a lie you keep telling yourself. Promise me you won't go dating tonight, that you will go home."

"But it hurts."

Jolene seized Bernice's hands, entwined their fingers and squeezed hard.

"You've got to do this, honey. You can't accept this life. Promise me you will go home. Promise me, before I get on my bus and leave town."

"Okay, I promise, Jo."

"Swear."

"I swear, Jo."

Jolene hugged her tight.

But after getting into her taxi and traveling several blocks, Jolene was uncertain. She told the driver to go back so she could check on Bernice.

Sure enough, there she was. At the mouth of a dirty alley, on Niagara, hustling a date. The cab stopped at a light, Jolene gripped her door handle, bracing to jump out and haul Bernice off the street.

But she didn't.

To hell with that girl.

Jolene told the driver to keep going to the terminal. She didn't need this shit. Not now. She was leaving for Florida tonight to build a new life for herself and her little boy. Bernice was an adult, old enough to take care of herself.

Jolene had tried to help.

She really had.

But with each passing block, her guilt grew. Soon the neon blurred. Brushing away her tears, Jolene cursed. She couldn't leave Buffalo tonight with that last image of her friend standing in her memory.

Bernice was an addict. She was sick. She needed help. Jolene was her lifeline.

And tonight, every instinct told Jolene that something was wrong.

The driver muttered when she requested he take her back to the alley. But by the time they'd returned, Bernice and the man she'd been hustling were gone.

Jolene had a bad feeling.

But she knew exactly where they'd be.

Down here, by the creek.

Funny, Jolene thought, during the day this was a middle-class sanctuary where people walked, jogged, even took wedding pictures near the water.

And dreamed.

Most locals, living their happy lives, were unaware that after dark, their park was where hookers took their dates.

It was where you left the real world; where you buried your dignity; where each time you used your body to survive, a piece of you died.

Jolene knew it from her former life; the life she'd escaped when she had Cody. He was her number-one reason for getting out. She'd vowed he would not have a junkie mother selling herself for dope.

He deserved better.

So did Bernice.

She'd been abandoned, abused, but had worked so hard to get into college, only to face a setback that led to drugs, which pushed her here. The tragedy of it was that she was only months away from becoming a certified nurse's aide.

Bernice didn't belong in this life.

Date or no date, Jolene was going to find her and drag her ass home, if it was the last thing she did. Jolene was not afraid to come down here at night. She knew the area and knew how to handle herself.

She had her pepper spray.

She arrived at the dirt parking lot, part of an old earthen service road that bordered the pathway meandering alongside the creek. The lot was empty.

No sign of anybody.

As crickets chirped, Jolene took stock of the area and the treetops silhouetted against a three-quarter moon. She knew the hidden paths and meadows, where drugs and dates were taken and deals completed.

Through a grove, she saw a glint of chrome, like a grille from a vehicle parked in a far-off lot. Possibly a truck. Jolene headed that way. She was nearly there when a scream stopped her cold.

"Nooo! Oh God nooo! Help me!"

The tiny hairs on the back of Jolene's neck stood up.

Bernice!

Her cry came from the darkest section of the forest near the creek. Jolene rushed to it. Branches slapped at her face, tugged at her clothing.

The growth was thicker than she'd remembered. Her eyes had not adjusted; she was running blind over the undulating terrain.

She stepped on nothing and the ground rose to smack her.

She scrambled to her feet and kept going.

There was movement ahead, shadow play in the moonlight.

Noises.

Jolene didn't make a sound as she reached into her bag, her fingers wrapping around her pepper spray.

A blast to the creep's face. A kick in the groin. Jolene had done it before with freaks who'd tried to choke her.

She swallowed hard, ready to fight. Heart pumping, she strained to see what awaited her. Someone was moving; she glimpsed a figure.

Bernice? Was that her face in the ground?

A metallic clank.

Tools? What was going on?

The air exploded next to Jolene with a flap and flutter of a terrified bird screeching to the sky. Startled, Jolene stepped away and fell, crashing through a dried thicket.

She was unhurt.

The air was dead still.

A figure was listening.

Jolene froze.

The figure was thinking.

Her blood thundered in her ears.

A twig snapped. The figure was approaching.

She held her breath.

It was getting closer.

All of her senses were screaming.

Her fingers probed the earth but she was unable to find her bag. Frantic, she clawed the dirt for her pepper spray, a rock, a branch.

Anything.

Her pulse galloped, she didn't breathe. After several agonizing moments, everything subsided. The threat seemed to pass with a sudden gust that rustled the treetops.

Oh, thank God.

Jolene collected herself to resume looking for Bernice, when she was hit square in the face by a blazing light.

Squinting, she raised her hands against the intensity. Someone grunted, a shadow strobed. She ran but fireworks exploded in her head, hurling her into nothingness.

2

What was that?

The next morning, Jack Gannon, a reporter at the *Buffalo Sentinel,* picked up a trace of tension on the paper's emergency scanners.

An array of them chattered at the police desk across the newsroom from where he sat.

Sounds like something's going on in a park, he thought as a burst of coded dispatches echoed in the quiet of the empty metro section.

Not many reporters were in yet.

Gannon was not on cop-desk duty today, but he'd cut his teeth there years ago, chasing fires, murders and everyday tragedies. It left him with the skill to pluck a key piece of data from the chaotic cross talk squawking from metro Buffalo's police, fire and paramedic agencies.

Like a hint of stress in a dispatcher's voice, he thought as he picked out another partial transmission.

Somebody had just called for the medical examiner.

The reporter on scanner duty better know about this.

For the last two weeks the assignment desk had promised to keep Gannon free to chase a tip he'd had on a possible Buffalo link to a woman missing from New England.

He needed a good story.

But this business with the police radios troubled him.

Scanners were the lifeblood of a newspaper. And no reporter worth a damn risked missing something that a competitor might catch, especially in these days of melting advertising and shrinking circulation.

Did anyone know about this call for the medical examiner?

He glanced over his computer monitor toward the police desk at the far side of the newsroom, unable to tell who, if anyone, was listening.

"Jeff!" He called to the news assistant but got no response.

Gannon walked across the newsroom, which took up the north side of the fourteenth floor and looked out to Lake Erie.

The place was empty, a portrait of a dying industry, he thought.

A couple of bored Web-edition editors worked at desks cluttered with notebooks, coffee cups and assorted crap. A bank of flat-screen TV monitors tilted down from the ceiling. The sets were tuned to news channels with the volume turned low.

Gannon saw nothing on any police activity anywhere.

He stopped cold at the cop desk.

"What the hell's this?"

No one was there listening to the radios.

Doesn't anyone give a damn about news anymore? This is how we get beat on stories.

He did duty here last week. This week it was someone else's job.

"Jeff!" he shouted to the news assistant who was proofreading something on his monitor. "Who's on the scanners this morning?"

"Carson. He's up at the Falls. Thought a kid had gone over but turns out he dropped his jacket in the river. Carson blew a tire on his way back here."

"Who's backing him up?" Gannon asked.

"Sharon Langford. I think she went to have coffee with a source."

"Langford? She hates cop stories."

Just then one of the radios carried a transmission from the same dispatcher who'd concerned Gannon.

"...copy... they're rolling to Ellicott and the park now...ten-four."

Calling in the M.E. means you have a death. It could be natural, a jogger suffering a heart attack. It could be accidental, like a drowning.

Or it could be a homicide.

Gannon reached down, tried to lock on the frequency but was too late. He cursed, returned to his desk, kicked into his old crime-reporter mode, called Buffalo PD and pressed for information on Ellicott.

"I got nothing for you," the officer said.

All right. Let's try Cheektowaga.

"We got people there but it's not our lead." The officer refused to elaborate.

How about Amherst PD?

"We've got nothing. Zip."

This thing must have fallen into a jurisdictional gray zone, he thought as he called Ascension Park PD.

"We're supporting out there."

Supporting? He had something.

"What's going on?"

"That's all I know. Did you try ECSO?" said the woman who answered for Ascension Park.

A deputy with the Erie County Sheriff's Office said, "Yeah, we've got people there, but the SP is your best bet."

He called the New York State Police at Clarence Barracks. Trooper Felton answered but put him on hold, thrusting Gannon into Bruce Springsteen's "The River."

Listening to the song, Gannon considered the faded news clippings pinned to low walls around his desk, his best stories, and the dream he'd pretty much buried.

He never made it to New York City.

Here he was, still working in Buffalo.

The line clicked, cutting Springsteen off.

"Sorry," Felton said, "you're calling from the *Sentinel* about Ellicott Creek?"

"Yes. What do you have going on out there?"

"We're investigating the discovery of a body."

"Do you have a homicide?"

"Too soon to say."

"Is it a male or female? Do you have an ID, or an age?"

"Cool your jets there. You're the first to call. Our homicide guys are there, but that's routine. I got nothing more to release yet."

"Who made the find?"

"Buddy, I've got to go."

A body in Ellicott. That was a nice area.

He had to check it out.

He tucked his notebook into the rear pocket of his jeans and grabbed his jacket, glancing at the senior editors in the morning story meeting in the glass-walled room at the far west side.

Likely discussing pensions, rather than stories.

"Jeff, tell the desk I'm heading to Ellicott Creek." He tore a page from his notebook with the location mapped out. "Get a shooter rolling to this spot. We may have a homicide."

And I may have a story.

3

Gannon hurried to the *Sentinel's* parking lot and his car, a used Pontiac Vibe, with a chipped windshield and a dented rear fender.

The paper was downtown near Scott and Washington, not far from the arena where the Sabres played. The fastest way to the scene was the Niagara leg of the New York State Thruway to 90 north.

Wheeling out, with Springsteen in his head, Gannon questioned where he was going with his life. He was thirty-four, single and had spent the last ten years at the *Buffalo Sentinel.*

He looked out at the city, his city.

And there was no escaping it.

Ever since he was a kid, all he wanted to be was a reporter, a reporter in New York City. And it almost happened a while back after he broke a huge story behind a jetliner's crash into Lake Erie.

It earned him a Pulitzer nomination and job offers in Manhattan.

But he didn't win the prize and the offers evaporated.

Now it looked like he'd never get to New York. Maybe this reporter thing wasn't meant to be? Maybe he should do something else?

No way.

Being a reporter was written in his DNA.

One more year.

He remembered the ultimatum he'd given himself at the funeral.

One more year to land a reporting job in New York City.

Or what?

He didn't know, because this stupid dream was all he had. His mother was dead. His father was dead. His sister was—well, she was gone. His ultimatum kept him going. The ultimatum he'd given himself after they'd lowered his parents' caskets into the ground eleven months ago.

Time was running out.

Who knows? Maybe the story he needed was right here, he told himself while navigating his way closer to the scene, near Ellicott Creek.

It was on the fringes of a lush park.

Flashing emergency lights splashed the trees in blood red as he pulled up to a knot of police vehicles.

Uniformed officers were clustered at the tape. Gannon saw nothing beyond them but dense forest, as a stone-faced officer eyed his ID tag then assessed him.

"It's way in there. There's no chance you media maggots are getting any pictures of anything today."

The others snickered.

Gannon shrugged it off. He'd been to more homicides than this asshole. Besides, guys like that never deterred him. If anything, he thought, tapping his notebook to his thigh, they made him better.

All right, pal, if there's a story here, I'm going to find it.

After some thirty minutes of watching detectives in suits, and forensics people in overalls, walk in and out of the forest, Gannon was able to buttonhole a state police investigator with a clipboard heading to his unmarked sedan.

"Hey, Jack Gannon from the *Buffalo Sentinel.* Are you the lead?"

"No, just helping out."

"What do you have?"

Gannon stole a glimpse of the data on his clipboard. Looked like statements.

"We're going to put out a release later," the investigator said.

"Can you give me a little information now?"

"We don't have much, just basics."

"I'll take anything."

"A couple of walkers discovered a female body this morning."

"Is it a homicide?"

"Looks that way."

"What age and race is the victim?" Gannon asked.

"I'd put her in her twenties. White or Native American. Not sure."

"Got an ID?"

"Not confirmed. We need an autopsy for that."

"Can I talk to the walkers?"

"No, they went home. It was a disturbing scene."

"Disturbing? How?"

"I can't say any more. Look, I'm not the lead."

"Can I get your name, or card?"

"No, no, I don't want to be quoted."

That was all Gannon could get and he phoned it in for the Web edition, putting "disturbing scene" in his lead. In the time that followed, more news teams arrived and Lee Watson, a *Sentinel* news photographer, called Gannon's cell phone sounding distant against a drone.

"What's up, are you in a blender, Lee?" Gannon asked.

"I'm in a rented Cessna. The paper wants an aerial shot of the scene."

Gannon looked up at the small plane.

"Watch for Brandy Somebody looking for you," Watson

said. "She's the freelancer they're sending to shoot the ground. Point out anything for her."

When Brandy McCoy, a gum-snapping freelancer, arrived, the first thing Gannon did was lead her from the press pack and cops at the tape to the unmarked car belonging to the investigator he'd talked to earlier.

The detective had gone back into the woods. His car was empty, except for his clipboard on the passenger seat. Gannon checked to ensure no one could see what he and the photographer were doing.

"Zoom in and shoot the pages on the clipboard. I need the information."

"Sure."

Brandy's jaw worked hard on bubble gum as she shot a few frames then showed Gannon.

"Good," he said, jotting information down and leaving. "My car's over here, come on."

Twenty minutes later, Gannon and Brandy were walking to the front door of the upscale colonial house of Helen Dodd. She was a real estate broker, and her friend, Kim Landon, owned an art gallery in Williamsville, according to the information Gannon had gleaned from the police statements.

Gannon thought having Brandy accompany him would help. Barely out of her teens, she was nonthreatening, especially with that sunny gum-chewing smile.

As they reached the door, it opened to two women hugging goodbye.

"Excuse us," he said. "I'm Jack Gannon, and this is Brandy McCoy. We're with the *Buffalo Sentinel.* We're looking for Helen Dodd and Kim Landon?"

Surprised, the two women looked at each other.

"Would that be you?"

Kim nodded. Helen was uneasy. Both women looked as though they had been crying. Gannon didn't want to lose them.

"Can we talk to you a bit about this morning?" he asked.

"How did you get this address?" Helen Dodd wanted to know.

Gannon said, "Well, we just came from the park, talked to police sources and stuff. We understand you found the woman."

Awkward silence followed until Brandy punctuated it with a prompt.

"It must've been terrible."

Kim resumed nodding.

"It was horrible," Kim said.

"May I take notes?" Gannon asked.

"I don't know." Helen eyed their press tags. "You're going to put this in the *Sentinel?*"

"Yes, for the story we're doing," Gannon said.

"For as long as I live, I'll never forget it," Kim started. "At first we thought it was a joke. When you see something like this, it makes you appreciate what's important. It was just so horrible. I mean, neighbourhood kids play in that park."

"I hope they catch the monster who did it," Helen said. "I'm calling my home-security company to make sure they keep an eye on my house."

"Can you walk us through how you found her?" Gannon asked.

"We take a regular morning walk in that area and spotted it. Her," Kim said. "At first she looked like a mannequin, entangled in shrubs and small trees. We didn't get too close once we realized what it was."

"Can you tell me exactly what you saw?" Gannon asked.

"We'd heard stories about what happens in there at night, which I never believed until now. We saw condoms and hypodermic needles," Kim said.

"She was in a shallow grave," Helen said. "We saw dark hair, an arm bent over a head in a swimmer's posture, like she was breaking the surface of the earth."

After they finished, Gannon dropped Brandy off at the scene to keep vigil until they removed the body.

He had to get back to the newsroom.

This was shaping up to be a grisly homicide, he thought, settling in at his desk. While eating a club sandwich from the cafeteria, he checked regional and state missing-person cases posted online, using the detective's description of a white or Native American woman in her twenties as his guide.

So many of them fit the general description, he thought, wondering if there was any chance this was linked to that tip he wanted to chase about a missing woman from Vermont or Connecticut. He stared into their faces, reading their information.

Was he staring at the unidentified victim near Ellicott Creek? Who was she? And how did her life come to an end there? She was someone's daughter, maybe someone's wife or sister?

He was pierced by a memory of his sister, Cora.

And what became of her life?

He couldn't dwell on that now and forced himself back to his story.

"Do we have any idea who she is?" Tim Derrick, the assignment editor, had a habit of sneaking up behind reporters and reading over their shoulders.

"Not yet."

Gannon clicked onto the latest news release from the investigators. He touched his pen to the words "unidentified female, in her twenties."

"She was sort of half buried in a shallow grave," Gannon said.

"Cripes," Derrick said. "Well, we've got strong art from the air and the walkers. Front will take your story. Give us about twenty-five inches or so. Make sure the Web people get it."

"Sure."

Derrick patted Gannon's shoulder.

"And nice work."

"Hey, Tim. Anything more to the rumors going around about more cuts?"

Derrick stuck out his bottom lip, shook his head.

"The way things are in this business, those rumors never go away."

A few hours later, as Gannon was giving his story a final read through, polishing here and there, his line rang.

"Hi, Jack, it's Brandy."

"How you doing there?"

"The medical examiner just moved the body. I got some good shots and sent them in to the photo desk."

"Thanks, I'll have a look."

After he'd finished his story Gannon joined the night editor at the photo desk where he was reviewing the news pictures with Paul Benning, the night photo editor.

"It's all strong." Benning clicked through the best frames as he worked on finishing a milk shake.

Here was the sharp overview showing a brilliant yellow tarp isolated like a flag of alarm amid an all-consuming forest, Gannon thought.

Here was the medical examiner's team, grim-faced with a black body bag strapped to a stretcher, loading it into a van.

Here were Helen Dodd and Kim Landon, tight head shots, shock etched in their faces. Here was Kim, looking off, eyes filled with worry.

"Go back to the aerial," Gannon said.

Benning sucked the remnants of his shake through a plastic straw.

"You see something?

"Maybe. Can you blow it up?"

Benning enlarged it.

Click after click drew them closer to the tarp and a fleck of white near the left edge. Click after click and the fleck grew, coming into focus as a hand.

The woman's hand, reaching from the tarp.

Reaching from her grave, as if seizing him in a death plea to tell the world who did this.

Before they did it again.

4

Some thirty-six hours after it had been removed from its shallow grave, the body was autopsied at the Erie County Medical Center, on Grider Street off the Martin Luther King Expressway.

Death was classified a homicide.

Using fingerprints and dental records, the dead woman's identity was confirmed as being Bernice Tina Hogan, aged twenty-three, of Buffalo, New York. The facts of her death were summarized in a few sentences in a police news release.

Nothing about the pain of her life, Gannon thought as he worked on a long feature about her. After her name had been released, some of her former classmates had contacted him at the paper.

"Bernice had a hard life," one friend told him.

Bernice never knew her real parents. She'd been told she had some Native American blood, maybe Seneca, and had been raised, for a time, on a reservation. Maybe Allegany, or Cattaraugus. She wasn't sure. Bernice had never been sure about much in her short life, her friends told him.

Some sent him photos.

She stood stiff and shy in obvious embarrassment; a heavyset girl with low self-esteem who'd been abused by her foster father, who also beat her foster mother.

At first she'd overcome it all. Bernice did well in school, going on to study nursing at Buffalo State, nearly graduating before she was drugged and raped at a party.

"After that happened she was so brokenhearted. It was like she just gave up. She began missing classes," one friend said.

Bernice had grown addicted to crack. Few people knew that she'd slipped into prostitution as she descended down a path that ended in a makeshift grave under a thicket of twisted maple near Ellicott Creek.

Gannon wanted to talk to Bernice's family, but no one knew who her foster mom was, or where she lived. So he made a lot of calls over the next few days until he got a lead.

"You didn't get this from me, but her name is Catherine Field," a source at the city's Social Services and Housing Department told him.

Catherine Field was a widowed fifty-nine-year-old diabetic who lived alone on welfare in an older section of the city west of Main. Gannon had gone to the address several times but in vain.

No one was home.

But he refused to give up trying to find her.

Maybe today would be different, he thought as once again he rolled by the home where Catherine had raised Bernice. It was a small two-story frame house built with the optimism that had blossomed when the Second World War ended. Now, with its blistering paint, missing shingles and sagging front porch, it looked more like a tomb for hope.

It sat among the boarded-up houses near a vacant lot where several old men leaned against an eviscerated Pinto and passed around a bottle wrapped in a paper bag.

Memories of his sister rushed at him before he turned

his attention back to the story and the house, eyeing it intensely as he drove by. His hopes lifted when he saw a woman in the backyard.

This time he parked out of sight down the block and approached the house from a different street, coming to the back first, where he saw a woman in her fifties, tending a flower garden near the rickety back porch.

"Catherine Field?"

She turned to him, the toll of a hard life evident in the lines that had woven despair on her face. Her red-rimmed eyes stared helplessly at him.

"You are Catherine Field, Bernice Hogan's foster mom?"

"Who are you?"

"Sorry," Gannon fished for his photo ID. "Jack Gannon, a reporter for the *Buffalo Sentinel*."

As if cued, breezes curled pages of the *News* and the *Sentinel* that were on a small table between two chairs. Also on the table: a glass and a bottle of whiskey that was half-empty.

"I've been trying to reach you," he said.

"I was burying my daughter."

"I'm sorry. My condolences. There was no notice of the arrangements."

"We wanted to keep it private. My brother had a plot, a small cemetery on a hill overlooking an apple orchard."

"Where is it?"

"I don't want to say."

"I understand. May I talk to you about Bernice?"

"You can try, I'm not in good shape."

She invited him to sit on the porch. Gannon declined a drink. Catherine poured one for herself, looked at her small garden and spoke softly. She told him that Bernice's mother was a child, fourteen years old, when she gave her up for adoption.

But Bernice was never adopted. Instead, she was bounced through the system. Catherine and her husband, Raife, a carpenter, became Bernice's foster parents when Bernice was eleven. By then Bernice was aware that she'd been given up for adoption.

"I loved her and always felt like her mom, but she chose to call me Catherine, never Mom. I think it was her way of emotionally protecting herself because she'd had so many 'moms.' No one could ever really be her mother."

Not long after they got Bernice, Raife started gambling, and drinking. He became violent and abused Bernice and Catherine before she left him.

"I'll spend my life regretting that I didn't do more to protect her."

Catherine considered her glass then sipped from it.

"She was such a bright girl. Always reading. I was so pleased when she left home to get her own apartment and start college. So proud. She was on her way. She volunteered at a hospice in Niagara Falls. I just knew she was going to make it. Then the bad thing happened."

"Her friends told me about the party."

"They think someone slipped something in her drink. She never overcame it. She turned to drugs to deal with it. She wouldn't talk to me or anyone, but I heard that when she ran up drug debts, she turned to the street."

Tears rolled down Catherine's face.

"When was the last time you saw, or talked, to her?"

Catherine wiped her tears and sipped from her glass.

"She called me about a month ago and said she was going to try to get clean, try to get off the street. Some friends were trying to help her."

"Did she say who those friends were?"

Catherine shook her head.

"You can't print anything I've just told you."

"But I'm researching your daughter's death for a news story. I have to."

"No. You can't print anything."

"Catherine, I identified myself as a reporter. I've been taking notes. This tragedy is already public. Now, did Bernice say anything about anyone possibly harming her?"

"I'm not supposed to say anything. They told me not to talk to the press."

"Who?"

Catherine stood.

"Please, you can't print anything. You have to go."

"Wait, who told you not to say anything?"

Several moments passed.

"At least tell me who told you not to speak to the press about your daughter's murder."

She looked at him long and hard.

"The police."

5

Two days after her corpse had been identified, Bernice Hogan's shy smile haunted Gannon from the *Sentinel*'s front page.

Her picture ran under the headline:

Murder of a brokenhearted woman
Nursing student's tragic path

Here was a troubled young woman whose life held promise. A woman who, despite the cruelty she'd endured, had been striving to devote herself to comforting others. His compassionate profile was longer than his earlier news stories and contained information unknown to most people, including his competition.

Not bad, he thought, sitting at his desk, rereading his feature in that morning's print and online editions.

Tim Derrick swung by, drinking coffee from a mug bearing the paper's logo.

"Nate likes what you did," Derrick indicated the corner office of Nate Fowler, the paper's managing editor, the man who controlled the lives of seventy-five people in editorial. Invoking his name gave currency to any instructions as quickly as it made people uneasy.

Fowler was not a journalist. He was a Machiavellian bureaucrat and Gannon did not mesh with him as well as he did with the other editors.

"Did he say anything else?" Gannon asked.

"He wants you to stay exclusively on the murder story, do whatever you can to make sure we own it. He said we need hits like this to boost circulation and stay alive." Derrick pointed his finger gunlike at Gannon's old Pulitzer-nominated clips and winked. "And if anyone's going to take it to the end zone, it's you."

Gannon was not so optimistic.

He needed a strong follow-up today but faced a problem.

The New York State Police led the Hogan investigation and he didn't know the lead detectives. He looked at their names on the last news release, Investigators Michael Brent and Roxanne Esko.

He'd put in calls to them but none were returned. He could go around them, but it meant asking sources to go out on a limb by leaking information to him.

He had sources everywhere: the Buffalo homicide squad, Erie County, Amherst, Cheektowaga, the FBI, Customs and Border Protection, the DEA, the U.S. Marshals Service, pretty much every agency in the region.

But nobody was saying much.

Maybe it went back to what Catherine Field had said about the police telling her not to speak to the press. At first he hadn't been concerned because detectives often asked relatives of victims not to speak to reporters, especially during the early days of an investigation.

But now, as he sat at his computer searching for a new angle, he wondered if it was a factor here. He couldn't shake the feeling he was missing something.

"That Hogan case is sealed, man," one source had told him. "But I heard that some of the people close to it were rattled by what the guy had done to her. I heard that it pushes the limits of comprehension."

Another source said that a number of law enforcement agencies were called in to help, possibly because of the area where she was found, and possibly because of other complications.

"I'll tell you something nobody in the press knows," the source said. "There's a closed-door case-status meeting with a lot of cops from a lot of jurisdictions. It's been going on all morning out at Clarence Barracks."

Gannon grabbed his jacket.

He'd go out there and see if anyone would talk to him.

The New York State Police patrol east and northeast Erie County from the drowsy suburb of Clarence, east of Buffalo. Clarence Barracks was on Main Street, housed in a plain one-story building.

When Gannon arrived, the woman at the reception desk was twirling her pen and talking on the phone.

"I've been temping all week, just when they get this big case…meeting after meeting, people coming, people going—one second, Charlene." She clamped her hand over the phone. "May I help you?"

"I'd like to see Michael Brent or Roxanne Esko. I'm with the *Buffalo*—"

"They're all in the meeting, third door on the right." She pointed down the hall with her pen. "I'm supposed to send everybody there." She went back to her conversation. "What's that? She's pregnant! OH MY GOD! How many is that now?"

"But I'm with the *Buffalo Sentinel*."

Ignoring what he'd said, the receptionist pointed him down the hall.

"Go," she told Gannon. "It's all right. Everybody's in the meeting."

He hesitated for as long as it took the receptionist to buzz him through the security door. As he went down the hall he could almost hear the floor cracking under him for he was treading on thin ethical ice. Through innocent circumstance he'd gained entrance to the inner sanctum of the investigation of Bernice Hogan's murder. The door to the meeting was half-open. He could hear loud voices.

How should he play this?

He'd knock on the door, identify himself then request to speak to Brent or Esko. They'd likely shoo him away, have him wait at reception.

At that instant the door opened and a man he didn't recognize exited, talking on his cell phone. Gannon turned and bent over a water fountain as the man, his tie loosened, shirtsleeves rolled up, whisked by him to the opposite end of the hall talking loudly on his cell.

"Tell Walt this Hogan thing is going to be a ballbuster," he said into the phone. "No one will believe where they're going with it. Yeah, they're keeping a tight lid on this. Yeah, I got to get back."

The man returned to the room and Gannon inched closer to the door.

It remained partially opened. Voices of people arguing spilled from it.

"I don't buy it."

"Look at what we know so far."

"What you have so far is hearsay, Mike!"

Gannon's breathing quickened. As he inched closer he got a limited view of a large whiteboard. He glimpsed a patch of handwritten times, dates, streets, arrows, then a clear view of initials written in blue marker under the heading

"Suspect." The initials on the board were blocked by an open hand slapping it to stress the point someone was making.

"Given all that we've got so far, all that we're following up with, this guy is our suspect and the focus of our investigation."

The hand vanished.

Gannon's heart beat faster as he glanced around to be sure no one could see him. He stepped closer and saw the initials of the suspect.

K.S.

Who was that?

"It's bullshit, Mike, I'm telling you!"

For an instant Gannon caught sight of someone he knew.

"How can you be so sure? We just don't buy it."

"It's not a done deal. Listen, we've got a lot of hard work ahead of us, but based on what we've got, everything points to him. He's the key."

"Let's see if I have this right. Based on the things a couple of crack hoes on Niagara told you, you're telling us that a cop, a decorated detective, is your suspect for Hogan?"

A cop?

Gannon froze.

Then he felt a hand on his shoulder.

6

Gannon turned around to see the receptionist's puzzled face.

"Aren't you going to go in?" she asked, holding a stack of files she appeared to be delivering.

"No, I was just leaving." He kept his voice down as he walked to the door. "I have to go."

"Well, I forgot to have you sign in," she said. "But if you're done I guess it doesn't matter."

Gannon waved his thanks, headed to his car, hurrying when he got to the lot. He pulled away, a thousand concerns shotgunning through his mind as he struggled to concentrate on what he'd heard.

A detective was the prime suspect in Bernice Hogan's murder.

This was big. Huge.

He wouldn't alert the desk yet, not until he nailed it. He had to keep this to himself until he had it in the bag.

Never oversell a story.

First things first.

He had to confirm the name behind K.S. and the police department the suspect worked for. He had an idea and drove downtown to the headquarters of the Buffalo and Erie County Public Library system. The building took up two city blocks in Lafayette Square.

He went to the public computer terminals and logged into the databases for the city of Buffalo employee listings by department. The Buffalo Police Department was the area's largest police force.

Let's start here, he thought as he began searching the BPD's directory for all officers whose surname started with an S.

Damn.

They were not ordered alphabetically but rather by seniority. With more than eight hundred officers to check, this would take time. Page after page of names blurred before he found a K.S.

Ken Smith. Then another. Kim Sailor. Then another. Kent Sanders. And another. Kevin Sydowski.

By the time he was done, he'd mined nine possibilities from the Buffalo Police Department. He moved on to the database for officers with the Erie County Sheriff's Office. After searching some four hundred names there, he had three more candidates: Kal Seroudie, Kyle Sawchuk, and Keen Sanchez.

But there were numerous police departments that served greater Buffalo, like the Cheektowaga Police Department, the Amherst Police Department, Hamburg, North Tonawanda, West Seneca, and Ascension Park, to name a few.

He continued scouring the databases.

As time passed he realized that he would never get through them all. He stopped to think. So far, he had some sixteen possibilities, but this was turning out to be a needle-in-a-haystack search.

He needed help confirming the name.

He'd use another option.

He abandoned the computer, went to a public telephone and called the private number of the person he'd seen at the meeting. He hadn't talked to his source for some time and was reluctant to push, but the stakes were high.

No one answered.

He left a message then returned to the newsroom, which was in full midday mode with reporters talking on phones, or typing at keyboards, or huddled with editors discussing stories. Gannon had grabbed a BLT in the cafeteria and was threading his way to his desk.

"Hey, Jack, what've you got?" Tim Derrick held up his clipboard listing the stories for tomorrow's paper. "I'm heading into the meeting. I've got you skedded for a follow-up on the investigation into Hogan."

"I'm expecting more information. I'll let you know if it falls through."

"Remember, Nate's counting on you for a scoop."

As Gannon settled in at his desk and prepared to eat his late lunch, his phone rang. He answered after getting two quick bites down.

"Jack Gannon, *Buffalo Sentinel*."

"I got your message."

The caller's number was blocked but he knew the voice.

"Thanks. It's been a while," he said. "How are you?"

"Oh, you know me. Same old same old. And you?"

"I'm a bit under the gun. I need a favour," he said.

"Something to do with Hogan?"

"I understand they're looking at a cop for it?"

Silence hissed in his ear.

"Why ask me?" the caller asked.

"I figured you might know something. I'm poking around everywhere."

Another stretch of silence passed.

"Listen," Gannon said, "I need to confirm what I've learned. I think the suspect's initial's are K.S. and I need to clarify some details."

After considering the situation, the caller said, "Jack, you have to guarantee that you will protect the source of this information."

"You have my word."

"You don't give my name to anyone."

"That's right."

"It's true. Your information is solid."

He stared at nothing. His breathing quickened.

"And this is from inside the investigation?" Gannon asked.

"Absolutely. I was at a case meeting today."

"Who's the cop?"

"A detective with the Ascension Park Police Department."

"Got a name for me?"

"Karl Styebeck."

Gannon thumbed the cap off of his pen, found a fresh page in his notebook and started writing, oblivious to the newsroom activity.

Styebeck.

"I've heard his name before," Gannon said.

"Check your archives, he's some kind of hero."

"You're absolutely sure we can go with this in the paper?"

"Dead certain."

"Thank you."

Pen clamped between his teeth, Gannon launched into a search of the *Sentinel*'s news databases, the archives of every community newspaper in the region, the Web site of the Ascension Park Police Department and various community sites online.

Soon, he had enough from community papers for a short biography.

Karl Styebeck was a decorated twelve-year veteran who

coached children's sports teams, volunteered for charity runs and gave stranger-awareness talks in Ascension Park schools. On Sundays, he went to church with his wife, Alice, and their son, Taylor. Occasionally, he sang in the choir.

This guy's a saint.

Several years back Styebeck was off duty, returning from a Bills game, when he came upon a house fire. He'd rushed into the burning building and rescued four children. They'd been left alone by their parents who'd gone to a casino at the Falls. For his bravery, Styebeck was awarded a Chief's Citation.

Now he's suspected of murdering a nursing student.

Gannon had to confirm his information with the state police.

He called Clarence Barracks and asked them to convey an urgent message to Michael Brent, the lead investigator.

"What does this concern?" the duty trooper asked.

"Information about the Hogan homicide."

"I'll pass your message to him."

Five minutes later, Gannon's line rang.

"This is Mike Brent, New York State Police."

"Thanks for getting back to me. Sir, I'm seeking your reaction for a story we're preparing for tomorrow's *Sentinel* that will report that Detective Karl Styebeck, of the Ascension Park Police Department, is the suspect in the murder of Bernice Hogan."

Brent let several moments of icy silence pass.

"I cannot confirm your information," Brent said.

"Is my information wrong?"

Silence.

"I would hold off writing anything like that and save yourself a lot of grief."

"What? I'm sorry, I don't understand."

"I can't confirm your information."

"But you don't deny it?"

"I think we're done here."

"Sir, you have not denied the information that Styebeck is a suspect."

Brent hung up.

Gannon circled the few notes he'd taken from Brent and weighed matters. Brent wouldn't have warned him to hold off if his information was wrong. Because if it was wrong Brent wouldn't have cared, which told Gannon that his information had to be dead on the money.

No way was he going to sit on a story this big and risk letting the *Buffalo News* scoop him.

There was only one more person to confront with the story.

Karl Styebeck.

7

Karl Styebeck's address and phone number were not listed, a step most cops took to protect their families.

Gannon had a hunch.

After he finished eating his sandwich, he picked up his phone and punched an internal extension.

"Circulation, Ashley speaking."

"Hi, Ash. It's Jack in news."

"Jack Gannon?"

He'd dated Ashley Rowe a few times after meeting her at the paper's Christmas party. They got along but they didn't think it would go anywhere. They'd parted as friends, or so he thought.

"Hello, are you there, Ashley?"

"I'm here, Jack. What is it?"

"Can you check a name for me? See if they're a subscriber? Styebeck, Karl Styebeck. Karl with a K and last name spelled S-t-y-e-b-e-c-k."

"You know it's against policy for us to share the paper's subscriber list."

"I completely understand. But it's for a story."

Gannon heard an annoyed sigh then typing on her keyboard.

"I cannot tell you that yes, we do have a subscriber by that name and the number and address are as follows."

Gannon wrote the information down.

"I appreciate this," he said.

"I'm sure you do."

Gannon called Karl Styebeck's home. The phone was answered by a woman.

"No, I'm sorry, Karl's not here at the moment." She was pleasant. "He's coaching the game at the Franklin Diamond. May I take a message?"

"No, no message, thanks."

Gannon did not identify himself.

He made a copy of Styebeck's photo from a recent profile of him in one of the community newspapers then drove to Ascension Park.

It was an established middle-class neighbourhood of streets lined with mature trees that arched over well-kept homes. Franklin Diamond encompassed a playground, basketball and tennis courts that were busy with activity. The bleachers at the ball diamond were sprinkled with parents cheering the players of a game in progress.

He neared the benches, getting close enough to scrutinize the coaches until he was satisfied he'd locked onto Styebeck. The cop was leaning against a chest-high chain-link fence, drinking from a can of soda, watching his players in the field.

"Let's go, Bobbie!" he shouted to his pitcher. "Big swinger!"

Gannon sidled up to him then waited for a lull in the game. Styebeck pulled a rolled roster from his rear pocket when Gannon interrupted.

"Excuse me, Detective Styebeck?"

Deep-set intelligent eyes turned on Gannon from a face as cold and still as a frozen lake. The man was in his early forties, stood an inch or so over six feet. He had a medium build with firm, large upper chest and arms. He wore a ball cap, baseball shirt and jeans.

"Detective Karl Styebeck?"

Styebeck nodded.

"Jack Gannon from the *Buffalo Sentinel.*"

"The *Sentinel?* You guys never cover our games."

"I'm not here for that, sir."

Gannon nodded to an empty picnic table by a tree, thirty yards away from the first-base line.

"Can we go over there for a moment?" Gannon asked.

"I'm kind of busy. What's this about?"

"Bernice Hogan."

"You better show me some ID."

Gannon produced his press ID. Styebeck examined it, gave it back, then went to the picnic table with Gannon.

"What do you want?" Styebeck folded his arms across his chest.

"I need to ask you a few questions for the record."

Gannon extended his small recorder.

Styebeck looked at it but didn't move.

"Sir, I'd like your response to a story we're running tomorrow that will name you as a suspect in the murder of Bernice Hogan."

Styebeck's eyes narrowed.

"What? Is this some kind of joke?"

"I understand that you are a suspect in the murder of Bernice Hogan, the nursing student whose body—"

"I know who she is. I'm working the case with the state police. I don't know where this is coming from, but your information is unmitigated bullshit."

"I'm going to quote you, sir."

Styebeck crushed his soda can in his fist just as two boys wearing jerseys emblazoned with *Kowalski's Towing,* ran to them.

"Coach!" one boy said. "We're up! Who bats?"

Styebeck glared at Gannon.

"T.J. is up, Dallas is on deck."

"Coach, you're bleeding!"

The twisted metal had cut into Styebeck's fingers. Blood dripped from them, dampening the earth. Gannon looked at it, then at Styebeck, catching something cold threading across his eyes.

"I'm fine, fellas. Let's get back to the game."

Styebeck held back, leaned into Gannon and dropped his voice. "You better watch yourself, asshole."

Styebeck returned to the game. Gannon stood alone, puffed his cheeks and exhaled slowly.

Then he checked his recording and walked to his car.

When he'd returned to the *Sentinel,* Tim Derrick was collecting his briefcase and throwing off to Ward Wallace, the night editor.

Gannon went to them and told them what he had.

"The prime suspect in Bernice Hogan's murder is a detective working on the investigation."

Wallace and Derrick exchanged glances.

"Christ, that's a helluva goddamn story." Wallace waved over Ed Sikes, the front-page editor. They used the empty city editor's office for an impromptu conference.

Wallace removed his glasses, tapped them on his chin as other deputy and night editors joined them.

"This is dynamite," Derrick said. "How'd you get it?"

"I picked it up when I went out to Clarence Barracks. Then I went to a good source who confirmed it."

"Who's your source?" Sikes said.

"They're inside the investigation. I can't name them."

"Why not?"

"That was the deal."

"Policy requires you give us a name, Jack. Even if we don't use it," Sikes said.

"I know, but this is deep inside. Come on. I gave my word and this is exactly how we broke the jetliner story. We were tipped by an unnamed source."

"You also got the document that nailed it," Sikes said. "Got any paper on this tip? A warrant? A police report? A memo?"

"No, not quite."

"What do you mean, *'not quite'*?"

"My information is solid."

"Jack, is your source on this information a cop?" Wallace asked.

"Yes."

"With the New York State Police?"

"My source is a cop inside the investigation. That's as far as I want to go. I gave my word."

"This story's huge," Derrick said. "Who else did you call?"

Gannon told them.

"Christ." Wallace ran his hand through his hair. "We need a story like this. *He's got the investigator on the record, and the suspect.*"

"Alleged suspect," Sikes said. His eyes were like black ball bearings as they bored into Gannon. "You trust your source with everything, Jack? Because with this kind of story, if you're wrong, we could all pay dearly."

Gannon took stock of the faces staring at him. Beyond the office, a few reporters raised their heads to look at the sombre group, curious about what was happening.

"I stand by my story."

Sikes kept Gannon in his gaze for a long time.

"We're taking a risk here."

"I trust my source completely."

"Write it up," Sikes said. "I'll take it for front. Better find a picture of Karl Styebeck." Then he pointed his finger at Gannon. "You'd better be right about this."

8

That night in a quiet neighbourhood of Ascension Park, Karl Styebeck sat alone before his television.

It was the only light in his darkened living room. Flickering images lit up the creases of his taut face. As he surfed from channel to channel, he chewed on his thumb while his wife descended the stairs after checking on their son, who'd gone to bed.

"Goodness, why are you keeping it so dark in here?" She swept into the room and switched on a light.

"Keep it off, Alice."

"Why?"

"Just keep it off."

"Fine, you vampire." She smiled and switched the light off. "Don't you think you're taking this a little too seriously, Karl?"

"Taking what too seriously?"

"You lost the game and some of the parents got upset. Taylor told me what happened at the diamond."

"No. It was a good game, could've gone either way. Nobody got upset."

Alice retrieved her needlepoint from the sofa and tapped his shoulder.

"I'm going to need some light, here." She switched on a low-wattage table lamp and he didn't object. "Would you find something to watch. I hate it when you channel hop. Men. Sheesh."

Styebeck landed on a local channel just as it offered a brief news update between commercials, reporting, *"No new developments on the murder of Bernice Hogan, the former nursing student from Buffalo State."*

"That's such a sad case," Alice said. "Well, Taylor told me some guy you were talking to at the game made you mad."

"No, it's nothing."

"Is it work? You're awfully pensive these days."

"Something like that. I'm getting a drink, you want anything?"

"Some water would be nice, thanks."

In the kitchen Styebeck poured himself a glass of orange juice, stood at the window over the sink, looked out at his yard and continued ruminating.

Immediately after that reporter, Gannon, had confronted him, Styebeck made a round of calls on his cell phone to detective friends. It was odd. Few of them had time to talk, and those that did seemed cagey.

"Yeah," a cop from Erie County told him. "There was a joint-forces case-status meeting today out at Clarence Barracks. Hush-hush. Mike Brent was running it. You didn't miss much, just a bunch of wild-ass theories about suspects."

"Any names come up?"

"Names? No, Karl, they had no names on the board. As far as I'm concerned, Brent's a prick. They've got no evidence and the way he's headed, he'll never clear this. Sorry, Karl, I have to go."

Why hadn't he been called to that meeting?

Now, as he finished his glass, Styebeck asked himself again.

Why wasn't he invited to that meeting?

He didn't know Brent, but he'd talked to him and his

partner earlier about his theories on the Hogan homicide. They'd come to him because he had a lot of confidential informants downtown.

That's what they said.

Then this reporter, Gannon, bushwhacks him with this crazy allegation.

Where the hell was that coming from? What did he know?

"Oh, Karl, I forgot to tell you." Alice entered the kitchen, startling him. "Some guy called for you when you were out."

"Who?"

"I don't know. He didn't say. He didn't leave a message and the number didn't come up. I figured it had something to do with the game and told him you were at the park."

He said nothing.

It was likely Gannon, he thought. *Well, he wasn't worried. There's no way the* Sentinel *would run a story based on that B.S. he was peddling. No one could possibly know what he knew about Bernice Hogan's murder.*

"Karl, is something going on? We've had quite a number of strange calls over the last few weeks. And you've been so edgy. Is there something you're not telling me?"

Styebeck turned away from his wife and went back to searching the night through the kitchen window.

"No, Alice. It's all work related. Everything's fine."

9

Jolene Peller surfaced through the haze of semiconsciousness.

A low monotonous rattling sounded in her head as memory and awareness fell upon her in ominous drops.

Where was she? What happened?

Bernice.

She'd had a bad feeling and had gone to help Bernice; had followed her into the night where she'd heard pleading.

Bernice begging in the confusion then a scream.

The man.

Jolene had glimpsed him in the chaos *and he saw her;* hit her with a blazing light, blinding her, locked onto her, chased her, *hunted her.*

She ran but could not outrun the darkness.

It was a nightmare. She'd had a nightmare. Okay, then wake up.

Wake up!

SHE WAS AWAKE!

Jolene's heart thumped as her memory gave way to an onslaught of crushing fear.

What was happening?

Bernice? What happened to Bernice?

What's going to happen to me?

The blood rushing in her ears roared with the droning.

What was that noise?

Why was this happening?

Why her?

The air smelled of old wood, cardboard and something foul. Oh God. Oh God. She trembled, her stomach roiled. She kept her eyes shut tight, fought to stem her mounting hysteria and clear her mind.

Think.

You're alive.

You've got to get out of this.

She was lying on something padded. A disgusting-smelling mattress. Her tongue burned with an awful aftertaste and her jaw ached. Something between her upper and lower teeth was splitting her mouth open. It felt like a leather belt strapped so tight to her head her eyes hurt.

She raised her hand to try to relieve the pressure, but her hands were welded together by something cutting into her wrists. Some sort of binding.

Breathe.

The stench of the air was choking.

Jolene clawed at the buckle at the back of her head in vain. Her nose was clear. If she stayed calm she could breathe.

Did she dare open her eyes?

She had to.

Okay. All right. Easy. Breathe.

She opened them wide to absolute blackness.

She raised her hands to her face and saw nothing. It was as if she'd been disembodied.

As if she were dead.

She was terrified of the dark.

Terrified of being buried alive.

Overcome with vertigo, she was consumed by a sickening sense of whirling and falling. A muffled whimper escaped from deep in her throat and echoed in the silence.

Breathe, she told herself. Stay calm.

You're alive.

If you're alive, you can fight to survive.

Be strong. Don't cry. Fight.

The earth shifted.

Jolene was jolted across the mattress. Humming, hissing and, now, mechanical grinding grew louder.

What was happening?

The world started moving.

Jolene's dark prison was now mobile and gathering speed.

10

The next morning, victory called out to Gannon from his front-page story.

On every street corner with a *Buffalo Sentinel* newspaper box, his exclusive took up six columns on page one, above the fold, under the headline:

Hero Cop Suspected in College Student's Murder

This was a clean kill against the competition, the *Buffalo News.* Those guys had squat. Looking at the bank of news boxes while waiting for a downtown traffic light to change, he savored the rush of pride.

Don't get cocky. Glory was fleeting in this business, where you're only as good as your next story.

But a cop? Man, he'd hit this one out of the ballpark.

His story was the line item in the *Sentinel*'s morning edition. It went to homes, stores and news boxes across Buffalo, across Erie, Niagara and eight other counties; everywhere the *Sentinel* battled the *News* for shrinking readership. It also anchored the *Sentinel*'s Web site, where most people went for their news these days.

He had scored. No doubt about it. Buffalo radio and TV morning news led with the story, wire services picked it up.

It was the win he needed.

The light changed and Gannon continued through traffic, turning into the *Sentinel*'s parking lot, concentrating on the reason he'd come in early today: to work on a follow-up. Beating the competition always meant they'd come back at you big-time.

He was not going to lose this one.

He grabbed a paper from the security desk in the lobby before stepping into the elevator. Ascending alone, he studied the front-page photo of Styebeck's handsome hero face next to one of Bernice.

What a heartbreaker.

During his years on the crime desk, he'd encountered tragedies every day: the deaths of children, school shootings, gang murders, fires, wrecks, calamities, manifestations of evil in every form. He went at things wearing emotional armor.

But something about Bernice Hogan's tragedy got to him.

Looking at her face, he vowed to see that, in death, she received the respect that had eluded her in life.

The elevator stopped and he went to the newsroom kitchen for coffee.

The best follow-up to this morning's exclusive would be a feature on Styebeck. He'd go into Styebeck's life, his upbringing and how he came to be a hero cop and suspected killer. Maybe he'd call some criminal profilers, talk about cases of murderers leading double lives.

He'd need a few days but it might work.

"You're in early." Jeff kept his eyes on his computer screen where he was playing solitaire.

"Anything going on out there?"

"It's deadsville, Jack. Nice hit on the cop. You blew away the Buffalo Snooze." Jeff nodded to the managing editor's glass-walled office across the newsroom. "Nate's been trying to reach you."

"About what?"

"Don't know. Can't be good. I'd give it a minute."

Gannon didn't like the scene he saw playing out in the office. Nate Fowler kept jabbing his finger at Ward Wallace who kept throwing up his hands. Their voices were raised but Gannon couldn't make out what they were saying. As night editor, Wallace never came in at this hour unless there was a problem.

A serious problem.

"What's going on in there?" Gannon set his coffee down. "What's Wallace doing here?"

"Beats me. Oh, and there's a lady here to see you. I told her you usually get in later, but she's been waiting in reception for about an hour."

"She say what she wants?"

"No. I'll get her."

Gannon did a quick check of e-mails and sipped some coffee before he saw Jeff direct a woman in her fifties toward his desk.

She wore no makeup, had reddened eyes and unkempt hair. Her sweater and slacks had frayed edges. She held a slim file folder, her fingernails were bitten.

"You're Jack Gannon, the reporter?"

"That's me. And you are?"

"Mary Peller, and I really need your help, Mr. Gannon."

"It's Jack." Gannon cleared a stack of justice reports from an extra chair for her. "How can I help you?"

"My daughter, Jolene, is missing."

"Missing? How old is she?" Gannon fished a notebook from a pile, flipped to a fresh page.

"Twenty-six."

"Twenty-six? What's the story?"

What came next was a tale Gannon had heard before. Jolene's dad walked out on them when Jolene was eleven. When Jolene hit her teens, Mary lost her to drugs and the street. A year ago, after Jolene nearly died from overdosing on bad drugs, she started going to church and decided, for the sake of her three-year-old son, Cody, that she had to get clean.

Jolene got a fast-food job, took night courses, and through a service, landed a junior motel manager position in Orlando.

"Jo was over the moon because it was her chance to start a new life. She wasn't proud of the things she'd done to get drugs…" Mary Peller's voice trailed off and she stopped to regain her composure. "We don't have much money, Mr. Gannon. Jo left last week on the bus to Florida. She was supposed to set herself up then return for Cody. But I haven't heard from her."

"Nothing?"

"Not a word. She never arrived. She should've been there days ago. It's like she's vanished."

"Did you call the police?"

"Police here, police in Florida, social workers. Nobody cares."

"You consider hiring a private detective?"

"I can't afford it."

She passed her folder to him.

"I was hoping you could do a story, it might help me find her. You're good at finding things out. Please, Mr. Gannon, you're my only hope."

Gannon looked at the folder's contents, beautiful pictures of Jolene and Cody, some letters, personal papers, numbers, addresses, more pictures. One photo stopped him.

Man, she looks like Cora in this one.

A shadow fell over them. When Gannon lifted his head, Nate Fowler was there.

"Excuse us, ma'am," Fowler said, turning to Gannon. "I need you in my office, now."

Fowler left.

Gannon closed Mary Peller's folder, gave her his card and stood.

"Can you leave this file with me?"

"Yes."

"I won't guarantee I'll do a story. But let me look it over. I have to go. One way or the other, I'll call you."

Mary Peller took his hand and shook it.

"Thank you. Thank you for listening."

"Jeff will show you out."

In Nate Fowler's office, Ward Wallace's haggard face conveyed the climate. Gannon had stepped into a shit storm.

"Shut the door." Nate twisted a rubber band around his fingers while staring at Gannon.

"Jack, as managing editor of this paper I sit on the boards of many charitable organizations that do a lot of good work for this city. Did you know that Detective Karl Styebeck is also a board member of some of these groups?"

He didn't know that.

"And did you know, Jack, that I was reminded of that fact this morning when I got a wake-up call from the publisher, who got a wake-up call from a police commander, who said your story was wrong?"

"Wrong?"

"He called it a fabrication and demanded a retraction."

"You've got to be kidding."

"Am I smiling?"

"My story's not wrong."

"It should've been verified before the presses rolled. I should have been called."

"We called you, Nate," Wallace said.

"I got in last night off a late flight from Los Angeles and had no messages." Fowler glared at Wallace, then Gannon. "Give me your source's name so we can confirm and stand by the story. Otherwise we run a retraction."

Gannon swallowed, took quick stock of Fowler's office, the citations, framed news pages, including Gannon's for the Pulitzer nomination. There were photos of Fowler with city, state and federal politicians. His wife had a power job with the New York State attorney general's regional office. His brother was married to the publisher's daughter.

Fowler was a political player and Gannon didn't trust him.

"I can't give you my source's name."

Nate looked at Wallace then back at Gannon.

"You can't? Did I hear you right?"

"My source has too much at stake."

"And you don't?" Fowler glared at him. "Do you have any documents supporting the story?"

"No."

Nate Fowler glared at Ward Wallace then Gannon.

"Jesus. So we have nothing in our possession. No warrant, no affidavit, no court record?"

Gannon shook his head.

"Do you have a source or not, Jack?"

"I have a source, but I can't give them up to anyone. I gave my word. You have to trust me."

"The hell I do! As an employee conducting business for this company, you are required to advise your managers of your source, or be considered insubordinate."

"Jack," Wallace said, "just tell us who your source is and where they work."

"I can't. My source would lose more than their job."

"Job?" Fowler said. "Let me tell you about jobs,

Gannon. If we print a retraction, we rupture the paper's credibility at a time of eroding readership. At a time of possible staff cuts. Do you understand what's at stake here?"

"I do. I swear my story's good."

"Is it? Without so much as a thread of evidence, you've accused an outstanding member of this community of murder! A man recognized for putting his life on the line, a man who volunteers to help street people. Your story claims he killed a goddamn prostitute!"

"A human being. A troubled nursing student, that's what she was."

"A drug-addicted hooker."

"My story's not wrong, you have to trust me."

"Trust you? We're way beyond that." Fowler thrust his finger at Gannon's face, then the door. "You're gone!"

"What do you mean?"

"I'm suspending you indefinitely, effective now and without pay."

"My story's not wrong, Nate."

"Then give me your source."

"I can't."

"Then get the hell out of my newsroom."

11

Gannon left the *Sentinel* struggling to make sense of what had hit him.

Blood drummed in his ears as he walked through the parking lot to his car. He rested his arms on the Vibe's roof, letting time pass as he contemplated the building and his options.

He had none.

He'd given his word that he would not give up his source to anyone. Not even his editors. There was too much on the line.

Sentinel workers were arriving. Oblivious to his trouble, some waved. As he watched them, Nate Fowler's ominous words about staff cuts made his stomach tighten and he drove off.

Navigating through Buffalo's downtown traffic, he dragged the back of his hand across his mouth, adrenaline still rippling through him.

The fact was Nate Fowler refused to believe his story. The guy had no respect for his own reporters. He didn't care for the truth. He kowtowed to politics and could not be trusted with sources.

Gannon recalled the advice of Sean Allworth, the paper's Washington bureau chief, when they'd teamed up last month for a story that never saw publication. It was on state and county real estate contracts.

Fowler had spiked it and that set Allworth off in one of their calls.

"Jack, never give that guy your sources. He's a snake. When I broke that land development story last year, I had to give him my source. A week later, Fowler's brother bought some key property. The whole thing stunk."

Allworth said he'd heard rumors that Fowler was going to run for some state office, and through his wife, was cozy with big backdoor players. "He'll give up your sources to build alliances. Be careful."

A popular hero cop like Karl Styebeck could give Fowler a ton of community support, Gannon figured as he stopped at a 7-Eleven lot.

Okay, he was suspended, so now what?

He'd pursue the story on his terms, as an outcast.

Start at square one.

He made a call from a public pay phone and it was answered by the third ring.

"It's Gannon, you read today's paper?"

"Yup. Big story."

"I need to see you."

"All right, the usual spot, say, half an hour."

He took the New York State Thruway south to Lackawanna, the former steel town, which was now harvesting the wind. When he got there, he entered the south section of Holy Cross Cemetery.

One of the area's largest cemeteries, it held over one hundred thousand graves, including those of people who had built this part of the country, immigrants who'd helped dig the Erie Canal, or worked on Great Lakes steamers or in the steel mills.

A good place to bury secrets, he thought as he drove

slowly along the graveyard's eastern edge, to the Garden of Consolation. After parking, he sat on a bench near a stand of oak trees and waited.

Within ten minutes he saw a familiar Chev Impala stop some distance away. A woman got out and started toward him. A white woman about his age, dressed in a lavender T-shirt, dark blazer, jeans and navy leather flat shoes. Her auburn hair was pulled up in a neat bun.

This was Adell Clark, a former FBI agent.

Two years back, he'd covered a botched armored-car heist at a strip mall in Lewiston Heights. The FBI had been tipped to the robbery and moved to thwart it. Clark was on the scene and was shot twice. She returned fire, killing the two suspects, aged twenty and nineteen. They were brothers from Philadelphia.

In the days that followed, Clark agreed to be interviewed. He wrote a feature on the case and they'd kept in touch ever since.

Her recovery had been rough. A bullet was still lodged in her lower back, forcing her to walk a little slower than most people, or endure a lot of pain. "Pills make me loopy, so I never take them." To this day, the full terms of her disability claim remained tied up in red tape.

Clark was a divorced mother of a little girl who needed expensive drugs to cope with a rare medical condition. They lived in a seventy-year-old two-bedroom house with a leaky roof on Parkview in Lackawanna where Clark ran a one-woman private-detective agency.

She used him as an investigative resource. And he used her. That's how it was.

Clark lowered herself carefully onto the bench.

"So, Jack, talk to me. How'd it go?"

"I need you to reassure me that our information is solid, Adell."

"This stays here with you, me and the dead," she said.

"Of course."

"After they found Bernice Hogan's body, SP's lead detectives called a multi-agency meeting with Buffalo homicide, Erie County, Amherst and several local and federal agencies, including the DEA, BATF, the border people and the FBI."

"Why?"

"They brainstormed with anyone who'd ever investigated anything linked to prostitution in the Buffalo area," she said. "I was called in because I'd been involved with the INS on cases that had involved East European gangs smuggling prostitutes into the U.S. across the Canadian border at Niagara Falls."

"So what about Styebeck?"

"His name came up as a suspect through a vehicle connected to him. By the way, how did you get his initials?"

"Let's just say I had another source," he said. "Can you tell me how they connected Styebeck to the case?"

"That information came from hookers. First they saw Bernice arguing with another woman, then they saw Styebeck talking with Bernice Hogan before she vanished. The car's plate was recorded through a security camera from a building on Niagara. The vehicle was a rental and the rental agency confirmed the renter was Karl Styebeck."

"So, there's no doubt he was on the suspect list?"

"None. Zero."

"But Styebeck's friends at the meeting got pissed off, said Brent's statements came from crackhead hoes, and discredited the information. They said Styebeck was likely doing outreach work for his church, or one of his charities. The guy's a beloved hero. Anyway, his pals appear to be winning support to downplay, or even remove, Styebeck as a suspect."

"This is dangerous stuff."

"I thought so, and what troubled me was that I'd heard similar accusations about Styebeck years ago from my confidential informants when I was working the INS case," Clark said. "I talked to Styebeck back then and got a bad read off of him. Hero or not, he gave me the creeps."

Clark gazed at the headstones.

"Believe it or not, I was going to call you," she said.

She gave Gannon a few moments to absorb everything.

"Jack, what's going on?"

"Somebody high up in police circles called the publisher this morning. They said my story was a fabrication and pressed the paper to retract it. My editors wanted me to name my source."

"Did you?"

"No. Normally, I would. I'm supposed to tell an editor."

"So why did you protect me?"

"I don't trust Nate Fowler, my managing editor. Rumor is, he's going to make cuts at the paper then take a hefty severance package. A while back, our Washington bureau chief told me Fowler's going to make a run for office. Maybe the senate or Congress. I think that if I gave him your name, Adell, he'd give you up to ingratiate himself with influential law enforcement types."

"I could be charged, you know."

"I know."

"I could lose custody of my daughter, lose my disability benefits, which are still in dispute. I'd lose everything."

"That's why I refused to give you up."

"So what happened?"

"I've been suspended without pay."

Clark looked off into the distance.

"I'm so sorry, Jack."

"Don't be."

"No matter what anybody says, Styebeck's a suspect. That's a fact. And it remains a fact unless they clear him or charge him."

Clark pressed her hands against the bench, leaning on it hard as she stood.

"At that meeting," she said, "I was afraid that they were not going to look hard at Styebeck and I started to feel guilty."

"Why?"

"When I'd heard these stories about Styebeck before, I did nothing. Now…" She turned away. "Jack, if you saw the crime-scene pictures of what Bernice Hogan's killer did to her… I can't explain it. Dammit, I helped you because I believed it was the right thing to do."

A few tense moments passed.

"Thank you for protecting me."

She touched his shoulder, offered him a weak smile, and then made her way to her car.

Gannon watched her drive off.

He sat alone in the Garden of Consolation, where stone angels watched over him and the dead as he contemplated his next move.

His cell phone rang.

"It's me," Adell Clark said. "Just heard on WBEN that there's a news conference at eleven on the Hogan murder, out at Clarence Barracks."

"Any idea what it's about?"

"I don't know, maybe they've got a break in the case."

"Thanks, Adell. Gotta go."

As he jogged to his car, Gannon checked his watch. He had just enough time to get out there.

12

The lot at Clarence Barracks was filled with TV trucks and news cars from the *Buffalo News, WBEN,* Niagara Falls, Batavia, Lockport, campus newspapers and the community *Hornet* chain, when Gannon arrived.

Indignation pricked at him when he saw a car from the *Buffalo Sentinel.* Who'd they send? Walking by the *Sentinel*'s Saturn, he glanced inside for a clue as to who it might be. He saw nothing. *Forget it.* Besides, he was here on his own, a freelancer.

Inside, he went to the woman at reception, who'd replaced the one he'd encountered earlier.

"I'm here for the news conference."

"Just sign in and go that way," she said.

Nearly two dozen news types were stuffed into a small meeting room. A forest of TV cameras on tripods lined the back. Operators made final adjustments as reporters in folding chairs gossiped, gabbed on cell phones, checked Berrys or made notes.

At the head of the room, three men and one woman, each stern-faced, sat behind a table heaped with microphones and recorders.

Bernice Hogan looked upon the gathering from her Buffalo State ID photo, which had been enlarged and posted on the big tan tackboard behind the officers.

A few hundred yards from the room where Gannon stood was a church and the upscale neighborhood of Serenity Bay, with its custom-built homes, clubhouse, tennis courts, beaches and residents who had little interest in the region's latest murder.

While a few miles west, hidden in the woods near Ellicott Creek, was the shallow grave where Bernice was found.

A sad juxtaposition, Gannon thought, looking from the picture and opening his notebook.

"Let's get started," the white-haired man at the table said. "For those who don't know me, I'm John Parson, captain in command of Troop A, Zone 2. To my left is Lieutenant David Hennesy. To my right, from our Bureau of Criminal Investigation, Investigators Michael Brent and Roxanne Esko, who are heading the investigation into the homicide of Bernice Hogan.

"Lieutenant Hennesy will give you a status update, then we'll take a few questions."

Hennesy summarized the case.

"To date we've received twenty-seven tips and are following all leads. Of importance are reports of a blue truck, a big-rig tractor without a trailer, possibly with unique markings on the driver's door. It was seen several times in the Niagara-Lafayette area of Buffalo, prior to Bernice Hogan's disappearance on the tenth of this month. If anyone has information on a vehicle fitting this description, we're asking them to call us."

Murmurs rippled across the room and pages were flipped.

A blue rig. This was new.

"Thank you, Dave," Parson said. "We'll take a few questions now. Yes, Cathy from the *Observer.*"

"Do you have more details on the blue truck?"

"The driver is believed to have had conversations with Bernice Hogan before her disappearance. However, we have no description on the driver, or the year and model of the truck. So we're appealing to the public."

"Hold on a second," Gary Golden, a TV reporter, held up a copy of the *Buffalo Sentinel.* "With all due respect, seems we're avoiding the elephant in the room. Is Detective Karl Styebeck of the Ascension Park Police Department your prime suspect? Yes or no?"

After a chorus of throat clearing and an exchange of glances among the four police officials, Michael Brent leaned into the microphones.

"Detective Styebeck is not the focus of this investigation."

"Is he now, or has he at any time, been a suspect?" Gannon said from the back.

Heads turned to Gannon.

"He is not the focus of this investigation," Brent said.

"That's not a denial," Kip Ramon, from the *Buffalo News,* said.

"Reports suggesting Karl Styebeck is the key suspect and focus of this investigation are wrong," Parson said.

"Do you have other suspects? This mysterious blue truck, for instance?" That question came from Pete Martinez from the *Sentinel.*

"As Dave said, we're following nearly thirty tips and we have some promising leads."

"Has Karl Styebeck been ruled out?" Gannon asked.

"We've answered that," Parson said.

"Sir," Gannon pressed, "you have not answered that question."

"Has Karl Styebeck been questioned?" Golden asked.

"We're not going to publicly discuss all details of this case."

"So you have questioned him?" Golden said.

"Next question," Parson said, pointing to a reporter from one of the Niagara Falls news stations. "Go ahead, Loretta."

"Did you find any DNA, fingerprints or usable trace evidence?"

"We're not going to go into that here," Parson said. "I think we'll conclude this for now. We'll keep you apprised of any developments."

Several reporters tried to get in last questions. The investigators waved them off as they gathered file folders and left the room. As the conference broke up, Martinez called to Gannon, pointing outside to talk privately.

Martinez was a seasoned general-assignment reporter who could cover anything, a good-natured guy who got along with everyone, including Gannon. They walked alongside the building, to the rear, where they could be alone.

"You're playing with fire being here, being suspended and all, Jack."

"Guess you heard what happened?"

"There are no secrets in a newsroom."

"Well, my story's not wrong, Pete."

"I'm not going to judge you, buddy," Martinez said. "Before you got here, I was talking with Golden and Ramon from the *News.* Seems nobody can find Styebeck. Any chance you could share any other contact data, Jack?"

"I don't have anything, sorry. I'm here as a freelancer."

"Really, for who?"

"I don't know yet."

"Watch yourself. You're persona non grata." Martinez looked around, then stepped closer and dropped his voice. "Nate fully intends to run a retraction if you don't give up your source. That's what I'm hearing."

"I can't do that, Pete."

Martinez's cell phone rang. "I don't care what you do. I'm just keeping you posted." Martinez shook Gannon's hand, answered his call as he headed for his car.

Gannon reviewed his notes, considering the new lead on the blue truck as the sunlight dimmed.

"Well, look who we have here. Mr. Jack Gannon, the legend who almost won a Pulitzer. At last we meet, in the flesh."

Michael Brent and Roxanne Esko were now standing next to him. He glanced around. No one else was in sight. Esko had car keys and a file folder in her hand.

"Quite an interesting story in your paper today," Brent said. "Unnamed sources say the darnedest things. Well, we heard something, too."

Gannon let Brent fill the silence.

"We heard you got fired or something for writing fiction. Care to comment?"

"I stand by my story. I trust my source. It's that simple."

"No, it's not," Brent said. "Because you and your 'source,' whoever they are, don't have a clue about what's going on. You don't know jack shit, Jack."

Gannon flipped to a clear page, poised his pen.

"Why don't you enlighten me, Investigator."

Brent stared at Gannon's notebook, then at Gannon.

"Enlighten you? I think you have a hearing problem. Seems when you called me, I told you to hold off with your little tale there, said you'd save yourself a lot of grief."

Gannon shrugged.

"So, how's that grief working out for you today, Slick?"

Gannon didn't answer.

Brent's jawline tensed, then relaxed as he stepped into Gannon's personal space.

"You'd better get ready for more grief," Brent said,

"because I'm going to find out who your source is, and when I do, I'm going to make sure they face the consequences of obstructing our investigation."

13

Gannon left that mess with the state police behind him in Clarence and drove to the Great Lakes Truck Palace at Interstate 90 and Union Road.

He needed to check out the revelation on the mystery rig.

After navigating his small car through a realm of eighteen-wheelers, with their hissing brakes and diesels spewing black smoke, he parked at the office of general manager Rob Hatcher.

"I'll help you if I can. A crying shame about that girl," Hatcher had said on the phone.

Gannon knew him from earlier stories he'd written on a couple of bad wrecks and had called him after the news conference.

Now, with Gannon watching him, Hatcher clicked his pen repeatedly as he gazed upon Bernice Hogan's picture in the *Sentinel,* which was spread across his service counter.

"So, you really think a cop did it?"

"He's a suspect."

"Well, two state police investigators came in three days ago, maybe four. They asked us to help them locate a blue truck."

"Did they say why?"

"Naw, they didn't provide much information."

"Did they ask you anything about this guy?" Gannon tapped the paper on Karl Styebeck's face.

"Nope."

"What did they say about the blue rig?"

"All they said was that the truck had unique writing and art on the doors."

"What kind? Did they give you any more details, like a plate?"

Hatcher shrugged.

"They didn't specify. They asked us to alert them if we saw a rig fitting that description."

"That's a pretty general description."

"I know."

Hatcher chuckled and nodded to the lot.

"We've got forty acres out there, partner. We run one of the largest operations in western New York. Seven or eight hundred trucks pass through here every twenty-four hours. Finding that rig is like finding a needle in a haystack. But the word's gone out."

"Will you call me if something breaks on this?"

"I can do that."

Gannon left the Truck Palace and spent the rest of the day working the street for data. He went to downtown coffee shops, hotel lobbies and taxi stands and talked to waitresses, doormen and cabdrivers for anything new on Bernice Hogan's murder.

At one point, Adell Clark sent him a text message.

FYI: Crime scene should be released by tonight.

Could be something for later, he thought as he entered Kupinski's Diner. Stan Kupinski, a former navy cook, ran a twenty-four-hour greasy spoon off Niagara that was a favorite of blue-collar workers and street types.

The smells of frying bacon and coffee greeted Gannon as he slid into a vinyl booth. He took stock of the checkered floor, the chrome stools at the worn counter with take-out containers towering to the ceiling.

He ordered a club sandwich and in no time at all Kupinski tapped a bell with his spatula, then left a heaping plate of food at the pick-up window. Lotta, the ample waitress—regulars called her Whole Lotta—set Gannon's food before him. He invited her to sit at his booth and talk about the murder. Since she needed to take a load off, she agreed.

"As a matter of fact, darlin', I did hear things about that little girl, Bernice," Lotta said. "I heard she and some other girl got into a little spat the last night anyone saw her."

Gannon's eyebrows climbed and he got out his notebook.

"Any idea what they fought about?"

"Maybe leaving, or something," Lotta said then stole a fry.

"Did you tell the police?"

"Police didn't come in here asking, like you."

"You know who the other girl is?"

Lotta's earrings swung when she shook her head.

"I can ask around," she said.

"Thanks—" Gannon put a five-dollar tip in Lotta's hand "—because I'd like to find her."

It was getting late but Gannon would try one more thing.

Experience from working on investigative stories had taught him that you should always keep tabs on your subject. It could yield a break, he thought as he headed to Ascension Park and Karl Styebeck's street.

Styebeck's house was a well-kept colonial with a two-car garage. It sat far back from the street, deep into the lot as if isolated within the neighborhood.

Gannon parked several doors away and watched it from his rearview mirror as he considered the story.

Why did the police consider Styebeck a suspect behind closed doors while not confirming it publicly? Where was the pressure to discredit his story coming from?

Was this the home of a monster?

Hold on.

The garage door was lifting as Karl Styebeck got into one of the two cars a dark sedan alone, then drove out.

Gannon started his Vibe's engine and followed him from a distance.

14

After leaving his house, Karl Styebeck waited at a traffic light, determined to fight his way out of this crisis.

Everything was on the line.

Jack Gannon's story in that morning's *Sentinel* had exploded in his home, claiming his wife and son as collateral damage.

Alice had buried her face in her hands

"Oh my God, Karl! This can't be happening!"

Taylor, his twelve-year-old son, was scared. "Why is Mom crying, Dad?"

Styebeck struggled to explain the story.

"It's wrong," he'd told them. "This guy, Gannon, screwed up. I'm helping with the investigation. His information is dead wrong. I'm going to straighten this out, okay?"

That seemed good enough for Taylor, who worshipped his dad. Still, Alice kept him home from school, and later she pulled Styebeck aside.

"Is this story true?" She glared at him. "We've had strange phone calls the last few weeks. You've been on edge and moody lately, tossing in your sleep. You tell me right now if you had anything to do with this girl's murder! You tell me, Karl!"

What could he say?

He stood before his wife, trying not to remember what he was and what he had come from.

"I swear to you, I did not kill that woman."

Alice's eyes searched his for a trace of deception until she was satisfied there was none.

As the hours passed, her fears were somewhat mitigated by the steady flow of friends calling and e-mailing their support, especially the volunteers with Styebeck's charity and outreach groups.

And the fact that the state police challenged the accuracy of Gannon's story at a news conference that morning had helped. Styebeck's lieutenant got behind him after calling to say, "Somebody got their wires crossed. Hang in there, Karl."

The police union offered legal help, which he declined. It wasn't needed. He'd booked off several days of saved vacation.

He'd take care of this himself. His way.

Night had fallen now as he cut across the city to his destination in the Delaware district. It was one of Buffalo's most prestigious communities, an area of mansions built in the late 1800s and early 1900s.

He went to the side door of a grand Victorian home and rang the bell. The door was opened by Nate Fowler.

"Thank you for seeing me privately, Nate."

"Certainly, please come in. Right this way." Fowler led him to a room with floor-to-ceiling bookcases, a fireplace and a grandfather clock. "Can I get you a coffee or anything?"

"No, thank you, this won't take long."

"I want to assure you that nothing you say leaves this room."

"As I mentioned in my call this morning, your reporter,

Gannon, ambushed me. I tried to reach you before the story ran."

"I was traveling. It was unfortunate for both of us. My apologies."

"This story has hurt me and my family, Nate."

"I understand, given your outstanding reputation."

"As you know, I have confidential informants on the street. Rumors get started and make their way into investigations. Things get misconstrued, things get leaked and fiction becomes fact. The truth is, I'm assisting the state police with the Hogan homicide. I can understand how a reporter trying to find a good story could get carried away."

"It happens, yes."

"I want you to know I had nothing to do with the homicide. It's ridiculous."

"Today the New York State Police publicly disputed our report on you. And given the circumstances under which our story made it into print, I think a full retraction and apology is necessary."

"Thank you."

"Additionally, we'll find the source of this injurious information. I trust that would be useful to you?"

Relief spread across Styebeck's face.

"That would be helpful."

"You don't deserve this, Karl. You're a hero in the eyes of this community. A great number of people admire you. I enjoy the charity work we do together and want to maintain our relationship."

As Styebeck stood to leave, his attention went to the woman who'd entered the room.

"Karl, this is my wife, Madeline, with the State Attorney General's Office."

"Yes, we've met at functions." Styebeck shook her hand.

"Maddy," Fowler said, "I was just telling Karl how I value our relationship."

"He thinks the world of you, Detective." She smiled. "Did he tell you he's willing to underscore that point at your fund-raiser this week?"

"No. That would be appreciated."

"In fact—" Fowler put his hand on Styebeck's shoulder as they walked to the door "—and this is confidential, please. But I'm considering a run for public office and would like to know that I can count on your support."

"I see…" Styebeck hesitated. "I don't really get involved in politics."

"I understand completely, Karl," Fowler said. "Not asking you to do or say anything. Just think about it. Besides, I'm taking steps to ensure this unfortunate matter will blow over."

"I need for that to happen."

"Now," Fowler said, "I know it seems the obvious move for me would be to fire Jack Gannon."

"I didn't want to raise that, or my legal options, here."

"Right. Just so you're aware, I can't fire him. Gannon's Pulitzer caliber, one of my best reporters. I almost lost him once. And while he's a zealous crusader, the fallout at the paper if I terminated him now would cause me too much grief with the news guild, just as we're positioning to sell the paper. That's confidential."

"Of course."

"I've pulled Gannon off this story and suspended him. One wrong move on his part and he's gone. That should keep him out of your business. How's that sound, Karl?"

"That sound's fine, Nate."

The men shook hands at the door then Styebeck got into his car.

Unseen, in the park across the street, Jack Gannon watched Styebeck leave Nate Fowler's house.

15

Gannon couldn't believe this.

Why was Karl Styebeck visiting Nate Fowler?

He doubted they were discussing their charity work.

Gannon walked from the park to his car then roamed the city, chewing on what he'd just witnessed, wondering where, or if, it fit with the latest aspects of the story. There was the mystery truck, the argument Bernice Hogan had had with another woman before she vanished, and the state police discrediting his reporting on Styebeck.

And now Styebeck pays Fowler a late-night visit.

Piece by piece a picture was emerging. Something large was percolating beneath the surface, but he didn't know what it was.

Was a cop suspected of murder being protected?

All right, better let things simmer, he told himself as he got to Cheektowaga, one of Buffalo's first suburbs. He lived in Cleveland Hill, a working- and middle-class neighborhood of proud, flag-on-the-porch homes built after the Second World War.

Mostly Polish-American families lived here, going back two and three generations. But he hadn't gone very far either. He'd grown up on the fringes of Cleveland Hill, near the Heights, a rougher district.

Buffalo was his home. A place he loved.

It was also his prison, he thought as he pulled into a parking space at the building where he lived, a tired-looking apartment complex built in the 1960s. He grabbed his bag, got his mail and took the elevator to the sixteenth floor.

His building had more good tenants than bad. There were a few noisy neighbors and a few creeps. And sometimes the halls were heavy with the smells of exotic cooking. But generally people left him alone.

He liked that.

His apartment had a large, sweeping view. The wind often charged off Lake Erie and rattled his windows, but it was warm in the winter.

He sat on his couch and sorted through his mail. There were mostly bills, then a letter from Ron Cook, an old reporter friend, who'd quit his job at the *Detroit Free Press* to teach English in Addis Ababa.

"Buddy, here's an application if you're looking for a career change and an escape from the snow!"

Gannon pondered the idea for a moment, but he had too much going on here to give it serious consideration.

No, thanks, Ron.

Then he came to a letter from the lawyer handling his parents' estate, reminding him that the anniversary was coming up for payment on the unit where he'd stored their belongings. Did he want to pay for another year, or did he have other plans for his family's property?

He'd deal with that later.

He tossed the letters on his coffee table, opened his bag, and had started reading the file Mary Peller had given him on her missing daughter when his cell phone rang.

"Gannon."

"It's Fowler. We've got a substantial retraction going in tomorrow's edition. In thirty minutes we start rolling it off the presses."

"You didn't call to tell me that."

"Give me your source and I'll kill the retraction."

Gannon said nothing. Now more than ever he didn't trust his managing editor.

"Jack, give me your source and we can all have our lives back."

"Does Bernice Hogan get her life back? Why does Styebeck get a free ride?"

"The police have publicly pissed on your story and the *Sentinel* today. You were wrong. We have to swallow that and move on."

"I was not wrong. And I can't give up my source."

"Think about what you're risking. Your job is hanging by a thread, Gannon. You've got about twenty-nine minutes to think it over."

Gannon didn't call.

He took a hot shower, dressed and got into his car.

Freeway traffic was light as he glided along Interstate 90.

He left the interstate and got on Genesee. As he headed into the heart of the city, Buffalo's skyline rose before him: the HSBC Center, the Rand Building and City Hall.

He found himself at the *Sentinel*'s loading docks, an area bordered by a chain-link fence that trapped stray papers and flyers. The air smelled of newsprint and exhaust as trucks and vans performed a marshaling ballet in and out of the ten bays, laden with damp copies of the first edition.

He was watching an act in the swan song of the newspaper industry, an industry in which he'd invested everything.

But he was not giving up.

He parked and went to the gate. Holding up a dollar bill, he flagged down a van departing for its route.

"Sell me a copy?"

The driver had a scar on his cheek. He snatched Gannon's buck then reached to his passenger seat, grunted and handed him a fresh copy of the *Buffalo Sentinel.*

The retraction was there on the front page, framed in a shaded box with a different font. He scanned, "*Sentinel* offers its apology…" "Uncorroborated information…" "Erroneous reporting…" "Taken action…" "Suspended…" The words landed like punches until he heard a clank down the street at a row of newspaper boxes.

A carrier was loading a box for the *Buffalo News.* Gannon went over and bought a paper. The *News* had clobbered him with their front-page coverage, giving him his comeuppance in a column under the headline:

The Pulitzer Finalist Who Got It Wrong

The item pontificated about the journalistic failing of rushing to be first at the expense of getting it right. Gannon lowered the papers, like flags of defeat.

What happened?

Less than twenty-four hours ago he owned the news in this town. Now his world was collapsing.

He nearly vanished in the dust that swirled around him as the delivery trucks thundered by. A cold wind kicked up from Lake Erie and he retreated to his car and drove away, traveling back through his life.

Being a reporter was all he'd ever wanted to be.

He was a blue-collar kid. His mother worked long hours as a waitress, while his father worked hard shifts in a factory on the lakeshore that made rope. Both of them were newspaper readers, a trait they'd passed on to him.

Enthralled by life's daily dramas, he read the *Buffalo*

Evening News and the *Buffalo Courier-Express*. And when the *Courier-Express* folded, he read the *Sentinel,* which rose from its ashes.

And he dreamed about seeing his own stories in print.

When his parents worked late, his big sister, Cora, would take him to the library and get him books by Jack London, Stephen Crane and Ernest Hemingway.

"This is what a future reporter should be reading, Jackie," she'd said.

Cora was five years older than him and nurtured his dream. She convinced their parents to buy him a second-hand computer and encouraged him to write. They were as close as any brother and sister could be. But their age difference would have a bearing on their relationship and eventually Cora grew apart from him and her family.

She changed.

It hit him the night police brought her home after she'd got drunk with friends who'd stolen a car. She'd grown into a different person, one who argued constantly with Mom and Dad. So many nights were filled with screaming, slamming doors, heart-breaking silence and tears. Cora started taking drugs, which led to more arguments until the day she ran away.

All she'd left was a note saying she could no longer stand living under "their fascist rules."

She was seventeen.

Friends told his parents Cora had gone to California with an older guy who was a heroin addict. When his father got an address, he flew to San Francisco and looked for Cora.

It was all in vain.

They never saw her again.

They hired private detectives, flew to cities when they had tips. It was futile. He ached for her to come home.

Then his anguish turned to anger for what Cora had done. Later, there were times he'd search for her on online databases. He even asked police friends to do whatever they could.

Not much came of it.

Cora was out of their lives.

Or dead.

Accept it and leave the past in the past, he'd always told himself.

Miles and time swept by as he searched the night for answers.

He drove through older neighborhoods; the best and the worst of Buffalo. Here were the abandoned factories, the shut-up mills and forgotten stores, reaching from the wasteland of the rust belt like a death grasp. And here were the new bohemian communities that resurrected historic, near-dead buildings and revived the never-say-die attitude of Buffalo.

After Cora left, he'd worked brutal summer shifts on assembly lines in Buffalo factories to put himself through college because his parents had spent nearly all they had looking for her.

When he found time, he reported for the campus paper, and freelanced articles to the *Sentinel* and the *News.*

All the while, he yearned to escape Buffalo for New York City and a job with a big news outlet. After he graduated from college, he worked at small weeklies then landed an internship with the *Buffalo Sentinel.* Impressed by his determination, the paper gave him a full-time reporting job.

The *Sentinel* would be his stepping stone out of Buffalo.

Then, while dispatched to cover a shooting in Ohio, he'd met Lisa Newsome, a reporter with the *Cleveland Plain Dealer.* She was a sharp-witted, brilliant writer. He remembered the way her hair curtained over her eye when she wrote the stories she'd cared about.

She told him that she'd fallen for his edgy charm and "*that Matt Damon thing you got going in the looks department.*" She wanted him to move to Cleveland and work at the *Plain Dealer,* or she'd offered to move to Buffalo because she yearned to have kids and settle down.

He didn't, so they broke it off and Gannon threw all he had into his reporting.

Two years back, his talent was tested when a charter jet en route to Moscow from Chicago plunged into Lake Erie a quarter mile off Buffalo's shoreline. Some two hundred people died.

While the world press speculated that the cause was terrorism, Gannon found a Russian-speaking man in the *Sentinel*'s mail room. They worked the phones and the Internet, locating the pilot's brother who was living in St. Petersburg, Russia. Turned out the brother had received the last e-mail the pilot had sent but refused to share it. *"Think of the dead, their families deserve to know the answer. Think of the dead, their ghosts will haunt you,"* Gannon and the Russian-speaking *Sentinel* worker kept telling the brother before convincing him to give them the final e-mail. It detailed the pilot's plan to commit suicide by crashing his jet because his wife had left him for a woman.

The story was picked up around the world.

It led to Gannon's Pulitzer nomination. He didn't win the prize, but he got a job offer in New York City with the World Press Alliance, the global wire service.

His dream had come true.

Then fate intervened.

About a week after the offer came, his mother and father were driving to see an old friend about another tip they'd had about Cora's location. Even though she'd be close to forty years old, Gannon's mother and father refused to give up searching for her.

"She may have children, we have a right to find her," his mother said.

They never made it. A construction worker who'd spent the afternoon in a bar slammed into their car.

They both died instantly.

Gannon blamed Cora.

It was a horrible time.

Gannon was in no shape to do anything and declined the New York offer. Why didn't he leave afterward? Maybe he stuck around to be closer to the memory of his parents. Maybe he thought Cora would miraculously appear. Even now, he didn't know. It didn't matter. In the end, the New York job never materialized.

So where did he go from here?

He eased his Pontiac Vibe to a stop at the edge of a park alongside Ellicott Creek. As the Vibe's engine ticked, he sat behind the wheel staring into the night.

Everything he was, everything he dreamed of, was on the line.

In his heart he knew he was not wrong on his reporting of Detective Karl Styebeck's link to Bernice Hogan's murder. Call it fate, destiny or a cosmic force, but something had guided him to that meeting-room door that day at Clarence Barracks and pointed to Styebeck.

But all he had left were more unanswered questions about the case.

There was only one thing he could do now.

He reached to the floor behind the passenger seat for his lantern flashlight. It had a new six-volt battery and an intense-focus beam. The light was strong.

He left his car and headed for the woods. If he was going to search for more answers, the shallow grave where they'd found Bernice Hogan's corpse was the place to start.

16

Jolene Peller's body swayed rhythmically to the low drumming of big wheels rolling at high speed.

As she floated in and out of consciousness, she tried to seize upon a way to claw out of the darkness.

She needed to think. Think of what she knew.

Her prison—or tomb—whatever it was, was still moving.

She knew she'd been abducted.

But who had done this? And why?

Someone had bound her hands, gagged her and imprisoned her. She had muzzy memories—or was it a dream?—of someone removing her gag, feeding her bread, chocolate bars, giving her water. Giving her a plastic bucket for a toilet, ordering her to relieve herself. There was tissue, but her hands remained bound with tape.

Mercifully the bucket had a lid.

Then she was forced to swallow capsules.

Drugs?

Someone was keeping her alive.

Like a captured animal.

Who? Who was doing this and what was he going to do to her?

Or had he already done something to her while she was unconscious?

The image made her retch. She swallowed. Please no. Jolene pushed back her tears.

Please.

What did he do to Bernice?

Jolene had no concept of where she was, or how long she'd been here. She was wearing the same clothes she'd worn when she tried to help Bernice.

She wanted to shower, to cleanse herself of this foul, stinking nightmare.

She knew by the steady drone that she was still moving. Maybe this was her chance to do something.

But what?

She was gagged. Her hands were bound, but not her legs or ankles. She was free to move, but she was blind in the absolute darkness. Maybe her abductor was watching her now with some sort of high-tech equipment? Maybe if he saw that she was awake he'd come to her?

To do what?

Jolene's breathing quickened.

She was so scared. She whispered a prayer.

Stay calm.

Using her fingertips, she felt in her pockets for her cell phone. It was gone.

Take it easy.

She steeled herself then probed the soft pad. Feeling its indentations, quilting and seams, she concluded that it was a mattress.

Single-size.

Pushed against a wall.

Jolene drew herself into a sitting position. She was woozy. She waited and breathed slowly. Then she ran her fingers over the walls. They were solid wood with a rough pitted surface. At times, she felt the steel hardware of a hinge-and-bolt assembly. Felt the line of a door frame. But it was shut up so tight, no light, or hope, leaked through. At times she felt the head of a nail or screw protruding from the wall.

It was familiar.

In high school, when she was a part-time supermarket cashier, she'd helped inventory all the departments, even the warehouse. The big storage containers and trailers smelled like this and had the same rough surface.

They were heavy, insulated, sound-absorbing walls, like those in a cooler. It was not refrigerated but it was cold. Near her were old blankets that smelled as if they'd been used for horses.

Jolene stood.

Waves of dizziness rolled over her and she steadied herself against the wall, waiting for them to subside.

She raised her restrained hands above her head, felt nothing but air.

Then carefully, starting with the nearest wall, she began inching her way around the boundary of her prison, steadying herself against the to-and-fro motion as she felt for a latch, a light switch, a door, a window, anything.

As she groped cautiously, her fingers brushed against the chain bearing her locket. A gift from her mother. She stopped, found it in the dark, and while her bound hands made the simple movement awkward, Jolene touched it to her cheek.

Cody.

It gave her strength.

It fueled her determination to get home to her little boy, who needed her, and to her mother, who'd be worried to death.

What if her mother thought she'd run off? Got stoned, abandoned Cody.

What if she died here and that was the last thought—the last memory—her mother had?

No, no, *NO!*

Jolene couldn't bear the heartbreak for her mother. Her mother, who'd stood by her and supported her when everyone else had written her off.

I love you.

At that moment, Jolene promised her mom and Cody that she'd find a way out and back to the new life she'd worked so hard, so damn hard, to build for them.

Jolene Peller's life would not end in this dark stinking box, or hole, or whatever the hell it was. She'd been through too much, worked too hard to just give up to some crazy motherf—

Jolene tasted the salt of her tears as she completed moving around the perimeter of her cell. About eight-by-eight, she guessed as she blinked back her fear and braced herself in her starting corner. Moving blindly and slowly, she cut across the floor. She extended her right foot, then her left, to feel for a trap door, or anything on the floor.

She was strong, smart and would fight, she told herself in the instant before her heart smashed against her chest and she froze.

Jolene's foot had hit something.

Something that moaned.

17

Gannon started walking along the water's edge.

It was close to 3:00 a.m., the area was deserted. Breezes fingered through the elm and maple trees. After nearly a hundred yards, he came to the hilly bend where the two women had made the discovery.

His flashlight captured a patch of shimmering yellow, a strip of flapping police tape knotted to a branch.

It beckoned him to the grim scene beyond. But he didn't move. He felt he was being watched. He swept his light beam up high through the trees.

A pair of eyes glowed back at him.

An owl hooted.

As Gannon took stock of the area, he moved his light lower toward the spot where they'd found Bernice Hogan's corpse.

Trees and branches obscured the reach of his light.

He proceeded.

He left the footpath, going deeper into the woods. Few people knew that the scene had been released earlier tonight, after it had been processed by the State Police Forensic Investigations Unit, dispatched from troop headquarters in Batavia five days ago.

They'd seized it for longer than usual.

Maybe they'd had problems with this one?

Now the tape was gone and all barriers had been removed.

No one was here.

The burial site was some thirty yards from the footpath, along hills and valleys, amid a stand of maple and shrubs. It was a long shot that the women would have spotted it, but conditions and lighting must have been just right.

Or maybe the killer wanted it found? The area was popular with walkers, hikers, birdwatchers.

During his time on the crime beat, Gannon had studied the same textbooks detectives studied to pass their exams. And he'd researched and reported on enough homicides, and murder trials, to know the procedures of an investigation and the collection of evidence.

He knew that buried-body cases and outdoor crime scenes posed problems. Weather conditions can harm any trace evidence, blow it or wash it away. Animals can damage a body, or carry evidence far from a scene. The perimeter can be impossible to establish.

Still, the investigators would have been thorough. They would have gridded the area; would have done a lot of things, like look for tire impressions back at the parking lot, or foot impressions here.

As he walked, he raked his light over the ground in front of him, looking at the flattened trail that was likely used by investigators as the entry-exit path to the scene.

He found nothing else in the empty forest. The state police had not released details on the cause or location of Bernice Hogan's death. Early rumors held that she was killed elsewhere and dumped near the creek. But later, Adell had told him that they believed she was murdered here, given the amount of blood that had soaked into the ground.

While Gannon continued, meticulously sweeping his light everywhere, he tried to imagine Bernice Hogan's last moments. As he ascended a small rise, he inched his light forward until—*Jesus, there it is.*

The hole in the ground was about six-by-two feet and about three feet in depth, a rounded, cup-shaped withdrawal of soil clawed from the earth.

This was the work of the scene experts.

To the right of the hole lay a neat mound of fine, dark soil. To the left, a neat pile of branches and twigs. A few fragments of white string were present, likely used to section the site and screen soil excavated from and around the grave. All in keeping with the transfer theory, which arises from the fact that a killer will always leave, or take, some sort of trace evidence from a victim or a scene.

The area had been methodically cleaned by the unit.

Gusts hissed through the treetops, tumbled down to the site, hurling grit into the dark forest and into Gannon's eyes.

He sat down on the rise nearby overlooking the grave.

Remnants of torn-off police tape waved from trees, like the aftermath of an explosion of the monstrous act committed here.

A human being was murdered right here.

In the distance, he saw the lights of the suburbs, rows of safe middle-class homes twinkling in a different world that was light-years away from Bernice Hogan's.

He looked down at her grave.

What a lonely place to die.

Did she glimpse heaven in her last moments?

He set his flashlight on the ground, pulled his notebook from his rear pocket, snapped through it until he found clear pages.

Soon, more people would come to the site. A parks crew would likely arrive first to restore it. That was the usual way things went in cases like this. They'd fill the hole, disperse the twigs.

Then morbid attraction would play out.

Neighborhood kids, the little ones, would dare each other to venture here. Teenagers would buy beer to party here and scare each other. Walkers, joggers and the like, would point respectfully and say, "They found her out there."

Gannon sat on the rise asking himself if there was more he could do as songs from warblers and field sparrows coaxed the sun to come up.

Stiff, he rubbed his eyes and stood. All he could do was search the edges of the area. It was not likely that the scene people had missed anything, but you never knew.

He walked in a spiral pattern, expanding it as he circled the grave site. He kept his eyes to the ground, scanning it for anything that might have been overlooked.

As he walked, faraway noises of dogs barking, a car horn, the sounds of the city waking echoed while he searched the ground.

Maybe Brent and Esko had some key fact evidence they were holding back.

It was a safe bet that Karl Styebeck would be familiar with this area. But so would plenty of other people. It was the suburbs, a metro area just minutes from the Canadian border.

Then there was the mysterious blue rig with unique writing on the door. And what about the angle that another woman had argued with Bernice Hogan the night she vanished, according to Lotta, the waitress at Kupinski's?

As Gannon continued circling the scene in an ever-widening pattern taking him to the park's outer limits, he found discarded items: beer cans, whiskey bottles, take-out containers, cigarette wrappers, a rusted license plate, a bicycle wheel and an old tire.

They were such a long way from the scene he wouldn't expect that the unit missed them, or that they'd be a factor.

Still, he noted their location on a crude map, with a brief description.

His body was heavy with exhaustion.

Time to pack it in, head home, have a hot shower, get a few hours of sleep and start fresh. As Gannon turned to leave, he saw another scrap of trash, a piece of paper caught in some shrubs.

Looked like some sort of receipt.

He yawned.

Might as well check it out.

Removing it from the branches, Gannon saw that it was a ticket for a one-way bus trip.

Buffalo to Orlando, Florida.

Hold on.

Somewhere, in the far recesses of his memory, a tiny alarm began sounding a short, high ring, telling him this was important.

Why?

The ticket was unused. There was no name on it. It was bought a week ago, almost the same time Bernice Hogan had vanished.

The pinging in Gannon's brain was getting louder.

Why was this important?

He should know. He should know.

He did.

Yes. He did know.

Peller.

His heart beat faster as he flipped back through his notes, back to Mary Peller who'd come to the newsroom to plead for help finding her daughter, Jolene.

Jolene, whom she'd lost to drugs and the street.

Jolene, who'd done things she was not proud of for money, like prostitution, maybe?

Jolene, who was twenty-six and missing.

All right, this was stupid. Her name was not on this ticket. No one's name was on it. He'd found it, what? Sixty, seventy, eighty yards from the scene?

He was beyond tired.

He took out his cell phone and photographed the ticket, then the location.

All right, he needed to find out exactly who had purchased this one-way ticket to Orlando, Florida.

He needed help and he needed it now.

He dialed a phone number.

18

Adell Clark had risen early with a knot in her stomach.

She pulled a robe over her T-shirt and sweats. She went to the bedroom across the hall. Crystal, her seven-year-old daughter, had Ralph, her stuffed bear, in a choke hold and was sleeping deeply.

Good.

Adell went to her home office in the corner of her living room. It consisted of a polished sheet of cherry wood atop two second-hand steel file cabinets she'd gotten from a veterinarian who'd retired to Tempe, Arizona.

Time for the moment of truth.

She switched on her laptop and called up the *Buffalo Sentinel*'s Web site. The retraction dominated the page. She read it then read the news story on the "mystery truck." Next, she went to the online edition of the *Buffalo News* and read their coverage, including the column attacking Gannon's credibility.

Gannon had shielded her.

He'd sustained the suspension, the humiliation and the professional ridicule to protect her. He'd put it all on the line.

What she couldn't fathom was why Michael Brent, or whoever was behind it, had gone out of their way to kill Gannon's story and practically clear Styebeck. There had to be a deeper thread to the investigation that Brent was holding back, she thought as her phone rang.

"Clark." A habit from her days at the bureau.

"It's Gannon."

"Speak of the devil."

"Did I wake you?"

"No. I just read today's papers. Thank you seems inadequate."

"Forget it. I need your help again. I'm at the Hogan crime scene. I've been here all night and I think I found something."

"Were the forensics people sloppy?"

"No. Listen, can you get to your e-mail?"

"Got it right here."

"I've sent you some pictures of a ticket. Have a look. I need to confirm who bought it."

Adell opened the e-mails. As she studied the photos of the scene and the ticket, Gannon told her about Mary Peller's visit to the newsroom, her worries about her daughter Jolene's disappearance, street talk about Bernice Hogan having argued with another woman before she'd vanished and what Bernice's foster mom had said about people trying to help Bernice get off the street.

"So, can you help me?"

Adell enlarged the images. The ticket had a number that could be traced to the point, time and date of purchase. Records would show the method of payment. If it was a credit card or bank card, the identity of the cardholder would be easy to trace. If it was a cash purchase, records would still confirm the date and time of purchase, which might, in a perfect world, be linked to captured security-camera images.

"Can you help me, Adell?"

"It's going to take a few calls. Where are you going to be in the next couple of hours?"

"Getting some sleep. Get back to me if you find anything."

* * *

On his way home, Gannon stopped off at a drive-thru for some breakfast. As his car crawled along the waiting line he tried focusing on what he should do next, but exhaustion dulled his thinking.

At his apartment he showered, got into bed and read through his notes until he fell asleep. Sometime later, he was looking around the bedroom trying to determine what had awakened him when his phone rang again.

"It's Adell."

"What do you have?"

"I had to call in a lot of favors."

"I appreciate that."

"The ticket was purchased for Jolene Peller."

"*For* Jolene?"

"Yes, it was charged to a credit card belonging to the Street Angels Outreach Society."

"It sounds remotely familiar."

"Check it out, Jack, I have to go."

He made a pot of strong coffee and began researching the Street Angels. He put in a few calls to city hall administration then started digging online. It didn't take long before he'd confirmed that they were a tax-exempt nonprofit association. A few archived news stories characterized their mandate as reaching out to help addicts and homeless people improve their lives.

He dug into the group's charter and administration pages and his jaw dropped.

Karl Styebeck was a board member.

And the group's biannual open fund-raiser banquet was tonight.

The banner on the events page said: *Tickets still available at the door.*

19

"This is Jolene at six."

A big-eyed girl in a flower-print dress and pigtails smiled at Gannon. Then the plastic cover sheet crackled and Mary Peller flipped through the album to more images of her missing daughter's life.

"When she was six, Jo fell from a swing in the park and fractured her skull. I was so afraid I was going to lose her then. But I didn't."

Mary covered her mouth with her shaking hand.

"But now. Oh God, this is so bad."

Mary looked at the bus ticket Gannon had set on her kitchen table. Her daughter's ticket.

She stared at it as if it were a death warrant.

As a reporter, Gannon had seen fear exact different reactions. Some people punched walls, or other people. Some insisted the facts were wrong, or a lie. Some collapsed to the floor.

Some prayed.

Others performed acts of faith in the face of looming tragedy, as Mary Peller did now. She'd reached for a cherished album, for comfort and confirmation that she'd confronted and triumphed over fear before.

See, like the time Jo fell off the swing.

Gannon understood.

But they weren't talking about a six-year-old girl. And they weren't talking about falling from a swing in the park.

Jack, if you saw the crime-scene pictures of what Bernice Hogan's killer did to her...

So Gannon let Mary Peller take her time to absorb the significance of the ticket as he walked around her modest apartment. It was on the third floor of a four-story low-rent building in a struggling working-class area near Schiller Park.

It was clean, tidy, and filled with Jolene's presence. Certificates for completion of her night-school courses and recognition for her "outstanding" work at her restaurant job hung on the wall. On the floor, a plastic ring-toss game and several picture books belonging to Jolene's son, Cody.

Gannon peered down the hall to a door partially opened to a bedroom where the three-year-old was napping. He saw his small face, cherubic calm amid tornados of curls.

Prior to arriving nearly half an hour ago, Gannon had grappled with how much he would tell Mary about his discovery of the ticket and its possible link to Bernice Hogan's murder.

Investigators needed to know about it.

Mary Peller deserved to know about it.

It was at the instant when Mary opened her apartment door to him and he looked into her worried eyes that he'd decided to tell her everything and ask for her help.

Now, after he'd explained all that he knew, after he'd given Mary time to process the twist in her daughter's case, Gannon had to push things.

"I know this looks bad, Mary."

"Jolene's not dead."

"That's right. Until we know the facts, anything is possible."

Mary glanced around her kitchen, helpless.

"Mary, I need you to think hard about my questions. I know they're painful but I need to know the truth so I can help you, okay?"

Mary agreed.

"When you first came to the newsroom to see me about Jolene, you told me that she wasn't proud of some of the things she'd done to get drugs. I'm sorry, but I have to ask—did she ever work downtown as a prostitute?"

Anguish creased her face.

She looked away to the window, then her focus returned to the photo album and the picture of Jolene at six in pigtails. Then she looked at the gold-framed photo on a bookshelf near the living room. It was Jolene smiling with Cody laughing in her arms.

"Mary?"

"Yes."

"Did Jolene ever work as a prostitute?"

"Yes, to pay for drugs."

"Did she know Bernice Hogan?"

"I don't know."

"Did she know Karl Styebeck?"

"I don't know because she never talked about that part of her life. It was like she wanted to rip it out of her past and move on. She'd worked so hard to crawl out of the hell she was trapped in."

"She must've known people with the Street Angels Outreach Society," he said, "given that they bought the bus ticket for her."

"I didn't know this. I thought she'd bought the ticket with money she'd saved. All I know is that she had some help from some groups." Mary touched a tissue to her eyes. "Some things she wouldn't talk about."

Mary's knuckles whitened. She clasped her hands together as if to keep herself from coming apart.

"I'm so scared. You found this ticket at the murder scene. I have to find my daughter! I have to find Jolene!"

Mary stifled a sob with both hands.

"I don't know what to do. Help me, please!"

"Take it easy, Mary. Try to think hard about my questions and listen to me again. I'm going to tell you what you should do, but I also need your help, okay?"

She nodded as she regained her composure.

"I'm going to leave the ticket with you in the envelope. Try not to touch it. I'm the only one who's handled it. I've got a copy. I left details on how it was discovered and my card in the envelope. Call the FBI field office and also call Investigators Michael Brent and Roxanne Esko with the state police in Clarence. Then call the county sheriff's office. Tell them about the ticket being found near the Hogan scene. It will get their attention."

Mary nodded as Gannon stood to leave.

"They're going to be angry at me for not coming to them first. Let me worry about that, okay?"

"All right."

At the door, Gannon gave Mary another business card to ensure she had his cell and home numbers.

"Now, I need you to promise me that whatever you learn from anyone on Jolene's case, you'll share with me and no other reporters. And I promise to share anything I find with you."

"You're the only reporter I trust."

Gannon nodded his thanks as his cell phone rang.

"Excuse me, I'll take this outside. I have to go."

Mary took his hand and shook it. "Thank you for helping me."

Gannon answered his call as he headed down the stairs.

"Gannon."

"Hey, this is Lotta, from the diner."

"What's up?"

"Got a working girl who wants to talk to you."

"Really?"

"She's got information about Karl Styebeck that you should have."

"I'll talk to her, tell me where and when."

"I'll get back to you with the details. But Jack, you have to know something about her."

"What's that?"

"She's scared to death."

20

The hooker's name was Tuesday. And she wanted to meet Gannon at the Compassionate Virgin's Redemption Church.

He considered the irony.

The location venerated purity and forgiveness. It was also a sanctuary, a smart choice for someone afraid of the secret they possessed. And given what was emerging, a church in the middle-class suburb of Tonawanda seemed like a safe place to reveal the truth.

Especially if it was tied to Bernice Hogan's murder.

The fifty-year-old building had been designed in the postwar modernist style. An enormous cross rose from the center section, which resembled a book standing with its covers open to embrace worshippers.

Gannon parked down the street under the shade of a willow tree. Walking to the main door, he read the church's outdoor sign, which gave mass times and other messages. He noticed that confessions were being heard today from 2:00 to 3:00 p.m.

His meeting was for 2:30 p.m.

The church had a center aisle with pews on each side. Light bled through its stained-glass windows that depicted the Stations of the Cross. The walls were interrupted with alcoves sheltering statues of the Holy Family, the apostles and saints.

At the front was the altar, graced by a massive crucifix suspended behind it and flanked by magnificent stained glass that ascended from the floor for several stories. The air held a mix of furniture polish, candle wax, incense and piety.

The building was empty but for a few people scattered among the pews, or waiting to enter the confessionals. Others found unoccupied pews where they said their penance while rosary beads clicked softly.

How egregious were the sins committed in this white-bread suburb? Gannon wondered as he went to a pew near the front right section, next to a replica of the pietà. The area was vacant. The bench seat of the wooden pew creaked when he sat down.

This was where he was instructed to meet Tuesday.

While he waited, he checked his phone.

No messages.

He set the ringer to vibrate and read his notes for several minutes, until his pew creaked.

A white woman in her late twenties sat next to him. She was wearing a charcoal business suit and tank top. The ensemble flattered her figure. Her dirty-blond hair was pulled up into a bun held with a hair clamp. Her face had the pallor of a woman averse to daylight, a condition she'd compensated for by applying a little too much makeup. Her eyes were blue, and Gannon noticed the scent of roses when she nodded to him.

"Are you Tuesday?"

"I'd like to see some identification," she said.

He showed her his press ID from the *Sentinel,* which she studied for several moments. Then she took stock of the area. Satisfied they were alone in their corner of the church, she kept her voice low.

"Lotta said I can trust you, is that true?"

"Trust me with what?"

"My life."

"Because of what you know about Karl Styebeck?"

"I don't want to end up like Bernice."

"I understand."

She looked around.

"You don't have a photographer hiding around somewhere with a big lens or anything?"

"No."

"Swear to me that no one will ever know what I'm going to tell you came from me. Give me your word."

"I don't reveal sources."

"To anyone?"

"To anyone. No one will know we talked."

Tuesday searched his face. Whatever internal security screening she possessed, whatever defence mechanism she'd engaged, Gannon had passed. Her face softened a degree; she spoke in a hurried whisper.

"After what happened to Bernie, my girlfriends and I read all your stories. You had the best information. Then things got weird."

"Weird? How?"

Gannon took out his notebook. Tuesday looked at it, hesitated.

"Do you have a hidden recorder?"

"No. Look, you called me. How can I be sure that what you're going to tell me is the truth?"

"Because it is."

Now it was Gannon's turn to decide if she was helping him, or playing him. That would depend on what she said.

"Tell me what you know about Karl Styebeck," he said.

"He was down on Niagara the night Bernice vanished, and when the detectives came around we told them about all the wack jobs and creeps who were down there, including Styebeck."

"Styebeck was known to the girls?"

"Big-time. But first there's nothing in the papers about it. Even right after they found Bernice."

"I had it."

"Yeah, you did. A few days later, we all thought, *Great! Yes! Nailed Him!* And you were, like, a hero. This Gannon guy's good. He prints the truth, you know."

Gannon didn't say anything.

"Then your paper prints a correction, retraction thing, like the stuff about Styebeck was all a big mistake, and we're all, like, 'what the—?' Know what I mean? What happened?"

"The paper was told that Styebeck was downtown that night doing some community-outreach work for a charity and wrongly got caught up in the investigation of Bernice's murder."

"That's a crock of shit."

"What do you mean? He goes down there to help, right?"

"Yeah, right. This is what he does, every month or so. Styebeck comes down there and first he gets in our face. He calls us whores and wants to save us. We tell him to go f—," Tuesday caught herself. "We tell him to take a hike."

Gannon took notes.

"He goes away then he comes back, and it's like his whole personality's changed. He wants to date some of the girls, but he asks for girls who are shaved."

"Shaved?"

"No hair down there because he likes them 'young and clean,' he says."

Gannon flipped quickly to a clear page.

"Anything else?" he asked.

"One girl said he once told her that he knew he was sick for what he was doing, and that he was that way because of his father."

"His father? Did he say any more about that?"

"No, that's all I'd heard," Tuesday said.

"What about the night before Bernice was killed?"

"He was bothering Bernice that night. He was in her face. We told the detectives. And he was asking us about some stupid truck. Some of the girls said they saw it."

"What kind of truck?" he asked.

"I don't know. It was in the news—a blue truck with writing on the door, or something."

"What about Jolene Peller?"

"Who?"

"Jolene Peller. She had a little boy and was trying to get out of the life."

"You talking about J.P. Got a boy named Jody?"

"Cody," Gannon said.

"That's her. Yes. I heard she left town."

"She was supposed to leave for Florida the night Bernice disappeared from the street. Jolene's mother says she never got there and she hasn't heard from her."

"Oh Christ, does anybody know what happened?"

"No. Did anyone see her talking to Bernice that night?"

Tuesday shook her head.

"I can ask around." She sifted through her bag for her wallet and then showed him a snapshot of her laughing with Bernice Hogan in front of Toronto's skyline.

"That's us a few months ago. We went shopping in Canada. Bernie was like a little sister to a few girls on the street. She didn't belong there. I mean, who does?"

Gannon nodded.

"I grew up in St. Paul, Minnesota, where my family was a freak show. Got pregnant by my stepdad, who turned me out to his two friends for drugs. By the time I was sixteen, I'd had two abortions. One day, I stole all the cash I could find and just left on a bus to anywhere. We all make mistakes. We all mess up."

Tuesday's eyes teared as she placed her photo back in her wallet. "Your job is to tell the truth, right?"

Gannon nodded.

"People think we're garbage," she said, "that we deserve the life we're in, that we're something you scrape off of your shoe. Nobody deserves what happened to Bernice. You've got to tell the truth about what's happening with Styebeck, because if you don't do it, who will? And if the truth doesn't come out, who's gonna stop him?"

"I'm just a reporter."

"Yeah, well, what's that old saying about the pen being deadlier than the sword?"

"Mightier."

"Mightier. Well, remember that, Gannon."

Tuesday accepted his card and left.

When Gannon headed to his car, he noticed a sedan that had wheeled off a block away.

It looked like an unmarked model used by detective units.

21

Harding Community Hall was in the heart of Ascension Park.

Inside, on the entrance walls, there were large portrait-photos of laughing babies, smiling seniors and volunteers comforting people in tragic circumstances.

Here was the work of the Street Angels Outreach Society.

A blowup of an older news picture was showcased in a glass frame. It showed Karl Styebeck in the back of an ambulance, his face masked with soot as he looked over the stretchers bearing the children he'd just rescued from a burning house.

The guy's a god here, Gannon thought while he queued with well-attired strangers to buy tickets. He adjusted his suit, feeling his notebook and recorder in his breast pockets. He was ready to confront Styebeck with what he'd learned today.

"How many, sir?" asked the woman seated at the ticket table outside the hall's banquet room.

"Just one," he said.

The lights were dimmed over some twenty formally set round tables that filled the room. Soft classical music mingled with cocktails and the conversations of some two hundred people.

Gannon avoided everyone, weaving through the group for half an hour until he spotted Styebeck in the distance, making his way with others to the VIP table on the riser at the head of the room.

Gannon found a seat at the far back of the hall with several older couples. He was careful not to reveal his name as they talked politics and art. No one broached the subject of Karl Styebeck, murder suspect, including Gannon.

"I'm just a writer, and like everyone else, I'm here to do my part for the cause." He smiled over dessert as Rona Nicole, the society's president, took the podium. She began with the usual jokes and calls to applaud event organizers and catering staff.

"Before we move on to achievements and our charity auction, we're going to address something," Nicole said. "As you know, Street Angels helps people who are facing the most difficult times in their lives. Well, now we're going to put to rest an issue that has distressed a few people in this room. I'm talking about the unfortunate events involving my fellow board member, Detective Karl Styebeck."

Nicole smiled at Styebeck.

"I've spoken with Karl and he would like to say a few words to you."

A quiet fell on the room, punctuated with nervous coughing and throat clearing as Styebeck leaned into the microphone and looked out to the gathering.

"Thank you, Rona. Ladies and gentlemen, on behalf of my family, I want to thank everyone for their calls of support. These past forty-eight hours have been a trying time for us, to say the least."

He glanced to his wife who blinked back tears as he continued.

"The fact is, I am assisting in the investigation of a terrible case, but I'm sure you'll appreciate that I can't say much more beyond that. However, through confusion, a painfully damaging allegation was made, one that has since been corrected. I want to apologize to the society for any undue anxiety its members may have experienced and assure you, there is a silver lining to this, as my special guest tonight will tell you. Nate."

Styebeck turned to the end of the VIP table. Gannon craned his neck and was incredulous at what he saw.

Nate Fowler was moving to the podium.

"Thank you, Karl. Everyone, I am Nate Fowler, managing editor of the *Buffalo Sentinel.*"

Someone booed and Fowler smiled, held up his palms in surrender.

"As you know, in the news business we're under a lot of pressure to get the story. In this case, we succumbed to it without getting the facts. In rushing to beat the competition we got it wrong. That error hurt people, but it was corrected in today's edition of my paper."

Applause rippled around the room as Fowler continued.

"As some of you know, I sit on the boards of other charitable organizations with Karl Styebeck. I know Karl and can attest to his unimpeachable, altruistic character. Gosh, look at that inspiring news picture of Karl out front in the hall, taken by a *Sentinel* photographer, I might add."

A few people chuckled.

"Folks, if we are to learn anything from this recent unfortunate situation, it is that anyone can find themselves in dire straits at any time. This only underscores the need for your group, the fine work it does and continues to do. So, Rona, before you move on to the auction, allow me, as a sign of good faith, on behalf of the *Buffalo Sentinel,* to present you with check for fifteen thousand dollars."

Amid the applause and ovation, Fowler raised his voice. "And my wife, Madeline, and I will personally add an additional five-thousand dollar-donation."

Dumbstruck, Gannon stood with the others, not to praise what had transpired but to convince himself that he'd actually witnessed it. He couldn't believe it. Fowler had just crapped on his own paper like a guy campaigning for public favor.

For the rest of the evening, Gannon struggled to sort things out while searching for the right moment to get Styebeck alone. It came when Styebeck was making his way to the men's room. Gannon caught him before he entered.

"Detective Styebeck?"

His smile twisted into a scowl when he recognized Gannon.

"What the hell are you doing here?"

"I need to ask you a few questions for the record, given recent events."

Gannon extended his small recorder and Styebeck's jaw pulsed, as if inviting Gannon to take his best shot.

"What recent events?"

"I understand there are people who witnessed you with Bernice Hogan the night before she disappeared from Niagara."

"Look, asshole, I don't know who your sources are, but you've got things all wrong. I tried to help Bernice."

"So you confirm you had a relationship with her?"

"I knew her and tried to help her."

"Help her do what?"

"Get off the street. Get clean. Get a life. It's what my group does."

"Were you with her the night she vanished?"

"Yes, I just told you, I was trying to help her."

"Did you kill her?"

Styebeck's face was blank, void of emotion.

"No, I did not kill her. Why the hell would you even ask me that?"

"What about Jolene Peller? Do you know her?"

"Who?"

"She's a former prostitute. Did the society help her leave Buffalo?"

"Maybe. We help a lot of people."

"Did you ever meet Jolene Peller, or J.P., as she is also known?"

"I don't know where you're going with this."

"Then I'll tell you. Women who work as prostitutes in downtown Buffalo say you are known to them."

"So? Why would that be unusual? I'm a detective. I have informants who are hookers. Besides, we offer them support through our group. I admit knowing prostitutes. Is that headline news, Gannon?"

"But sir, they've identified you as a client, a customer with special preferences. What's your response to that?"

"It's bullshit."

"Is it? They seem to know a lot about you, that you prefer them young, clean, and that you specify that they be shaved. And you once called yourself sick and blamed it on your father. What's up with that, Detective?"

Gannon had crossed a line. Something slithered across Styebeck's eyes.

"They're lying."

Gannon sensed a presence and turned toward a woman standing behind him. Other people had gathered behind her, concerned.

"This is my wife, Alice. Alice, Jack Gannon from the *Sentinel* has paid us an unannounced visit and seems determined to twist fiction into fact."

Undaunted, Gannon pressed on. "What did you say to Bernice Hogan the night before she was killed, Detective?"

Styebeck's gaze locked on Gannon.

"I think you should leave. Now."

Styebeck's anger bored into Gannon, and for the benefit of those who were watching them, he said, "Do you believe this guy? He's supposed to be suspended. Yet he comes over here to continue to publicly humiliate me and my family. Do I have to seek a restraining order, Jack?"

After Gannon glimpsed Fowler weaving through the crowd and nearing the scene, he left, throwing a parting glance over his shoulder.

He saw Styebeck watching him, his wife rubbing his arm, while several other people stood behind them.

Gannon drove around the city analyzing his read of Karl Styebeck. Over and over, he kept coming back to that split second when something cold had flitted across the detective's eyes.

Like a secret had been revealed.

And a dark force had been unleashed.

22

Styebeck sat alone in his living room, tie undone, a glass of scotch and ice in his hand, the banquet reverberating in his head.

It had been an hour since Alice had finally gone to bed after wrestling with her anger and fear over what had happened that evening.

"I can't believe the gall of that reporter! Karl, people told me we should sue him."

Styebeck had agreed with her, the scene had been upsetting, but sleep was the best thing for her right now, he told her.

He'd get them through this mess.

But would he?

Gannon was getting close to the truth.

The ice clinked in his glass as Styebeck sipped from it.

He had to get a handle on the situation. Alice was a loving, supportive wife. Taylor trusted and idolized him. He'd worked so hard to build a good life and he would protect it.

At any cost.

Gannon was trying to pry the lid off the casket of secrets he'd buried.

No one knew.

No one must ever know that he was living his life in a

constant battle with dark urges that arose from his past, urges that forced him to do the most despicable things with women.

Not with Alice.

Other women.

Because he paid them to satisfy the all-consuming demands of his secret compulsion. For years, he had kept it caged, but it gnawed at the edges of his control, growing intense, ravenous. His ears would ring, his head would throb, until it took over.

He would drive into the night.

Hunting.

Some women on the street were shocked by his needs, so he'd move on until he found the kind of women who could gratify him. Women who guarded secrets, especially when he paid them with extra cash, or with favors. Like, getting a pimp to back off. Or dealing with an abusive john, a crooked landlord. Or supplying drugs.

And so many times his relief gave him so much pleasure he lost consciousness.

That had been his secret life.

It worked because he was a good husband, a good father, a community hero whose group helped troubled women.

And it worked because he was a respected detective.

Often the women gave him information on a case. And that made him look good. Oh, it had worked so beautifully.

Bernice Hogan knew the real Karl Styebeck. How he missed her, sweet, sad Bernice. She guarded his secret. So did several others, including Jolene Peller.

But J.P. was strong. She'd managed to get out of the life. On the surface, Styebeck was glad. Deep down he still craved her and wasn't sure he could let her go. But he had to contend with his mixed feelings privately because J.P. had earned the right to something better.

Sure, some of them deserved it.

Some of them didn't.

Because of what they were.

Sinful whores who deserved—

Stop.

He was in trouble. Far greater trouble.

It began with the letter several months ago.

Then the phone calls started after that, long before they found Bernice.

At first they were hang-ups. Wrong numbers. The ID was always blocked. Then came the call that stopped him cold.

It came a few days before they'd found Bernice.

"Guess who, Karl?"

A call from the pit; the pit Styebeck had crawled from a lifetime ago.

His gut twisted. Even across decades of estrangement he'd recognized his brother's voice, almost jubilant on the other end of the line. Styebeck said nothing as the feigned warmth of his brother's tone dropped several degrees.

"Did you really think that we'd never find you, Karl?"

"What do you want?"

"I've been watching you, your wife, your boy, for a spell. I know all about you. You think you're better than us. But I know what you do, Karl."

"If you come near my family, I swear, I'll—"

"We don't care about them. You know who sent me and you know what you have to do."

"You're out of your mind. I'm not like you."

"You're one of us. It's time you admitted the truth and faced your responsibilities."

Like a scab being pulled from an old wound, Styebeck confronted the painful memories of his family's disintegration.

"She's dying, Karl. We almost lost Belva but I saved her. You got her letter. She told you what to do. Your time is running out. Are you going to do it before it's too late? You've got twenty-four hours to give me the right answer, Karl, or I will pass judgment on one of your whores and give you a world of trouble."

Styebeck relied on his training as a cop.

Don't panic. Assess. Act. Resolve.

He did the only safe thing he could do.

That night and the next he patrolled Niagara in a rental and kept a vigil for anything threatening the women. He talked to each of them.

No one had seen anything, other than the regular jerks.

"Oh, there's an asshole in a semi-rig, just the cab, acting a bit creepy," one of the girls told Styebeck. "Got something on his door. Something about a sword. He was talking to Bernice last we heard."

Alarm rang in Styebeck's ears.

Don't let it be his brother.

Styebeck had to handle this himself. He couldn't risk calling in uniforms or backup; it was all too close to home. He'd spent the night searching for Bernice, for the rig. He went down to the park by Ellicott Creek.

But he saw nothing.

He searched the surrounding forest with his flashlight.

All in vain.

Then he went home.

That's what happened.

That's what he believed had happened, wasn't it?

Because sometimes when his compulsion took control he would black out, lose track of time, suffer memory loss.

No! Not this time! That's what happened. He'd tried to help!

Then Bernice Hogan's murder hit the news.

Brent and Esko from the New York State Police had called him in for help on the Hogan murder. But Styebeck didn't trust them. He'd sensed they knew something they were holding back. And why wasn't he invited to join the task force? That's when his friends, who didn't know the truth, had stepped up. It helped, but it didn't take care of all the heat.

Now Jack Gannon was getting closer.

Then he got the call that had pushed him over the edge. It came a few days after they'd found Bernice, on the night he'd clashed with Gannon.

"Look what you did, Karl. Everybody knows now," his brother said.

"That was you. Not me."

"You sure about that?"

Silence passed.

"Are you going to come back to us, Karl?"

Another moment passed.

"Think it over, I'll be in touch."

After the call, Styebeck felt the walls of his life closing in.

Brent and Esko were onto him.

Jack Gannon was onto him.

Everything he'd worked so hard to build was collapsing around him.

Styebeck froze.

A noise was coming from the back of the house, a tapping or ticking on glass. He went to his gun safe, got his Glock and slipped into the kitchen.

A man was standing in the breezeway between the kitchen and garage. *Why didn't his motion detector light this guy up?* Styebeck switched on the floodlights, opened the door and stepped out, keeping his gun at his side.

The man had his back to him and was calmly smoking a cigarette.

Styebeck took stock of his snakeskin cowboy boots and jeans. He wore a T-shirt that flattered his well-toned upper body, and a ball cap. The man stubbed his cigarette into a patio tile and turned to face his brother.

They were boys the last time they'd seen one another. They stared at each other for a long moment, taking stock of the men they'd become.

Styebeck tightened his grip on his gun.

"I told you to never come here, Orly."

"You've grown into a disappointment, Karl," his brother said, glancing at the gun then shaking his head. "A big disappointment."

"I told you not to come here. Ever."

"There's not a lot you can do now, is there?"

"It's over. I'm going to bring you in and tell them everything about where we come from and what you did."

"What I did?" Orly laughed.

"You're sick. You need help."

"I'm afraid it's a little more complicated than you think. You see, I took precautions in case you were planning to turn me over to your police friends. No matter what you do, you're involved now. Up to your eyeballs." Orly stepped forward. "It's time you paid some respect, Karl. Time you own up to your responsibilities because I fixed it good."

"There's no way you can implicate me."

"No? Give this a whirl." He tossed a DVD at him. "Your whore's last words. I saved them for you. Now, you give it a spin and I'll keep in touch, hero boy. Shee-it!"

Orly Styebeck's laughter faded as he sank into the darkness.

"Karl?"

Alice was approaching from the living room to the breezeway; Styebeck slipped the DVD into his pocket.

"I heard voices. Oh my God, why do you have your gun? Karl, what's going on?"

Alice's hair was messed, her eyes red rimmed, worry etched in her face as he backed her into the house soothing her.

"Who were you talking to just now?"

"It's nothing. A cat tripped the motion sensor. It's nothing. We're all on edge, Alice. Take a pill and get back to sleep, honey. I'll double-check the locks and be right up."

She looked into the night, seeing nothing, hearing only crickets, before she returned. "Promise me you'll be right up."

"Promise."

Styebeck went to his study, turned on his computer and played the DVD, which displayed shaking images of a forest at night then blurry pictures of a woman.

It was difficult to distinguish what was unfolding.

But then he recognized the woman's voice as soon as she spoke.

"Mr. Styebeck, please, I beg you…oh God no…please, Karl…NO!"

It was Bernice Hogan.

In the final moments of her life.

23

As Jack Gannon showered the next morning, needles of hot water revived his tired muscles but didn't thaw his impression of Styebeck.

As cold as an executioner.

Did that make him guilty?

And something unholy was going on between Styebeck and Fowler.

The new facts took this story into a wicked realm, making him wonder if Ascension Park's hero detective was a Jekyll-and-Hyde case, especially considering Tuesday's information that Styebeck admitted his desires "were sick" and had blamed his father.

His father?

As Gannon dressed he decided to dig deeper into Styebeck's past. He was going to dissect his career, climb up and down every branch of his family tree.

He started making a full-court press on all public, federal, state and local records he could get. Then he made calls to sources, starting with a woman he knew in the Ascension Park personnel department who owed him a favor. After launching his research, he made coffee and had just grabbed a bagel when his phone rang.

"Gannon?"

"Yes?"

"It's Fowler. Can you come into my office now?"

He'd expected this call.

"Is this about last night?"

"Just get in here."

Thirty minutes after the call, Gannon was in the newsroom.

As he headed to Fowler's office he sensed an undercurrent; something grave was going on. Conversations halted; people in the middle of phone interviews gazed at him.

"Gannon!"

Fowler was cutting across the metro section toward him, tie loosened, collar button undone, sleeves rolled to the elbow. A clipboard listing the morning's assignments was in his left hand, which he'd raised to point to his box-shaped, glass-walled office.

"In there. Now."

Fowler shut the door behind him.

"Give me your *Sentinel* cell phone."

Gannon put it on the desk.

"And the paper's credit card."

"Is this about last night?"

Gannon produced the plastic card he'd used for trips and expenses. It snapped when he put it on Fowler's desk next to the phone.

"You going to tell me what's going on?"

"You're going to stand there and act like you don't know?"

Fowler slid the surrendered items into the top drawer of his desk.

"Know what, Nate?"

Fowler waved to Kathy, his assistant. She entered with an envelope, handed it to Fowler then left, keeping the door open.

Fowler gave the envelope to Gannon.

"What's this?"

"You're fired."

"What?"

"There's severance pay and vacation."

Two uniformed security officers filled Fowler's doorway.

"I didn't want to do this, but you left me no choice. Your actions are indefensible and do not represent this newspaper. Kathy will collect your personal items from your desk and send them to you later."

Fowler nodded to the security guys, big, unsmiling strangers.

"Hold on, Nate. I don't understand."

"You're unbelievable, Gannon."

"Come this way, sir," one of the security men said.

At that moment, Paul Capresey, a news photographer, fired several frames before Gannon and the officers got into the elevator car. It was a tense silent descent. Gannon could smell cologne. A tattoo of a spiderweb reached above the neckline of one of the officers.

The doors opened to the lobby where Gannon was met by Pete Martinez, a *Sentinel* reporter, who held a small recorder in front of him. Martinez walked quickly alongside Gannon as the security people hurried him to the *Sentinel*'s glass doors.

"Pete, what's going on?"

"Jack, I need your reaction to Styebeck."

"What reaction? For what?"

At that instant Gannon saw a tangle of reporters in the street, people he knew. News cars and vans were parked behind them.

Was that a satellite truck?

The officers released Gannon and bright camera lights blazed, cuing the press pack to advance. Microphones, lenses and hardened faces lurched at him with an eruption of questions.

Gary Golden fired first.

"Jack, what's your response to Karl Styebeck's wife?"

"What about her?"

"She overdosed last night."

"What?"

"According to Styebeck, it happened after you crashed a fund-raiser and publicly accused him, in front of his wife and friends, of visiting hookers and murdering Bernice Hogan."

24

Jolene Peller was not alone in her dark prison.

Her encounter had sent her scurrying back to her mattress.

She'd pushed herself hard into her corner, trembling as she contended with the fact that a few feet from her someone else was alive.

Enemy? Or ally?

Jolene's nostrils flared as she panted.

Adrenaline rushed through her body, giving rise to the primal instinct to fight. But at the same time Jolene struggled to be rational.

It could be Bernice.

Ashamed and angered at herself, Jolene tore at her gag with such ferocity she loosened it just enough to allow her to breathe easier.

And to speak.

Her jaw welcomed the relief and she swallowed several times before she whispered.

"Bernice?"

Jolene crawled through the blackness to the person moaning on the floor.

"Is that you, Bernie? It's Jo. It's going to be okay. I'm going to get us out of here. Be calm while I try to help you, okay?"

A muffled moan—the soft tone of a female—rose

from the floor as Jolene's bound hands explored the stranger's body.

She felt fabric. Thin fabric. There was warmth under it. A T-shirt. She felt sturdier fabric. Denim. Legs. Shoes. Sneakers, or tennis shoes. Legs and ankles unbound. Moving upward she felt a flat stomach. Curves. The ridged outline of a bra. This woman had a larger bust than—*this wasn't Bernice.*

Jolene felt warm skin. Arms, leading to binding and thick coils of duct tape around the wrists, just like hers.

Jolene felt the woman's neck then the binding around her mouth, a dampened rag wedged between her upper and lower jaw, knotted tight as a cord behind her head.

"Let me help you."

Jolene tried to slide the rag down at the back of the woman's neck. The woman rolled her head from side to side, resisting Jolene's help.

"Honey, be still, let me help. I'm your friend. I'm going to help."

Jolene could feel the woman's entire body shaking. She was in shock. Jolene tried to soothe her but the woman flinched.

"Take it easy," Jolene said. "Let me try to loosen the gag on your mouth."

The woman moaned but stilled herself long enough for Jolene to work on the gag. Firmly Jolene pushed and pushed until she managed to slide it lower, so that it loosened and the woman drew air into her mouth.

Jolene stroked her hair.

"Isn't that better? It's better, right?"

No response.

Time was impossible to measure.

Jolene had no way of knowing how much of it had

passed. She felt like they were underwater in a dark river, rushing into the eternal night. As they drifted in and out of consciousness, Jolene wondered about the other woman.

Who was she? How did she get here? Did she know about Bernice? Or who had kidnapped them? Where were they going?

The stranger was in worse shape than Jolene.

The woman never spoke.

She would come to, roll her head and groan.

"That's okay," Jolene said. "We're in this together. I can be strong for both of us. I've got a good mother. I've got a beautiful little boy. I've got a new life waiting for us in Florida. I've been through some tough times and I'm not going to let my family down. Or you. You'll see."

The woman never responded.

"I'm going to see what you have in your pockets," Jolene said. "Maybe you've got something in there that can help us."

Like a cell phone. Keys, a knife. Jolene turned the woman on her side and checked her rear pockets. Nothing. Then she checked her front left pocket and found a small plastic box. She shook it. By the sound and cinnamon smell, she guessed it was breath mints.

Jolene felt something hard in the woman's right pocket, managed to slide her fingers in and tugged out something metal, jingling.

Keys.

Good.

Jolene felt the key ring, a few metal keys and a small cylinder. Her fingers assessed the cylinder. It had a smooth tip, like glass, a button like a—Jolene pushed—small flashlight!

A flash of bright light burst on the horror.

Jolene gasped.

The woman's face was a surreal stew of bloodied torn flesh; her T-shirt and jeans were brown with dried blood.

Then all went dark again.

The flashlight's tiny batteries had slipped from the cylinder, clunked on the floor and rolled in the darkness.

"No!"

Jolene groped for them.

She pawed the floor for the longest time but it was futile. She could not find them. Maybe they'd rolled into a crack, or a seam, or deeper into hell.

Jolene cursed.

The keys chimed as she put her head in her hands, the image of the woman's face seared in her mind.

What sort of monster had done this?

And why?

What had he done to Bernice?

Would she ever see Cody and her mother again?

Jolene crawled back to her corner and cried until she lost consciousness.

25

Bernice Hogan is standing alone on Niagara Street. A rig—just the tractor, no trailer—rolls by then vanishes. A few minutes later a car emerges and stops. Looked like a Chev Malibu? Bernice leans into the window, hustles the driver. The car leaves without her. Then a man walks up to her. Is it Karl Styebeck? Impossible to say; traffic obscures the view. Then Bernice disappears into the darkness.

Like she was never there.

Michael Brent, New York State Police investigator, took a moment to absorb the scenes he was reviewing on the security videotape.

Had he just watched Bernice Hogan meet her killer?

As Brent drank coffee from his Buffalo Bills mug, he glimpsed Bernice Hogan's self-conscious smile from an open folder. He didn't see a hooker whose lifestyle invited her death. What he saw was a young woman who deserved better and he vowed to avenge her murder.

But why had her killer marked her?

Brent pondered the key piece of evidence that he and Esko had kept from nearly everyone, a cryptic message the murderer had carved into Bernice Hogan's body.

What did it mean?

He'd grappled with these questions ever since the autopsy.

The job was all he had going these days, he thought as he watched the tape again. His stomach tensed the way it always did when his gut told him the answers were in front of him.

But he was missing them.

"Who is that guy?" Brent asked the screen as he replayed the tape, losing count of how many times he'd rerun the footage.

It was 10:30 p.m. in the Bureau of Criminal Investigation offices of State Police Clarence Barracks, Troop A, Zone 2. He was working with Roxanne Esko, preparing for the next case-status meeting of the task force investigating the homicide.

The video's quality sucked. It was like looking through a snowstorm. The forensic guys in Batavia had tried to clean it up, but it was still terrible. Going public with it would not have helped. So they kept it as holdback, a card to be played later.

The tape had been volunteered by Samson's Music Mansion across the street from Bernice Hogan's corner at Lafayette. Samson's sold used guitars, drums and keyboards at a run-down store that had an outdated security system.

The angle from the store's camera had captured partial images of Bernice. *The last pictures of her.* The minutes, hour and date running across the bottom were key to establishing a time frame for her disappearance but little else. Brent shifted his gaze to Esko, who'd stopped watching it to review the files.

"Your neck muscle's pulsating, Mike." Esko worked at her computer. "What're you thinking?"

"Jack Gannon's an asshole."

"I know he's a pain, but he's just doing his job. Or was."

"He messed up my case."

"Let it go. Being pissed at him is a waste of time. He's gone. Fired. We've been at this since 6:00 a.m. Why don't you take a break while I finish up."

Brent shook his head.

He came from a long line of dedicated police officers who were not inclined to take breaks. His great-grandfather, Stanislaw Brentkozeska, had been a cop in Warsaw before arriving in the U.S., where an immigration officer at Ellis Island shortened his name.

"Welcome to America, Mr. Brent."

Brent's grandfather and father were cops and Brent kept with tradition when he joined the New York State Police, a decision that had nearly cost him his life.

He was working as a trooper near Watertown when he stopped a car for speeding. While writing the ticket another car struck him. The accident had left him with a lifetime of back trouble and a sour attitude.

Then his heart broke last winter when his wife died of cancer. Her loss was evident in his weary eyes and fugitive smile. Brent thought of her every day. He dreaded his retirement in a few months. He was a solitary investigator but found that working with Esko made his life bearable.

Roxanne was happily married to a furniture-store manager she had met while shopping for a bed at the Eastern Hills Mall.

While Esko entered data on her computer keyboard, Brent removed his bifocals, then reread his notes.

They had known about Karl Styebeck from the get-go, about the community-cop hero and his volunteer work. But Brent also had statements from hookers alleging Styebeck's habit of first trying to rescue them, then insulting them. And about his disturbing preference for "young ones."

Was he some kind of predator?

The women had witnessed Styebeck on Niagara talking to Bernice the night she vanished. One recorded a plate number for a rental, which they'd traced to him.

Why use a rental? Why not a departmental unmarked?

Styebeck was vague but admitted he'd talked to Bernice; claimed he was on the job talking to informants. Styebeck said he was asking about a strange truck, whose driver had creeped out some of the girls.

Really? Nobody got the plate? And why would Styebeck care? Protecting the girls is something pimps do.

That's when the partner theory arose. *Maybe Styebeck and another person were responsible. And maybe Styebeck was protecting them.*

It was tricky but Brent shifted gears. He'd thanked Styebeck for clearing things up and requested his help on the case. Brent couldn't let Styebeck know that he was a suspect; he even made a cop-to-cop joke about it, while secretly they focused on him.

They wanted to know his link to Bernice and to the rig. They had partial tire impressions from the unpaved parking lot near the murder scene. They had taken casts of them and of larger tire impressions, consistent with the tires on a rig.

Brent requested the rental-car company retrieve the car Styebeck had rented from circulation and return it to Buffalo so the lab could analyze it. The company was cooperating, but it would take time.

The car was in Pittsburgh.

At this point they still had no solid evidence.

The District Attorney's Office had advised them that they didn't have grounds to charge Styebeck, or even enough leverage to question him.

Not yet.

Brent wanted to put Styebeck under surveillance, build a case. Then Gannon blew everything with his front-page story and Brent damn near put his foot through a *Sentinel* news box. He wanted to know Gannon's source, wanted to know who in the task force had compromised his investigation.

As Esko's keyboard clicked away in the empty office, Brent poured himself fresh coffee and considered Jolene Peller's file.

It was a missing-person case that took on a chilling dimension, thanks to Gannon's discovery of Jolene's unused bus ticket near the scene. A ticket to Orlando that had been purchased by Styebeck's outreach group.

They were working with the FBI on Peller's case.

Brent couldn't believe Gannon's tenacity and, privately, he was developing a begrudging respect for him. Hell, he could've built a bridge with Gannon that would've served them both.

The demand for a retraction hadn't come from Brent or Esko. Brent didn't know where the demand had come from. There were rumors that either Brent himself, or the D.A.'s office, had leaned on the *Sentinel.* Styebeck seemed to be cozy with Fowler, the paper's managing editor, whose wife, Madeline, worked with the Attorney General's Office.

It got strange last night when Styebeck's wife OD'd after mixing booze and pills following the fund-raiser where Gannon showed up to take another shot at Styebeck while his boss was praising him.

Which reminded Brent…

"Rox, did you call the hospital to find out how Alice Styebeck is doing?"

"She's not out of the woods yet." Esko kept working at her keyboard.

"What about Karl? We need to talk to him again."

"That's not going to happen for a while. He's with his wife at the hospital."

Brent checked his watch.

"How are you doing there, Rox?"

"Almost done."

Esko was working on their submission to the Violent Criminal Apprehension Program.

She scrolled through the form on her computer monitor. ViCAP was the nationwide database that gathered and analyzed details of missing-person cases and violent crimes, specifically murder, and linked them to others with similar patterns.

Brent's case would first go to the New York State Police Forensic Investigation Center in Albany. The center administered the state's ViCAP system and worked with the FBI in Quantico, who operated the national system.

Esko was a great believer in ViCAP.

The program's goal was to detect signature traits that could pinpoint crimes committed by the same offender. Some detectives were anxious about giving up all of the critical key fact evidence and often held back stuff that no one but the primary investigators, or the offender, would know.

Esko reread the autopsy report, inhaled slowly and flipped through the crime-scene photos of Bernice Hogan.

In her career, Esko had seen horrible things up close. But nothing, nothing compared to the Hogan case. Esko had fought to maintain her professional composure and kept her game face on for the sake of the other guys at the scene.

At home, she'd lost it in the shower.

The photos brought it all back.

She swallowed hard and closed them.

They had to catch this guy.

"Ready to submit it, Mike."

"You put in all our holdback, the details on the message?"

"Yes."

"Okay."

Esko submitted the case then massaged her temples.

"Mike, do you think our guy's done this before?"

"I don't know." He studied Jolene Peller's file. "At this point I'm only concerned with stopping him from doing it again."

26

Gannon gazed at the suds sliding to the bottom of his glass.

Sorrow hung in the stale air, rippling up to the bar from the blues singer on the lower stage. Gannon tapped the rim.

"You really think you need another one, sir?" the bartender asked.

Gannon let the question slosh around in a head numbed by the wreckage of recent catastrophes.

"Yes, I do."

"I'll give you one more, but it'll be your last."

Gannon tried to remember how long he'd been here. His new home. Moved in, what, eight beers ago? It's starting to look good. Not as empty as the old place. He liked the diamond pattern of the scuffed linoleum floor, the worn wood paneling, the old jukebox and the black-and-white photos of Buffalo's history.

That's Mark Twain. He used to own a newspaper here.

Jack London did a bit of jail time here.

And that's some president waving from a train.

Goodbye.

So long to the great Jack Gannon, who almost got a Pulitzer.

Hello to the loser people blamed for driving Styebeck's wife to overdose.

He didn't mean to hurt anyone.

Goodbye, Jack. The writing was on the wall and in the letter he reread from his pal in Ethiopia and the application form. Maybe he *would* chuck journalism and teach English in Africa.

"Last one," the bartender said.

Gannon gripped the sweating glass and thought, here's to loss. Loss of a career, loss of ten years, loss of his parents, loss of his sister, loss of a dream.

Loss of himself.

He took a long gulp.

Local news flickered on the muted TV above the bar. Gannon saw a still of Styebeck's hero-cop face, then footage of Bernice Hogan's crime scene, a still shot of her college-ID photo, then footage of himself in front of the *Sentinel* building after being fired.

Gannon turned away and swallowed more beer.

What went wrong?

In the far reaches of his mind the remotest grains of self-doubt began to squirm. Was it possible that maybe, just maybe, he was wrong about Styebeck?

He downed the remainder of his glass. His stomach roiled; his head lolled. His vision blurred but he saw it all clearly.

He was not wrong.

Styebeck was involved in this. He's living some sort of double life. Gannon had to stop feeling sorry for himself and break this story.

Gannon started ringing.

He tried to find his cell phone. It rang and rang. He shoved both hands in his pants pockets. No phone. Where was it? The bartender retrieved it from Gannon's shirt pocket, answered, then handed it to Gannon.

"Hullo. Jack Gannon, formerly of the *Buffalo Sentinel.*"

"Jack, it's Adell. I'm calling from a pay phone. There's been a break."

Gannon said something before his phone, then his head, hit the counter.

He could not remember falling asleep.

He woke with a short-lived memory loss of where he'd been, what he'd done. He was on a strange sofa, under a quilt, in a small pleasant living room with the shades drawn. He was in his clothes, his shoes on the floor beside him. His mouth was dry. His head was nestled in a soft pillow that was hurting him.

Coffee. He could smell coffee.

He saw Adell Clark in the adjoining room.

Bar.

That's it. He'd gone to a bar to mourn his termination. He'd gotten drunk. Adell had called.

"Morning, Jack."

"How did I get here?"

"The bartender picked up your phone and told me about your troubles. You were blathering to him all night. I drove down. We loaded you in my car and with some effort I got you here to sleep it off."

"Thank you."

"Sure. Eggs?"

"God, no."

"Coffee?"

"I need your bathroom first."

Gannon washed up and returned to the kitchen where he saw his wallet, and its contents, stacked beside it, on the counter.

"It fell from your pocket on my driveway last night. Thought you'd want to organize your stuff." Adell set a cup of black coffee before him. "I wasn't snooping, but I saw the pictures of your parents and Cora. Are you still looking for your sister?"

Gannon stared at the age-worn snapshots before sliding them back into place.

"No, not really." He drank some coffee. "You said something about a break on the case?"

"Out-of-state calls on Jolene Peller's phone have been made after her disappearance. And you won't believe who they were made to?"

Gannon looked at her, waiting for the answer.

"Karl Styebeck," she said.

"That means Jolene Peller could be alive," he said.

"It means Styebeck has to be tied to her disappearance."

27

Alice was going to make it. She had to make it.

The room where Karl Styebeck waited was oppressive with antiseptic smells. He stared at the cheerless walls, the drab vinyl couches, the outdated copies of *Reader's Digest* and *People,* as the clock above the nurses' station swept time forward.

How long had it been since this morning when Alice wouldn't wake up?

She just wouldn't wake up.

Sirens screamed when the ambulance came.

It appeared to be a bad reaction to an accidental but dangerous mix of pills, alcohol and anxiety, the doctor had said.

"Will she recover?" Styebeck asked him now.

"She's stable, but it'll be touch-and-go for the next few hours."

Styebeck sat down, ran his hands over his whiskered face and inventoried the calamities mounting against him. The murder, Gannon's accusation, his brother's recording of Bernice Hogan's dying words implicating him.

Now, outside his wife's hospital room, he accepted that for all these years he'd been wrong to think he was free of his father's curse.

He had to end it himself.

To prepare for that moment, he had to confront the greatest pain of his life. He had to take his mind back through time and exhume a long-buried ancestral secret. He had to return to the root of the evil in his blood.

He had to imagine 1937, Brooks, Alberta, Canada….

Majestic dust clouds ascended from the parched earth as a lone farm truck cut across the desolate prairie.

Norris Selkirk drove while his mother, Vida, sat next to him; the sky and worry were reflected in her eyes as she searched the endless horizon.

Not a sign of life for miles in this quarter of dry grassland where the Blackfeet Nation once hunted the great buffalo herds before treaties were signed and the white homesteaders arrived.

This morning Vida had told her husband that she needed their son to take her out to the Rudd place.

"What for? I need Norris here, to help me with the tractor."

"Clydell and Eva weren't at church. The younger ones weren't at school. And remember, that killer escaped from Stony Mountain prison in Manitoba and was supposed to be headed west."

"Vida, we got our own business to mind."

"You mind it. I'm going out to see if Eva needs help. Maybe they're sick."

Vida's husband grunted the way most men did whenever they considered Clydell Rudd and anything related to him.

The Rudd place was at the edge of Newell County where Clydell kept his wife, Eva, their five daughters and young boy, Deke, isolated from the community.

Except for church and school, they rarely left their property.

Clydell never permitted his girls, including the two who were full-grown and unmarried, to go into town.

Clydell didn't care for other people, which suited other people just fine.

Earlier on, there was talk that one of the Rudd girls had become pregnant, then came rumors that Clydell had a criminal past, or owed money to the Chicago mob. Somebody claimed that some nights people had seen Clydell drunk on his own brew, running naked on his land raging at the moon.

No one knew the truth about Clydell Rudd.

Vida didn't care. She put no stock in childish folklore. She wanted to be sure Eva and her kids were all right. That's what you did out here, where living could be hard with men who couldn't understand a woman's heart.

Vida took stock as the Rudds' ranch house with its peeling paint came into view. Their battered green Dodge was there all right, but no clothes were pinned to the line.

Odd.

With five children, you could count on Eva and the girls doing a wash every day.

Norris halted the truck, shut it off, got out and released a whistle that normally summoned the dogs.

Nothing.

The chickens seemed agitated, clucking up a storm in the coop. As Vida approached the house, the air felt wrong, like something had been taken. The front door was open, swaying and creaking, as if beckoning Vida to continue.

Or warning her to turn right around and go home.

"Eva?" Vida called. "Clydell?"

No one responded.

Three fat mice darted out of the house, over the threshold.

"Anybody home?"

Nothing.

Passing through the door, Vida and Norris met a wave of foul air.

"Whoa," Norris said.

As their eyes adjusted to the light, they moved through the small living room. Vida's calls filled the quiet. Nothing seemed out of place but for the stillness. It was too quiet, as if all life in the house had stopped.

Then they heard the humming.

Vida and Norris exchanged a glance.

As they approached the first bedroom, the humming grew louder. Norris pushed the door open wider and they saw the source of the sound.

Vida's scalp tingled.

Norris felt the little hairs on the back of his neck stand up.

Flies encased the two figures on the bed.

Vida's first thought was how they looked like macabre scarecrows hastily assembled by a lunatic.

Reddish-brown matter laced their wide-eyed faces and upper bodies so that Vida could barely identify them as belonging to Clydell and Eva. Splatters and ribbons of blood cascaded down the wall above the headboard and streamed down the painting of the Rockies that Eva had treasured.

"Jesus H. Christ!" Norris said the same way his father cursed.

Vida covered her mouth with both hands in time to stifle a sob.

Moving to the next bedroom, they found the three youngest girls in the same manner lying in their small beds. A little rag doll stared back wide-eyed from under the arm of one.

Vida gasped as they moved down the hall to the little

loft with the bed where the thirteen-year-old boy, Deke, slept.

It was empty.

No bloodstains. Norris touched the sheets. They were cool and dry.

"Deke!" he called, moving quickly to seize an iron poker.

There was no response as they moved on to the last bedroom, the one used by the two older girls. The smell and the scene were the same. It was as if pails of red paint had been hurled in anger at the two young women and the walls surrounding their beds.

"Look!" Norris pointed.

One of them seemed higher in her bed, seemed to rise and fall as her body trembled. Norris spotted an extra arm, hand, another pair of eyes staring back.

Someone was under her—alive!

"It's Deke!"

The Rudds' only son had survived by hiding under the corpse of his murdered sister.

In the aftermath, it seemed that the world had descended on the Rudd place north of Brooks.

First came members of the Royal Canadian Mounted Police arriving out of nearly every detachment from Calgary, some eighty miles west, and Medicine Hat, about the same distance east. A team from the Calgary Medical Examiner's Office arrived, then forensic experts. Then came reporters from the big newspapers and radio stations in Calgary, Toronto, Vancouver, even the United States. And the wire-service syndicates sent correspondents. Their first reports brought the public, who drove in from Edmonton, Red Deer, Swift Current, Winnipeg, Montana, North Dakota and Minnesota.

They had to see.

7 Family Members Slaughtered
Boy, 13, Survives by Hiding Under the Dead

The press left within days of the funerals, which were even more heartwrenching because not a single relative of the Rudds, on Clydell or Eva's side, attended.

They had no other family.

Vida Selkirk wanted to take Deke into her home but they couldn't afford to raise him. The law made him a ward of Alberta's social services, which set out to find him a home. In the time after the tragedy, caseworkers got Deke counseling and helped him to help the Mounties investigating the case.

"All I remember was noises and shadows. Then it got all quiet. I got up and went to each bed. I shook everybody, tried to wake them before I knew they were all dead. My mother, my sisters. I got scared. The dogs run off. I was alone. I was the only one left. I thought whoever done it was coming for me. So I hid under my sister and played dead until somebody come to help."

The investigators held the theory that the killer overlooked Deke because the boy slept in the loft, which could be easily missed in the dark.

They showed him pictures of the escaped killer from Stony Mountain, who was still at large. Deke could not identify him.

"It was dark."

The first reports on the death toll were wrong.

While Deke was the only survivor, not every member of his family died that night. Tilley Rudd, his oldest sister, thought dead, was found to be alive when help came. She was taken to the hospital in Calgary where she slipped in and out of a coma before she died of her injuries.

Given the circumstances and publicity of the case,

many people wanted to give Deke a home. Ultimately, quickly and with no publicity, he was adopted by an American pastor and his wife living in Brooks at the time.

"Hello, Deke, my name is Gabriel Styebeck," the pastor said.

He was a tall man with a beard like Abraham Lincoln's and a face so stern he looked to be hurting when he smiled.

"This is my wife, Adolpha. We'll be your new mother and father."

Adolpha nodded and cupped Deke's face in her hands.

They were ice cold, like those of his dead sisters.

A few months after the Styebecks adopted Deke, they moved to Texas, near Lufkin. They sent Deke to a special bible school, where male instructors would hit him with a yardstick when he failed to learn Scripture. He wanted to drop out and fight in the war, like some of the older boys in town, but it never happened.

After he graduated from high school, Deke moved out on his own and got a job with the state of Texas as a corrections officer in Huntsville. It was the perfect job for him, for he would secretly scrutinize the case of every inmate he encountered, vigilant for any chance, however remote, that he might find the one who'd murdered his family.

Like his father, Deke kept to himself and was a bachelor for several years until he couldn't live with the loneliness anymore. So one night he got up the nerve to go to a summer social near Trinity. There he saw a young lady standing against the wall. He smiled at her, told her she was pretty and asked her to dance.

Her name was Belva Denker.

They began dating.

Belva was a schoolteacher. Her father, a farmer, had been killed when his tractor rolled on top of him. And her mother had passed away two years later. Belva taught elementary school and lived alone in a room downtown where she dreamed of having a family.

Deke wanted a family, too. Like Belva, he felt alone and they made each other happy. He was the only man who'd asked her to dance, the only man who'd ever smiled at her and told her she was pretty.

Deke told her how he was orphaned at the age of thirteen after a stranger had come into his family's home and murdered his father, mother and five sisters. The killer had never been found. Deke told her about his secret search for the killer.

Belva believed in his cause but never realized its intensity until he took her swimming and she saw the words tattooed across his back.

"And I will execute great vengeance upon them with furious rebukes," she read aloud.

"It's from Ezekiel," he said.

Belva traced her fingertips over the words. Awestruck, she regarded Deke Styebeck as a warrior against all the bad in this world. Her hero.

A year after they met, they were married.

After several years, Belva gave birth to their first child, a son.

Karl Styebeck.

Two years later, during a difficult delivery that nearly killed her, Belva gave birth to a second son.

Orion Styebeck.

They lived a quiet life on a farm in a wooded, secluded tract outside of Huntsville.

During that time, Deke was promoted to a post on the prison's execution team where he took great pride, some said pleasure, in escorting men to their deaths....

* * *

"Excuse me, Mr. Styebeck? You can see Alice now," the nurse said.

"Will she be okay?"

"She's groggy, but she'll be fine. Her heart rate is normal and all of her vital signs are normal."

"Thank you." Styebeck embraced the positive news.

He'd use it to prepare for the battle of his life.

28

Jolene Peller's silver cell phone sat in front of Anthony Sloan.

Its fading power light pulsed like a telltale heart.

FBI special agent Ron Garvin and New York State investigator Mike Brent faced Sloan across the polished table in a brightly lit meeting room of the FBI's new Las Vegas Field Office, near Martin Luther King Boulevard. The building's air-conditioning system hummed.

Sloan was sweating.

"Where's Jolene Peller?" Brent asked.

"I told you, *I've never heard of her.*"

"When are you going to tell us the truth?" Brent asked.

"What about you? You show up at my hotel, flash your badges, ask me to come here to help you on some urgent matter," Sloan said. "I cooperate fully. Let you look through my things. But for the last hour you refuse to tell me what this is really about."

"You know what this is about, Tony," Brent said.

"The phone?"

"You see," Garvin said, "with that kind of phone, when it's on and roaming, we can pretty much get a location, which led us to you."

"How did you get the phone?" Brent asked.

"I told you, I picked it up somewhere by mistake. It's identical to mine."

"Identical?" Garvin placed a slimmer black phone on the table in front of Sloan. "That's your phone, Tony. No resemblance."

Brent's forefinger jabbed the silver phone.

"Jolene Peller is the owner of this phone. She's a single mother, from Buffalo, New York, and she's missing. Her disappearance is tied to a homicide in Buffalo. You're a mechanic from Illinois, in Las Vegas, making calls with a missing woman's phone and lying to us."

Sloan swallowed.

"You hear that, Mike?" Garvin said. "I think Tony's sphincter just tightened."

"Where's Jolene Peller?"

"I don't know."

Brent put Jolene's picture in front of Sloan, who shook his head.

"I swear, I don't know who you're talking about."

"Why did you call Karl Styebeck's home?"

"Who's he?"

Brent put Styebeck's picture in front of Sloan.

"This phone's been used to call Karl Styebeck's home in Buffalo. How do you know him?" Brent asked.

"Never saw him before in my life. Never heard of him."

Brent nodded and considered another avenue to the truth.

He paged through his notes and a file folder of documents the FBI had faxed him before he and Esko flew to Nevada on a bumpy late-night flight out of Buffalo via Detroit.

"Bet you consider yourself a successful man, respected in the community," Brent said.

Sloan didn't answer.

"Started as a mechanic, now you own a six-bay shop in, where is it again?" Brent asked.

"Naperville," Garvin answered.

"Naperville. Worked hard to build your business up from nothing, I bet. You come to Vegas this week to meet some buddies and to have a good time. You make some calls, a couple of 900 numbers." Brent scanned a page. "We got all the calls here."

Sloan was silent.

"Your wife's a teacher. Your daughter's a Girl Guide. Son's in Little League. You help coach his team, you said on the ride over."

"Sounds like you're living a nice life there, Tony," Garvin said.

"But that little ditty about what happens in Vegas staying in Vegas," Brent said, "ain't true for everybody. Now I want you to give it some thought. Try to envision how it's going to play with your wife, your kids, your business when it gets out in Happyville that the FBI has charged you—"

"Charged me? With what? Using a lost phone?"

"When the FBI charges you with obstruction of justice and it gets in the *Happyville Times* that Tony Sloan got himself mixed up with this missing single mom in Buffalo."

Brent slid Jolene Peller's picture closer to Sloan. Next came Bernice Hogan's college ID.

"And tied to this woman who was murdered. Horribly murdered."

Next came crime-scene photos of Bernice's body in the shallow grave.

"Christ!" Sloan looked away. "This is some mistake. I've never been to Buffalo in my life! I don't know this woman."

"Then tell us how you got her phone!"

Sloan held back.

"How did you get Jolene Peller's phone?"

"I took it."

"From Jolene?"

"No. No one. It was just left and I took it."

"Where? When?"

"At a truck stop, just before I flew here. I was driving to O'Hare. I needed gas and filled up before I parked at the airport."

Brent took notes.

"After I filled up and paid, I went to the head and there it was. Someone had left the phone on the shelf over the sinks. Must've forgotten it."

Sloan gazed down at it on the table.

"No one was around. I picked it up and was going to the office to turn it in when I got a stupid idea. Why not keep it and have some fun? So I did. On an impulse I brought it with me to Vegas. Turned it on, made some calls. I was going to leave it in the john at McCarran. I don't know anything about those people you're talking about. That's the truth, I swear."

"Be more specific about the truck stop," Brent said.

"It was the Thousand Mile Truck Stop, where I-294 meets the Ike, near the turnpike by the North Avenue West Lake area."

"Did you see Jolene Peller or Karl Styebeck at the truck stop?"

"No. How would I know if I did? I don't know these people."

"Did you pay for your gas with your credit card?" Brent asked.

"Yes."

Garvin slid a pad and pen to Sloan.

"Write down everything—dates, times, credit-card number. Give us a full statement about how you obtained the phone and used it," Garvin said.

* * *

A large two-way mirror filled the wall at the end of the room. It was connected to an unseen darkened office. Inside, FBI special agent Reba Jensen worked at a computer checking information arising from Sloan's interview. New York state investigator Roxanne Esko worked alongside her, talking softly on a telephone and making notes.

When Sloan completed his statement, Brent and Garvin joined them in the office. The two men talked over the phone to FBI agents who were on-site in Illinois at Sloan's auto shop and to those en route to the Thousand Mile Truck Stop. Brent and Garvin also talked with police back in New York State.

During the next three hours the team of investigators corroborated Sloan's account. And they confirmed that for the period of time between Bernice Hogan's disappearance and leading up to her murder, Sloan was in Naperville.

He was driven back to his Las Vegas hotel without being charged.

In Chicago, FBI agents set out to intensify their investigation on the Illinois truck stop to determine if Jolene Peller or Karl Styebeck had been there, or find out who may have left her cell phone in the men's washroom.

At 11:45 p.m. that night, a twin-engine MD-80 lifted off from Las Vegas bound for Chicago with a connection to Buffalo. Once the jet leveled, Brent fell asleep while Esko switched on her laptop.

She spent a long time staring at a picture of Bernice Hogan and thinking about the horror they'd found near Ellicott Creek. She was meticulous as she updated Jolene Peller's file, reminding herself to check with ViCAP. When she'd finished, she went back to the phone.

How had Jolene's phone surfaced in a Chicago truck stop? Who called Styebeck? Were they going to find the corpse of another young woman?

Esko was exhausted.

She put her work away and stared out beyond the starboard wing.

29

Jack Gannon needed a job.

It was the only way he could break the Styebeck story.

But the woman who answered his third call of the day to Kirk Tatum, assistant managing editor for the *New York Daily News,* didn't care.

"Yes, he's got your messages from this morning, Mr. Gannon."

"I can freelance a major exclusive on the unsolved murder of a nursing student. I have inside information. The story will have national interest."

"So you told us. One moment." Gannon heard a keyboard clicking above the newsroom clamor. "Kirk sent something, here it is. He said he was sorry about your situation at the *Sentinel.* A *damn shame,* he wrote here."

"He knows about that?"

"Apparently. He also said that he can't accept your freelance offer. His budget's tight and he has no openings for reporters as these are tough times for newspapers."

"That's it?"

"Sorry."

Gannon hung up, drew a line through Tatum's name on his pad.

Over the last few days, since learning that Jolene Peller's phone was used to call Styebeck's home, he'd pitched the story to the *New York Post, USA Today,* Reuters, and the Associated Press.

No one wanted anything to do with him. He was a pariah, ignored by people he respected, editors like Kirk Tatum.

After Gannon's Pulitzer nomination, Tatum had called him at the *Sentinel. "Congratulations on the nomination. I'm impressed with what you did on the plane-crash story. Win or lose, you're Pulitzer caliber. Anytime you want to talk about coming to the* News, *call me."*

Now Tatum wouldn't even take his calls.

And Gannon couldn't believe the response he'd received from Melody Lyon, a senior editor with the *World Press Alliance,* the international wire service. She was legendary for finding talent and guiding reporters to produce award-winning work.

The WPA operated a bureau in every major U.S. city, and two hundred bureaus in seventy-five countries around the globe, providing a nonstop flow of fast, accurate information to thousands of newspapers, radio, TV, corporate and online subscribers everywhere.

After his nomination, she'd flown him to New York and over lunch at the Plaza offered him a position as a national correspondent based at the WPA's world headquarters in Manhattan.

"I'll call you to confirm things in a few days, Jack," Lyon told him.

One week later, a New York state trooper stood at Gannon's apartment, hat in hand, explaining how a pickup driven by a drunk driver had smashed head-on into his parents' Ford Taurus killing them both.

Gannon went numb and had to steady himself against the door.

His parents had heard through friends that Cora might

be living in Canada and were driving to the friend's house in Orchard Park to learn more.

Later, when he was able, he called Melody Lyon, explained his situation and declined the job, *for the time being.*

Lyon had understood.

Weeks after the funeral, after he'd settled most of his parents' affairs, he'd followed up on the job offer at WPA. Melody Lyon was in Europe. Gannon spoke to an editor who worked with her.

"Unfortunately, Jack, our staffing needs have changed," the editor said.

Gannon couldn't understand what had happened and confided to Stan Baker, a grizzled night copy editor at the *Sentinel,* who'd known his dad. No one knew that Gannon was going to leave the paper for a job in New York. Baker was the only person Gannon trusted. After Baker "quietly poked around some," he pointed to Fowler.

"Word is Nate may have caught wind of your desire to leave when WPA was doing reference checks in town," Baker said. "You know he can't afford to lose his best reporter."

Gannon couldn't believe Fowler would somehow stand in his way.

And now, Gannon refused to believe that Melody Lyon would not respond to his calls. He'd checked with WPA. She was not sick. She was not on vacation, nor was she out of town.

Finally, after a few days, he got an e-mail from her.

Sorry about your situation with the retraction and everything. And I'm sorry I don't have any suitable openings at the moment. Stay in touch. M.L."

What the hell was this?

He shook his head.

Why couldn't any of these editors see through the bullshit he'd faced at the *Sentinel* and trust that he had the inside track on a major story? This tip on the calls took it to a whole new level. Styebeck was not only linked to Bernice Hogan's murder, but he was tied to Jolene Peller's disappearance.

This story was going to explode.

But no Buffalo news organization had broken this new angle.

Yet.

It was all his. But if he didn't break it soon, someone else would.

He monitored newscasts and Web sites, anxious to hear from Adell.

She'd learned nothing more on the case from her sources. There was a tight lid on the investigation. All she knew was that Brent and Esko had traveled out of state on the phone break.

She was trying to find out where.

So was Gannon.

He took a moment to review his financial situation. He had his severance and vacation pay, and some money from his parents' estate, but not much. He was good for three, maybe four months.

Then he would need income.

Deal with that later, he told himself, resuming his examination of his growing stack of hard-copy files on Karl Styebeck. *Who was he? Where did he come from?* Styebeck had blamed his father for his dark side.

What's the story there?

Gannon had started digging into Styebeck's family history. So far, he'd learned that Karl Styebeck had been raised in Texas. That his father, Deke Styebeck, had been a cop, or something like that, before he died.

Gannon didn't have much more on Karl Styebeck's background, like how he came to be a cop in suburban Buffalo.

Or how his old man died. Was it in the line of duty?

Gannon had a number of searches going. He concentrated on Texas because Styebeck had grown up somewhere between Houston and Dallas.

As Gannon worked alone in his apartment, scrutinizing his files for any angle or lead, his phone rang.

"It's me," Adell said. "The calls to Styebeck on Jolene Peller's cell were made in Illinois from a Chicago truck stop. Got a pen?"

"Fire away."

"The Thousand Mile Truck Stop, not far from O'Hare."

"Anything else?"

"All I know is they're going to dig into the truck stop."

As Gannon assessed the lead, his pulse quickened. The guys at the *Chicago Tribune* and *Sun-Times* would take this story from him if they found out what was happening in their yard.

This was his story.

Gannon tapped his pen, thinking that Chicago was, what? An eight-, ten-hour drive?

He slid his laptop and files into a bag and packed.

30

"Eighty for two nights. Best I can do."

The motel clerk resumed working on his crossword puzzle and the cigar in the corner of his mouth.

"Eighty. Take it or leave it."

Welcome to suburban Chicago.

Gannon had driven all day and into the early evening, making only food and washroom stops. After almost nodding off at the wheel on the Eisenhower Expressway, he started searching for a motel.

He'd made it as far as Hillside where the better chains were charging a hundred bucks a night. The Hillside Sea of Tranquillity Motel, offered "dirt-cheap rates"—and free wireless Internet.

Gannon was an out-of-work freelancer traveling on his own dime now.

"I'll take it for two nights." Gannon put his credit card down. "Can I get a room on the upper level?"

The clerk grunted.

Gannon's room smelled of a war among cigarettes, pine air freshener and—what was that—*vomit?* The toilet was hissing.

He was too tired to care.

He showered then turned on his laptop. Waiting for it to warm up, he recalled reading that Al Capone was buried in a Hillside cemetery. He considered a travel feature to sell to magazines, but set the idea aside as his laptop beeped to life.

Surprise. His Internet connection worked.

He had a number of responses from the libraries and genealogical societies he'd reached in Texas for help on Styebeck. Not much was useful.

He read until he fell asleep.

The next morning he bought a four-dollar breakfast at the convenience store across the street from his motel: an egg burrito heated in the store's microwave oven and a jumbo coffee.

While eating in his room, he read a new e-mail that had arrived from Rob Hatcher, who ran the Great Lakes Truck Palace in Buffalo.

Hey Jack, just heard new details on the writing on that blue rig you're looking for. Something relating to a sword. A "quick sword." Thought you'd like to know. Stay safe, pal. Rob

Gannon thanked him, closed his laptop, grabbed his car keys.

The Thousand Mile Truck Stop was a few miles away, a 24-7 operation with twenty-two fuel lanes and parking for more than four hundred trucks. Massive American, state, county and corporate flags waved from chrome-tipped poles that reached high above the main building.

Inside, he went to the office of the manager, Kevin Mawby. He was on the phone but waved him in, halted his call, clamped his hand over the mouthpiece.

"Can I help you?"

"Jack Gannon, I phoned you yesterday. Freelance reporter."

"The guy from Buffalo?"

"Right."

"Kevin Mawby. Have a seat, be done in a minute." Mawby went back to the call. "So that shit-for-brains thinks he's going to sue us because his piece-of-shit rig catches fire at my fueling station?"

Mawby wore a checkered shirt and jeans and rocked in a chair behind a large computer screen. His credenza had two more. Above them was a bank of security monitors, changing pictures every few seconds.

On one wall, there was a large map of the U.S.

Gannon glimpsed business cards on Mawby's desk but pretended he didn't notice that two of them bore the FBI's seal.

He had to be careful here.

"Okay." Mawby ended the call and smiled at Gannon. "You're doing a story about trucks? You were vague, as I remember."

"Well, there's a bit more to it."

As Gannon explained about Bernice Hogan's murder, Jolene Peller's disappearance and a tip that calls from Jolene's cell phone were made at Thousand Mile, Mawby's smile dimmed.

He started shaking his head when his phone rang.

"I have to take this."

In one smooth, subtle motion, while reaching for a pen, Mawby made the FBI cards disappear in his hand as he swiveled away from Gannon, who was looking at the wall map, letting on like he didn't notice.

Mawby made some notes and the new call ended abruptly.

"I'm sorry, Jack. I can't help you. Sounds like a sad case."

Gannon nodded but didn't push it. Mawby was battling other matters. The timing for this was all wrong.

"I see. Well, mind if I walk around, talk to a few people?"

"To what end? We don't know anything about your story."

"I'm also researching a color travel feature about the area, Al Capone's grave, truck stops, truckers who see things most travelers miss."

Mawby shrugged.

"It's a free country."

They shook hands.

Gannon found a private spot, flipped through his notes, then put in a call to the clerk at the county court to see if any search warrants had been executed recently for the Thousand Mile Truck Stop.

"I'll have to get back to you, I'm due in court," the clerk said.

Gannon began approaching truckers, showing them Jolene's picture, asking if they knew a rig with reference to "quick sword," or anything related to Bernice Hogan's homicide in Buffalo.

He talked to drivers in the lounge, the billiards room, the stores, the CB-repair shop, the Laundromat, the business office, the freight brokers, the hair salon, the chapel and the arcade.

No luck.

He went out to the lot and fuel lanes, roaming in an ocean of big rigs, with their growling diesels and hissing brakes. He went from rig to rig, driver to driver, showing pictures, asking questions. All he got were headshakes and head scratching.

And a whole lot of nothing as the day blurred by.

Back inside, he made another round of inquiries, going table to table through the restaurant. Nothing. He sat on a stool at the counter and ordered a club sandwich.

While waiting, the court clerk called back, informing him that no warrants had been executed on Thousand Mile.

Another strike. Mawby could have volunteered any potential physical evidence to the FBI, like video security tapes, Gannon thought, feeling a sense of defeat settling upon him as the waitress set his order before him.

"You're that reporter asking about a missing girl and a sword truck?"

"That's me."

"Tell me a little more about it? I might be able to help."

As Gannon told her the story she nodded.

"Yup," she said. "Two FBI agents were here the other day asking the same sorts of questions, asking us to keep quiet about their inquiries. But you seem to know as much as them."

Gannon started eating as she continued.

"This morning, I got thinking I should've told them to talk to my brother, Toby. He works at the Central Cargo Depot."

"The Central Cargo Depot?"

"It's a big cargo-warehouse place. I'd say half the trucks that come here usually pick up or drop loads at Central. You should go there."

She pulled out her order pad and drew a map.

"It's off the Ike. You can't miss it, it's huge. Ask for Toby Overmeyer. Show him this." She wrote: *Toby, help this reporter. Big Sis.*

Gannon thanked her then followed her map.

In a few miles, the complex of warehouse buildings stretched out before him. He went to the main office, to the service counter, and asked for Toby Overmeyer.

It was busy with drivers coming and going. Gannon estimated some twenty people were processing data at computer monitors. A Willie Nelson song filled the air. The walls had murals of American vistas, the Pacific Ocean, the Rockies, the Grand Canyon, the Florida Keys and Great Plains.

Barely in his twenties, Toby Overmeyer came to the counter. He studied the note and listened as Gannon explained his story once more.

"That's my big sister, Darlene," Toby said. "Always wants to help."

He told Gannon that the Central Cargo Depot had ten warehouse buildings, with tenants from major corporations, including a couple of shipping companies that housed and loaded for distribution goods from a spectrum of customers. The shippers used fleets from major trucking operations and hundreds of independents and subcontracted carriers.

"In total, we've got one hundred and sixty loading docks and trucks coming and going nonstop. We're a major hub for the central U.S."

"Any way you can check for companies or trucks where the word *sword* figures in the name?" Gannon asked.

"Sure, wait here."

Toby went to a terminal and worked quickly at a keyboard, then came back to the counter with a printed page, shaking his head.

"We got Sawyer, Simpson, Simon, SASX, SWWK, SWANE, SWISTER, nothing specifically with *sword,* although we don't get all subs."

"Subs?"

"Subcontracted carriers, hauling for other companies listed. Smaller independent operators."

"Mind if I walk through the complex, check out trucks, talk to the guys?"

Toby hesitated.

"You can't enter the warehouses. What you see mostly are empty trailers backed to loading docks, either being loaded or unloaded."

"That's fine with me."

Gannon thanked him and set out walking through the complex. The buildings were identified with large numbers.

For as far as he could see, trailers were backed tight to the loading bays. Every type of merchandise imaginable was loaded, or unloaded, amid the creak and clank of forklifts at work inside the trailers and the constant thunder of trucks rolling in, or out, of the depot.

Gannon had to get out of the way whenever a diesel roared, and brakes knocked as tractors hooked the trailers then maneuvered to begin a long haul across the country.

He found nothing that looked like a blue truck, or trailer, with "sword" in the name, logo or brand. Like searching for a needle in a haystack, he thought as he checked each dock, slowly working his way to Building 2.

Time tumbled by.

Outside, at the edge of Building 5, a group of warehousemen were seated at a picnic table on a break, watching two guys toss a football. Gannon approached them, told them that he was a reporter researching a story and asked them about Jolene, the truck, Buffalo, everything.

Again, his inquiry resulted in a lot of head shaking.

"Sorry, dude."

"Heads up, buddy," one of the guys holding the football said.

As a truck rattled past Gannon, he got a quick look at the door.

He froze.

The rig moved fast without a trailer as it swung around the building, disappearing into a dust cloud that hurled grit into his eyes, temporarily blinding him.

It was blue. Wasn't it?

And wasn't there something written that said "sword"?

Or was it "swift"?

Rubbing the grit from his eyes, he wondered if he was losing his mind.

"Did you guys see that? Was that a blue tractor?"

The men were returning to the warehouse, disinterested in Gannon.

Determined to investigate, he trotted after the truck. As he rounded the building, he thought he saw a dust cloud in the distance at the corner of Building 7.

It must've turned in there.

He started to run when he came headlong to a sedan, the light bar on its roof brilliant with flashing yellow and white, like a squad car.

"Hold it right there, sir!" The driver was wearing dark aviator glasses. He held up his hand.

Gannon stopped.

"Sir, your presence here violates our security policy. Do you have identification?"

Gannon passed him his New York State driver's license.

"I was told at the office I could conduct research here."

"I have authority out here." The man was making notes on a clipboard. "And I'm going to escort you out of the complex now, Mr. Gannon."

"But I just need to talk to the operator of the blue rig."

"That is not going to happen." The man had to be six foot six inches tall. He was holding the back door open for Gannon. "Get in, please, I'll take you to your vehicle."

Gannon glanced toward Building 7.

Damn.

"Sir," the big man said, "get in or I'll report you to the Chicago PD as a trespasser."

Gannon got in.

31

Jolene Peller was rising.

Surfacing gradually, her senses adjusting with every breath she took.

The droning had halted. Her mobile prison had stopped dead.

The other woman hadn't stirred.

All was still.

The darkness roared with Jolene's breathing and heartbeat.

Wait.

She held her breath as she noticed the far-off sounds of machinery. Growling engines, creaking, hissing. Big machinery but far away.

So distant and faint.

Where were they?

Jolene pressed her ear tight to the wall, straining to listen.

Voices! Muffled but definitely people far off!

"HELP!" she called. "HELP!"

Jolene's pleas were absorbed by the heavy insulated walls of their small space as something stirred near her in the dark.

The other woman began groaning to Jolene.

"Nooooo."

Jolene moved to her.

Time had loosened their gags. Their captor didn't seem to care, or bother to secure them whenever he'd stop to toss a half-eaten hamburger, cold fries, chocolate bars into their chamber, just enough food to survive their nightmare.

He seemed to be less vigilant.

Jolene seized the chance to attract help.

But now the other woman was panicking.

"No, it's okay," Jolene said. "It's good. I hear voices. We're near people. They can help." Jolene turned to the wall and screamed: "HELP! PLEEEEASE HELP US!"

"No," the woman rasped. "Stop…must be quiet."

"No, it's okay. Try to stay calm."

Jolene resumed fumbling around for the flashlight batteries. Maybe by shouting and creating a ruckus she could draw attention.

"I've got to find the flashlight batteries. I haven't looked under you," she said. "I'm going to feel under you."

The roar of engines rose and fell, delivering hope as Jolene's fingers felt for the batteries. She found a small round tube, then another.

"Yes!"

Fumbling for the batteries' button top Jolene inserted them into the flashlight. But as her thumb held them in the cylinder, she realized that the light wouldn't work without the tiny contact cap to keep them in place.

How would she ever find it in the dark?

Jolene cursed then screamed.

"HELP!"

She got to her feet.

"OH PLEASE HELP!"

Exhausted. Terrified. Thirsty. Hungry. Filthy. Angry. Jolene gave in to an emotional, uncontrollable outburst and slammed her shoulder into the wall, screaming, pounding, kicking.

"Noo. Stop!" the injured woman pleaded.

But Jolene ignored her, until she felt something tighten around her ankles. The woman had gripped Jolene.

"Stop!"

"Honey, we have to scream for help!"

"No." Her grip on Jolene was hurting.

"Honey, let go." Jolene lowered herself to the woman. "It's okay."

"No, if he hears, it will be bad. I've seen what he does."

"Then we have to fight. We have to get out."

"No. If you try to escape, it will be worse than anything you can imagine." Her voice broke. "I've seen what he does. I've felt it!"

"But if we do nothing then we make it easy for him and I refuse to let the freak do what he likes. Not without a fight."

"You don't understand what he did to me."

"No, *you* don't understand! All my life I've had to fight. Honey, I understand that you're hurt, you've been through hell. I need to get you to a hospital. Now, I'm telling you that crazy son of a bitch does not get me without the fight of his sick life."

Broiling with rage, Jolene pulled away as the woman pleaded in vain.

Jolene removed her shoes and used them to hammer the walls with unrestrained fury.

"HEEEEEELLLLLLLP!"

32

"*The Killing Floor." Here we go, baby. Can you dig it?*

As Jack Gannon saw the depot vanish in his rearview mirror, Ross Lowe—listening to Jimi Hendrix on his mp3 player—jumped from his forklift truck to size up his last order in Building 7.

Oh man, this one was Brownie's job, not his, Lowe thought.

Why did he always catch that slacker's work at the end of his shift?

Lowe bit down hard on his pen and repositioned his earphones. While Hendrix raged through the classic Howlin' Wolf tune, Lowe studied the shipment's bill of lading.

Look at this thing. It's a freakin' mess.

The operator's an independent. Rolled up to dock 75 a few days ago, partially loaded from Buffalo and Rochester, and waited for the rest of his freight, which took a couple of days to arrive at the depot and process.

Then this guy's got to pinball over the country hauling deliveries once he got him loaded. Lowe didn't know what sort of cargo the dude was already carrying and he didn't care because now he had to drive his forklift to the extreme end of Building 7 for the goods to load on the trailer.

Look at this.

Tires, cosmetics, chairs, tables, books and clothes—all

in the far end of the building. Lowe cursed. He was going to be late for his band rehearsal tonight. Why did they dock him way the hell up here at 75. Probably because nobody looked at the bulletin.

Thank you, Brownie, you useless goof.

Lowe spit into the steel trash bin then slapped his gloved palm on the red button, activating the dock's automatic door.

It rose to the yawning maw of the forty-foot trailer, releasing a rush of rank air that enveloped Lowe. As he stepped into the lip to take stock of its darkened reaches, The Who pumped "Won't Get Fooled Again" into his earphones.

He hit the floodlights and got a better look. Large crates, resting tight up front. The trailer was only a quarter full. Its walls, scarred from loading grazes, were white and insulated. A converted reefer, he thought, nodding with the music.

He started back to his forklift when something caught his eye. Light-colored replacement boards in the trailer's blackened floor, the telltale sign of rotting wood.

Lowe had the fresh memory of the time a trailer's floor collapsed and his forklift sank partway though. Scared the hell out of him. He'd jumped off without getting hurt. A close call he never wanted to repeat, so he walked into the trailer to check the floor, bouncing up and down on it.

Solid.

Curious about the crates, he continued on when the trailer tremored.

Christ, what was that?

Lowe yanked off his earphones.

What the hell was that?

Still ringing from Keith Moon's drumming, Lowe's ears adjusted to the outside noise of rigs navigating throughout the depot. Their rumbling was muted by the trailer's insulated walls.

No.

Whatever that was, it came from here. And he'd felt a slight vibration that seemed to have originated from inside one of the crates.

Was this guy hauling a living, breathing item?

He remembered the time Perkins found that anaconda that got out of its box and everyone came running to see before animal control came.

Lowe tensed as he placed his hand on the crate to sense more movement.

Nothing happened.

He saw no airholes or shipping stamps. No markings on the crate.

Weird.

Maybe it was a load shift? But this thing's been here for days.

Lowe found a foothold and heaved himself up to see if he could find any markings topside of the crates. There was nothing but shadow in the one-foot gap between the top and ceiling.

"What are you doing with my load?"

A man stood at the back of the trailer, silhouetted against the blinding floodlights.

"I thought I heard something," Lowe said.

"I don't think so."

"No, really."

At that moment a semi clamored by. It took several seconds before the deafening work of a rig grinding through lower gears subsided.

"Get away from my load."

Lowe approached the man.

"Know what I think, sport?" the man said. Tendrils of smoke curled from his cigarette and the tip glowed red. Smoking inside the depot was a violation. "I think you were fixing to steal from me."

"No, I wasn't. I heard something."

"Shut the fuck up."

Normally, Lowe could deal with anything truckers dished out, but something about this guy, something about his ice-cold calm, was threatening.

The cigarette dropped and a large snakeskin boot crushed it.

"Get on your forklift and do your job before I report you to your supervisor."

The man tapped a steel tire billy in the palm of his hand.

Cursing under his breath, Lowe inserted his earphones and continued on without ever looking at, or speaking to, the trucker. When he finished, and after both men had signed the bill of lading, the stranger edged his rig forward enough to close his trailer's doors. Lowe clamped on a seal then watched the guy walk to his cab.

What a prick.

The driver's door swung open; Lowe glimpsed the writing on it: *Swift Sword Trucking.*

I'm going to remember you, asshole.

33

East of Buffalo, at State Police Clarence Barracks, Karl Styebeck sat in an interview room.

Interview room was a euphemism.

Investigators knew the intent of such rooms. Small and sparse, with hard-back chairs, a table and white cinder-block walls that seemed to be closing in on you. These were battlefields where truth waged war against deception.

Michael Brent, having returned from Las Vegas with Roxanne Esko, wanted to tear answers from Styebeck.

But Brent knew better as he inventoried the detective from Ascension Park PD sitting before him. Styebeck's eyes were webbed with red threads. Strain was carved deep into his face, accentuating whiskers his razor had missed.

This was a man bearing a shitload of stress.

Or guilt.

Forget the hero crap, Brent regarded Styebeck as a disgrace, a man who'd lied to them about his ties to Bernice Hogan and Jolene Peller.

Brent wanted to rip the truth out of Styebeck. But Robert Kincaid, the district attorney, was not making things easy for Brent. He'd cautioned him: "You still lack a solid case for me to take to a grand jury. You've got no DNA, no strong physical evidence linking Styebeck to

Hogan's murder." And Kincaid, now watching with Captain Parson and Lieutenant Hennesy from behind the one-way mirror, added: "Despite the break with Jolene Peller's cell phone, everything you have is circumstantial."

All they could do was try to pop Styebeck, making it Brent's job to outmaneuver another detective.

"We appreciate you coming in, Karl."

Styebeck nodded.

"Hope you don't mind us talking in here, it's more private." Brent raised his head from his files.

"We just wanted to update you on the Hogan case. You know, get your thoughts," Esko said. "We're sorry about what happened with Alice after your last round with Jack Gannon, that idiot from the *Sentinel.* How's Alice doing, Karl?"

"She's fine. Thank you."

"Given all you've been through," Esko said, "we appreciate your agreeing to help us."

"I want to help."

"Good, Karl. That's good because we need it." Brent said. He had to be careful with the information they had and how they revealed it to Styebeck.

"As you know, Bernice Hogan's friend, Jolene Peller, was seen talking to Bernice the night before the body was discovered."

"Yes, I've got that from the missing-person's report on Jolene."

"You said you were on Niagara that night talking to Bernice. Did you have any contact with Jolene that night?" Brent asked.

Styebeck's bottom lip shot out before he shook his head.

"I don't think so. As I recall, Jolene had left the street some time ago. Our group had helped her out."

"You also told us that you were down there that night

before Hogan was found, looking out for the girls on Niagara because a strange truck was *'creeping them out'*?"

"I was collecting information from CI's and heard there was some guy in a truck, yes. I told you that before."

"Why were you on Niagara in a rental, if you were on the job?"

"Well, I'm not going to use my personal vehicle, and criminals can easily spot a tag on a departmental unmarked."

"Why not take a vice, or seized drug car? Or an abandoned impound?"

"Nothing was available."

"I see." Brent touched the tip of his forefinger to his tongue then touched it to another page in his file to flip it. "Understandable."

Styebeck nodded.

"What I don't get, Karl, is why some of the women allege you're a client, and others say you insult and harass them?"

Styebeck's face cracked with a grin that spread as he shook his head.

"Mike, come on. I get intel from them. I try to broker deals, favors. Some of them don't like it. Some bullshit me, hoping I'll help them with a beef. Some of them get pissed off, they'll tell you lies. *You have to look at what they are.*"

"And what's that, Karl?" Esko asked.

Styebeck's eyes met Esko's. Then went to Brent.

"'Whores, drug-addicted scum, a waste of skin, society's excrement in need of flushing.'" Esko read from her notes. "That's what some of the women claim you call them, Karl."

"They're tragedies. Every one of them. It is a brutal life down there. I accept they'd be pissed at me when I can't make their dreams come true."

Styebeck looked into his empty hands and swallowed.

"I've got a family. A job I love. I work hard as a cop. I believe profoundly in the outreach work my volunteer group does. Then—" Styebeck clapped his hands together, startling Esko "—this reporter, Gannon, and his paper destroy everything!"

"Do you know where Jolene Peller is, Karl?"

"I wish I did. Maybe she knows something about Bernice."

"Well, did you ask her when she called your home on these dates?"

Brent slid a page bearing the call history from Jolene's cell phone to Styebeck. Beautifully played, Esko thought, just beautiful.

"Because," Brent said, "it would help us to know what she said to you and where we can locate her."

Brent had just paid out a little rope for Styebeck to hang himself.

"Yeah," Styebeck said. "She was stoned, almost incoherent. I tried to make sense of what she was saying, where she was, but I couldn't."

"Why didn't you tell me, Roxanne or the task force about these calls, what with Jolene being a material witness and all? We could use the help, and you're a smart crime fighter, Karl."

"I know. I know. I got all tripped up. *Man, the* Sentinel *was accusing me of murdering Bernice Hogan!*"

"Did you kill her, Karl?"

"What?"

"Maybe she made you angry," Brent said. "Maybe you lost it, things got out of hand. You're thinking, who'd miss the dirty little drug-addicted whore? Am I right?"

"I know the game, Mike. No, I did not kill Bernice Hogan. You want to polygraph me?"

"It's an option," Esko said.

"But you did in fact talk to Jolene Peller, the woman reported missing?" Brent said.

"Yes."

"And you told no one?"

"She wanted to keep it confidential."

"Excuse me? *She wanted to keep it confidential?* Karl, do you do that with every person who is key to a homicide investigation? Hold back information from the primary investigator in a manner that could be construed as obstruction?"

"Obstruction? Are you nuts? Look, I've been through hell and I wasn't thinking right."

"In that case, how about you volunteer all your phone, credit-card, banking and personal-computer activity for us to review, to ensure you haven't overlooked anything else that might help us?"

"Or," Esko said, "we could get warrants, but you know how the press likes to jump on those things."

Styebeck swallowed.

"I got to think it over, do it right, maybe with a lawyer."

"A lawyer?" Brent said. "Why would a solid, dedicated cop—a hero, like you—need a lawyer to help us investigate the murder of a woman you were with the night before her body was discovered? You need a lawyer to help us investigate the disappearance of her friend, who just happened to call your home a few times? Have I got that right, Detective?"

Styebeck tapped his fingertips on the wood-veneer table as he looked at the walls.

Those white cinder-block walls seemed to be getting closer.

34

Jack Gannon returned to his apartment, dropped his bags on the floor and fell onto his sofa.

He wasn't certain he'd actually seen a blue rig with "sword" on the door at the Cargo Depot in Chicago.

But his gut told him he was close to breaking this story.

Setting his laptop on his chest, he checked the *Sentinel* and *Buffalo News* Web sites for anything new on Styebeck, Bernice Hogan or Jolene Peller. Just superficial updates. He called Bernice Hogan's foster mother, then Jolene Peller's mom, for any developments.

Nothing.

He scrolled through his e-mails for anything new on the document searches he had going.

Not much there.

He took a shower. Revived by the hot water, he decided to pursue another angle into Styebeck's past.

While eating a ham-and-cheese sandwich, he flipped through his hard-copy files, this time concentrating on the fat folder of news stories that carried any mention of the Ascension Park Police Department for the last seven or eight years.

After some forty-five minutes of reading small items, Gannon grew drowsy thinking it was futile. All of this stuff was inconsequential.

Then he sat upright.

An article had seized his interest. The story went back four years.

How did he miss this one?

Vic Trainor, a veteran detective with the Ascension Park PD, had been charged with criminal possession of cocaine and heroin.

There were a number of clips from Trainor's indictment, his trial and his conviction. Gannon read them quickly. He hadn't covered the story but he recalled the case as he picked out the information he needed.

Trainor was tried for allegedly supplying hookers and pimps with dope that arose from an organized network out of Newark, New Jersey. He pleaded not guilty and throughout the case Trainor's lawyer argued his innocence.

Trainor lost.

He was convicted and sentenced to two years in prison and a year of post-release supervision.

One article in the *Buffalo News* said the case was chiefly built upon evidence presented to the D.A. by Trainor's former partner.

Detective Karl Styebeck.

"Well, now. Isn't this interesting," Gannon said to himself.

The item said Styebeck attended his ex-partner's trial for one morning, never testified and refused to comment outside the court.

Gannon wanted to talk to Trainor about Styebeck.

The ex-cop would have been out for about two years now, Gannon figured, setting his laptop on his kitchen table to start searching for him. He expected Trainor would keep a low profile, so this might not be easy.

The first online search yielded three Victor Trainors: one died in Knoxville in the early 1900s, another was in a retirement home in Europe, and the last was a teenage soccer star in Miami.

Phone-number searches for New York State gave Gannon seven residential listings. They were in Albany, Rochester, Syracuse and four in New York City. None of them were for Victor or even V. Gannon called them anyway, starting with Albany.

No one answered there.

The Rochester number for Phillip Trainor was answered by a man with a small, high, soft voice.

"Victor Trainor? I'm afraid he's not at this number."

"Sorry to disturb you."

Gannon was about to hang up when the man said, "Vic lives in Niagara Falls, I think."

"Do you have a number?"

"This is embarrassing, seeing that he's my cousin, but we lost touch. I think he runs a garage or body shop. Something with Eagle in the name. Try there."

Gannon went back online and found a Niagara Falls listing for Golden Eagle Collision and Repair.

The man who answered practically shouted Golden Eagle.

The loud staccato whine of a power wrench, hammering, tools clanking on a concrete floor and a radio playing seventies classics all spilled into Gannon's ear.

"Would Vic be there? Vic Trainor."

"Hang on. *VIC! PHONE!*"

Gannon heard "Born to Run" before the line was picked up.

"Trainor, how can I help you?"

"Mr. Trainor, this is Jack Gannon. I'm a freelance reporter in Buffalo. I'm researching Bernice Hogan's murder and Jolene Peller's disappearance."

Trainor said nothing.

"Sir, you may know that there's some question of Karl Styebeck being involved in these cases."

The noise of the shop filled Gannon's pause before he continued.

"I know he's your ex-partner and I was wondering if you might have a moment to talk to me, confidentially, about his background?"

A moment passed.

"You know," Gannon said, "kind of enlighten me a little about him."

Maybe it was the rhythm of Trainor's breathing, or something emanating through the line, but Gannon sensed that years of pent-up bitterness had been made molten and started to ooze from him.

"Go along the river about three miles south of the Falls, across the street from the Mobil. There's a place called Rachel's. Meet me there tomorrow at one. I'll be wearing a T-shirt that says Golden Eagle on it."

Rachel's Diner was a clean, quiet place run by a long line of owners since it opened in the fifties. An original neon beer sign hung inside the entrance where Gannon spotted Trainor alone in a booth.

"Vic?"

Trainor studied Gannon, nodded then shook his hand.

"Thanks for meeting me," Gannon said.

Trainor's eyes were cold black cherries. His muscular arms were laced with tattoos and a stud earring glinted in his left lobe. Whatever special hell ex-cops endured in prison, Vic Trainor had emerged a harder man.

"I can give you fifteen minutes." Trainor took a hit of coffee.

Gannon waved off a menu from the waitress.

The only thing he wanted was information.

"Let's get to it then. Tell me what I should know about Styebeck."

Trainor snorted, turned to the window and contemplated the Mobil station across the street.

"He set me up because I'd learned the truth about him. He's whacked."

"The truth? Do you mind if I take notes?"

"I don't care."

"So what's the truth?"

"He was banging young hookers and feeding them dope," Trainor said. "He's a cobra. Keep your distance from him."

"What do you mean?"

"Look, it's a long story, but I knew what he was doing when we were partners. He claimed he was getting good intel from his CI's but I knew he was getting more than that. I knew the truth about him."

"Did you threaten to expose him?"

"No. First I told him to shape up, that he was risking his job, family, everything. Then bam, before I know it I'm being read my rights. Erie County's finding drugs in my home, my locker, my car. I'm dead. It's over."

"But couldn't you have told Erie County what you knew?"

"I tried. Nothing I had could be used in my case, never allowed in court. And none of the girls would confirm a word because they feared Karl." Trainor looked out the window. "And I had a complaint from my university days, got drunk and shoved my girlfriend. Styebeck had that. Man, he had me by the balls and squeezed because I threatened to expose the hero as drug-dealing scum."

"Anything else you can tell me?"

"He was an iceman. When we were partnered he rarely spoke, barely acknowledged me. But he'd stop at nothing to save himself."

"What about now? Didn't the detectives come to you for help on the Hogan murder?"

"That's funny. I'm an ex-con, an ex-cop with an ax to grind. Ain't nobody coming to me. Besides, I'd refuse. I want nothing to do with any of them. I lost my wife, my kids, my job to a system that thinks the sun rises and sets on Karl Fucking Styebeck."

"Can you tell me anything about Styebeck's past, his family?"

"I gotta go."

"Wait, please. I'd heard he blamed his father for his troubles."

Trainor glanced at his watch.

"There was this one time. We were sitting on a house, waiting in the car all night. Karl starts opening up to me about how his old man was a guard on the execution team in Texas and was responsible for some terrible tragedy that haunted Karl every day of his life. He blamed his old man for his own problems."

"Any idea what the tragedy was?"

"Nope, he clammed right up, like he'd said too much. Went back to being an iceman."

"Do you know his father's name, or when this happened?"

Trainor shook his head.

"All I know is there's something seriously wrong with Karl Styebeck. I've read your stories. Sooner or later it's all going to come to an end. My question is, how many people will he take with him?"

35

The night after Brent and Esko had taken a run at him, Karl Styebeck was in his garage making preparations.

He wrapped duct tape around a small box he'd covered with a plastic trash bag, grabbed a shovel and a flashlight then headed into his backyard.

Brent, Esko, Gannon; all of them were getting close. But he remained calm. He wouldn't get a lawyer. That would look like he had something to hide. He'd volunteer, cooperate.

Then he would do whatever he had to do.

His shovel bit into the earth behind the shrubs at the far corner where he started digging.

Everything he'd built was at risk.

Like a ghost, Orly had stepped from his past and intruded into his life, threatening to pull him back down into the world he'd buried long ago… Back to…1964 in Huntsville, Texas…

Karl and his younger brother, Orion, were in the empty prison cemetery, known as Peckerwood Hill.

White crosses pierced the morning mist.

The boys stood before a grave, freshly dug by inmates for Vernon Lugo, sentenced to die for murdering two Dallas police officers in a bank robbery.

Karl was nine years old. Orly—nobody called him Orion, except their mother when she got impatient with him—was seven.

Their daddy, Deke Styebeck, towered over them, contemplating the hole and the neat mound of red earth on the well-tended green grass. Deke was now boss of the execution team that would take Lugo to the electric chair.

"Boys, I brought you here to teach you something important before it's too late. Do you know from your bible class where evil comes from?"

"Hell, Daddy," Orly said. "Evil comes from hell."

"That's right. And it's my sworn duty to send evil back to hell. For the likes of Vernon Lugo the doorway is through this grave. And I guarantee you, come tomorrow, Vernon Lugo is going to pass through it."

Deke considered his sons, deciding that now was the time; they were old enough. Bending his knees, he lowered himself.

"Karl. Orly. You're going to find out soon enough that in this life, some people are defective. They come into the world damaged, not fully human on the inside, like Vernon Lugo, and most of them others out at Ellis on death row. These men have done evil, such terrible evil that the law has sentenced them to pay with their life for the wrong they've done, for all the hurt they've caused. That's what we call a death sentence. And I am authorized by this great state to ensure the sentence is carried out. Do you understand what I'm saying?"

"Yes, sir," Orly said.

"Never forget, I am at war with evil. Now there's talk that up in Washington they're fixin' to change the law. My hope is that reason will prevail, but what's going on is all politics and not for us to worry over, understand?"

"Yes, sir," Orly said.

"I brung you here to promise me on this spot today that, no matter what happens, when you grow up you will carry on my battle to remove the blight of evil. It is a righteous lifetime job and I want you to do your daddy proud."

"I promise, daddy," Orly said.

"Good."

Deke placed his big hands on their little shoulders, the same hands that would position Vernon Lugo into the electric chair, which everyone in Huntsville called "Old Sparky."

"Karl, you're being awfully silent. What's on your mind?"

"I'm just wondering, is all."

"About what?"

"Daddy, how does it feel when you kill them in Old Sparky?"

The question stung.

Blood drained from Deke's face. The warmth of his hands on his sons' shoulders turned cold as he removed them, stood and gazed upon the crosses, reflecting on all the condemned men he'd dispatched.

"I don't kill anyone," he said. "I carry out the court's order. I do what the people want, according to the law of the land." He looked at Karl. "But if truth be told, I feel it is a privilege and a great honor to wield the sword of justice."

The sword came down the next day.

Vernon Lugo gave the last of his private property—a radio, a watch, a model ship—to other death-row inmates at Ellis Unit, located on the old Smither Farm. Then Deke's team put him in shackles and got him into a prison truck. It rolled beyond the dark river, the forest and farmland. No one spoke. All that was heard in the truck was the clink of

Lugo's chains for some twelve miles as they traveled south to Huntsville.

At The Walls, they placed him in the death house and under the death watch.

When Lugo's time came, the warden told him all legal avenues to delay his sentence had been exhausted. The governor would not intervene. Lugo had to face his fate like a man. As Deke Styebeck and his team walked him from his death cell toward the gray steel door, it opened to the small room with the electric chair. Lugo's legs gave out, but Deke and his men kept him standing, kept him walking.

Then Deke and his team strapped Lugo into Old Sparky. The electric generator hummed like a requiem hymn as the chaplain read from the Bible.

When Deke finished inspecting all the straps, he whispered into Lugo's ear, "I'm sending you back to hell where you'll burn for all eternity."

Moments later, the warden read the sentence then nodded for the switch to be thrown. Lugo's eyes bulged and his body fought in vain against the restraints. Then the doctor pressed his stethoscope to Lugo's steaming chest and confirmed death had arrived.

A thunderstorm let loose afterward as Deke walked in triumph to the administration building with the paperwork. Another one done. He glanced back at the prison's gothic clock tower three stories above the north entrance. Sheets of rain raked across the brick walls, turning the runoff red.

As if the building were bleeding.

I have seen the glory, *Deke thought.*

A hearse delivered Lugo's body to the local funeral home. No one claimed his remains. His body was put into a suit then a coffin, both of which were made in prison shops.

Then, just as Deke had guaranteed, Lugo was interred in the very grave Karl and Orly had stared into at Peckerwood Hill. To the inmates who tended it, the graveyard was known as the cemetery of the unwanted and unloved.

As was his custom after an execution, Deke affirmed his devotion to his duty by reading Scripture by candlelight with his wife, Belva.

Sometimes they held hands as they read.

But tonight, after Lugo was executed, Belva felt the first prickle of trouble coming from deep in the shadows of Deke's eyes.

"You going to tell me what's bothering you?"

"All this talk coming out of Washington about stopping the death penalty and we got Gaylon Melk next week. His lawyers just launched three last-minute appeals."

"Lawyers appeal all the time, Deke. And so far the law hasn't changed. It's not your worry."

"But I can't help it, Bel, when you look at what he done. I swear it's just eating me up inside, just tearing at me."

The next week came, bringing Melk's death date closer. As no court had issued an order to delay, Deke's team headed to Ellis to transfer Melk to The Walls.

At this point, most inmates were usually resigned to their fate, scared but dignified in their cooperation. Not Melk. He sneered and smirked throughout the entire process. In the van he sang vulgar songs, grabbed his groin and taunted Deke and his men.

"Shut up and behave!" Deke said.

"Or what?" Melk giggled. "What will you do, boss?"

As Melk laughed, Deke seethed, thinking about Melk's crimes. He'd abducted three children, raped them, killed them, then decapitated them.

Deke's anger bubbled as he looked upon Melk, thinking

that this "thing" disguised as a human being needed to be returned to hell.

At The Walls, they put Melk into the death cell where he talked in hushed tones with his lawyers, two crusaders up from Austin. Melk declined a last meal or a visit from a spiritual adviser.

Some twenty minutes before Melk's execution was to take place, one of the two dedicated telephone lines rang. The warden took the call and absorbed the clerk's message from the court of appeal.

"Melk's been stayed. The district judge says it's all tied up with that Supreme Court business in Washington. Everybody stand down. Deke, allow your prisoner time with his attorneys before you transport him to Ellis."

Deke's team escorted Melk into a small, secure room for five minutes of privacy with his lawyers. Melk's whooping escaped into the hall.

"What the hell's that all about? His stay won't last long."

"I don't think that's it so much," J. D. Priddy, one of the guards, told Deke. "I read in the Houston Chronicle *today that they figure all executions will soon be declared unconstitutional by the Supreme Court." Priddy watched Melk through the door's secure viewing window. "Could mean a halt on all death sentences while they sort this out. Could mean commutation to life."*

"What?"

"Melk's likely just got hisself a free ride," Priddy said. "Likely what his lawyers are telling him right now, Deke."

"That's not right."

Deke's keys jingled as he unlocked the door.

"Time's up."

"Can we have a few more minutes?" one lawyer said.

"Time is up, sir."

After the lawyers said their goodbyes and left the area

with one of the guards, Deke and the other guards entered to collect their prisoner.

"It's a beautiful day." Melk stood, thrust two middle fingers at Deke, exposed his jagged tobacco-stained teeth with a grin. "Ain't nobody can touch me now, boss. I'm going to outlive your sorry low-paid dog ass and there's not one damn thing you can do about it. And just think, them kids I done. They coulda been yours, boss, so you chew on that, then you can chew on this."

Before Melk could grab his groin, the room exploded with the sound of keys, shackles and snapping bones as Deke tackled Melk then beat him with his chair until the other guards pulled him off.

Deke's attack left Melk in a coma for seven days.

Melk had cheated death twice but emerged a mute, for Deke's beating permanently destroyed his ability to speak. Melk's lawyers tried to have Deke criminally charged.

They failed because the other guards said Melk "threatened" Deke.

But Melk's lawyers persisted, and using the account of a spiritual counselor who'd walked by the room at the time of the attack, they succeeded in getting Deke fired.

He'd lost all the time he'd put in, all his benefits, his pension, his moral standing as the man who wielded the sword of justice. Belva helped him land a job as a school janitor and they scraped by, but bit by bit Deke started to unravel.

He'd go out to his workshop in the barn and sit in the dark for hours with a bottle of whiskey between his legs. Sometimes Belva would go out there with a Bible and candles and get him to read and talk.

Karl and Orly spied on them from the window, listening to everything. It's how they learned the stories of their daddy's righteous job and his tragic downfall. Sometimes

Deke slurred and Karl told Orly, "Daddy's a bit drunk," as he unburdened himself to his wife.

"I can hear 'em Bel. The voices of all those vile creatures on the row at Ellis. I hear them cacklin' now because the moratorium has come to pass."

"It's out of your control, Deke."

"No. No, it's not. I'm fixin' to do something about it. I have seen the glory!"

"The glory? Deke, I don't understand. I've begged you not to drink."

"It helps me see. Look."

He lifted his lamp so the light lapped on the barn wall illuminating the list of names of every prisoner he'd executed. Deke's list ended with a question: "Who is next?"

"See, Bel. It's not over. Our war is eternal. This is all part of His plan. See now, it's up to you and me to carry out prosecutions against them all."

"Against who, Deke?"

"The wicked. Every last one of them...."

After Styebeck patted the earth in his backyard, he lit a fire in the old steel drum in the corner of the yard where he incinerated trash. He went into the garage and got several items he'd hidden under his workbench.

One of them was the DVD of Bernice Hogan begging for her life.

Flames lashed from the drum when Styebeck tossed them in, deciding at the last moment to rescue one from the fire. Watching the rest burn, he took stock of his home and the life he loved.

He would protect it, as he'd done before. As long as he took care of matters his way, nothing would stop him.

Still as a statue, Alice stood at the window of their unlit kitchen.

She'd risen from bed to get a glass of ginger ale. She'd been there long enough to secretly witness Karl burying something in their yard then burning something in the trash.

Cold fear coiled up her spine as she returned to bed before her husband.

36

Melody Lyon held the power to change Jack Gannon's life.

She was quite aware of that fact as she dripped cream into her tea and resumed reading files on her BlackBerry.

The legendary news editor was sitting alone at the Wyoming Diner in Manhattan. It was late afternoon and the lunch rush had ended. A tired-looking waitress and a bored short-order cook chatted at the counter over coffee.

Savoring the quiet, Lyon returned to her dilemma.

Should she offer Gannon a job, or write him off as a tragic figure?

Scrolling through his news articles, she reviewed his brilliant work on the jetliner crash, which had earned him a Pulitzer nomination, her respect and a job offer.

Gannon was an outstanding reporter. He had the innate talent, instincts and drive to excavate a good story. Skills Lyon searched for to strengthen her special-investigation team at the worldwide wire service.

She was disappointed that it never worked out after Gannon had declined her job offer. Strangely, around that same period, when they were checking Gannon's references, the WPA got an anonymous tip alleging Gannon had a drug problem. She'd always questioned the validity of that claim and the timing of it.

It was as if someone was trying to prevent him from leaving the *Sentinel.*

But that was then.

Now, Lyon found herself in a new predicament with Gannon.

She and her fellow editor, Carter O'Neill, had one opening on their special-investigations team. They'd nearly come to a decision among four strong candidates, a reporter from Seattle, one from Berlin, another from Toronto and one from London. Each was a seasoned, award-winning journalist of the highest caliber.

Then, only days ago, Gannon had resurfaced, calling out of the blue, offering to freelance a story to her.

Most people in the business knew he'd been fired from the *Buffalo Sentinel.*

"Forget about him, Mel," Carter said. "Given the recent history of scandals at major newspapers, the last thing we need is to bring in a tainted reporter. Our SI team is the best of the best."

Still, Lyon, a well-connected force in the craft, remained skeptical because she knew Nate Fowler, the *Sentinel*'s managing editor, had a reputation for being slimy.

When Lyon measured what she knew about Fowler against what she knew about Gannon, it didn't add up. Not in her book.

Sirens echoed near Madison Square Garden as Lyon walked west along Thirty-third Street back to her office.

She thought carefully about Gannon's controversy. It concerned his reporting of a cop under suspicion for the murder of a Buffalo nursing student, which had led to a retraction and Gannon's termination.

If Gannon was wrong, he was finished as a reporter. If Fowler had somehow pressed him to back off, then there was every chance a bigger story and, more important, an injustice, would go unreported.

How this would unfold was anyone's guess, Lyon thought as she passed a private academy. It was a beautiful stone building a block from the World Press Alliance.

The WPA was situated in a twenty-story building in midtown Manhattan's far west side, in the heart of the Hudson Yards. It was close to Penn Station and the Lincoln Tunnel, and offered views of the Empire State Building and the Hudson River.

In the lobby, Lyon swiped her ID badge at the security turnstile and stepped into the elevator.

She was fifty-four years old. Widowed at age thirty-one. Never had children. She'd been a journalist most of her life, reporting on every major story around the globe. Her news judgment rarely—some said never—missed. And people who crossed her did so at their peril.

Lyon lived a private life but kept a tight circle of friends that included former heads of state, film stars, billionaires, as well as goatherds, seamstresses and children living with AIDs in the poorest regions on earth.

Journalism was not just her life, it was her lifeblood. She had earned her place as one of the world's top editors running one of the world's largest news services.

While its push for excellence had earned the WPA twenty-two Pulitzer Prizes, Lyon was wary of its global competition, chiefly: the Associated Press, Reuters, Agence France-Presse, Deutsche Presse-Agentur, Bloomberg, China's Xinhua News Agency and Russia's fast-rising Interfax News Agency.

Lyon got out of the elevator at the sixteenth floor, the need to make a decision on Jack Gannon weighing heavily on her.

She embraced the pride she felt passing through reception; the walls displayed WPA news photos of the world's most compelling moments captured over the last one hundred years.

Lyon walked across the thick gray carpet of the newsroom, with its low-walled cubicles and polished wooden desks where reporters and editors worked nonstop, under flat-screen monitors streaming video and data from around the world.

Arriving at her corner office, she stood at her desk and was considering calling the number she'd jotted on a pad next to Jack Gannon's name when she was interrupted by two soft knocks at her open door.

Carter O'Neill entered.

"Ready?" he asked.

"Ready?"

"Mel, I don't know where the heck you've been, but we're supposed to meet now to decide on that reporting position for Special Investigations. Don't tell me you forgot?"

Lyon flipped through her calendar.

"That's next Tuesday, Carter."

"No, it's today. We've already delayed. Let's get to it."

Keeping his eyes on the pages in the folder he was holding, O'Neill flopped into the plush sofa chair in the small meeting area of her office, unbuttoned his collar, loosened his tie.

"Now," O'Neill sighed. "I told you I really like Dieter, the guy from Berlin. I had Thomas at our Bonn bureau confirm his references. And this woman, Dianne Gray, from Toronto, is very impressive. Are you with me, Mel?"

Lyon was tapping her pen on her calendar and checking her cell phone.

"Carter, I'd like to delay filling the post for a couple more weeks."

"Delay? What the hell for? We're already a month behind on this."

"I know. Look, I've got a meeting at the *Daily News* in thirty minutes. Then I have to fly to D.C."

"Hold on a sec." O'Neill looked hard at Lyon. "You're still considering Jack Gannon in Buffalo, aren't you? I thought you were kidding after you told me he'd contacted you."

"Carter, we've made no decisions on the position yet."

O'Neill left his chair, stood before her and removed his gold-rimmed glasses. He was a former war correspondent and she regarded him as a professional equal, but she outranked him in the WPA's management hierarchy. His cold blue eyes held hers.

"I know you helped build this team, Mel. But you would be going out on a limb bringing a guy like Gannon into our organization. Hell, he's just been fired for fucking up a story. That kind of thing does not usually get you a better job. How can you give him any serious consideration? Remember that tip we got about Gannon's rumored drug problem?"

"I smell Nathan Fowler all over this thing at the *Sentinel* and the claim about Gannon using drugs. Look at Gannon's work. Come on, Carter."

"Even if you're right about Fowler, do you want to bring the *Sentinel*'s problems here? We don't need it. And, need I remind you, this is an unforgiving business. Managerial mistakes are expensive."

"I have a gut feeling about Gannon," she said.

"Are you going to risk your own reputation on it? And maybe more? You'd better think long and hard about the implications here, kiddo."

"I have. I want to delay for two more weeks. I want to see if Gannon can pull himself out of this nosedive. See what he's made of. Two weeks, Carter, that's all I'm asking."

O'Neill replaced his glasses, closed his folder and shook his head.

"Fine, but it's your funeral."

37

Jolene Peller felt hope slipping further and further away.

Minute by minute, mile by mile. Abandoning her to fall deeper into the never-ending darkness, the divide between life and death closing on her like massive jaws.

No. Please.

She drifted in and out of sleep as they rolled to the uniform rattle and hum of what had to be a large truck. To where, she didn't know. For how long, she didn't know.

It could've been days.

She gave up trying to guess. There were no clocks in this hell. No minutes or hours. Time here was measured in torment and agony.

How long had it been since they'd heard voices and machinery so near to them? One, two, three days ago?

No one had heard her cries for help.

No one came.

At times she questioned whether it had ever happened. Was it some sort of illusion? Was she losing her mind in this rotting hellhole?

She ached everywhere. She was hungry. Thirsty. She smelled bad. She was unclean. Soiled. Her teeth were caked with something disgusting.

She was too damn tired to fight anymore.

A low sound of pain rose from the floor.

The other woman stirred again.

The woman was terrified, in shock, and her condition was worsening. Jolene wanted to help her but could do nothing. Hot tears ran down Jolene's face. As she lifted her heavy, bound wrists to brush them away, she felt her locket.

Her beautiful locket.

A gift from her mother for turning her life around.

Clenching her fist around it filled Jolene with love and strength. She was not giving up.

Not while she was still alive.

She had to find a way out of this.

Think.

Think of the positives.

Their gags had loosened more, making it easier to breathe and talk. And the salt of her sweat had loosened her bindings, although the duct tape still held her wrists like a vise.

Jolene summoned a mantra from her school courses: Plan your work then work your plan.

She patted her pockets. She had the flashlight and the keys. Tools. She stood and ran her hands over the familiar rough walls, touching protruding nails, then metal seams and hinges indicating a door or window. *Find the contact cap for the flashlight. Inspect the hinges. Use the keys to work on removing them.*

Jolene crawled on her hands and knees, her fingertips feeling for the cap. She felt again under the other woman, who groaned.

"Carrie."

Jolene stopped.

"What?"

"My name is Carrie May."

"Hi, Carrie May. I'm Jolene Peller."

"I remember."

"Remember what?" Jolene continued feeling for the cap.

"What happened. How he got me."

"Tell me."

Carrie coughed and began to speak slowly.

"I was done my shift at the drugstore at the mall. I needed a ride home but all my so-called friends were gone."

"Where was that?"

"Hartford, Connecticut. I'd argued with them. It was my third shift at my new job. They wanted to go downtown and do drugs, I didn't. You know, at some point you just want to grow up. They took off and left me. So I walked to the truck stop across the turnpike. I had other friends there."

"Is that where he was?"

"Yes. It was real foggy that night. When I got there, my friends weren't there. I was pissed off. I bought a six-pack for my dad then tried to figure out how I was going to get home—walk or take the bus. When I came out, he was there hanging around the door."

"Do you know him?"

"No, God no!"

"What happened?"

"He started talking to me, saying he was worried about the sick little girl he had in his truck. Said he had no health insurance and saw me in my uniform and begged me to come see his little girl."

"Uniform?"

"My white drugstore smock. I figured that to him I looked like a nurse, or something. I took it off and put it in my bag. I told him I worked in a drugstore not a hospital. But he was desperate and sounded so convincing. A little voice told me not to go, but he had a little girl. Against my better judgment, I walked off to the far end of the truck stop to his rig. It was so dark."

"Did you see a girl?"

"No. I never even saw his face. He had his ball cap pulled down. The last things I remember were his boots, his keys jingling and him saying that for me to buy beer was 'mighty sinful.' Then everything went dark."

"How long ago was this?"

"I can't tell. Two or three weeks, maybe longer. Everything just went black, and when I woke up here in the dark, he was inside yelling at the other girl."

"Me?"

"No, before you. Another girl."

"Was her name Bernice?"

"No. Melissa maybe. That's all I know."

"What happened to her?"

"She's gone." Carrie's voice broke.

"But what happened?"

"I think he killed her."

Carrie sobbed. As Jolene moved to comfort her the truck jolted, its air brakes swooshed. They slowed and turned onto another road. Gravel pinged against the undercarriage as they went for what seemed like half an hour, maybe longer, then turned again onto a softer road. They could hear weeds and brush slapping against the truck.

Jolene's breathing quickened.

She sensed they were driving deep into an isolated area. As she began to struggle with her mounting fear, she felt a small point at her ankle and reached down.

She'd found the flashlight contact cap.

It took a few seconds of fumbling but she screwed it into place, switched on the light, pointed it to the floor.

Blinking at the hope, or horror, it would bring, Jolene swallowed.

"Carrie, I know he hurt you. I need to look at your injuries, see if I can do anything."

The truck was now crawling, like he was strategically positioning it.

Jolene moved the small beam of light toward Carrie's face, revealing a bloodied patchwork of abrasions, contusions and torn flesh. One eye was swollen shut; her lower lip bulged abnormally.

"You see?" Carrie sobbed. "What he does?" Carrie's good eye released a tear.

"Wait," Jolene's fingers hovered over Carrie's forehead. "I see letters written on you. Let me figure out what it says."

The truck stopped. He killed the engine.

Carrie nodded, her good eye widening with terror.

"He marks you."

"Why?"

"For judgment."

Jolene read the letters and gasped.

"Turn the light on yourself," Carrie said. "He marked you, too."

At that moment they heard someone directly outside.

A man's humming, the swish of tall grass, then the clank of steel tools being dropped on the ground. The jingle of keys, locks being unlocked, the squeak and metallic roll of a door being opened, allowing the dim illumination of twilight and fresh air to rush in.

Any thought of hope died.

Gloved hands gripped the frame. One of them held a steel pipe. No. Not a pipe. Jolene had seen that before. A cattle prod.

Carrie whimpered, rushed to a dark corner, wedging herself into it.

A snakeskin boot balanced on the lip of the door.

A man hoisted himself inside.

38

After meeting Styebeck's ex-partner, Jack Gannon intensified his digging into Karl Styebeck's family history.

What was the deal with Styebeck's old man?

To find out, Gannon had put in calls to Huntsville and Austin requesting Texas officials confirm the employment of people with the family name of Styebeck in the state-prison system.

The next morning he got a callback from Austin.

"Mr. Gannon, this is Bobby Sue Yarrday, with the Texas Department of Criminal Justice, responding to your request."

"Yes."

"A preliminary search of our records shows that a Deke Styebeck was employed by the Texas Department of Criminal Justice as a correctional officer in Huntsville until 1964 when he was terminated."

"Can you tell me the reason for his termination? Or provide copies of his file, or any disciplinary proceedings?"

"I am unable as of yet to determine the circumstances of his dismissal, but I will continue to look into it and see about records."

"Thanks. What about other information, like his date of birth, marital or family status? Does any of that show?"

Bobby Sue hesitated.

"Because they are confirmed as deceased, I can tell you that Deke Styebeck's parents were Gabriel and Adolpha Styebeck. That's Pastor Gabriel Styebeck."

"Pastor?"

"Yes, of Shade River, Texas. That's in Angelina County, near Lufkin."

Now Gannon had another key piece of data.

He called the *Huntsville Item* and requested a news-library search of any archived reports naming Correctional Officer Deke Styebeck. Gannon wanted the period from 1960 to 1967 checked.

"It's fairly urgent," he said and provided his credit-card number.

Then he went online, found listings for churches in Shade River, Texas. He sent e-mails and made calls starting with the office of Pastor O. B. Woodridge at the Southern Church of the Spirit.

"Hello?"

"Is this Pastor Woodridge?"

"No, I'm his son, Willard."

"Jack Gannon. I'm calling from New York. I'm a freelance writer and I'm conducting some historical biographic research. I was wondering if you could point me to anyone who might recall Pastor Gabriel Styebeck and his wife, Adolpha?"

"No, doesn't ring a bell. I think you'd have better luck with Yancy, our local historian."

"Yancy?"

"Yancy Smith on Hickory Road. He's in the book."

Gannon found the listing online and called. The phone was answered promptly on the first ring.

"'Yellow."

"Yancy Smith?"

"You got him."

Gannon repeated his request and was heartened by Smith's answer.

"Yes," Smith said. "Pastor Gabriel Styebeck. He was with the Shining Glory Church. Yes, his wife was Adolpha. They had a son, Deke. A bit of a tragic story, actually."

"Tragic, why?"

"Well…" Smith paused. "Sorry, I should be getting ready for a specialist's appointment in Dallas this afternoon. My daughter-in-law is driving me."

"Wait, please. Can you just give me a quick summary?"

"Well, no one really knew the details. I believe Deke was part of the execution team at The Walls. Word was he was a difficult man to live with before he died."

"How so?"

"They said it had something to do with Pastor Gabriel and Adolpha and a strict upbringing. But Deke was adopted by the Styebecks when they were ministering in Canada."

"Adopted? Do you know much more on that?"

"I think we have some old church bulletins from the Shining Glory Church. Can you hang on? My files on all of Shade River's churches are in the other room. Just hold."

Gannon heard a dog yelp, heard Smith go into another room, say something to someone. Several moments passed before Smith returned.

"Hello?"

"Still here," Gannon said.

"I found something, but I'm afraid it isn't much."

"Go ahead."

"There's mention in a bulletin from 1937 welcoming the return of Pastor and Mrs. Styebeck, and *their boy,* Deke. They'd been in Alberta."

"Alberta?"

"Yes, Brooks, in the southeastern part of the province.

The bulletin welcomes them and their new son. See, Deke was thirteen. He was adopted because Adolpha couldn't bear children. Most of Shade River knew that. But soon the rumors started to fly that they got Deke after some terrible tragedy in Alberta. The pastor and his wife never spoke of the circumstances of the adoption. Guess they wanted to protect their boy."

"Can you scan and e-mail me that bulletin?"

"I think so."

Now Gannon had another piece of the Styebeck puzzle.

Without stopping, he began contacting newspapers in Alberta, big ones in Calgary, small ones in Brooks and Medicine Hat. He was trying to reach retired reporters or historians who could help him research a tragedy that happened near Brooks, Alberta, in 1937.

During the next few hours, as he waited for responses, the *Huntsville Item* sent him a small news clipping from 1964 that reported on the dismissal of Deke Styebeck, a guard at The Walls, after an altercation with a condemned inmate following a stay of execution.

That doesn't tell me much, Gannon thought before his phone rang.

"Gannon."

"Mr. Gannon, Ross Sawyer. I'm told by some news friends that you might want to talk to me about what happened in 1937." The man cleared his voice. "I was with the *Alberta Tribune* back a bit, before I retired."

"Yes! Mr. Sawyer. Thank you. Can I ask you a few quick questions?"

"You sure can. I was just sorting through some old files and notes right here. Family's been at me to write my memoirs. I turn eighty next month and promised to start."

"Yes, Mr. Sawyer, I need to know all about Deke Styebeck's connection to Canada."

"Deke Styebeck. Yes, you're talking about the murders."

"What murders?"

"You're talking about the Rudd massacre in '37 out by Brooks."

"A massacre?"

"Seven members of the Rudd family were murdered. Deke Rudd, the thirteen-year-old boy, was the only survivor. He was adopted by an American pastor and his wife. This all happened before my time. But I interviewed Superintendent Ian Macdonald a few years ago, before he died. His son's a Mountie at the Brooks Detachment, you know."

"Superintendent Macdonald?"

"At that time, Ian Macdonald was a rookie and part of the investigation team on the Rudd-family killing. He was quite forthright in recalling the case because I was going to write a book on it. Guess I got a lot of books to do." Sawyer laughed at himself.

Gannon had a quick, wild thought.

"Mr. Sawyer, if I came to Alberta, could I impose upon you to let me review your files and point me to Brooks where this all happened?"

"I'd be happy to help you out. When you coming?"

"Just as soon as I can."

39

Before the New York State Police came to search the home of Detective Karl Styebeck, he'd taken precautions.

That knowledge passed unspoken between Brent and Styebeck like a bluff between players at a high-stakes poker table as they watched investigators examine the house room by room.

Brent regarded Styebeck as a liar who was shielding himself with deception, and he expected the search to yield nothing of use to his investigation.

For her part, Alice Styebeck struggled to be cordial as strangers wearing latex gloves probed their rooms, their furniture, their clothing, their lives.

"I volunteered to let them search without a warrant. It's necessary for me to help the investigation because of the people I deal with, Alice," Karl had told her earlier.

His face betrayed nothing now as he watched them search his garage, but his breathing quickened slightly as he watched them sift through and collect the ashes of his steel trash drum.

No one understood that he would take care of things his way and everything would be resolved, everything he'd carried all these years.

Watching them he knew this was his crucible and it took him back to the crucible he'd faced as a boy in Texas, in 1969….

* * *

The rapid whirring of his father's table saw drew Karl to the barn.

The smell of lumber, the snap of a measuring tape, and nails being hammered signaled that something was being created.

Returning home from school, hope rippled through Karl, for his father had spent the past few years mourning his prison job and deluding himself into thinking he would return to it.

Every time he got word of a reinstated prison official, Deke would go on at the supper table about his belief that "at long last" his situation would be reviewed and his termination overturned.

When it didn't happen, Deke went out to the barn alone and listened to the radio with a bottle between his legs. Karl and Orly would slip out of their beds and watch him through the barn's weather-worn planks. Some nights Belva would light a lamp and sit with her husband. They'd read Scripture. Deke would write on the barn walls, covering them with passages and apocalyptic ramblings.

Sometimes Deke would drive off into the night, or to town, and stare at the prison like a ghost.

At fourteen, Karl knew his father was contending with a prolonged breakdown. But on this day, Karl's hopes were lifted by the sounds of carpentry. When he entered the barn, shafts of light caught the sawdust that flecked his father's hair and moist face.

The light illuminated his younger brother, Orly, sitting there in a big chair their daddy was making.

Not just any chair.

An exact copy of Old Sparky, the electric chair used to execute prisoners. Karl had seen pictures. Everybody knew the most infamous chair in all of Texas.

"Hey, Karl!" Orly was twelve and his arms looked small on the rests; his feet dangled down but did not reach the ground. "I'm going straight to hell!"

Karl searched for wiring and saw none. He looked at his father.

"What're you making this chair for?"

Deke's stare went clear through him.

"For my work." He pointed the handle of a clawhammer at Karl. "And you can help by keeping your mouth shut. Nobody outside this family needs to know our business. Got that?"

Deke then pointed the hammer at Orly and repeated, "Got that?"

Orly said, "Yessir."

Karl grew uneasy.

But he didn't press the matter with his father, choosing instead to raise it privately with his mother that night when she was cleaning up after supper and Deke and Orly had gone out to the barn.

"I just don't understand," Karl said to his mother, after asking why his father was building a death chair in their barn.

Belva stopped her work, dried her hands on her dish towel and clasped her son's shoulders.

"Your daddy's had a vision."

"What do you mean?"

"It's too complicated to explain." Belva's face was serene, like she was in another place. "But I trust in it. We have to help your daddy answer to it. Now, Karl, just like you, people won't understand it. The best way to help your daddy is to hush up about it, okay?"

He was confused.

"Karl?" His mother smiled and searched his eyes for a connection.

"Yes, ma'am."

"Now you don't breathe a word of this to anybody, understand?"

"Yes, ma'am...."

Several hours passed before the investigators finished their work at the Styebeck home.

Alice Styebeck blinked back her tears, thankful Taylor was in school, thankful no press had been around, although she saw neighbors gawking at all the unmarked vehicles.

As the detectives left, Karl put his arm around her waist, assuring her it was all part of his work on the investigation.

"We're going to get the guy who killed Bernie Hogan," he said.

Looking into his face, Alice struggled to believe him.

40

"What do you think, Paul?"

Michael Brent was on his cell phone to Paul Labray at the lab. Esko was driving.

Brent and Esko were returning to the State Police Barracks at Clarence. They'd just finished an interview in downtown Buffalo with a pizza-delivery driver.

"I maybe might have seen that girl that got murdered talking to a man that night. Maybe. I'm all mixed up, man. Sorry."

Brent was cursing the pizza guy's unreliability.

It had been a day since they'd searched Styebeck's home and things didn't look promising. But now the lab in Olean had something on the rental car Styebeck had used. Labray gave Brent a quick summary. The tread of the tires on the Malibu rented by Karl Styebeck were consistent with the casts taken from tire impressions near the Hogan murder scene.

"I think," Labray said, "this puts Detective Styebeck closer to the homicide."

"A lot closer," Brent said. "Nice work, thanks."

Brent hung up, punched in Lieutenant David Hennesy's number and relayed the update. Esko's eyebrows climbed as she listened to Brent's end of the conversation.

"Okay," Hennesy told Brent. "We'll set up a conference call. Our place at four. I'll advise Parson, call Kincaid and the lab."

Brent slid his phone into his pocket and watched the suburbs roll by.

"This is something, Mike."

"It's something, all right. Have to see what Kincaid makes of it."

An hour later, Brent, Esko and several other state police investigators gathered in a meeting room at Clarence Barracks. They'd all reviewed the attachments on the tires Labray had sent to them prior to the call.

At 4:10 p.m., Kincaid was still running late and kept the others waiting on the line.

"Hang on." Kincaid's voice crackled through the speaker with tinny crispness. "I've just returned from a pretrial motion on another case. Lieutenant Hennesy briefed me on the new evidence. Bear with me while I get up to speed with the material you've sent me. Give me a minute."

Moments passed. While the others looked over files, Esko tapped her pen and glanced at Brent. He didn't look optimistic and she didn't blame him. For they'd drawn Bob "Slam Dunk" Kincaid as the D.A. for the Hogan murder.

Kincaid, an assistant district attorney, was one of the state's heavy hitters. He handled violent crimes and rarely lost because he made near-impossible demands on detectives to make his case a slam dunk, absent of all reasonable doubt.

"Okay," Kincaid could be heard flipping papers. "Good work on the tires."

"So, do we bring Styebeck in now?" Brent asked.

"You mean charge him?"

"Yes."

"With what?"

"First-degree for Hogan. This puts him at the scene and we've got the phone calls from the missing woman."

"Slow down, there. You're forgetting Styebeck has admitted contact with Bernice Hogan and Jolene Peller. Styebeck has a right to rent a car. This evidence puts his rental car *near* the scene. This break does not make the case. It's a building block."

"Look," Brent said, "we've got witnesses putting him with the victim and the missing woman."

"Mostly prostitutes with axes to grind. And Karl Styebeck, being a detective with confidential informants on the street, has reason to be on Niagara talking to people. As I've said, he's not challenging the fact that he had contact with Bernice Hogan and likely Jolene Peller."

"What about Peller's relationship to Hogan and Styebeck?"

"What about it? That Peller was helped by Styebeck's outreach group is circumstantial. That Peller's mother reported her missing is also circumstantial given the woman's background."

"What about Peller's cell-phone calls to Styebeck?"

"No question, you've hit on something there. That Peller's phone surfaced in Las Vegas after calls were placed from a Chicago truck stop to Styebeck is a compelling piece of evidence. Like the tires. They are both building blocks but not enough to make the case."

"Well, he's refused a polygraph after indicating he would take one," Brent said.

"That's his right, Mike. But so far, he's cooperated without playing the lawyer card. Look at his ties, his community work with his outreach group to help the girls. His contact with them. All reasonable."

"You're making this harder than it needs to be, Bob," Brent said.

"If Styebeck gets an attorney, he'll knock us on our asses based on what we've got so far. He'll point to the fact that Styebeck's cooperated. He's volunteered his phone, bank, credit-card and computer records. He's allowed you to search his house and his personal vehicles."

"Of course," Brent said. "He's smart. He's likely got rid of anything hot. He wouldn't have volunteered if there was anything incriminating to be found."

"So, what did you find?"

"Some calls to him from public phones all over the place."

"And?"

"He said they're from informants, or associates," Brent said.

"To his home?" Kincaid said. "I thought you guys used safe phones."

"Not all the time," Esko added. "Depends on the cop and the informant."

"Some of the calls," Brent said, "were from phones at, or near, truck stops."

"Wasn't there a suspicious truck seen the night before the murder?" Kincaid asked.

"Yes."

"And the cell-phone calls came from a Chicago truck stop?"

"That's right," Brent said.

"You're close, guys," Kincaid said, "but it's just not there. His appearance of cooperation will go a long way in front of a jury. And he is considered a community hero. At this stage, we have not removed all reasonable doubt."

"What do we need?" Brent asked.

"Irrefutable evidence. You've got some strong pieces, but not enough. You need something like a confession, or DNA. Or something we haven't yet thought of."

"You're talking about a lucky break," Brent said.

"That's correct, if you want to make this a slam dunk."

41

"Justin! Wait up!"

Zach Miller was pedaling as fast as he could, fighting to keep up with his big brother. Justin resented how their mother kept forcing the little geek on him whenever he wanted to hang with his friends.

"You can't keep excluding him, Justin, it's not fair."

All right, he thought, looking over his shoulder, but the little geek was going to pay a price.

Justin signaled to his pals and they all accelerated their bigger bikes, speeding through the treacherous terrain of Clear Ridge Crossing, the new subdivision being carved out of farmland at the southern edge of Wichita, Kansas.

"Justin!" Zach's voice grew distant. "Wait for me!"

"Go home if you can't catch up, Zachary!"

But Zach had reached the point of no return. Not yet close enough to be part of Justin's posse, and too far from home to ride back alone. All the boys knew the psychology at work here. Zach would have to earn his right to ride with them. Prove himself worthy, or go home like a baby.

Zach gritted his teeth, squeezed his handlebars and pumped, hell-bent on being accepted by the older boys. But they had vanished ahead of him behind the tall scrub of a downhill slope into the next valley.

That did it.

Zach invoked the power that ruled over him and his big brother.

"I'm telling Mom!" he yelled.

"Go right ahead, you little shit!" Justin yelled back.

"I'll tell her what you're really going to do in the woods! I will, Justin!"

Defeat blossomed across Justin's face. He rolled his eyes, then locked his brakes, grinding everything to a stone-spewing, dust-churning halt.

"Jesus, Zach!"

Justin's cohorts, Brody, Devin and Aaron, stopped out of duty to their leader. Like outlaws on the run, they leaned on their handlebars and caught their breath as they watched Zach bring up the rear.

"Little guy rides pretty fast," Brody said.

Justin half grinned, begrudging Zach a modicum of respect for his perseverance. It grew into pride watching how he put his whole heart into a hard ride just to keep up. For deep down he loved his little brother who'd always had to battle the odds.

One night when Zach was two, he'd stopped breathing. Mom and Dad freaked out. Mom rode in the ambulance. They got him breathing but the people at the hospital couldn't tell them what the problem was. His parents prayed for a miracle and Zach pulled through.

But then came all those years when Zach used to wet the bed and their family learned a couple of new words.

Nocturnal enuresis.

Justin would never forget Zach's shame and anguish. Night after night Justin watched him sleep on the floor of their room and cry himself to sleep. Justin helped clean up, promising him that it would get better.

And it did.

Zach hadn't had any trouble in nearly three years now.

Except for Justin. Who gave him a hard time. Every time. To make him stronger. Out of love.

Justin was Zach's protector.

The bond between him and his little brother was unbreakable. And Lord have mercy on anyone stupid enough to harm a hair on Zach's head.

Zach's gasping filled the air when at last he joined the older boys.

He was red-faced and on the brink of tears at having nearly been abandoned such a long way from home.

Clear Ridge Crossing was new territory for him.

As far as they could see, cookie-cutter houses were in stages of evolution. At one end, rows of finished homes lay adjacent to lines of wooden skeleton frames of homes in progress. Next to them, an expanse of open grassland was undergoing transformation into earthen lots.

Columns of dust dimmed the sky as the racket of hammering and sawing blended with the diesel roar of battalions of graders, loaders, earthmovers and convoys of big trucks rolling in and out of the zone. It was dotted with the portable white trailers of contractors' offices that backed onto a marshaling area where all kinds of material was stored.

The southeastern fringe was lush with dark forests, an inviting haven for Justin and his friends.

"So, what is it you think we're going to do?"

Zach pushed his glasses back up his nose, sniffed, then nodded to Brody and Aaron, who had their school packs strapped to their bikes.

"You're going to drink beer you took from Brody's dad's fridge and watch movies of girls doing sex stuff Aaron downloaded off his brother's computer. I heard you talking back when we started. Devin's voice is loud."

Justin absorbed the information then held his fist under Zach's chin.

"You can come but if you tell anybody about this I'll hammer you."

"I won't tell anybody."

Justin then led the group along a network of earth roads at the edge of the subdivision. They slipped deep into the woods where the boys had built a tree house using scrap wood they'd taken from the site.

With the din of the work softening behind them, they dismounted at the base of a thick hardwood tree. An uneven ladder of mismatched wood ascended the trunk to a crude structure affixed and hidden among the branches twenty feet up.

Aaron and Brody unfastened their backpacks from their bikes and slid them on. Then, like small soldiers, they climbed up the ladder with commando precision. Devin went next, then Justin, followed by Zach, who, being a first-timer, smaller and nervous, took his time.

Zach was excited by his initiation into his big brother's group. But just as he reached the entry, he was barred.

"Not yet," Justin said.

"How come?"

"You gotta get some wood so we can make a seat for you. Got to do your share to help build our fort."

"Where do I get it?"

Justin pointed to an area in the forest thirty yards off where he and the others had hidden the discarded scraps they'd carried from housing sites.

"Find four boards as tall as you and bring them back here. We'll drop the rope for you to tie around them, so we can haul them up one at a time."

Zach climbed down, never suspecting Justin's goal was to keep him out of the tree house. He dutifully navigated his way through the forest stepping through patches of creeper, sumac and dogwood as he searched for the cache.

But he couldn't find it.

He'd lost his bearings.

He glanced back and upward toward the tree fort, but it was obscured by the branches and leaves of other trees.

He turned and moved on in another direction.

After taking a few steps, he froze.

At first he thought it was a trick of the sun, the way rounded spots of color played in light and shadow.

Just old branches, bushes and leaves.

Right?

But what he was seeing, hearing and smelling was real.

The drone of flies was as loud as his pulse thumping in his ears.

Zach was transfixed by what he saw.

Gooseflesh rose on his arms.

As he slowly backed away, Zach shut his eyes but the image burned before him.

Is that a human?

The tiny hairs at the back of his neck stood up. All the saliva in his mouth evaporated, muting his cry for help.

Then a familiar warm fluid ran down his legs.

42

A few hours after Zachary Miller made his discovery, the Wichita Police Department's blue MD 500E thudded high over Clear Ridge Crossing.

Detective Candace Rose squinted up at it from her car.

The chopper was photographing the site to help determine the size, scope and boundaries of the crime scene.

Rose, the rookie homicide detective, was the primary. Lou Cheswick, the veteran, was her partner.

Outdoor scenes were problematic. And based on what the young Miller boys had already described to them, and what the responding officer had told them, this one was bad.

Real bad.

They'd interviewed a teary Zachary Miller in one of the job-site trailers, where the boy's shaken mother—"Dear Lord, I can't believe this. A dead person! Are you sure it's not an animal? Dear Lord!"—had brought her son a fresh change of clothes.

Then Cheswick drove their Impala to a ridge that was a natural gateway to the site and waited for the assessment. As the chopper's rotor sliced the air, Rose called her husband, an engineer at Cessna.

"You and the kids pick up a pizza. I won't be home for dinner tonight."

"You don't sound so good. Did you catch one?"

"I did."

"And are you the primary?"

"I am."

"Good luck. I'll pick up some butterscotch ripple for you. For later. I'll wait up, if you like."

"No, no need to wait up. I'll be fine with the ice cream. Thanks."

Rose's walkie-talkie crackled in her hand. She held it to her ear as the spotter above guided them to the best point of entry to the scene.

Cheswick slipped their sedan's transmission into drive.

As they crept along a bumpy worn path that stretched across the earthen plain, Rose looked into her side mirror and was assured by the small convoy. Some marked units from Patrol South Bureau stayed back at the ridge to establish an outer perimeter. A couple of cars followed her and Cheswick in. The uniforms would tape off and secure the scene.

The CSI vehicle was with them, along with K-9 and some search boys if they needed to grid the area.

The flat wide stretch took Rose back to her childhood. She'd grown up in the heartland, a farmer's daughter, in Comanche County. Through high school Rose worked part-time in the sheriff's office, then studied law enforcement at college before joining the Wichita PD.

She'd worked a beat and met her future husband after giving him a traffic ticket. She hit the books and became a detective with the Sex Crimes Section. And when Homicide Section's caseload strained, she was called in to assist with murder investigations.

The lieutenant liked her work and suggested she apply for a vacancy that had opened up in Homicide. Rose scored high on her exams and won the job. Two weeks ago she was partnered with Lou "The Legend" Cheswick.

"Welcome to the few, the proud, the sleep deprived. Next case that comes our way is yours," he'd said.

After six years as a street cop and four years as a sex crimes detective, Rose had seen enough misery to last a liftetime or two—savage abuse of children and women, the aftermaths of suicides, fires, car wrecks and murders.

But taking the lead of her first homicide? This was nerve-racking.

It was bad enough that it had an outdoor crime scene as big as all Kansas. But to be so grisly, and have it be a little boy who'd made the find…

Zachary Miller's voice was fresh in her ears.

"Is it human? Was it really a person?"

Rose reviewed her mental checklist: reread her statements and start her log, noting the time, weather and temperature and the relation of the scene to its surroundings.

Now she puffed her cheeks and exhaled slowly as they neared the solitary patrol car that had responded to the initial 911 call. She parked and got out.

"Take your time, Rose," Cheswick said, "because you only get one chance at a first-time at the scene."

They opened their trunk. As they slipped into white coveralls with shoe covers, then tugged on latex gloves, Rose took in the area, absorbed the conditions, atmosphere, its isolation, until they were approached by the responding officer who had preserved the scene. His name was Smart; he'd already suited up.

"We spoke on the phone, Detective."

"Yes, thanks. Did you take in or remove anything from the scene?"

"No."

"Anyone else go in there besides you and your partner?"

"No."

"Good. Would you take us in now."

"Right this way, and you should brace yourself."

The others held back as Kern led Rose and Cheswick into the woods using what would become the path of entry for investigators.

Branches and shrubs slapped against them. They stepped carefully into the darkened forest whose moist, rich smells mingled with birdsong.

It wasn't long before a low monotonous drone rose from the darkness ahead. A breeze delivered an offensive smell as they stopped to behold the horror: a puzzle of flesh, mud and blood suspended crucifixion-style a few feet from the ground.

A long moment passed in silence, save for the flies, the birds and the distant hum of the housing construction. All three cops stood there, reaching deep within themselves, ensuring that whatever moral substance they safeguarded in their most secret corners remained untouched as they looked upon the outrage.

It was Cheswick who went first.

"What a wonderful world we live in. Times like this challenge my faith in humanity."

"Those poor little boys," Rose said.

"Let's get to work."

Before they allowed the CSI people, the forensic photographer and the people from the coroner's office access to the scene to process it, Rose and Cheswick inventoried the area, took notes and digital photos, and searched the immediate scene for any sign of evidence—waste, condoms, a weapon. They searched for clothing, anything that might contain a suggestion of ID as to who the victim might be. Rose wrote down a description of the victim: white female in her twenties.

As she stepped closer, she noticed a brief metallic flash near the victim's right hand, which was closed into a fist.

A fine chain hung down from the victim's hand.

Jewelry.

"Lou, check this out. She's got something in her hand."

Cheswick stepped up.

"Take pictures, Candy, then see if you can pry it out."

She clenched her eye behind her small digital and took several photos before reaching for it with her gloved finger. She loosened the grip, allowing the item to fall into her palm.

"A tiny locket."

It was inscribed.

"Love Mom."

Rose opened it to a photo of a little boy.

43

"Mom, help me!"

Somewhere in the night at the edge of Buffalo's Schiller Park, the distant howl of sirens nudged Mary Peller from sleep to partial consciousness.

Voices and images continued streaming through her mind.

"Mom, help me find it."

It was Jolene. Always Jolene. At various stages of her life.

Mary holding her in the maternity ward looking into her tiny scrunched face and meeting a pair of blazing little eyes.

"Mommee, slow down!"

Mary fleeing with little Jo into the street after Mary's worthless husband began smashing furniture in a drunken rage over burned potatoes.

Mary working full-time as a supermarket clerk. Finding an apartment.

Jolene in a new dress Mary made for her first day of school.

"But I don't want to go away from you!"

She's so pretty. So heartbreakingly pretty.

"Your daughter's been in an accident!"

A halo of blood grows around Jolene's head after she's fallen from the swing in the playground. Ambulance. Hospital. Antiseptic smells. Doctors being paged. Serious fracture to her head.

"Her condition is critical, Mrs. Peller. I'm so sorry but you should brace for the possibility you could lose her."

Jolene skipping classes in high school. Hanging out with kids who did drugs. Arrested for shoplifting. A parade of loser boyfriends. Mary pleading.

"Jolene, please listen, I love you. You can't go on like this!"

"Stay out of my life!"

Jolene dropping out of high school. Running away. Drifting in and out of Mary's life. Making demands.

"Do you have any money? I need a place to stay for a while."

Mary finding drugs hidden in her dresser.

"Stay out my life!"

Jolene living on the street. Living in a vermin-infested house with street people, gang members, drug dealers, prostitutes and addicts.

Year bleeding into year.

Then Jolene at her door.

Pregnant.

"Who's the father?"

"I don't know. I'm raising it myself."

Mary holding her grandson in the maternity ward, looking into his face and meeting a pair of little diamond eyes.

"I'm naming him Cody. He's my lifesaver."

Hope, love, maturity and determination light in Jolene's face.

"I have to pull my life together for him. Will you help me, Mom?" Tears, so many tears. "Please, Mom, will you help me?"

Jolene struggling in vain with her addiction. Back on the street searching, fighting to get clean until an overdose nearly kills her.

"I'm here, Jolene."

Mary at her bedside in the hospital.

"Please help me, Mom. It's so hard. I need to get clean, for Cody."

Jolene and Cody moving in with Mary. Mary taking overtime shifts. Jolene in rehab and going to night school. Going to church. Working with outreach groups. Surviving. Winning.

Getting clean.

Getting a job in Florida. A new life in the sun.

Mary's gift to her.

The locket.

Jolene stronger. Jolene, a reborn young woman with a job waiting.

Jolene at the door with her bag and bus ticket to Orlando—the last time Mary saw her daughter.

"Call me every day. Promise me, Jo."

"I'll call you. I promise. I love you so much, Mom."

Mary so proud they'd worked through it all together.

A telephone not ringing.

No calls. Nothing.

"I'll call you. I promise.

Nothing.

"Help me, Mom. Help me find it."

Jolene's so near. She's here. In the living room! Mary can sense her presence. Jolene is sitting on the sofa.

"I'm so sorry. I tried to call you, Mom. I'm doing my best."

Jolene crying.

Mary reaching out, aching to hold her.

"Oh honey, that's okay. You're here. You're safe."

Jolene shaking her head.

"I'm not, Mom. I lost it. Help me find it."

"Find what, sweetheart?"

"My locket. I can't find my locket. Mom, I'm so scared!"

"I'm right here."

Mary reaching out.

To nothing.

Screams pierce the night.

Mary Peller sits bolt upright, her heart pounding.

Cody is standing next to her bed in the soft light, wide-eyed.

"I miss Mommy."

Mary takes her grandson into her arms, holding him tightly to keep both of them from falling off the earth.

44

The jet's wing tipped slowly, giving Jack Gannon a spectacular view of Calgary, a city of one million nestled in the foothills of the Rockies.

It was dusk.

Once he landed, he rented a compact car then checked into the Radisson, near the airport, where he'd reserved a room.

"We have a package and a message for you, Mr. Gannon," the clerk said.

It was a brown envelope thick with files, old clippings and yellowed typed notes. The message was from Ross Sawyer.

> Welcome to Alberta, Jack. Thought you'd like to read these over before we head out in the morning. My daughter will drop me off at your hotel at 8:00 a.m. as we discussed. I'll be wearing a navy windbreaker. This old reporter is always ready to chase a good story. R.S.

Gannon ordered a cheeseburger from room service and ate while working. Sawyer's files included articles on the murder, isolated societies, psychology, and theories about the killer.

In the morning Gannon didn't recognize Sawyer in the lobby. With his thick white hair, rugged features and trim build, he looked like a man closer to sixty-five than eighty.

They took the Trans-Canada Highway east, with Sawyer telling him about regional history during their two-hour drive.

"Drive several more hours east into Saskatchewan and you'll come to the spot where Sitting Bull led his people into exile after Little Big Horn."

They cut across gentle hills that soon flattened to the horizon for as far as Gannon could see.

"I called Lorne Macdonald like you suggested," Gannon said. "We'll meet him at the detachment and he'll take us out to the house."

RCMP sergeant Lorne Macdonald was dressed in jeans and a plaid shirt. He was an imposing man close to retirement who gave Gannon a crushing handshake. Brooks was a small prairie city known for agriculture, gas and oil, he told Gannon as they got into his unmarked Chev.

"Beyond town there's not much," Macdonald said.

The geography outside of Brooks was an eternal rolling treeless plain. After following a ribbon of paved highway with next to nothing in sight, Macdonald turned onto a dirt road to nowhere.

"These are service roads for underground gas and oil operations," Sawyer said.

Macdonald had called the gas company that now controlled the land under "the old Rudd place." The manager had OK'd a visit. Dust clouds rose behind them, as if taking them into another realm, another time, Gannon thought.

It's like this part of the world's been forgotten.

After twenty minutes the skeletal remains of a dilapidated ranch house came into view as Macdonald brought his car to a halt.

Overgrown dry grass laid claim to the place now, left empty and neglected for decades.

"Hold it," Macdonald said as Gannon approached the yawning doorway. The Mountie tossed a couple of rocks that thudded into the empty house.

"Might be coyotes."

An owl lifted off through the window.

The place reeked of mouse and bird shit, wind buffeted against the loosened boards of the ramshackle walls. Gannon had a good idea of what had transpired here in 1937, but walking on the creaking floorboards, in the steps of a mass murderer, brought it all to life.

As they went from room to room, Gannon envisioned the carnage.

"After it happened, no one ever lived here again," Sawyer said. "I think the mattresses and furniture were burned. People were spooked."

They entered the last bedroom, at the end of the hall.

"This is where they found Deke, hiding under his dead sister," Macdonald said. "I'll tell you what my dad told me about this case a month or so before he died."

Gannon nodded.

"Not all of this is in any file. And since everybody involved is now dead, it's really a matter of history." Macdonald said the case had haunted his father.

"He had several theories about what happened. The Rudds were killed with an ax. The doors were never locked, so anyone could have entered easily. One theory was that a stranger, possibly a convict who'd escaped from Stony Mountain in Manitoba at the time, was responsible. The convict was looking for food or money and murdered the family."

The speculation was that young Deke survived because he slept in a loft and was missed.

Deke Rudd was traumatized. Over several interviews, he said that after he'd gone from bed to bed and discovered his family dead, he'd hid in fear underneath one of his sisters.

"It explained the blood trails, the blood on him and his clothing, and his condition," Macdonald said.

The murder weapon was never located. The suspected escaped convict was arrested in Quebec and it was determined that he'd never set foot in Alberta. The killer of the Rudd family had never been found.

An unknown and disturbing element concerned the eldest Rudd sister, who, contrary to press reports, had survived in hospital for a few days before she died of her injuries. The Mounties kept her survival secret, hoping to obtain information from her that would help them find the killer. Half of her face had been severed from her skull. She was medicated and emerged periodically from her coma to give a hazy, piecemeal deathbed account.

"My dad interviewed her and she revealed to him that Deke was not her brother, but her son," Macdonald said.

"What?" Gannon said. "And that was never made public?"

"No," Macdonald said. "She told my father that Clydell Rudd abused all of his girls, said the Bible gave him dominion over his women. Some of them had babies by him, but the babies, all girls, died and Clydell just buried them at night somewhere out on the land. Deke was the only boy."

"That's incredible," Gannon said.

"Clydell Rudd was an evil, evil man," Sawyer said.

"He said he'd kill his daughter if she ever told anyone about the abuse and that she would burn in eternal flames," Macdonald said. "She thought that young Deke had overheard her arguing with Clydell one day and learned the terrible truth about who and what he was."

Even at Deke's age, he probably reasoned that his parentage was wrong. "That's what my father figured," Macdonald said. "The girl told my father that Deke had grown sullen and withdrawn. It gave her reason to believe that Deke had learned what most of his family knew."

"What was that?" Gannon asked.

"That they lived with the devil."

Sawyer said that he'd researched the subject of incest and found that inbreeding was common in small, isolated communities and cultures.

"In some cases, there was no impact on health, but in others, there were terrible health problems, including some theories that inbred offspring were susceptible to catastrophic psychiatric problems."

"Such as Jekyll-and-Hyde behavior?" Gannon asked.

"Who knows for sure," Sawyer said.

"You said your father had several theories about what happened?" Gannon said to Macdonald.

"My father's second major theory in the Rudd massacre was that young Deke Rudd had murdered his entire family."

Gannon was stunned.

"And," Macdonald said, "given what he knew of the case, my father came to believe it was the most likely scenario."

The wind moaned through the gaps of the death house as Gannon absorbed the revelation and its impact on his story.

This was the gene pool from which Karl Styebeck had emerged.

45

The day after Zachary Miller found the victim, her corpse lay under a tissue-paper sheet on a cold stainless-steel tray in the autopsy room of the district coroner's office in Wichita.

Detective Candace Rose looked upon her.

For Rose, this woman was more than her first homicide. Judging from the little face in the locket, she was somebody's mother.

For a heartbeat, Rose thought of her own children.

"Ready?"

Coroner Russell Pratt and his assistant, Nancy Treggo, adjusted their aprons and surgical face shields as they prepared to begin the procedure.

Rose and her partner, Lou Cheswick, were also gowned and protected with gloves, surgical masks and face shields.

Rose was no stranger to the aftermath of death: bodies entwined with the twisted metal of car wrecks; bloated weeks after drowning; burned beyond recognition; people reduced to brain and viscera splattered on living-room floors and bedroom walls.

And the worst of them all: babies, the corpses of babies. The little ones who never had a chance.

That was what she'd seen as a street cop and it forged what she knew: that death, the great equalizer, was now her formidable foe.

Rose braced to look upon her Jane Doe.

This was her first homicide case but not her first autopsy.

She was acquainted with the room's chill, familiar overpowering smells of ammonia and formaldehyde. The victim had already been washed, weighed, measured, photographed and x-rayed.

"Go ahead," Pratt nodded to Treggo, who slowly drew back the sheet.

Rose's nostrils flared, her breathing quickened.

She stared at what was on the table: an act that had obliterated the barrier between what was human and what was depraved. For, this woman had not been murdered. She had been destroyed.

The mutilation had rendered her face unrecognizable.

Treggo removed the brown paper bags around the victim's hands, and fingernail scrapings were collected before taking fingerprints. Pratt inspected the arms, wrists and hands for any signs of defensive wounds. Pratt and Treggo were meticulous.

Then they moved on to the internal examination.

Pratt made the primary Y incision as he proceeded.

As they worked, Pratt spoke aloud for the overhead microphone recording the process, pausing occasionally to consult a plastic-covered clipboard. At times, when Pratt exchanged observations with Treggo, Rose heard terms like subclavian, femoral, clavical and femur.

They were nearly finished and reviewing aspects when Treggo's brow wrinkled. She concentrated on the woman's forehead.

"Wait, Russ."

Treggo spotted something amid the network of abrasions that laced the victim's flesh, something she'd missed. A jumbled line of letters below the hairline had been carved into her skin.

A white-gloved finger pointed to the word they spelled. "See that?"

Pratt and Treggo invited Rose and Cheswick to move closer and Rose read the word.

GUILTY.

After finishing, Rose and Cheswick deposited their gowns, gloves and masks in the trash. They got some fresh air then joined Pratt in his corner office of the Sedgwick County Regional Forensic Science Center.

It was spacious and neat with a number of thriving ferns and a pleasant scent of potting soil and coffee. Rose detected a hint of cologne as Pratt typed at his computer keyboard finishing his preliminary report.

His printer hummed then he passed copies to the detectives.

"Let's go through it," Pratt said. "You have a white female. Five feet five inches. Approximately twenty to thirty years of age. One hundred twenty pounds. Brown hair, blue eyes. No confirmed identity."

"We have this." Rose presented a color page of an enlarged clear photo of the locket. "She was clutching this locket in her left hand."

"So noted," Pratt said. "And Nancy's taking care of the prints for you."

"Thanks." Rose opened her notebook. "We'll run those through AFIS."

"And," Pratt said, "I've got a forensic odontologist coming in. He'll help prepare a dental chart for a comparison."

"DNA?" Rose asked.

"We'll start a kit for the DNA database, but it'll take three or four weeks before they process our submission. The fingerprint database might be faster for identification."

"What can you say about cause, time and location?"

"Indications are that the decedent died where she was found, within thirty-six to forty-eight hours prior to discovery."

"And the cause?"

"As for cause, the decedent suffered tremendous blunt-force trauma to the entire body and head, something consistent with a heavy metal tool such as a pickax. In my estimation the dece—" Pratt stopped, removed his glasses. "In my estimation, this woman suffered approximately sixty to seventy blows, half of them piercing her body. It would have caused massive hemorrhaging that would have been fatal."

The silence that followed Pratt's assessment may have been a moment of respect, but it allowed Rose to catch up with her note-taking before Pratt continued.

"No defensive wounds were evident. Markings on her wrists and remnants of duct tape suggest she was bound. We should have more on stomach contents, toxicology and other analysis later."

Rose looked out Pratt's large window toward the University of Kansas School of Medicine before releasing a flood of questions.

"Why the overkill? What am I supposed to make of his message? Guilty. Who is guilty? And guilty of what?"

"I'm not a profiler," Pratt said, "nor an expert in criminal psychosis. But I would think it all has to do with his fantasy, or maybe diminished mental capacity. Perhaps he's under the influence. The savagery and the ritualistic display could mean he's on a mission and the message is his signature. Or perhaps I'm completely wrong. What do you think, Lou?"

Cheswick had said little because beneath the surface he was seething at the violation. Furious at the arrogance, the indignity of this killer.

"Don't worry about the hows and whys, they'll only divert you," Cheswick said. "We find out who she is, how she got there. We work the case and we hunt the animal down. Because this guy's out of control. He's right off the chart. I'm sure as hell he's done this before and I will bet you my pension that he'll do it again."

46

That afternoon, Rose and Cheswick joined grim-faced detectives at the City Building downtown for the first case-status meeting.

Investigators from several agencies settled into high-backed chairs at a large table in a sixth-floor meeting room of Wichita's Homicide Section.

Rose cleared her throat.

"We have the ritualistic mutilation murder of an unidentified white female discovered yesterday by boys playing at Clear Ridge Crossing. You all have copies of the coroner's preliminary report."

Rose typed a few commands into a laptop keyboard and an aerial image of Clear Ridge Crossing surfaced on the big screen reaching down from the ceiling at one end of the room.

"I'll summarize the case. Could someone dim the lights, please?"

Rose clicked through large, crisp photographs of the massive new subdivision, the crime scene, the victim and pictures taken by the coroner.

Profanity rippled around the table.

"Identification is a challenge," she said. "We've obtained her fingerprints and run them through AFIS. So far we've got nothing. They've had technical problems with their mainframe and will run them again."

Questions came to her from the dimmed light.

"What about clothing? A wallet, shoes, jacket?" a detective asked.

"Nothing like that was recovered."

"Time of death?" he asked.

"It's estimated she was murdered at the scene thirty-six to forty-eight hours before Zachary Miller found her. We're hopeful we can also obtain a dental chart for comparison."

"Was she sexually assaulted?" another detective asked.

"No."

"What about traces of alcohol, controlled substances or medication? Any impairment?" someone asked.

"Toxicology results are still coming."

"Says here the injuries are consistent with a pickax?"

"That's right."

"Art," Rose said to the Wichita detective who'd led the team that canvased contractors and workers on the site. "Anything come up with the canvas?"

"No, ma'am. Nothing specific."

"Anybody see or hear anything that might help us?"

"Nope. The job site has a lot of traffic from builders, suppliers, workers, subcontractors. Lots of trucks coming and going from all over. And it's easily accessible to the Kansas Turnpike. Some folks said out-of-state long-haul truckers will arrive at all hours and park overnight in that area waiting to be offloaded in the a.m."

"What about in that particular area and the scene?" another detective asked. "Did CSI get casts from tires, or footwear?"

"They did, and we'll use them for comparison," Rose said.

"Start a second canvas," the Captain said. "And let's get

a list of all suppliers. Use it to build a pool of everyone who ever had access to that site. We'll cross-reference vehicles to the tire casts, get employee lists linked to the vehicles, and driving and criminal records. That's one avenue."

"We'll also run it against the registered-offender database," Cheswick said. "Our guy could've somehow got off on his act."

"What about DNA?" asked an investigator.

"The coroner has started a kit and will work with you to submit it to CODIS," Rose said. "And we'd like some help checking all missing-person cases in Kansas and beyond, see if Jane Doe fits with any."

"Dobson and Wurlitz, that's you with the FBI," the lieutenant said. "Candy, let's get to the key fact and hold back. I want to remind everyone that nothing, absolutely nothing, leaves this room."

Large, sharp photos of the locket filled the screen.

"She was clutching this in her left hand," Rose said.

The inscription *Love Mom* was clear, as was the photo of a toddler.

"Candace, that could be your key to identification," one detective said. "Maybe you should run this through the FBI's Jewelry and Gem database, see if it's been reported stolen."

"The FBI no longer maintains it," FBI special agent Nick Vester said. "It's now run by the industry. But looking at the locket, it would appear to have low dollar value and might not be included. However, we know the operators of the database make case-by-case decisions depending on the circumstances. We'll check for you."

"Thanks," Rose said then clicked to a gruesome image—the word carved into the victim's forehead.

"Gee Zuss," someone said.

"This is also holdback," Rose said.

"What's that all about?" one detective asked.

"I think we should go back to Agent Vester to give us his thoughts." The captain nodded at Vester, who'd spent last summer at the FBI's academy at Quantico studying psychological profiling of ritualistic violent crimes.

"Off the top, just based on what we know here, it's clearly ritualistic. It exhibits his control. It's organized, almost ceremonial, as if he was adhering to a procedure. The gross mutilation, the overkill, and the obvious message let people know he's justified in his crusade. Something is raging internally."

"The coroner suggested something along those lines," Rose said.

"I'd suggest you submit your case, key fact evidence and all, to ViCAP. If you fill out the form I'll submit it at the field office as soon as I can."

"Do that, Candace," the Captain said. "Okay, people, you've got your assignments. Next meeting in twenty-four hours."

It was early evening by the time Rose got to the ViCAP form. She was a true believer in the system, having learned more of its history when she had studied for the homicide detectives' exam.

The idea for the FBI's Violent Criminal Apprehension Program emerged over fifty years ago with an LAPD detective who was pursuing a killer who lured women to their deaths by placing ads for models in newspapers. After taking their photographs, he would rape, then hang them.

The investigator was convinced that the murders in Los Angeles were linked to those in other area cities and searched for patterns by studying similar murders reported in out-of-town newspapers at the public library. The detective discovered enough links to track down his suspect.

The killer was convicted and executed.

Years later, the FBI helped develop the concept into a computerized data system for police to quickly share information on mobile suspects.

Now, as Rose completed the form, she hoped ViCAP would help her with her first homicide. She answered some one hundred detailed questions on every known aspect of the crime scene and the victim, including key fact, or holdback evidence, which most cops rarely shared.

After Rose's case was submitted to the database, FBI analysts would compare it to all other submitted files. Like the LAPD detective half a century earlier, they would look for patterns, matches or signatures linked to other crimes in other jurisdictions. The ViCAP analysts never revealed holdback, but when they got a hit, they alerted the case detectives and advised them to talk to each other.

It was late when Rose finished and hand delivered the form to Vester at the FBI's field office, which was on her way home.

Vester, working late himself, assured Rose her case was a priority and that within twenty-four hours it would be submitted "and in the mix" at the FBI's ViCAP database in Quantico, Virginia.

When Rose arrived home, she found her husband asleep on the couch in front of the TV while John Wayne looked for his abducted niece in *The Searchers*.

Rose walked softly to her son's bedroom. Jesse was asleep. She watched him breathing for several moments before bending down and tenderly touching his head. He smelled of shampoo, assuring her that her husband had gotten their youngest in the shower.

Then she went to her daughter's bedroom. Emily's

place was a mess, typical of a girl on the cusp of her teens. Rose abandoned the thought of tidying and kissed Em's cheek.

She then went downstairs, kissed her husband, who woke up and dragged himself to bed. Then she took a hot shower, washing away the autopsy, the day. Her husband was snoring when she slid into bed next to him. Rose couldn't sleep. She was determined not to drop the ball on her first case. She switched on her reading light to look at the enlarged photo of the locket.

The bright-eyed boy stared back at her.

Who do you belong to, sweetheart?

Someone was holding you so tight, so tight they'd never let go. They must have loved you so much.

So much.

47

Valerie Olson cupped her hands around her mug then left the office kitchen for her desk at the FBI academy in Quantico.

Olson took in the view of the Virginia woods surrounding the secure facility. She was an early riser who loved her job and always started long before her shift began. Today, a note from her supervisor greeted her from her keyboard.

Val, got a new one last night from Wichita. John

"All right," Olson said to herself as she logged on to her terminal. She was a case analyst with the FBI's Violent Criminal Apprehension Program. ViCAP was headquartered within the Critical Incident Response Group in what was known as the CIRG building.

Olson had always thought the program could have passed for the claims department of a large insurance company, or a major call center. For nothing betrayed the enormity of the work beneath the clicking keyboards and quiet telephone conversations of the three dozen crime analysts. It was here that they searched ViCAP's ever-growing database for serial patterns among violent crimes across the country.

The program divided the U.S. into six regions and each region had analysts and supervisory agents assigned to them: W-1, W-2, W-3 for the western half, E-1, E-2, E-3 for the eastern.

Olson, a seasoned Minneapolis homicide detective, took the job just over a year ago, not long after she'd retired.

"The program's always looking for someone with your expertise, Val," the FBI recruiter, an old college friend, had told her.

Olson's husband, a retired airline pilot, encouraged her to go for it.

"Milder winters and closer to Florida," he said. "Besides, I don't think you're done pursuing justice."

Her husband was right.

Olson embraced the work, loved helping put the pieces together, loved using her years as an investigator to assure passionate detectives that their cases were safe in her hands.

"I've been in your shoes," Olson would tell them. "My job is to help you find the links that will lead you to your killer. We're in this together."

Olson sipped her tea as she began studying the new case. She was attached to the eastern region, which encompassed much of the Northeast, the Great Lake states and the Rust Belt.

All of ViCAP's regions would be analyzing the new submission from Wichita, comparing it with others from their areas of responsibility. Like most cases the program received, this one was gruesome.

Olson read over all the known details. Horrible, just horrible, she thought as she moved on to focus on the key fact evidence.

She concentrated on the word *GUILTY* crudely carved

into the victim's forehead then queried the system. While awaiting the results, she checked the submission's source. Detective Candace Rose, Wichita PD, Homicide.

Olson reached for her tea but stopped.

She'd gotten a hit.

"All right. Let's see."

Olson entered her security codes to gain access to the other file.

The hit linked the Wichita case to one submitted recently by Michael Brent, an Investigator with the New York State Police. In the New York case, the victim was also a female. Also slain in a ritualistic manner. Body was found by walkers in a wooded area near Buffalo.

Olson's pulse kicked up as she went to Brent's evidentiary key fact mode. Her keyboard clicked and she almost smiled at what she read.

"Bingo."

In the New York case, the word *GUILTY* had also been cut into the victim's head just under the hairline.

The victim was identified as Bernice Tina Hogan, a twenty-three-year-old nursing student from Buffalo, New York.

In the Wichita case, the coroner estimated the victim's age at being twenty to thirty. Identification had not yet been confirmed. Other key fact evidence in Wichita included a locket bearing the inscription *Love Mom,* which contained the photograph of a small boy.

Olson was typing and reading as fast as she could now.

The New York case had supplemental information of a potential link to the homicide: the missing person case of Jolene Peller of Buffalo, New York. Peller was described as a white female, aged twenty-six. One key descriptive in the file—

Olson gasped, covered her mouth with her hand and continued reading.

The key descriptive: a locket bearing the inscription *Love Mom,* containing the photograph of a small boy, Peller's three-year-old son, Cody.

Olson reached for her phone.

48

The rising sun broke the horizon at Ellicott Creek.

Bernice Hogan had been murdered less than fifty yards from the bench where Michael Brent sat alone reviewing the case. As he gazed at the sky's reflection on the serene water, he grilled himself again.

What was he missing?

The Hogan homicide was all he could think about. He couldn't sleep. But when he did, he woke up exhausted. He'd lost his appetite, lost weight. And after his shot at Karl Styebeck a few days back, Brent suffered a burning sensation in his stomach.

His ulcers had returned.

This morning before leaving his empty house, he'd drunk a quart of milk.

He didn't give a damn about his physical discomfort.

Comes with the job.

It was his sworn duty to see justice done. He needed to clear this homicide before he hung up his badge. He already faced the rest of his life without his wife. How could he bear the torment of letting a killer go free?

He couldn't and he wouldn't

He vowed to close this case.

The pages of his notebook fluttered as he went through his notes again.

Over the last few days he'd believed, truly believed, that he was close. But since he'd questioned Styebeck at the Barracks; since their futile search of Styebeck's house, vehicles, records; since the breaks on Jolene Peller's cell phone and the tire impression, they'd made little progress.

Brent knew in his heart that Styebeck was lying. Knew in his gut that Styebeck was linked to Bernice Hogan's murder and Jolene Peller's disappearance.

All he had to do was prove it.

As Brent flipped pages he reminded himself to be flexible and not get so mired in his theories on Styebeck that he forgot the other aspects.

The angle of the mystery truck.

He reviewed everything related to it. The girls on Niagara had reported seeing "a creepy guy in a big truck." Jolene Peller's cell phone was found in the Chicago truck stop. Other calls to Styebeck's home came from public phones. Maybe Brent should adjust his thinking.

His cell phone shattered the morning calm, startling him. The number was blocked. He answered with one word.

"Brent."

"Investigator Michael Brent with the New York State Police?"

"Yes, who's calling?"

"Valerie Olson with the FBI's Violent Criminal Apprehension Program in Quantico, Virginia."

"ViCAP?"

"Yes, sir, and I think we have a very strong link to the case you recently submitted concerning the homicide of Bernice Tina Hogan."

"That so? And where would that be?"

"Kansas."

"Can you tell me what the strong link is, exactly?"

"I can't, as you know we respect everyone's key fact

evidence. But when you're ready to copy, I'll give you the contact information for the detective on the Kansas case. They've got a very recent homicide and you should talk."

Brent flipped to a clear page, clicked his pen, noted the date and time.

"Go ahead."

In Witchita, Candace Rose was in the shower when she was interrupted by her husband's loud knocking on the bathroom door.

"Phone, Candy! New York State Police. Something about ViCAP."

It took Rose less than thirty seconds to towel off, throw on her bathrobe and grab the phone in her bedroom. Within minutes of Rose talking to Brent, the two detectives agreed their cases were linked.

Forty minutes later, Rose was at her desk in the Homicide Section and back on the phone with Brent. Half a continent apart, the two investigators were simultaneously looking at the two homicides on their computer monitors. As they compared their cases, it was clear that Bernice Hogan and Jane Doe in Kansas were murdered by the same person.

Both victims were females in their twenties. Both had shoulder-length dark hair. Both were discovered in outdoor crime scenes amid wooded sections of metropolitan areas. Both scenes, while hidden, were easily accessible by the public. Both involved ritualistic display.

"It's like he wants his work discovered," Rose said.

She shared photographs of the signature cut into the victim's forehead under the hairline: *GUILTY.*

Brent sent her the crime scene and autopsy photos of Bernice Hogan bearing the single word *GUILTY,* carved into her forehead under the hairline.

"Now, this next item is the one you said may help us

ID our victim here," Rose said as they came to enlarged photographs of the locket.

"Yeah. We think that locket belongs to a woman who was Bernice Hogan's friend. We have witnesses who saw her with Bernice the night before Bernice's body was discovered."

"And that would be Jolene Peller, according to the missing person's file you sent me, Mike."

"Her mother reported her missing a few days after the Hogan murder. Peller was headed to Florida to start a new job, but she never arrived."

"And she's a single mom with a three-year-old boy, Cody. The little boy I'm looking at right now."

"That's right."

"The locket from our case is identical to the one described in Jolene Peller's missing-person's report. Our Jane Doe's age, height and weight are consistent with Peller. We're still working on obtaining a dental chart."

"We have a dental chart and fingerprints for Peller. I'll send them to you this afternoon for comparison as soon as I do the paperwork."

"We'll be standing by."

But that afternoon, shortly after Wichita's Homicide Section received Jolene Peller's fingerprints and dental chart, tragedy struck on an interstate just outside the city.

A van carrying twelve high-school cheerleaders to a competition in Wichita blew a front tire and swerved into the path of an oncoming dump truck. The van ignited, killing six people trapped inside.

Two others were ejected.

The shock of the accident reverberated across the entire state. Confirming the identities of the dead superseded all other cases for the coroner's office.

Identifying the female homicide victim was delayed, Rose told Brent in Buffalo.

After five minutes of consideration, Brent made a phone call. Then he collected his files and summoned his partner, Roxanne Esko.

"I don't know, Mike," Esko said as they drove to Mary Peller's apartment in Schiller Park. "Is this a good idea? Shouldn't we wait?"

"We can't risk this leaking out before she's been told."

After arriving and parking, they went to Mary Peller's door.

Among Brent's files were enlarged photographs from the Wichita Homicide Section of the locket the victim in the Kansas case had been holding.

Brent was going to show them to Mary Peller.

Then he would gently destroy her world by telling her to brace for the worst. The search for her daughter had likely ended in a wooded area of Wichita, Kansas.

49

Jack Gannon returned from Alberta with more than his luggage.

He'd unearthed disturbing facets of Karl Styebeck's life.

That Styebeck came from an incestuous bloodline, and that his father may have murdered his family, was chilling.

Little by little something was taking shape. Should he confront Styebeck now, or keep digging?

Gannon thought it over while driving home from the airport.

It was early evening, traffic was light. He'd eaten and slept on the flight and arrived at his apartment energized. He checked for messages, e-mails and for any developments from the *News* or *Sentinel.* There was nothing. Adell Clark was still out of town on one of her own cases.

Okay, so his trip to Canada had paid off.

He had something but was unsure what his next move should be.

He was frustrated.

While he'd uncovered a terrifying chapter on Karl Styebeck's father, Deke, he still hadn't found much more on Karl, other than the fact that he was married to Alice, a bank teller, and they had a son, Taylor. Styebeck coached ball teams, worked for charities, went to church. He was a small-town hero who'd grown up in Texas, the son of a prison guard. And he'd joined the Ascension Park Police Department some twelve years ago.

Gannon knew nothing more of Styebeck's earlier life.

His search of records had yielded nothing so far.

It was like Styebeck's past was a secret.

Gannon's phone rang with a blocked number.

"Hello."

"Is this Jack Gannon, the reporter?"

He didn't recognize the male caller. He'd always kept his name and number listed but not his address. He suffered the whack jobs for the occasional story.

"Yeah, who's this?"

"I don't want to say. I live in Ascension Park and have been following the murder of that college girl and this Karl Styebeck business."

"Yes."

"Styebeck lives down the street from me and the other day I was walking my dog when I counted six unmarked police cars parked at his house. Guys who were not in uniform, but obviously cops, were coming and going. It's like they were searching for something."

"Did you ask them what was happening?"

"Nobody would talk to me. There was nothing in the news, which burns me. I thought we lived in a democracy. Anyway, I thought you should know, seeing how you wrote up a big story about him a little while ago."

"Thanks."

"Maybe you can put something in the paper?"

"I don't work for the paper anymore."

"What? I thought—"

"Thanks for the call."

Gannon grabbed his jacket and keys.

It sounded like they'd executed a warrant on Styebeck.

Now that things were moving faster, he couldn't risk sitting on what he knew.

As he drove to Styebeck's house in Ascension Park, he considered how to play his information. Given that he was not Styebeck's favorite reporter, Gannon figured he should just hit him with Alberta and hope that he'd talk about Deke, maybe reveal other information.

It was a long shot.

Gannon rang the bell. A boy opened the door.

"Hi, I'm Jack Gannon. May I speak to your dad?"

The boy's face tightened slightly as he and Gannon recognized each other from his first confrontation with Styebeck at the ballpark. The boy kept his hand defensively on the door, his eyes on Gannon, and shouted, "Mom!"

"Who is it, Taylor?" His mother's voice came from inside the house.

"Mom, you better come!"

Footsteps, then Alice Styebeck appeared, drying her hands on a dish towel, her chin lifting in subtle defiance.

"Yes."

"May I speak with Karl, please?"

It struck Gannon that Alice Styebeck was struggling with her answer, as if she *wanted* Gannon, *the enemy,* to visit her husband.

Taylor shot her a look of surprise when she said, "He's in the backyard. You can go around the side."

What just happened there? Was she sending him to his doom, or was something else at work? Gannon wondered.

He heard thumping as he went round the house.

Karl Styebeck was splitting logs with a long-handled ax.

Thud-crack-thud-crack-thud.

Sweat dripped from his face, blotching the neck and underarms of his T-shirt.

Thud-thud-thud.

"Detective Styebeck?"

He looked at Gannon.

"What the hell are you doing on my property?"

"I wanted to talk to you about your father, Deke. I've just returned from Brooks, Alberta, and I know."

"You know what?"

"I know everything, sir."

"You don't know shit!"

"I do. I know about your blood and the speculation of what Deke did all those years ago."

Styebeck's knuckles whitened as he gripped his ax and pointed the blade to the street.

"Leave, Gannon!"

"Tell me, Karl, does it run in the family?"

Styebeck's face twisted with rage and he invaded Gannon's space.

"Get off my property now or I'll get my gun."

Gannon stood his ground long enough to let Styebeck know he didn't fear him. Then Gannon turned to see Alice Styebeck glaring—not at him, but at her husband.

That night in his apartment Gannon tried in vain to sleep.

He tossed and turned, questioning himself over and over about the way he'd approached matters.

What did he learn from his idiotic confrontation with Styebeck? Nothing. He'd committed the sin of prematurely tipping his hand. He was stupid, stupid, stupid!

His phone rang.

"Mr. Gannon?"

"Yes."

The woman on the line was crying.

"This is Mary Peller."

"Mary? What is it? Are you all right?"

"They found Jolene!"

"They found her?"

"She's dead! My daughter's dead!"

50

A pure and overwhelming calm had descended upon Schiller Park and the low-rent building where Jolene Peller's mother lived.

Gannon looked up at her third-floor unit. Faint light filled her window like an unyielding flag of hope in the final hour before dawn.

Mary Peller's words—*"my daughter's dead!"*—still rang in his ears.

In calling Gannon, Mary had invited him to her apartment as soon as possible. Half an hour after her call, he brought his car to a halt in front of her building.

He headed for the entrance thinking how much he hated this, just hated this part of the business. As a reporter, he'd been to countless places of mourning and each time it cost him a piece of his heart.

Locks clicked.

Jolene Peller's mother opened her door, surprising him when she fell into his arms, sobbing.

A wave of alcohol rolled over him. He saw the opened Jack Daniels' bottle on her coffee table.

"I'm so sorry, Mary."

She pulled herself away and gestured to the couch.

"Thank you for coming. Daisy made fresh coffee."

"Daisy?" He saw no one else in the apartment.

"My friend downstairs. She's stayed with me ever since the two detectives arrived. I just sent her home because you were coming."

"And Cody?"

"He's sleeping."

Mary may have been drinking but she was not drunk.

"I'm sorry. I'm not being a good host at the moment. You'll have to help yourself to coffee. Everything's there."

Gannon fixed himself a cup then joined Mary on the couch. Jolene smiled at them from photographs covering the coffee table. Mary moved the bottle and glasses aside to an end table.

"This is hard for me, Mr. Gannon."

"Take your time. And please call me Jack."

"The police told me not to tell anyone what they said about Jolene. They said it might not be safe because the killer might still be around. They don't want anything leaking out about what they found."

He was bursting with questions but restrained himself.

"I don't care what they said because I trust you," she said.

"I understand."

"You're the first person who gave a damn when I was looking for her. That day at your paper you gave me your time. You showed me respect. I just knew you were a good man. I want to tell you what the police told me."

Gannon nodded.

"The man, Brent, did most of the talking. He was kind and all, telling me they had some news and to brace myself for the worst."

Mary covered her face with her hands, inhaled then exhaled.

"They said the body of a woman fitting Jolene's description had been discovered. *Fitting her description?* I said, are you absolutely certain? I said, show me a picture."

Gannon cast a glance at the coffee table.

"They didn't have any pictures of the victim. Well, none that they would show me. They said it was all very bad with the body."

Mary stopped to breathe.

"Excuse me." She took a sip from the glass in her shaking hand. "They said they'd sent Jo's fingerprints and her dental records, which I'd provided when I made my missing person report, to the police for confirmation."

"Did they confirm the identity?"

"Not yet. They said it's all being—being *processed,* that was the word. They said they wanted me to hear about it all from them first before any of it got out."

"Mary, if they haven't confirmed yet, then maybe there's a chance—"

"They showed me these."

Mary reached around for a file folder of enlarged, sharp color prints of a locket. The pictures had dates and evidence numbers in the corner.

"See the inscription? See Cody? I gave Jo that locket. My gift because—" Mary took a breath "—because she'd turned her life around. Jo loved it and wore it all the time. All the time."

"The police gave you this picture?"

Mary nodded. "To identify it as belonging to Jolene." Anguish webbed across her face.

"Where did they find this locket?" he asked.

"In Jo's hand. See, she was hanging on to Cody. Never giving up." Mary gasped. "Mr. Gannon, I have to see her for myself. Unless I see it, it can't be true. I keep praying that it's all a mistake. But it's like the nightmare I had where Jo lost her locket."

"Where did they find her?"

"Kansas."

"Kansas?"

"In Wichita. Little boys playing in the woods found her."

"Did the police tell you anything else?"

"They're convinced the person who did this is the same person who killed Bernice Hogan."

51

Later that morning in Manhattan, senior editors gathered in the sixteenth-floor conference room of World Press Alliance headquarters.

Strands of conversations on breaking news, sports, travel budgets and plain old gossip faded as they settled around the polished table.

They'd set down coffee mugs, notepads, copies of the *New York Times,* and the *Wall Street Journal* as they commenced the day's first national-story meeting. There would be other national- and international-story meetings throughout the day and night. Being a twenty-four-hour global news service meant the flow of information never ceased.

"Roll call," Carter O'Neill, who ran the meeting, said loudly for the benefit of the WPA's domestic bureau chiefs who were participating through the teleconference hookup. After a string of voices from across the country checked in, O'Neill took attendance around the table.

The editors reviewed printouts of the morning's national-news agenda and discussed only the bigger stories emerging from across the country, those that the WPA was offering subscribers everywhere.

As usual, O'Neill led off with major stories out of New York City.

"Okay, we've got ongoing coverage of the murder of two

rookie NYPD patrol officers, the Wall Street investment scandal and the new network and Internet deals for the NFL."

"Questions?"

"It's Nan in Miami. We're hearing that the CEO may be charged in the investment fraud. He's got family in South Florida."

"Nan, it's Gord. We're on top of the potential charges," the New York bureau chief said. "But we may need some help. Word is he may take the corporate jet to Boca Raton, then to the Caymans."

"Other questions?" O'Neill said. "No? Okay, on to the bureaus, to those of you who've been flagged. Martin in Washington, you're up first."

"We've got new testimony on the '77-91' Lobby Gate mess."

"Let's hope we hear something substantial," O'Neill said. "I think the committee's scraping the barrel. Vince in Chicago, you're next."

"We're on the trial of the two ex-soldiers who robbed the armored car."

"That's getting a lot of pickup," O'Neill said. "Questions?"

"Your team's been doing nice work on that, Vince," executive editor Beland Stone said.

"Thanks."

"Next, Houston."

"Still have the huge refinery fire. Still burning but its contained."

"What's the toll now, Wes?" O'Neill asked.

"They just updated. Eleven."

"Next, Hector in Los Angeles."

"The gang shooting in the school yard."

"How young were those kids?"

"Eight and nine. We've got a good followup coming."

"Next, Brad in Wichita."

"We're following the crash with the cheerleaders. A sad story. We also may have something else brewing with a homicide."

"A homicide?" O'Neill asked.

"A woman's body dumped in the woods. So far, she's a Jane Doe."

Melody Lyon lowered her printout, concentrating over her bifocals.

"Brad, it's Melody. Why raise a homicide? What do you have there?"

"Wichita police are not saying anything on this. We're hearing rumors that the homicide was ritualistic and tied to another case out of state."

"Brad?" Lyon said. "We'll talk off-line immediately after the meeting."

Less than fifteen minutes later, Lyon was at her desk, typing on her keyboard, searching for a recent e-mail.

"Gotcha," she said to herself when she'd found it. "Here we go."

She called Brad Roth, the WPA's bureau chief in Kansas. As the line rang, Carter O'Neill entered Lyon's office. Lyon moved her hand in a sweeping motion signaling him to shut her office door.

He did, then sat in one of her cushioned visitors' chairs.

Lyon switched her phone to speaker mode and adjusted the sound.

"Hi, Melody," Roth said.

The WPA's Wichita bureau had a staff of five: Roth, two other reporters, a freelancer and a photographer.

"Okay, Brad, what can you tell me on this homicide?" Lyon asked.

"Not a whole heck of a lot more than what I said on the meeting call. The police have shut everyone down on this."

"What about the *Eagle?*" O'Neill asked. "What have they got?"

"Bare-bones stuff, here. I'm rereading it. We know what they know. They're trying to ID this Jane Doe, who was discovered by some little boys playing in woods near Clear Ridge Crossing, a new subdivision."

"So what're the rumors? What're you hearing?" Lyon asked.

"The scene was disturbing. Extremely grisly. The little boys who made the discovery are getting counseling. We're also hearing that a task force has been formed because they think this is linked to the homicide of another woman across the country."

"Where?"

"We don't know. Maybe east."

"Good work flagging this. It could turn into something. Stay on it and keep me posted," Lyon ended the call and gestured for O'Neill to come closer to see what she had up on her monitor. "Look at this e-mail I got from Jack Gannon this morning."

Melody:
Still hoping you might have time to talk to me. I've got some new and disturbing information concerning the murder of the Buffalo nursing student, including a tip from a solid source that it may be linked to the murder of another woman found in another state. *I know exactly where it is,* but you can appreciate why I'm holding back. Gannon

O'Neill whistled through his teeth.

"I think Gannon's case *is* the Wichita case," Lyon said. "And I think Gannon knows way more than everyone else."

"What do you plan to do about it?"

Lyon steepled her fingers and touched them to her lips. "I need to think."

"If you're thinking of involving Gannon, you'd better be careful."

She nodded at O'Neill's warning.

At the same time, her instincts were screaming at her.

With Gannon, they could have the inside track to a huge national story.

52

Jack Gannon watched the ground drop and felt the jet force his body into his seat as the A320 climbed from the airport.

Destination: Wichita, Kansas.

He checked his watch. It'd been three hours since he'd left Mary Peller grieving in her apartment. As metropolitan Buffalo blurred below him, he vowed to stay ahead of this story and somehow get it out.

Just before boarding, he'd e-mailed editors at *Vanity Fair, Esquire* and *Penthouse,* pitching an investigative article.

He knew it was futile with the big magazines.

In desperation, he'd e-mailed a cryptic pitch to Melody Lyon at the WPA.

He looked out his window, knowing that in a few hours he'd be at the death site of a second murdered young woman. His job was to show the world the link between these murders and Detective Karl Styebeck.

The jet turned and Gannon's body shook from his lack of sleep, his adrenaline and an overdose of black coffee.

But he couldn't rest. He had to work.

When the plane leveled he turned on his laptop. For a moment, he thought of his sister, Cora, *out there somewhere,* but had to set his thoughts of her aside for another time.

Jolene Peller's face appeared on his laptop screen.

Then pictures of her locket.

How did Jolene end up in Kansas?

What did police have at the Kansas scene that convinced them that the same guy killed Bernice in Buffalo and Jolene in Wichita?

Jolene knew Bernice. They both knew Styebeck.

Styebeck?

It was wild. A hero cop, a *detective,* murdering women.

If it was Styebeck, how did he get Jolene to Kansas? Did he chase her? Meet her there? Did he fly there? How is he involved?

And why the hell hadn't Brent and Esko charged him yet?

Gannon reviewed files and notes until his jet landed in Chicago.

At O'Hare, he'd fallen asleep in the preboarding area with his ticket peeking from his pocket and would've missed his connecting flight to Wichita if the attendant had not nudged him.

"Mr. Gannon, it's last call for your flight."

During the next flight he bought a prepacked sandwich on board and resumed working, reviewing what he knew of Styebeck's past.

Did any of it have any bearing on what was happening now?

As the jet began its descent into Wichita Mid-Continent Airport, Gannon reviewed all the articles he'd bought online from the *Wichita Eagle.* It was superb, well-written stuff, but the purchased items didn't contain graphics or photos. Thankfully, Gannon's request for the *Eagle's* news library to send him scanned pages of the actual print edition had come through.

They were perfect.

At the car-rental agency's airport desk there was a backlog due to an air-industry conference in town. Gannon used the delay to grab a burger and coffee, and study his Wichita map and the *Eagle's* locator graphic pinpointing the crime scene. He also examined the online edition of the *Eagle* for any developments, relieved nothing new had emerged because it meant his exclusive was still valid.

He drove directly to Clear Ridge Crossing, hoping that the crime scene had been processed and released. When he arrived he was astounded by the scale of the new subdivision.

Nothing but stages of housing development for as far as he could see. And everywhere in all directions he saw equipment and trucks rolling in and out. He drove to a ridge that, by the maps, seemed to be the entrance to the area where the body was found. He saw nothing in the dusty distance that indicated a crime scene, let alone a point of entry into the dense forest that bordered the vast section.

He drove to the row of temporary construction-site offices. He came up to a couple of men in jeans, plaid shirts and hard hats, carrying rolled white pages of plans, and asked for directions.

"Yeah, you got the right place," said one. He had a salt-and-pepper beard and the name Burt on the crown of his hat. "See that taller grove?"

Burt aimed his tube of rolled pages to the hazy distance, which Gannon followed to the jagged tree line.

"Where, exactly?"

"Where the taller trees form a teepee shape."

"Oh right, yeah."

"Go in there."

"Thanks."

"The guys tell me the police cleaned everything out."

"That's fine. Thanks again."

Gannon wheeled the Toyota around.

Driving with confidence now, he left the trailers behind. As he bounced and jolted across the vast stretch of land, he recognized a chilling reality: he was following the killer's path.

No patrol units were posted when he arrived at the edge of the forest. Not a car. Not a uniform. Not another soul.

It was a remote area.

No one around to hear screams.

He looked back at the dust clouds billowing over the busy construction zone then stepped into the woods.

Birds chirped as he moved through the darkened thick growth of shrubs and towering trees. From time to time he came upon a discarded section of yellow plastic crime scene tape, reminders of the violence that had exploded here.

Gannon pushed his way through the branches that snagged his shirt and jeans, as if imploring him to reconsider going farther.

But he progressed to the scene then held his breath to absorb it.

It had been processed.

The large tree before him was marked with bright green fluorescent paint. Small circled x's formed a triangular shape.

Good God, did he suspend her on the tree?

All around the tree's base, a number of squared sections of the earth had been removed. Like Bernice Hogan's shallow grave, they'd been carefully excavated and sifted.

Was she alive here? Did she know she was going to die here?

A wave of sadness swept over him. Here he was at a second murder scene, a thousand miles and a time zone away from the first. He stood in respectful silence for several moments before taking out his notebook. He wrote details and sketched what he saw.

He'd just reached for his small digital camera to take pictures when he heard the thud of car doors and voices.

Men and women approaching.

Gannon stood his ground waiting, until he recognized New York State Police investigators Michael Brent and Roxanne Esko. They were with another man and woman. Possibly Wichita homicide detectives Candace Rose and Lou Cheswick, Gannon guessed, from his memory of the *Eagle's* news photos.

"*Gannon?* What the hell is this?" Brent said.

"You know this guy?" Cheswick said.

"He's a reporter from Buffalo," Brent said.

"Jack Gannon," Gannon extended his hand. No one took it.

Cheswick didn't like the situation. He was a case-hardened cop who'd worked with his share of showboater cops with big egos, who tipped the press for profile to enhance a career.

He'd only met Brent and Esko that morning and was now wary.

"So he just decided to come all the way from Buffalo to this spot?" Cheswick said. "I wonder who gave him that idea."

"Not us," Brent said, "but I have a few people in mind." Then to Gannon, "Who tipped you?"

"I don't give up sources," Gannon said.

"I'd like you to leave our scene," Cheswick said.

"Unless you're protecting it with invisible police, it's obviously been released."

"Get the fuck out of here," Cheswick said.

"That's a fine welcome to Kansas," Gannon said. "I'll go but I've got a few questions."

"You deaf, asshole?" Cheswick put his hands on his hips, spreading his jacket, revealing his badge and the butt of the gun in his shoulder holster.

"Take it easy, Lou." Rose turned to Gannon. "Ask your questions."

"Do you have a suspect?"

"No comment at this time," Rose said.

"How is this case linked to the homicide of Bernice Hogan in Buffalo?"

"No comment at this time."

"Can you confirm to me the identity of the person murdered here?"

"No comment at this time."

"So this is how you guys are going to play this?"

"Leave now," Cheswick said.

Gannon closed his notebook, looked each detective in the eye then shook his head.

"Guess your idea of catching a killer, *or protecting him*, is making sure nobody knows a damn thing about him."

"Why, you prick! You don't know squat!" Brent stepped toward Gannon.

"Mike!" Esko stopped him.

"Mr. Gannon," Rose said, "you asked your questions, I answered them. Please leave."

Gannon nodded and headed out.

"If I was the killer," he said, "I'd be mighty thankful you'd kept everything out of the papers. Allows me to do my work without interruption."

"Wait," Rose said.

The other detectives shot her looks as Gannon turned to her.

"We expect confirmation of identity later today. There'll be a press conference this afternoon downtown at the City Building. Four fifty-five North Main."

"Thank you."

"And Gannon?"

"Yeah?"

"Welcome to Wichita."

53

"This will be short," said Lieutenant Gil Clawson, commander of the Wichita police Homicide Section.

He'd taken his place at the table in the department's fifth-floor briefing room, where reporters and photographers had gathered for a late-afternoon media briefing.

Jack Gannon sat apart from the group, taking notes as Clawson introduced the other officials at the table.

Clawson summarized the case of the unidentified body of a white female homicide victim discovered at Clear Ridge Crossing.

"Through dental records and fingerprints we've confirmed the identity of the victim as Carrie May Fulton, twenty-two, of Hartford, Connecticut.

What? Gannon was stunned.

That can't be right. It's Jolene Peller.

He looked to the wall where Brent, Esko, Cheswick and Rose stood, expecting them to correct the mistake.

They ignored him.

It was no mistake.

A uniformed officer wheeled out a bulletin board displaying an enlarged head-and-shoulders photograph of Carrie Fulton. She bore no resemblance to Jolene.

It's not Jolene Peller? What about the locket? Why are New York State cops here? What's going on?

Gannon tried to grasp what Clawson was saying now.

"We're passing out a flyer with more information."

Fulton was reported missing by friends nearly three weeks ago from the vicinity of the Settlers Valley Mall in northeast Hartford, Clawson said.

"We're asking for help from the public. We're interested in talking to anyone who may have had any contact with Carrie Fulton. We'll take a couple of questions now. Yes, Scott from the *Eagle,* go ahead."

"Lieutenant, we're hearing that this was a ritual killing and that it's linked to another murder out of state. Can you confirm that?"

"I'll let my federal colleague take that."

"As is routine in cases where the victim is from out of state, the FBI works jointly with all law enforcement agencies. In this case, we are working with the Hartford PD and Connecticut agencies through our field office in Hartford."

"That doesn't answer the question. Is Fulton's homicide linked to any other murder?" the reporter asked.

"We can't confirm that now, but we're not ruling out the possibility," Clawson said, then acknowledged a TV reporter. "Tom, yes."

"Why have you formed a task force?"

"We haven't." Clawson looked at his colleagues. "We're working together as we routinely do on cases."

"Can you tell us the cause of death?" the reporter asked.

"We're not confirming that at this time."

"Any suspects?"

"It's early and we'll be working closely with Connecticut authorities to establish Carrie Fulton's activities before her body was discovered."

"Did you find a weapon?"

"No."

"Do you have any idea what it is?"

"We have an idea."

"Will you elaborate?"

"No."

"Do you have any DNA, trace or physical evidence?" the Associated Press reporter asked.

"We won't discuss that."

"Any theories on how she got to Wichita? Any family? Friends? What's her connection to the city or state?" the reporter continued.

"Those are things we're trying to determine."

"Who made the discovery?"

"Some young boys. They were quite shaken by it, so we're not releasing their names," Clawson said. "I believe the *Eagle* had something on that."

Gannon needed to ask questions but didn't want to reveal what he knew to the other reporters. He didn't even want them to know he was there from Buffalo. Throughout the conference he weighed the wisdom of approaching Candace Rose. Of all the detectives on the case, she'd been civil to him.

"Do you fear Fulton's killer may kill again, sir?" a radio reporter asked.

"We fear that of every suspect until we arrest them," Clawson said. "All right, before we close, we want to invite any member of the public who might have a tip or lead to call Crime Stoppers, e-mail us, or send us a letter the old-fashioned way. The contact information is on your handout."

"Have you received any tips so far?" one reporter asked.

"A few, yes. We're following them up," Clawson said. "Okay. The next media briefing will be announced when we have additional information to be released. Thank you."

As the briefing broke up, Gannon saw Rose leave the room alone.

He caught up with her in the hall as she rounded a corner and prepared to make a call on her cell phone.

"Excuse me, Detective Rose?"

She turned without making her call, not smiling but not frowning, either.

Gannon double-checked to ensure they were alone.

"I didn't see or hear anything about the locket," he said.

"The locket?"

"What was Carrie Fulton doing with Jolene Peller's locket?"

Rose said nothing.

"I didn't hear anything about a truck or any connection to Chicago or a cop back in Buffalo."

"What do you want?"

He handed her a page from his notebook.

"All I'm asking for is a card, to allow me to keep in touch with you. Sometimes trading information can be helpful."

Without touching it, Rose looked at the folded slip of paper Gannon was offering. She let a moment pass before closing her hand around it.

"Do you have a card you could give me, Detective?"

She passed it to him.

"Will you be leaving Kansas soon?" Rose asked.

"Tomorrow morning."

"Have a nice trip."

That night Gannon lay on his bed with his laptop on his stomach.

He tried to work as he grappled with sleep, the lingering smell of cigarettes and the rhythmic mattress squeaking in the adjoining room.

The thin walls of his cramped room were stained with something brown. A TV was blasting from the room below. And despite his hammering on the wall, whatever was going on next door—a woman was now moaning and shouting—was not stopping.

Most of the letters in the neon sign over the motel he'd found on Wichita's outskirts had burned out. Something suggesting *"heaven,"* but Gannon's thirty-two bucks had bought him a night in hell.

He returned to his work, concentrating on Carrie Fulton and Jolene Peller, who stared back from his screen. Then he reread the few short stories on Carrie that he'd purchased from the *Hartford Courant.*

His body ached from lack of sleep, jet lag and stress.

He shut down his computer.

The energy drink and coffee he'd guzzled were losing the battle to keep him awake and he was overcome with an utter sense of defeat.

The case was now tied to three women and reached into at least three states. Five, if he counted Illinois and Texas. And another country, if he counted Styebeck's family history. It had grown complex, involving more and more police agencies.

He was not sure what to do next.

As sleep arrived, Gannon tried to grasp the one bright spot amid his confused exhaustion.

Hope.

The tragic twist in the case had given Mary Peller a small measure of hope that her daughter was still alive.

For if the victim here in Wichita was Carrie Fulton that meant there was hope that Jolene was alive.

Which left Gannon with one last question as he fell asleep.

Where was Jolene Peller?

54

Jolene Peller was surfacing through fear until she woke in darkness.

Her heart slammed against her rib cage like a trapped animal. She thrashed against her bindings on the floor where she lay as she fought to remember.

How long had it been?

She didn't know…. Where…where was she? Still in the truck…but where? She didn't know…. They were moving… she recognized the drone…. Where…where was he taking her?

Her fear grew. Something had happened…something.

Carrie?

What had happened? A memory streaked…a scream echoed….

Carrie!

Jolene shouted her name, cried out to the blackness, to the silence.

To no one.

Her body sagged.

Jolene remembered light.

The door had opened to dim light…like after sunset… the door opened and she saw a dark figure…silhouetted against the twilight…saw his boots, his gloves…saw the cattle prod.

Noooo!

Carrie had screamed.

He'd come for Carrie as she'd crushed herself into the corner. He just walked to her, slapped her face, grunted and hoisted her to his shoulder as if she were cargo.

Jolene help me oh God please help me!

Jolene scrambled to her feet…steadied herself—*to do what?* She lunged at him, tried to head butt him… He turned, grunting as Carrie clawed at him then at Jolene, grasping in vain at her locket, pulling it until the chain broke.

Don't let him take me! Help meeee!

He pressed the cattle prod to Carrie, knocking her unconscious.

Then he pressed it to Jolene. The pain shot her to the floor. She cracked her head against the hard wood, hurling her back into the darkness.

Now, hot tears rolled down her cheeks.

She was aware.

Aware that she was alone.

Aware that death was near as vague memories assailed her. Memories of Carrie's distant screams that ended with the distant "thud—thud—thud," like some enraged force was pounding the earth.

"Thud-thud-thud."

In the dead silence that followed she thought, *He must've killed her!*

Jolene sobbed into her stinking mattress.

Why was this happening? Why? She couldn't bear the agony, couldn't go on. This can't be real. It only happens in movies, in books, in nightmares.

Wake up.

Wake up!

She was awake. It was real.

Was he going to kill her? She had to find a way home. Had to find a way out. Had to find strength. Something to hold on to.

Cody.

Jolene reached for her locket but found nothing.

Her deafening cry filled the darkness.

Carrie had taken her locket.

Stop it!

Stop feeling sorry for yourself. Carrie didn't die alone. She died with Cody in her hand.

Cody.

Jolene had to keep fighting for Cody.

She tightened her hands into fists and felt Carrie's keys. Felt the tiny flashlight. As if Carrie had bequeathed them. As if this was meant to be. For these tiny precious things were tools.

Jolene knew now.

She summoned the strength to think, to remember her plan. She summoned the courage, summoned the anger to not let that sick mother win. Not without the fight of her life.

For her life.

Jolene stood.

All right.

She ran her trembling hands along the walls, feeling, sensing, until she found it. The protruding nailhead. Sticking out about two inches. It felt about eye level. Okay. Jolene lifted her arms and began catching the duct tape on the nail head. Working it over and over, feeling the nail head puncture the tape binding her wrists. Sweating and sniffling, she repeated the action.

Each tiny tear, each small rip was a victory.

She refused to let up, kept the sawing motion going, pushing through the ache in her arms, feeling the tape weakening, loosening, until at last it released her.

Her teary squeal blended into a laugh as she massaged the soreness from her wrists, her arms, replacing it with strength and renewed determination.

Wait!

Flipping on the small flashlight, she replaced the spent tape so that it would appear she were still bound if she touched her wrists together.

"Okay, that's good."

Jolene then raked the small beam of light over the door and examined its hinges. Three steel hinges, secured by three flathead star-point screws. She positioned Carrie's car keys, separated the one with the largest thumb pad. Its sharp corner fit nicely into the screw head.

Using all of her strength she turned counterclockwise. Nothing moved. She tried again until her thumb and forefinger became numb.

She waited, taking deep breaths, then tried another.

The result was the same.

Jolene growled with frustration until she recalled something she'd seen on a home-repair show. She removed her shoe and began whacking the hinge and screw heads.

Then she began prying at the pin holding the hinge.

Nothing budged under the pressure she could apply with the small key.

But Jolene refused to stop.

She put her shoe back on and kicked at the hardware over and over.

Again, she wedged the key's corner into the screw head forcing all of her strength into the twist, cursing and begging for cooperation until she heard a high-pitched squeak.

"It moved!"

Her hopes soaring, Jolene stood and, with unrelenting determination, twisted the head a half rotation, then another half, then another and another until she removed it.

"YES!"

Okay, eight more to go.

At that moment, a sudden jolt staggered her as the transmission ground down and the truck decelerated.

55

Across the country, alone in his study, Karl Styebeck inserted a DVD into his computer.

He should've followed his first instinct to let it burn in the trash drum.

But a darker, stronger fire had raged within him and he'd plucked it from the flames.

He'd hidden the DVD under a shingle of his neighbor's garage roof.

Brent and the others never found it when they searched his house.

Styebeck had surrendered his personal computer to them, as a sign of his cooperation. Then he bought a new one, which he used now to review Bernice Hogan's last moments.

He needed to see her again.

Bernice was his favorite.

He ached to see her—even like this. He craved one last look.

He shouldn't do this.

This was a mistake. Destroy this DVD now. That reporter, Gannon, was getting too close. Orly had threatened to send Gannon a copy of this recording.

But there was still time.

Time to fix everything.

Time to enjoy one last session of pleasure with Bernice

while Alice was out. As the DVD loaded, his urges battled his conscience, tearing him apart. He had to take steps to protect his family, his life. Still, he yearned for Bernice and the other women because the murder had brought the dark side of his life to a standstill and he couldn't take it much longer.

Was he mourning Bernice?

Blurring images of her swam into focus before him. Her face, even though she was terrified, had ignited an explosion of wicked desire. Seeing her, hearing her, even in the throes of death…

"Mr. Styebeck please, I beg you… Oh God no… please, Karl… NO!"

This was wrong.

Get a grip, he told himself. Orly had forced her to use his name, incriminating him. He had to stop his brother, had to fight back, before he lost everything.

Something crashed.

"What are you doing, Karl?"

Startled, he turned to find Alice standing over the heap of groceries she'd dropped on the floor.

"That's the murdered woman! That's Bernice Hogan! Karl, what are you doing?"

He removed the DVD, slid it into his pocket and stood.

"This is part of the investigation."

"What? No, I don't understand. I just don't."

"Alice. I told you, its part of the investigation. Some of the people I deal with on the street want to hurt me."

"No, no, Karl, I don't understand. First we get strange calls, then that reporter writes that horrible story."

"Alice."

"Then I saw you with that strange man who came to our house that night. I pretended I didn't, but I saw from the window. Karl, you were holding your gun!"

"Alice, calm down!"

"Then the police search our home, and I see you burying things at night and burning things and now this!"

"Alice, I told you, I'm helping with the investigation. Some of my informants have accused me, they're trying to implicate me. And they've told Gannon lies. I've been working on this."

She stared at him hard then stared at the computer monitor where she'd seen and heard a terrified woman plead for her life. Then she looked back at her husband, as if seeing him for the first time.

"Tell me the truth, Karl, please."

He said nothing.

"I heard that reporter ask you if 'it runs in the family.' What was he talking about, Karl?"

"He was fed lies, Alice."

"Stop it, Karl! Answer me. Are you involved?"

"Yes."

Alice covered her mouth with her hand.

"Yes." He put his hands on her shoulders. "I knew Bernice Hogan. She was an informant. Yes, I was on the street that night trying to find her, trying to talk to her about a case. And I'm being implicated by people who are all linked to it all. But I did not kill her."

Alice took several moments to digest his explanation.

"Are we safe?" she asked. "Should I take Taylor with me to my sister's in Rochester?"

"That's not necessary. You have to let me handle this. I'm going to get us through this, okay?"

Alice nodded then bent down to pick up the groceries.

It was difficult because her hands were shaking.

56

The loud hiss of brakes echoed through the tranquil forested hills.

Dusk and an eighteen-wheeler arrived outside a tumbledown building that clung to Interstate 84 east of Portland, near The Dalles and the Columbia River. Not far from the end of the Oregon Trail.

A pair of snakeskin boots stepped from the cab.

Stones crunched under them as the driver walked across the gravel parking lot, approaching a line of pickup trucks. He shot a glance at the worn sign above the entrance: *Wolf Tooth Food & Beer.*

He horked and spat before he entered.

Inside, it felt as if the place were a mausoleum for motivation. A gloomy grocery store offered milk, bread, smokes and outdated magazines, then it morphed into a dark and dingy bar.

Unshaven men with stomachs straining plaid flannel shirts, and plain-faced women in tight tops and jeans, sat at Formica tables on hard-backed bingo-hall chairs. They joked between swallows of beer while a basketball game flickered on the muted set perched on a high shelf, next to the beer signs.

A country song sought mercy from a cracked speaker.

Five full minutes after the driver sat alone at a two-chair

corner table and memorized the laminated menu, the bartender decided to take his order.

"What'll it be?"

"Steak and eggs. Side of beans, coleslaw. White toast."

"To drink?"

"Coke and coffee."

"That it?"

"I'll also take a burger platter with fries to go with a bottle of water in a bag."

"Sure. Noticed your rig. Where you coming from, friend?"

The bartender saw smaller versions of himself reflected in the dark glasses that turned to him. The driver did not smile as an icy moment passed.

"What business is it of yours?"

"Just being friendly."

"I got a long way to go."

"I'll get that order up."

While waiting, the driver went to the bar's phone booth, stepped inside, closed the door, deposited a stream of coins and dialed.

Later, as he finished the last of his meal, the bartender left the bill and the grease-stained bag holding his takeout order. The driver probed his teeth with a toothpick as he reviewed his bill. Reaching into his pants for his cash, he was distracted by the woman who'd invited herself to sit in the empty chair facing him. Her ample breasts pushed her navy T-shirt and the words Let's Go Crazy at him.

"Got a minute, there, handsome?"

She was shapely, appeared to be in her early thirties. Could've been younger, for her face looked like it used to be pretty before something in her life broke. She had a butterfly tattoo on her neck and her left nostril had a diamond stud. She dropped a large bag at her feet.

"A minute for what?"

She leaned forward.

"I need to get out of this town and I'll make it worth your while if you take me as far as you can."

He began flipping through his thick roll of bills. Her eyes lingered on his tattoos, which transmitted *The Power and the Glory* across his powerful forearms. The guy looked like he was made of steel.

He left two new tens on the table.

"You'll make it worth my while, will you?"

"I'll blow your mind, buddy."

"That a fact?"

"Mmm, hmm."

"You live here?"

"Hell no. Got left here this morning. Just traveling through. Like you."

"Got some ID to prove that?"

"What? You a cop?"

"Nope."

"Well, I'm not showing you that."

"You already showed me a lot of nerve."

She frowned.

"What the hell." She fished a state-issued card out of her bag. He studied it. It looked recent. She was twenty-four years old and from Joplin, Missouri.

"Leeandra Lake," he said more to himself.

"I go by Lee." She snatched her ID back. "So, how 'bout it?"

"I'm going far."

"How far? Like Seattle, or San Francisco?"

"So far, you might never find your way back. Think it's wise for you to go down that road?"

Her smile was reflected in his dark glasses.

"You make me tingle, handsome. Take me with you."

He stared at her unsmiling.

"You know what you are, *Lee?*"

Her smile shrank a bit as he let a long moment pass, then another, enjoying the crimson blossoming in her skin.

"What am I?"

"My guest."

It was nearly dark as they walked across the gravel parking lot to his rig and to the passenger side of the tractor.

"Swift Sword?" She read the lettering on the door as he reached up to open it for her. "What's that?"

"That's what I am. Hop in there."

She climbed in. He shut the door then walked to the trailer's side. He opened the side inspection door. It swung out. Then he began opening the interior door, which swung in.

He pushed it and froze.

It felt different.

"Hey!" Lee looked back from the side mirror. "Whatcha doing, handsome? Let's go!"

He set the bag of food inside on the dark foul-smelling floor, closed the doors then climbed into the driver's seat. He started the rig's big engine, set it in gear and began to roll.

"You know, I never even asked you your name?" Lee said as she inventoried the truck's interior.

"It's not important. What's important is for you to accept what you are."

"I'm your guest," Lee said, gazing at the prism-colored sky over the Columbia River Gorge. "That's what you said."

"No. You're a goddamn dirty whore!"

She turned to see his face contorted with rage.

"Stop this truck," she said. "I want out now!"

He upshifted.

"Say it! Say, yes, Karl, *I'm a goddamn dirty whore!*"

Frantic, she tried to open the door but it was locked.

"Stop this fucking truck, asshole!"

"Say, *I'm a goddamn dirty whore and my judgment day has come!*"

As she struggled with the door he reached under his seat for the cattle prod. No one heard her screams as the truck vanished into the lonely Oregon night.

57

In suburban Buffalo, Karl Styebeck lying in bed next to his wife, opened his eyes to the glowing numbers of the digital clock: 1:07 a.m.

Alice barely stirred as the cordless phone on his bed stand rang again softly. He grabbed it.

"It's me," Orly said.

"Wait." Styebeck kept his voice low and moved to his den.

"I'm damn tired of shouldering the burden, Karl. When will you accept what you are and do your share?"

"Never. I'm not like you. Or her. Or like him. Turn yourself in."

"We're blood. You're no better than us, you're *exactly* like us."

"Why do you want to destroy me?"

"I'm trying to help you correct the error of your life before it's too late."

"What you're asking is wrong."

"*It's not wrong!* It's what we were put here to do. Belva is dying. Accept your responsibilities. We need to eradicate this world of the whores and whoremongers, which is what you are, Karl. I tried to help you in Buffalo and now my new work in Wichita should inspire you."

"Wichita? What did you do?"

"I have seen the glory, Karl! Listen!"

Styebeck's stomach lurched. Static hiss led into a recording.

"...Mr. Styebeck, please...oh God, let me go...Karl, I swear I won't tell a soul anything...about Bernice Hogan...about what you did to her in Buffalo...noooo! PLEEEEAAAASSEEE! OH GOD!"

The recording ended.

"Orly, turn yourself in."

"My work is righteous. And I got more coming."

"I'm coming for you. I'll bring you in, I swear."

"I don't think so, Karl, you'd go down with me. Your whores will tell them about you, like the one I judged told me before she died. And I'll see to it that the police get my recordings. And like I said, maybe that reporter that nailed you should see copies."

"Those women are being forced to make false statements, I am not involved."

"I've got you good Karl, because it is righteous to carry on with Deke's work. Belva needs to know where you stand before she passes on. You owe her. You owe him. You owe me. We have work to do."

"Deke was sick. You're sick. We're all sick. It's like we've been cursed. You need help."

"I have seen the glory, Karl, and I'm not going to stop until you do what has to be done! Time to come home, brother! Time to come home!"

The line went dead.

Styebeck switched on his computer then found news stories out of Wichita, Kansas. In less than a minute, Carrie May Fulton of Hartford, Connecticut, was staring out from the electronic pages of a Wichita newspaper. Above her face was the headline:

New England Woman Victim of Ritual Slaying
Police say ties to out-of-state killings "can't be ruled out"

"Oh Jesus."

His breathing quickened as he read. He was living a nightmare. He'd come from a bloodline that was cursed, a curse he had to escape.

Styebeck looked at the framed pictures of him with Taylor and Alice.

He got up and took down a large framed painting of a sunset. Hidden in the paper backing was a thick envelope of old files.

It was time.

He dressed then went to the garage for the bag he'd packed earlier. He got a trowel then went to the backyard and dug up a plastic-covered box containing several thousand dollars and a disposable cell phone.

Then he stood there in the dark staring at his home.

He saw Taylor's bicycle, the ceramic pots Alice was working on. He saw the dimmed lights of the appliances in the kitchen window. He knew the calendar on the fridge was marked with Taylor's games, games Styebeck might never see.

Then he picked out the bedroom he shared with Alice.

As a man, he knew he'd been blessed with fortune he didn't deserve.

As Deke and Belva Styebeck's son, he loathed himself for what he was.

As a cop, he knew how to travel without leaving a trace.

As he sank into the night, Styebeck braced for the battle ahead and replayed the one he'd fought against his father in Texas….

* * *

Karl tried to understand why Deke needed an electric chair in their barn. His concern grew.

But he told no one.

As time passed, Deke continued fussing over the chair while Belva helped by making the padded restraining belts. Then Deke came home with a huge diesel generator from military surplus hitched to his truck.

He positioned it in the barn, wired the switch box for the chair, then connected the box to the chair and the generator.

They tested the chair with an old scarecrow Orly had dragged in from one of the fields.

It was a grotesque thing.

Deke fashioned it into a satisfactory test subject. They dressed it in his old clothes, reinforced the arms and legs with stovepipes. A rusted metal bucket served as the head. Orly got a brush and can of red paint and carefully stroked the word GUILTY *on the bucket's face.*

Then Deke secured the "condemned" into the chair and fired up the generator. Its rumble was deafening. When all was set, Deke threw the switch. The generator kicked and growled. The scarecrow vibrated as if it were alive before it exploded into a sizzling, sparking cloud, splitting the bucket and rendering the torso a stinking, eviscerated, smoldering heap.

Deke Styebeck smiled.

Belva smiled, too.

When the remains cooled, Deke instructed Karl and Orly to haul them out to the woods. While Orly, who worshipped his father, was excited to be part of this exalted work, the incident had left Karl puzzling over how executing a scarecrow fit in with his daddy's mysterious vision.

It was at this time that Karl was grappling with his own

strange sensations toward girls at his school, the younger ones in the lower grades. His fantasies grew into agonizing urges that were hard to suppress.

What troubled Karl was that his desires had shocked his school buddies, when he told them. They'd even shocked the grease monkeys at Hank Jebson's gas station—and these were the men who'd shown Karl pictures of naked girls from dirty magazines.

So Karl just stopped talking about it.

But he never stopped thinking about it.

He was good at keeping secrets.

Not much happened after the scarecrow was put to death. Months passed until the night Karl awoke to what he thought was a muffled scream. At his window he saw silhouettes in the dim light of the barn.

Karl left his room, and amid the crickets, padded shoeless to the gaps in the barn's wall. He pressed his face to it so he could see.

As he focused on what was inside, the skin on his arms and neck bristled.

All the saliva dried in his mouth

A stranger was in the chair.

A woman. Her legs, arms, chest and head were bound by the chair's restraints. Her eyes were wide with fear. The woman whimpered as Karl's mother sat before her talking in the same soothing voice she used when he or Orly was sick.

"It's going to be all right, dear."

The woman was wearing a tight blue dress that showed her bare shoulders, the tops of her breasts. She was sweating and heaving, arousing an urge in Karl. She had big earrings and bright red lipstick. Her feet were bare and her dress was slit, showing more of her leg, all the way up to her hip.

"Don't worry," his mother told the woman. "You'll be fine, dear, he knows what he's doing. Shh."

Karl was frightened and fixated.

He felt something shift in his groin just as pain exploded at the back of his neck. A powerful force gripped him like a vise as Deke Styebeck's voice thundered from the darkness.

"What the hell're you doing out here playing with yourself, boy?"

Karl choked on his words.

Deke marched him back to the house efficiently, the way he'd escorted inmates. Using old prison-issue hardware, he handcuffed Karl, and Orly, who slept soundly, to their beds. Then he bent down and whispered into Karl's ear.

"You go to sleep now. And later, you don't tell nobody nothing, got that?"

"Yes, sir."

"It's just a bad dream, understand?"

"Yes, sir."

Karl never told anyone what he'd seen that night, yet he couldn't stop worrying about it. Days passed. He couldn't sleep or eat. When his mother finally pressed him about his torment, he told her about what he'd seen and his father's warning.

Karl's mother looked at him long and hard.

She sighed then took him out to the back porch where they could see Orly working with his father far off in a field. She sat in the big chair swing and patted the space beside her.

Karl sat with her.

"I think you're old enough to hear this." She gazed out at the field. "Promise me you'll never tell your father what I'm going to tell you."

Karl nodded.

"There was a woman your daddy brought here that night."

Karl said nothing.

"A young woman from Fort Worth, rife with sin. A street woman, or what the Bible calls a harlot. She did bad things. She needed help."

"But she looked so scared."

"She was terribly frightened, at first. But your daddy helped her with what she needed. She understood what had to be done."

"What's that?"

"He had to scare her, really scare her."

"Why?"

"He put her in that chair he built to show her where she was headed with her sinful ways. To show her what was going to happen to her if she didn't change. To frighten her into correcting her life before it was too late."

"But she's okay?"

"Oh, goodness yes. She's much better now. Your daddy sent her on her way. She's not going to sin anymore."

"And this is part of his vision?"

"That's right, Karl, and someday you and Orly can carry on."

Relief washed over him.

But it didn't last.

On a deeper level he could not help but feel something was still wrong. It was the terror he'd seen in the woman's face, the way she was bound and the fact he'd heard that big generator kick on that night.

It felt like something had been swallowed by the darkness.

No.

That part about the generator was not real. It couldn't be. It had to be a bad dream.

Still, it haunted him for days, until it struck him to look into his father's past. Deke never talked about his childhood, his upbringing. He was the only child of a pastor and his wife.

That was it.

But Karl figured there just had to be more to know. So one day when Deke, Belva and Orly went to town, leaving him at the farm to do chores, he began investigating. In his parents' bedroom closet, on a top shelf, there was a chest where his daddy kept all his legal papers and such.

It was locked. His parents hid the key in the kitchen. Karl knew where.

When he was younger, he had no interest to snoop but things were different now. Deep down, he feared something was not right with his father, his mother, and maybe even him.

It scared him.

He had no other relatives he could turn to. Or friends, for that matter. No one came to visit them. The Styebecks had always kept to themselves. His family's history was a mystery to him. Maybe he'd learn more if he could read his father's important papers.

The chest was heavy and jammed with envelopes and documents.

He flipped through property and tax records, the bills of sale for the truck and the tractor, a will, some health records, certificates from his mother's teaching job and his father's job at the prison.

Scraping to the bottom of the chest, Karl heard a hollow knock. Something loosened. The chest had a hidden shelf at the bottom. Carefully, he worked on jiggling the wooden base. It squeaked as he shimmed it open to find large envelopes with old papers yellowed by time.

There were news pages with stories about a family's

murder in Alberta, Canada. Who was the Rudd family? Something about a sole survivor. Then a church bulletin about a pastor and his wife returning to Texas from Canada with their son, Deke Styebeck. Old letters from the Royal Canadian Mounted Police. What was this all about?

This all looked important.

Karl blinked.

Unable to make sense of all the new information, he decided to take a risk. He'd take the envelopes from the chest without telling anyone. He'd keep them until he could read them and make notes.

He put everything else back exactly the way it was.

Then he placed the papers in a bag, grabbed a spade and hurried into the woods between the fields, to bury them near where he and Orly had dragged the remains of the scarecrow.

In the darkened forest he approached the broken parts of the executed scarecrow. Standing near it, he looked around for a good place to bury the papers.

He shifted his attention when the sun glimmered on a small shiny object.

Karl bent over.

It was an earring. Just like the one the woman in the blue dress was wearing when she was bound to the chair.

Karl stepped back.

The earth here was dark.

It had been freshly overturned.

58

Gannon found a letter from the Office of the Attorney General for Texas in his mailbox when he returned from Wichita. He read it in the elevator to his apartment.

Dear Mr. Gannon,

Your file has been assigned ID # 15894STYE.

With respect to your request for additional information concerning Deke Styebeck, who was employed as a correctional officer until his dismissal in 1964…

The letter said that Deke Styebeck was fired after a "physical confrontation provoked by an inmate." It provided no details, concluding that much of the personal information Gannon sought remained "excepted from disclosure under sections…"

A big zilch. Damn.

His other search options with sources and mining of records had also yielded little. This story was not getting any easier and time was hammering against him. Sooner or later some reporter somewhere was going to break this story, *his story,* wide open.

He tossed the letter on his kitchen table then made a ham-and-cheese sandwich. As he ate, he tried to determine where to go next. He needed to know more about Karl Styebeck's life to connect the dots linking him to the murders. All of the signs pointed to Styebeck being involved.

But how?

This was the mystery.

Gannon weighed everything he knew about Styebeck's links to Buffalo, Chicago, Texas, Alberta, Kansas, Connecticut.

Pieces.

That's all he had, really, pieces of information swirling in a maelstrom of unknowns. He exhaled slowly, asking himself where he was headed with this story. Seriously, who was he writing for?

No one was interested in his freelance offer. Well, he hadn't nailed it yet. He had to keep going.

Unless he was ready to quit journalism and teach English in Ethiopia?

No, that was not in the cards.

After finishing the sandwich, he made coffee, logged on to his computer and worked. Let's go back to where the trail was freshest, that's where you'll find the best leads.

So there was Jolene's locket.

How did Carrie Fulton, a woman from Hartford, come to have it in her hand when she was murdered? Gannon went online rereading stories from the *Hartford Courant* then he reread the Kansas handout.

Carrie May Fulton had vanished from the area surrounding the Settlers Valley Mall in northeast Hartford. The articles presented her as a troubled young woman. He called up online maps of the mall, and as the pages loaded, he wondered if Carrie knew Jolene.

Settlers Valley Mall was near a turnpike, which—he checked again—was near a truck stop. Jolene Peller's cell phone was used to make calls to Styebeck at a Chicago truck stop. And Gannon could have sworn he glimpsed a truck with "sword" on the door at the Chicago shipping depot.

In Wichita, there were a lot of trucks of all types rolling in and out of that development, which was off the Kansas Turnpike. In Buffalo, the girls on Niagara had reported seeing a creep driving a rig.

Did Karl Styebeck have a connection to that truck?

And was any of this tied to Styebeck's past? Did it have anything to do with Deke, or the Styebecks' twisted family history?

A bit of Texas gothic, there, but was it a factor?

Gannon didn't know.

He couldn't understand why he was having such a hard time finding out more about Styebeck's immediate past. He gathered all of his files, spread out all of his papers on the kitchen table. Then page by page he reviewed everything he'd searched, or tried to search: warrant files, genealogical records, census records, voter lists, criminal and court records, birth records, drivers' records, sex offender registries, property records, credit records, death records, divorce actions, military records, marriage records and on and on.

Virtually none of it helped him build a profile of Karl Styebeck's life before he'd joined the Ascension Park Police Department.

In this digital age, with access to instant information, Gannon couldn't understand why all of his online-data searches into Styebeck's past had yielded nothing. Even the professional online companies he'd paid to conduct records searches had struck out.

It was like Karl Styebeck had hidden his past—or buried it.

Hold on.

Gannon saw his note on the search he'd done of the *Huntsville Item.* He'd only specified a search of reports naming Correctional Officer Deke Styebeck for the period for 1960 to 1967.

What? No obit? There should've been an obit.

Gannon checked his notes from what the amateur historian in Angelina County, Yancy Smith, had told him.

"...Deke was part of the execution team at The Walls and word was he was a difficult man to live with before he died."

Died. Right. So there had to be an obit.

How could that have been missed? It's not a perfect world, he thought as he called the *Huntsville Item* news library to request another search for all archived articles on Styebeck, including an obituary.

"Get back to you within the hour, Mr. Gannon," the librarian said.

While waiting, he drank his coffee and looked at the faces of Bernice Hogan, Carrie Fulton and Jolene Peller peeking at him from the files.

Suddenly he pictured his big sister among them.

Cora is smiling at him. Her voice is crystalline. She is his protector as they go through the library and she finds adventure books for him.

You're going to be a great writer someday, lots of people are going to read your stories, Jackie. Wanna know how I know? Because you're so smart. I see it in your eyes. You don't let go. You don't give up.

The heart-deadening crash of a door.

He runs to his bed, stuffs his head under the pillow as Cora and their mother wage war over Cora "being late," over boys, over drugs, over everything.

Why can't they stop?

Cora, please!!!!

At the cemetery, in the silence, as the conveyor lowers his father's, then his mother's, casket into the ground, he hears the last thing his mother said to him before they drove away to find her.

She may have children, Jack. We have a right to find her.

Cora.

I see it in your eyes. You don't let go. You don't give up.

Gannon's computer trilled, alerting him to a new e-mail from the *Huntsville Item.* The obituary for Deke Styebeck had arrived, with a note.

Mr. Gannon, this obituary only appeared once, and we're sorry not all family members are listed. Back then, that's how they sometimes were submitted. Please let me know if I can help you further.
Nell Fernandez, Library Services, *Huntsville Item*

Gannon opened the attachment containing the scanned death notice for Karl Styebeck's father, printed it off and read the hard copy.

Styebeck, Deke.
Deke Styebeck, died April 17, 1968. He was 44 years old. He was the only son of Pastor Gabriel and Adolpha Styebeck, of Shade River. Deke and Belva Denker were united in marriage in 1952. He lived in Huntsville, Texas, where he was employed as a correctional officer with the Texas Department of Criminal Justice until 1964. He and Belva moved to Pine Mill in 1953. Deke worked as a custodian for the Pine Mill School District. His wife, Belva, and their two sons survive Deke. A private service was held April 20. Interment was at Pine Mill Cemetery.

After reading it, Gannon read it again and underlined *two sons.*

There it was.
The break he needed.
Karl Styebeck had a brother.

59

Jolene Peller did not move.

Death was near.

She held her breath, fumbling through the haze of her waking mind, tumbling through a galaxy of streaking images.

The door had opened.

He'd removed the tape from her mouth but never replaced it because he'd left food. Hot food. She'd devoured it and drank the water. Then she'd slept, but didn't know for how long.

Now, warnings were screaming at her.

Death was so close.

You're a hostage. He's killed Carrie. He likely killed Bernice. He's going to kill you. You have to get away. You have a plan. You've freed your hands. Keep yourself together. Work on the door.

But the truck had stopped.

The door had opened to darkness outside. A glimpse of stars, shadows. Grunting and something being hefted. Boots walking on the foul wooden floor. A body was placed next to her. The peel of duct tape.

Then several silent moments passed.

Crickets.

Fresh air.

The open door beckoned but Jolene's impulse to flee was reined in by a new reality.

He has another hostage.

He was right beside her fixing tape around the other woman.

That means—Jolene was next to die!

She feigned sleep.

Suddenly her face was crushed by a huge strong hand that seized it. Keeping her eyes closed, she groaned under an intense light. Was he inspecting her?

After a few seconds, the light was extinguished.

Boots on the floor. He grunted and jumped to the ground.

The door closed.

The mechanical grind, hiss and growl of the rig.

They were on the move again.

Now Jolene woke fully to controlled panic.

Calm down. Think. Breathe.

They were moving fast.

While they were moving she was safe to work on her escape plan. In the darkness, Jolene went to the woman next to her.

"Are you awake? Nod if you can hear me."

Jolene felt the woman move her head.

"My name is Jolene. I'm your friend. My hands are free. I'm going to help you. It's going to hurt but I'll take the tape off your face."

It took several long minutes for Jolene to loosen all the duct tape. To avert excruciating pain, she had to leave strips adhered to the woman's hair as the woman gasped and sobbed.

"Easy, take it easy," Jolene soothed her. "Tell me your name."

"Lee. Lee Lake. Oh Christ, he's crazy! What's he going to do?"

"Listen, calm down. Listen to me, Lee. We're going to escape. I have a plan. Did he hurt you? Are you strong enough to help me?"

"I think I can help. Oh Christ, all I wanted was a ride. I was stupid."

"Lee, listen. I have to remove your bindings from your hands and legs. It's going to be difficult because he's got so much tape on you. Do you have anything in your pockets? Anything sharp?"

"A metal nail file in my back right pocket."

The woman shifted, Jolene got the file. Again, long minutes passed as she used it to slice through the tape around Lee.

"Okay, listen, Lee. I've got a tiny light, but the batteries are weak so I'm saving them. There's a door that opens inward. I've removed half the bolts from the hinges. We need to get out the rest so we can remove the door."

"But there's another door that opens out. I saw it."

"I know. I've got a plan. Just work with me to hold the light. We have to hurry. We have to do this now, before he stops the truck again."

Working in the dim light, Jolene glimpsed Lee's face, wondering if the fear she saw in it was a reflection of her own.

"Jolene, there are letters on your forehead. It says GUILTY. Did he do that to you?"

"Yes. It's what he does."

"What does it mean?"

"It means we have to work faster." Another bolt squeaked loose. "Oh, thank God, this nail file is better than the key. We're almost done."

Gritting her teeth, Jolene worked through the aches

shooting through her fingers, wrists and arms. She barely comprehended the true horror they were facing, as if rejecting reality in a futile attempt to convince herself that this was one long nightmare.

But it was no dream. They were fighting for their lives.

Adrenaline shot through Jolene when she removed the last bolt.

Her joy soon died.

The heavy door was like a slab of granite and did not move. Jolene pried the hinges away from the wall and pulled with every ounce of strength, shifting the door, pulling it ajar but only slightly.

Lee tried, barely budging the door.

Jolene worked on the side opposite the hinges, finding knots in the wood that allowed her to hook three fingers against the door's lip, managing to feel the massive door shift as the truck hit a rough patch.

Jolene withdrew her fingers in time before they would have been crushed.

Construction zone.

"Come on, Lee, pull the hinge. The bumpy road is shifting the door!"

Jolene seized the upper hinges and both women pulled while the trailer shifted. The door began slipping from its frame, exposing the thick heavily insulated hinged side of their prison.

"Get out of the way!"

Jolene shoved with her palms then wedged her shoulder into the crack, forcing the door out of its holding. A loud bang reverberated as it crashed to the floor. The hum of the freeway filled their prison with hope. It streamed in with the light leaking from the frame of the outside door.

The women cheered and hugged.

Then Jolene took stock of the outside door, their door to escape.

"We're only going to get one chance to save ourselves. Now, this is what we're going to do…."

60

Michael Brent rubbed his bloodshot eyes.

He was alone in the boardroom at Clarence Barracks waiting for the next case-status meeting.

Since returning from Kansas he believed they'd dropped the ball. Images of what the killer did to Bernice Hogan and Carrie Fulton were seared in his memory and he seethed with anger.

He'd put in long hours working every aspect of the murders, Jolene Peller's disappearance and Karl Styebeck's involvement. He'd assessed the facts, the evidence and the pieces that were obvious. Then he reassessed them all until he grew embittered.

Styebeck was the key.

But Robert "Slam Dunk" Kincaid from the D.A.'s office kept pushing that key further away by demanding they magically produce the "irrefutable" piece of evidence that would make his job easy.

And apart from Kincaid, they had Jack Gannon in their face.

Shows up in Kansas. Freakin' Kansas. At the scene. And before *them.*

Gannon was becoming more than a pain in the ass and Brent wanted to know who his sources were. He was unlike any reporter he'd ever met.

Relentless. And very, very good.

They were lucky that nothing on the Buffalo-Kansas link got into the press. They needed to keep a lid on it so they could build their case against Styebeck—something Brent felt they'd achieved long ago.

But not Kincaid.

Well, somebody better damn well do something fast because the lid on this thing was loose and rattling.

"Let's get started."

Brent shifted his thoughts as Lieutenant Hennesy, the captain, the sergeant, Roxanne Esko and two other investigators joined him at the table. Hennesy entered codes into the phone and began the call.

"Hello, everybody," Hennesy said into the speaker. "We'll start with a roll call."

As the voices of two dozen investigators from Kansas, Illinois, New York and Connecticut made introductions on the line, Esko leaned close to Brent's ear.

"Mike, I know you're pissed off. Take it easy, okay?"

At that point, Esko felt a soft tap on her shoulder, and a large envelope was set before her by the officer manager. Styebeck's military records had arrived. Esko had been expecting the delivery and smiled her thanks then set the package aside to study later as Hennesy continued.

"All right, everyone's with us," he said, amplifying his voice. "We've got a lot to cover. I'm going to hand off to Roxanne to bring everybody up to speed with her summary."

"Hi, everyone," Esko said. "Everybody should have the basic info sheet that we sent around before the call. We have key fact evidence found at both scenes that confirms Bernice Hogan and Carrie May Fulton were murdered by the same person or persons. We also believe that the disappearance of Jolene Peller is linked to those murders. Peller is still missing. The NCIC file also has details."

In both homicides, time of death was estimated at being within twenty-four hours before discovery. Both victims were found in isolated areas, the first in a park, the second at a construction site near the Kansas Turnpike.

"And note, in the Hogan case, a bus ticket for her friend, Jolene Peller of Buffalo, who is also missing, was found at the site. A unique locket belonging to Peller was later found with Carrie Fulton, the victim in the Kansas case. No other trace of Peller has emerged," Esko said.

"In both cases, cause of death was attributed to blood loss and blunt-force trauma. In the first case, injuries were consistent with a weapon having a serrated eight- to ten-inch blade. In the second case, a heavy metal object consistent with a pickax.

"Both cases are characterized as frenzied overkill," Esko said.

"What about DNA, semen, trace?" an investigator asked.

"Nothing. No indication of any sexual assault."

Esko said that both homicides were ritualistic with the victims displayed, indicating an organized killer who sought discovery of his crimes and was likely on a mission or crusade.

"What about physical evidence at the scene?" a detective asked.

"We've outlined some of it—the locket, the bus ticket. We also have casts of tires that would be consistent with a big rig. That information's detailed on your sheet."

"What about your key fact?" the detective asked. "It's not on the sheet."

"An identical message was left in each case. One that we're holding back to protect the case."

"What about your suspect, Styebeck?"

Esko shot Brent a look, saw his jaw muscle pulsing.

"This is Brent," he said. "I'm the lead on Hogan. Walt Stanton with the Hartford PD has an update on something that was passed to the district attorney here in Buffalo—"

"Are you talking about my office, Mike?" Robert Kincaid said.

"Yes, Bob. Your office got it yesterday afternoon. Go ahead, Walt."

Kincaid's muttering could be heard as Stanton updated the group.

"Thanks, Mike," Stanton said. "We took the information Mike Brent provided and traced one phone call from Hartford to a residence in a Buffalo suburb. A call was placed using coins from a public phone at the Rolling Dog Truck Stop, which is located on the other side of the expressway from the Settlers Valley Mall. Carrie Fulton disappeared from the area within the time frame of when the call was placed."

"Care to tell us to what number the call was placed?" Brent asked.

"The residential number for Karl Styebeck."

"Can you provide me with some documentation on that?" Kincaid said.

"Your office has it," Brent said. "We have e-mail confirmation and a signed receipt for the courier, Bob."

"Okay, sorry, found it. I've got the information here from Hartford."

A long moment of silence passed; Kincaid was reading the material.

"I think this clearly establishes that Styebeck had some sort of knowledge of the crimes," Brent said.

"But Mike, as I said in our previous call, Styebeck cooperated, he surrendered his private records. I'm going to need a lot more before I can do my job."

"What more do you need?" Brent let loose into the

speaker. "We've got his association with the women. We've got witness statements. We've got Styebeck's rental at the scene, the locket and the phone calls to his goddamn house. We have waited too long and wasted so many opportunities because of you, Bob."

"Mike, settle down," the lieutenant said.

"No, I won't settle down. We've been at two scenes. How high does the body count have to get before Kincaid does his job? Huh? Tell us, Bob. Are you protecting somebody?"

"Hey!" Kincaid shot back.

"I understand you're pals with Nathan Fowler, the editor at the *Sentinel.* I understand his wife is high up the food chain with the Attorney General's Office. Word is you and Nathan both have some sort of political aspirations or affiliation with charity work Styebeck does. Could be seen as a conflict."

"Back off, Brent," Kincaid said.

"Still, to take down a cop for murder, you've got to have a sure thing, right, Bob? Got to have the old slam dunk. Meanwhile, it looks like we, the brothers in blue, are giving Styebeck, the 'hero cop,' a free ride."

The tension that followed was diffused by a new female voice.

"Excuse me, Mr. Kincaid?"

A grumbled response.

"Mr. Kincaid, Sheila Carruthers, with the Connecticut Chief State's Attorney. After reading over the case, I would think Styebeck's relationship to these women and the facts presented by the detectives demonstrate that Styebeck's knowledge goes beyond the investigation. You have enough to support an accessory-to-murder charge. You could use that to leverage more information."

"Bob?" Brent said. "Everyone has done their job, when are you going to start doing yours?"

"Mike!" Hennesy said.

"No, we've been busting our humps, going to Chicago, Wichita, now working with Connecticut, gathering evidence piece by piece. I think it's time for Slam Dunk to get his ass in the game, here."

"Robert," the captain's stern voice reached out to Kincaid. "Do we have enough to support a charge, or not?"

Kincaid released a long heavy sigh.

"In light of the latest information, I would support a charge of accessory."

"Very well," the captain said. "Let's get the ball rolling and go pick him up. And Mike, everyone, it's not over yet."

61

Gannon could not find Karl Styebeck's brother.

Nothing he'd tried had worked.

It was difficult because he didn't have a first name, and now, after some twenty-four futile hours, locating Styebeck's brother, even his mother, seemed impossible.

What was it with this family? Didn't they drive cars, own phones, use credit cards or vote?

Gannon's hopes had lifted when he confirmed that they'd owned property in Texas in the 1950s. But it was sold years later and he'd failed to find any updated listings for Belva Styebeck or any other Styebeck.

Was this a family of ghosts?

Calls to Huntsville, to Pine Mill, to the school district and county offices, had produced nothing. Either no one remembered, or they didn't know who he was talking about. "Sure you got the right area? It seems like a long time ago, son," one county clerk told him.

Gannon was exhausted.

His eyes grew heavy but snapped open when his computer ponged. He'd received an e-mail news alert from the service he'd subscribed to with the online edition of the *New York Times.*

To keep an eye on the competition Gannon had subscribed to a number of news-alert services, entering several key words from the Hogan, Peller, and now Carrie Fulton, cases.

The *Times* had filed a substantial staff-written investigative piece out of Wichita on Carrie Fulton's case. The thrust of it said police sources across the country confirmed Fulton's murder was thought to be linked to the ritualistic homicides and vanishings of women from several other states.

Dammit, had the Times *beat him?*

Gannon swallowed and read to the end.

Okay, the article did not name Buffalo, Bernice Hogan, Jolene Peller, or Karl Styebeck, Alberta or Texas.

But the *Times* had put the case on the national stage. It was a hair away from making the link to Styebeck and catching up to him. And if the *New York Times* was breathing down his neck, other major outlets would be right behind.

Gannon was going to lose his story. Damn. He ran his hands over his face, feeling his stubble. He had to do something.

But what?

He considered flying to Texas, when he realized he'd overlooked going back to Yancy Smith, the local historian in Shade River who'd helped him with Deke Styebeck's past. Maybe Yancy knew someone in Huntsville who could help.

He called Smith's line and a woman answered.

"I'm sorry," she said. "He can't talk to you. He's in the hospital recovering from surgery. This is Marla, his daughter. Can I help you?"

After Gannon explained, Marla asked him to wait while she flipped through her father's address book.

"There are a few people Dad works with on histories in Huntsville. They're a group of genealogists who've lived in that area a long, long time. They know just about everybody and everything about everybody."

Marla Smith gave him three names, numbers and rural addresses. He thanked her, made coffee, then made calls.

Sipping his strong brew, he was encouraged that he was now on the right track. The first number, for Lester Dunphy, went unanswered. The next, for J. T. Pruitt, went to an answering machine. Next, Gladys Howell.

"Hello?"

"Is this the Howell residence?"

"Yes."

"Jack Gannon, calling from New York. I'm a freelance writer and I'm conducting some historical biographic research on the Styebeck family who lived in your area."

"Who?"

"The Styebeck family?"

"Oh yes, the Styebecks. Heard of them but I don't recall very much. They kept to themselves. Try Pearl York's place, she's lived here longer than us. Want her number?"

Gannon dialed the number.

"Hello," a man answered, and Gannon gave his pitch while hearing what sounded like something sizzling in a pan before the man called, "Ma!" Then the phone was muffled as the man explained, "Some guy from New York."

"Yes, hello?"

Gannon repeated his appeal about the Styebecks to Pearl York.

"Oh my, yes, Deke and Belva, I think it was. I don't remember them very well. I think you'd be best to try Lester Dunphy, he's one of the best in this part of the state."

"Sure, thanks."

Hanging up, Gannon tried Lester Dunphy's line again.

He pushed his headset tighter when the line clicked and an older man answered.

"Lester Dunphy?"

"Yes."

Gannon repeated his request, explaining what he was looking for.

"Yes, of course, I recall the Styebecks. A shame."

"Why?"

"Excuse me, you said you're a writer?"

"Yes, a freelance journalist. I'm researching the history of the Styebecks. I understand the family has a tragic history."

"I see, right. Well, it's true. No one really knew what was going on in that family. Deke was part of the execution team at The Walls. Word was he loved his work. Had a zeal for it."

"Yes, I understand."

"And no one knew much about Deke's upbringing. There was talk he'd been adopted by a reverend in Angelina County. I don't know about that. But when Deke lost his job at the prison for beating a convict, they say he just fell apart. Stories went around that he'd deteriorated and put his family through hell."

"Like with drinking?"

"Not that so much. There were stories, just stories, mind you, that Deke had built an electric chair in his barn, just like Old Sparky at The Walls."

"What? Why would he do that?"

"Nobody knew. The family was so private. After Deke died, Karl, the older boy, moved away. Up north, did a short hitch in the military, I think. Then his brother, Orly—"

"Hold it, his brother's name is Orly?"

"I think it is actually Orion, like the constellation, but he went by Orly. He was a very quiet boy. Not quite right."

"What do you mean? Was he violent? Did he hurt people?"

"Not so far as I know," Dunphy said. "I can tell you that about a year or so back, I can't be sure, Orly ended up in a mental hospital or something."

"A mental hospital? Where?"

Dunphy let a long moment go by the way a person who'd said more than they should have wishes the silence to erase what they'd said.

"I don't know," Dunphy said. "You know how people talk."

"Is he still there?"

"I could not tell you. Like I said, it was a rumor and people talk."

"What about Belva Styebeck?"

"Might've gone into a home, or moved along. The Styebecks just faded away and no one ever heard of them again. Sorry, son, that's all I know. But I can ask around, see what I can find out."

"Yes, you can call me collect, or e-mail me. Mr. Dunphy, it's important and kind of urgent." Gannon gave him his contact information.

"I'll see what I can do," Dunphy said.

Gannon hung up, sensing that Dunphy knew more than he'd revealed.

The room turned icy as he stared at the papers of his research spread on his kitchen table, struggling to make sense of what he'd just learned about Karl Styebeck's family.

Less than thirty minutes later he received an e-mail from Lester Dunphy.

Mr. Gannon:
I spoke with my friend Julie Pruitt about your research.

She's willing to tell you a little more about what happened to Orly Styebeck, provided it remains confidential. Her daughter had some unpleasant dealings with him last year. Call Julie at 409-555-1212.
Les

62

In her office at the World Press Alliance in Manhattan, Melody Lyon watched helicopters lift off and land at the West Thirtieth Street Heliport near the Hudson.

Beyond that, she saw New Jersey and jets approaching Newark.

Lyon was under pressure to fill the opening she and Carter O'Neill had on their special investigations team. They were falling behind in the staffing schedule and could face a budget problem. But between meetings, calls and duties, Lyon searched the skyline for an answer to her quandary over Jack Gannon.

It had been a couple of days since Carrie May Fulton of Connecticut was identified as the victim of the murder in Wichita. While Kansas investigators would not rule out the "possibility" that Fulton's death was linked to homicides in other states, they'd refused to name one.

Lyon sensed a bigger story here; so did the WPA's competitors.

Which is why she'd ordered the bureaus in Wichita and Hartford to make the homicides a priority and push their police contacts.

But no one was talking. Nothing new had leaked in the past few days.

And since the *Times* released its speculative piece out

of Wichita, nothing about New York links to Kansas and Connecticut had hit the New York papers. Earlier that morning she'd called Ted Kollock, the WPA's Buffalo bureau chief.

"No, Melody, not a word here about any connection to the Kansas killing. And nothing new on Karl Styebeck in the *Sentinel* or the *News*."

"What're you hearing on Styebeck?"

"Not much. Word is he's keeping a low profile and might be getting ready to sue the *Sentinel*."

"What about the local murder of the nursing student?"

"Nothing new about the Hogan murder, or the disappearance of her friend, Jolene Peller, other than weak updates on inside pages, or metro briefs, you know."

"On another matter, and this is just between us, are you hearing any scuttlebutt in the wake of Jack Gannon's firing?"

"No, nothing."

"Did you ever hear anything at all about him abusing drugs or alcohol?"

"No, nothing like that. Just that he was a helluva good reporter who'd earned his Pulitzer nomination. Why?"

"Just curious. Thanks, Teddy. Keep digging. Something big is going to pop on this story. I can feel it in my bones."

It was Jack Gannon.

He'd made Lyon uneasy for so many reasons.

Asking her for a job in the wake of being fired from the *Sentinel*. Then there was Gannon's call about having inside information, his cryptic e-mail about the murder of Bernice Hogan and the possible link to the murder of another woman found in another state. Gannon's e-mail came before the Wichita story broke.

She hadn't heard from him since. Maybe she should call him. What if he was on the right track to breaking a major story? What if he was dead wrong and his career was about to crash?

Lyon's phone rang. The extension came up for Beland Stone, the WPA's executive editor. Her boss.

"Lyon."

"Got a minute to come and meet me and Carter in my office?"

"Yup."

Beland Stone was an institution.

Before rising to the WPA's top editorial position, he had been chief of the Washington bureau. He'd covered five presidential campaigns and won two Pulitzers for breaking international stories out of Africa. And he'd written two best-selling books on global poverty.

Tough, gruff and smart—that was Stone.

Lyon entered Stone's vast corner office with its panoramic view. Carter O'Neill was sitting in one of the plush visitors' chairs.

Stone was standing at his window pondering the Empire State Building while twisting a rubber band.

"You were supposed to fill that position on special investigations weeks ago." Stone turned from the window. "Carter says you're delaying."

Lyon shot a look at O'Neill.

"Don't blame him, Mel, I saw him in the hall and asked him. What the hell's the delay?"

"I'm considering Jack Gannon from the *Buffalo Sentinel*—"

"Formerly of the *Sentinel.*"

"We were going to hire him once. He was nominated for a Pulitzer—"

"I know about Gannon. He's a liability now because of that recent blunderfuck in Buffalo. Jesus."

"Nate Fowler runs that paper."

"I know. Fowler's a bit of a flimflam man. Never liked him. Tried to interest me in a timeshare when he worked at the Washington bureau."

"I think," Lyon said, "that in spite of everything, Gannon is onto breaking a major story."

"You got proof of that?"

"No, just a sense of it. Beland, I think he's so deep into it that it would be a mistake not to consider it."

"Well, consider this, Mel. The World Press Alliance has a reputation for excellence. It's our duty to uphold it. But if you want to risk your ass on Jack Gannon, then make your stand and do it. You know I respect people with a spine. If you're right, we bring him in, maybe break a story, and we'll all applaud your judgment. But given the current news climate, if you're wrong, Mel, you'll pay an enormous price. The board would ask for your head."

"I know."

"You've got three days to give me the name of your new hire."

63

In some far corners of northern California's Sierra Nevada region, the chug of a semi might be overlooked.

Take the isolated reaches between Yosemite and Desolation Valley, where paved roads thread through the forests of the glorious mountain range. The rumble of a big forestry truck, or a flatbed hauling heavy equipment for a road crew, wouldn't draw a second look here.

And so it was that no attention was given to the dull throb of the rig with out-of-state plates, its big diesel roaring, black exhaust pluming from its stacks, as it sliced along a deserted stretch of stunning mountain highway.

The people who lived here were physically, and psychologically, removed from those caught in the sprawl of the Bay Area and southern California. Here, neighbors kept to themselves and, depending on which parts you ventured to, the only sign of civilization was the occasional mouth of a private road that greeted visitors with a chained gate and a No Trespassing or Keep Away sign.

The truck moved on with purpose.

Only the driver knew its destination.

The crank and whine of its big engine scattered birds as it came to a stop. The driver then made a slow left turn into the forest, meticulously guiding the unit onto an unpaved road.

The entrance was invisible to an outsider's eye. Hidden by overgrowth, it was marked with a small faded sign that warned: Private—Keep Out.

The driver knew this area well, knew all the characteristics of its highways—140, 120, 4, 88 and 50.

And he knew this isolated property's history.

Formerly a long-abandoned gold mine, the property's title had changed hands countless times over the years, until the land was bought a decade ago by a Chicago lawyer intending to build a resort.

That dream died with the lawyer.

The land, forgotten by his estate, was isolated and neglected.

But eight years back, one of the lawyer's last actions had been to have the road graded. It horseshoed for about a quarter mile into thick forest and exited back to the highway, easily accommodating a large vehicle, if it was driven with care.

Now, as the rig proceeded, it was swallowed whole by the towering sequoia and pine. The sweet scent of the trees filled the air. Glorious shafts of light beamed through the forest.

The semi crept down the road that rolled and twisted along slopes and inclines webbed with old trails leading to lakes and streams, ancient camps and other forgotten places.

The loud grind and hiss of careful driving echoed through the trees.

After several minutes, the rig stopped in a meadow bordered by stands of lodgepole.

The driver set the brakes then killed the engine.

He stepped from the cab and stretched.

Then he took a long, relieving piss while enjoying the area's beauty until he finished.

Time to go to work.

He walked into the forest with a sense of complete freedom to do whatever he wanted as he scouted locations. Satisfied with the one he'd found, he returned to his truck, walked to the trailer and opened a lower storage box to withdraw tools and ropes.

Taking his time, he positioned them at the site then returned to the truck, humming. It was perfect weather. He'd enjoy today's judgment. His keys jingled as he approached the trailer's side inspection door.

He started unlocking the steel padlock, but hesitated.

Sounded like something had moved inside.

Something *felt* different. He blinked and thought. To be safe, he went to the cab, got his cattle prod and returned.

Be ready for anything, he cautioned himself as he finished unlocking the side door, grunting as he reached for the lower handle.

Weird.

Pulling it open, he found it moved freely—*like it was pushing from the other side.* Before he realized what was happening, the cognitive command to act was overtaken by the sudden, overwhelming force that fired from the truck directly at him.

Guttural screeching amid a typhoon of fists, fingernails and feet crashing into his face, throat, chest, hurling him to the ground.

The women were free.

The cattle prod rolled away, his head thudded. He saw an explosion of white, heard the women squealing, scrambling.

One was running off.

He managed to react, moving with lightning speed, reaching for the woman who'd fallen near him. He got his fingers on fabric, felt jeans, a belt loop, a leg convulsing, a foot kicking. His hands slid down, grabbing at a thigh, a calf, an ankle.

He seized hard on a foot.

"Jolene! Help! He's got me!"

He twisted the foot just enough to subdue her while he scanned the area for the other woman.

Futile.

He began dragging his screaming captive toward him, intent on smashing her face, binding her, then hunting down the other one and— *Something hammered the back of his skull and his thoughts vanished in a starburst.*

64

Jolene Peller stood over the prone driver.

She was still gripping the brick-size rock in both shaking hands, one thought drumming in her mind: *Run!*

Her heart was galloping, fueled by fear and the instinct to flee as Lee struggled to her knees then leveled a mule kick, driving her heel into the driver's temple.

"Kill him, Jolene! Smash his head!"

"I think he's dead!" Jolene tossed the rock and pulled Lee away. "Come on! We don't know if he's got friends here! Move your ass!"

Numb with shock, they fled, chanting the license plate of the tractor as they fled. *Did they have it right? Go back! NO!* They kept running.

Jolene glanced back.

Oh no! The driver was alive!

He'd staggered to his feet and was trotting after them.

"Faster!" Jolene jerked Lee's hand. "This way!"

They veered from the road into the thick, dark forest, stumbling down a steep incline. Underbrush and branches tore at their faces, hands, their clothing.

Pushing themselves, they moved faster, lurching toward the bottom of a slope. They crossed a clear running stream. The icy water took their breath away, cold shot up their feet and lower legs. They splashed ahead, steadying themselves on deadfall, and disappeared into the tangle of brush and forest on the other side.

They were running for their lives.

They didn't dare stop.

He could be a heartbeat behind them, he could have friends, a rifle.

Anything.

Their only advantage, the only way they could stay alive, was to keep moving.

The wild terrain with its exposed rocks, hidden cliffs and drops was dangerous and exacted a toll. Muscles ached, skin was ripped and bleeding. Their lungs burned, their bodies craved rest. Panting, gasping, they ran without stopping for half an hour.

As they crested a jagged rise, Lee cried out.

"Jo—stop." Lee collapsed. "My ankle!"

She'd twisted her foot in a narrow fissure.

"Oh God, it hurts! Owww!"

Jolene knelt down and helped Lee extract it. The skin had been scraped clean to the anklebone.

"Owww, it hurts, it hurts!"

Jolene tore off part of her shirt. Scanning the woods behind them, she saw no sign of the driver. She made a crude pressure bandage for Lee.

"Let's rest. Over there."

Jolene positioned Lee behind a thicket as they searched the view below while catching their breath. Jolene nodded to the peak of a rise forty yards ahead.

"Listen. I hear rushing water. I'm going to climb up there to look down the other side and see what's in the valley. Maybe there's a town or something."

Breathing hard, Lee nodded and massaged her injured leg.

Jolene scrambled to the top and studied the valley,

which was divided by a stream. Within seconds, the glint of sunlight on a mirror flashed to her.

The mirror belonged to a solitary white SUV, parked on a riverbank.

No sign of life near it.

A fisherman? A hiker?

Still, it was hope. Parked one hundred yards away.

Jolene returned to Lee.

"There's an SUV parked on the other side. I'm going down for help. You stay here, Lee. Stay low and don't move! No matter what, I'm coming back for you, okay?"

Lee nodded, tears filling her eyes.

"Just hurry! He could be gaining on us! Please hurry!"

Jolene clambered down the slope as fast as she could, navigating around jutting rocks and gullies. All the while, she eyed her surroundings for any sign of their pursuer.

The SUV was locked. It looked and smelled new.

Jolene shouted for help over the river's rush.

She froze.

What was that?

She thought she'd heard something just as a big black crow sped by, screeching. Feeling an unseen threat closing in on her, Jolene's pulse raced. She had to act. Had to do something.

What?

A note.

Leave a note with details. She glanced around and spotted a fast-food take-out bag and a tossed beer bottle. The bag was faded. Others had been here. People knew this spot.

Jolene's mind raced.

She had an idea—*a stupid one,* but an idea nonetheless. She smashed the beer bottle, cut her finger with a shard. Using a sharp-ended twig like a pen tip, she dipped it into the blood bubble on her finger and wrote a short plea for help on the take-out bag.

Jolene slowed her breathing and steadied her hand. All the while her brain screamed *Hurry!*

When she finished, she approached the SUV, seized a large rock, smashed the driver's-side window. Glass rained into the interior. The alarm and horn blasted and the lights flashed.

Jolene left her message on the driver's seat then fled back up the slope to Lee.

This was life and death.

As she scrambled up, her hand dripping blood, the alarm rose around her, filling the river valley. Jolene prayed the owner would come. She and Lee could watch from a safe distance. But while this may summon the SUV owner, it could also alert the trucker to their location.

Had she made a costly mistake?

She wasn't thinking.

Had she overlooked the chance to search for a spare key, a cell phone, or for someone who could help? Did she even know what to do? She fought back tears, her body quivering as she reached the peak.

Alarm rang everywhere as she trotted to the location where she'd left Lee.

She was nowhere in sight.

What happened? Where'd she go?

"Lee!"

This was the right spot. There's the bush! This was the spot!

"Lee!"

Jolene looked around then froze. There was no sign of Lee until a faint cry rolled across the land to Jolene.

She saw the trucker carrying Lee over his shoulder

just as they disappeared into the dark woods in the direction of his rig.

Jolene ran after them.

65

"Les told me you'd be calling. Something to do with your research on the Styebeck family," Julie Pruitt said on the phone to Gannon.

"Yes, there have been some tragedies in the New York and New England areas that may be linked to them. Can you help me?"

"I'll try. That family is well acquainted with tragedy."

"I'm interested in Orly. Les said your daughter had dealings with him?"

"That's right, but this must be kept confidential."

"Of course."

"Orly was a patient at the hospital where my daughter works."

"Where's that?"

Pruitt suddenly appeared to be besieged with second thoughts.

"I understand it was a mental hospital?" Gannon said.

Pruitt was pulling back on him.

"Julie, please, this is important."

"I don't feel comfortable telling you more. I'll call my daughter and let her decide. I'll call you back."

He was close. So close he could feel it.

Gannon inhaled then went to the living-room window

and searched for answers on the rooftops of his neighborhood.

Earlier this morning, the *Chicago Tribune,* following the *New York Times,* reported that the FBI was looking into links between a Chicago truck stop and the murder of Carrie May Fulton.

Other reporters were gaining on him. It was only a matter of time before someone put everything together.

His line rang. Pruitt had called back.

"My daughter said she cannot help you with Orly Styebeck, but she seemed interested in the new tragedies you'd mentioned. Her name is Crystal Palmer. She's at work at Ranger River Psychiatric Center. It's just outside of Houston. She's the assistant director of admissions. Here's her direct line."

"Thank you."

Gannon took down the number then called.

"Crystal Palmer."

"This is Jack Gannon, I'm a freelance writer."

"Yes, Mr. Gannon." Her voice was authoritative, officious. Her bureaucratic defense shields were up.

"I'm hoping you might be able to help me, in the strictest confidence, on the case of Orion Styebeck."

"I'm sorry, I'm forbidden by policy and law to confirm, or discuss, the files of any patients, Mr. Gannon."

"I understand, but as you may know, my inquiry arises from recent and disturbing tragedies that should interest you."

"No. As I said, I am forbidden from discussing our patients. I just wanted to make that clear to you. Have a nice day, Mr. Gannon."

"Wait. Please. I'll put all my cards on the table."

"I really don't have the time."

"This is extremely important. It's information you should know."

She sighed. "Please be brief."

"Thank you. And I'll ask you to keep this confidential," he said.

Gannon began with the discovery of Bernice Hogan's body and the link to Karl Styebeck, leaving nothing out, including his own firing. He told Palmer about Deke Styebeck's disturbing past in Canada and why he needed to know more about Orly.

"Do you have access to the Web?" Gannon asked her.

"Yes."

"Go to these links, write them down."

"Mr. Gannon, I really don't think—"

"Please, it's important and it won't take long. Go to them now."

One by one Palmer clicked on stories about Bernice Hogan's murder, Karl Styebeck, Jolene Peller's disappearance, the mention of a mystery rig, Carrie May Fulton's murder in Kansas, articles in the *Chicago Tribune* and the *New York Times.*

Gannon thought he'd heard Palmer's breathing quicken as she scanned through the stories.

"Now, you know more about Orly Styebeck than I do," Gannon said, "because you have his file. I need you to understand that two women are dead, a third, a single mom with a three-year-old son, is missing. All have a link to Karl Styebeck. All I am asking for is information about his brother, Orly, a man I'm trying to find right now. Of course your inclination is to not help me. When I hang up, you'll say, I've done my job, I've protected a patient's rights. And when another woman's corpse is found somewhere, you can tell yourself one more time, well at least I did my job and protected a patient's rights. And you can keep telling yourself that for the rest of your life. As you try to blot out images of grieving families at grave sites, you can be assured that at least your files were kept safe."

"Mr. Gannon—"

"All I am asking for, Ms. Palmer, is a summary of Orly Styebeck's case and information on where I can find him." He squeezed the phone. "Let me repeat, Ms. Palmer. Two women are dead, a third is missing. Now, it is clear by the fact I am unemployed that I protect sources, that I believe sometimes we must consider who we protect and who we hurt when we serve bureaucracy blindly and without question. I'm begging you to help me. If you need a reason, go back to those stories and look at the photos, the faces of the women who are now in the ground."

A long silence passed.

"Mr. Gannon, call me back in two minutes on another number…."

66

All of the official inflexibility melted from Crystal Palmer's voice when she answered on the second line.

She spoke firmly but from her heart. "Losing my job for telling you what I'm going to tell you is the least of my worries."

"I understand."

"No one must know where you obtained this information, understood?"

"Understood."

Gannon heard the clicking of keys on a computer keyboard.

"About eleven months ago, Orion came to us complaining about hallucinations arising from his family's history, a type of prolonged-grief reaction to his father Deke's death. He died suddenly a few years after losing his job as a correctional officer in Huntsville, where he escorted condemned prisoners to their executions. Orion said it was primarily the fact his mother was ill and dying that resulted in his voluntary admission. He was subsequently counseled, treated and, after three weeks, released."

"Is there anything in there about his brother, Karl?"

"He was estranged from Karl after his father's death. It was a source of continued anguish for him and his mother."

"Was Orion violent when he was with you?"

"Not physically, but he was verbally abusive to the female staff. Some patients are, but we cope with that."

"What did he say, specifically?"

The keyboard clicked.

"He called the doctors whoremongers, and the nurses, dirty whores who were guilty of sins for which they would be judged. I'm afraid I have a meeting. That is all I can tell you."

Gannon was taking notes.

"One last thing. I need to ask, is Orion Styebeck's profession listed? I assumed he was a guard or cop."

"Orion Styebeck is a truck driver. An independent, numbered company known as, wait—" Clicking on the keyboard. "It's Swift Sword."

Gannon froze.

"Jesus Christ," he whispered to himself.

"Mr. Gannon?"

"Do you have an address?"

"Yes, he's renting near Lufkin, Texas, north of Houston. Here it is."

Gannon took it down, thanked Palmer.

After hanging up he cupped his face in his hands.

That's it.

The last piece had fallen into place. Everything aligned. Everything fit. Styebeck's connection was through Orly, his truck-driving brother in Texas.

This was it.

It had to be.

Karl was either protecting his brother, or working with him.

He had to go to Texas to find Orly.

And fast, before somebody else beat him to it.

67

That afternoon, the streets surrounding the Styebeck home were sealed off by the Ascension Park police, the Buffalo PD and the Erie County Sheriff's Office.

All traffic was diverted from the area.

Officers refrained from using lights and sirens as they evacuated residents from neighboring homes in the line of fire. Police then set up an outer perimeter, clearing the way for the Buffalo FBI's SWAT team.

FBI sharpshooters settled into concealed, close-range locations and took aim at the doors and windows of the Styebeck house. Other SWAT members, clad in black armor, quietly took cover points against the house at the front, sides, back and garage.

An eerie calm fell over the property.

FBI SWAT commander Ben DeVoss observed it through binoculars from the hood of the command-post truck, among a clutch of other police vehicles down the street.

He turned to state police investigators Michael Brent and Roxanne Esko who had the warrant. The tactical arrest was needed, given that Styebeck was a cop and possessed weapons.

DeVoss made a number of whispered radio checks.

Everyone was ready. He nodded to Agent Daly, the SWAT negotiator.

"Make the call, Kern."

Daly called the number and after three rings a woman answered. Daly pressed her and she identified herself as Styebeck's wife, Alice.

"This is Special Agent Kern Daly of the FBI. We have a warrant for the arrest of Karl Styebeck—"

"Arrest?" Muffled anguish passed between them. "Arrest for what?"

"Ma'am, that will be explained to Mr. Styebeck. Right now, we advise that Mr. Styebeck immediately come to the front door with his hands raised, palms forward, and proceed to the front lawn."

The request was met by a long silence then sniffles.

"He's not here," Alice said.

They always say that, Daly thought, and had the nearest squad car sound a siren three times then repeated his request.

"This has to be a mistake. I told you, he's gone. This is crazy!" Her voice was cracking. "I don't know where he is. Please go away, you're scaring me. Please. Just go away."

"How many people are in the house, ma'am?"

"Just me. My son's at school. Leave us alone!" she sobbed. "I have to find my husband!"

"Ma'am, I want you to take a couple of deep breaths," Daly said. "For your safety, could you please exit now through the front door with your hands outstretched, palms facing forward, and we can talk."

Alice took a long moment to find a measure of composure then she cooperated.

The FBI took her into custody and into the command post while the SWAT team did a tactical room-by-room search of her home.

Distraught and trembling in the command-post truck, she told Brent, Esko and the FBI the little she knew.

"I don't understand anything. Karl left in the night yesterday. Or maybe it was the night before. Oh dear God." She thrust her face into her hands and shook her head. "He didn't talk to me about it, or say where he was going. Or why. He's been under so much pressure. It all started with that horrible story in the paper, accusing Karl of murder!" She touched the back of her hands to her eyes. "He tried so hard to help you, to help with the investigation."

Esko exchanged an *"are-you-buying-this-crap"* glance with Brent as Alice Styebeck continued.

"I'm so scared. We have to find him. All he left was this note."

She withdrew a folded piece of blue-lined schoolbook paper bearing the handwritten note:

I'm so sorry, I have to do this. I'll be back to explain.

I love you. Karl.

Radios crackled with an update from the FBI SWAT-team leader in the Styebeck home.

"The residence, garage and yard are clear. No one else here."

Alice searched the sober faces staring at her.

"What is my husband charged with?"

Karl Styebeck had slipped through their fingers.

Brent's anger strained the car's interior as Esko drove them back to Clarence Barracks. His rage pulsed under his taut jaw, but they rode without speaking. No words would help. Every creak, rattle and bump emphasized what had happened: a supreme failure.

For Brent, it was a matter of having to tell Bernice Hogan's mother, Candace Rose in Wichita, and detectives in Hartford, that Styebeck, the key to clearing the case, had fled.

After two hours of questioning Alice Styebeck, further checks with their bank, credit-card companies, phone and computer records, Brent was satisfied she knew nothing about her husband's sudden disappearance.

Styebeck knew how to vanish without a trace.

Now, it was all Brent could do to keep from driving his fist through the windshield.

"Mike," Esko started. "We'll find him. We'll blast out a bulletin, the FBI will put him on their Most Wanted. We'll find him."

Brent said nothing. Esko shook her head.

"It was Kincaid, Mike, holding us back, playing games."

"No, Rox. It was me. I should have pushed back." Brent looked at the world rushing by his window. "It was me. I dropped the ball."

Within one minute of their return to their office, Lieutenant Hennesy approached their desk.

"It's all bullshit, Mike. The captain's on the phone to Kincaid's boss."

Brent was removing his jacket and draping it over his chair.

"Call Walt Stanton in Hartford," Hennesy said.

"They know already?"

"I don't know. Stanton left a message, wants to talk to you ASAP."

After Hennesy left, Brent looked to Esko, who shrugged and opened the couriered envelope she'd received earlier. She'd meant to open it sooner, but they got consumed by the planning to arrest Styebeck.

Brent turned on his computer, then called Stanton in Connecticut, expecting a lot of grief at the other end. As it rang he glanced at Esko, who was studying documents with growing interest.

"Hartford Homicide, Stanton."

"Walt, it's Mike Brent. I guess you heard, Styebeck's a fugitive from us."

"Yeah, tough break but we've got something here that might help."

"We could sure use a break right now. What do you have?"

"I've sent you a file our ID guys just finished. Did you get it?"

"Hold on."

Brent slipped on his bifocals, searched his e-mail, found the file and opened it. It was a slide show of stills taken from a security camera.

"Got it. Pictures."

"Right. Taken from the truck stop near where Carrie May Fulton was last seen. The managers there are very good about keeping security footage. We scoured their archived stuff and compared it with the date and time the call was placed to Karl Styebeck's home in Buffalo."

"Right." Brent was encouraged. He glanced to Esko whose interest in the file she was examining was intensifying.

"See, Mike," Stanton was saying from Connecticut, "the cameras are superior quality. They picked up the guy at the public phone who made the call."

Tall, well-built guy in a checkered shirt, jeans and expensive-looking cowboy boots.

"This is good," Brent said.

"Keep going through the pictures. See, they also picked up our guy walking to his truck, checking a side inspection door of his trailer. See?"

"Yup."

"Now, Ident did some real nice work enhancing the frames, but see the name on the door of the truck?"

"Swift Sword."

"We got the tag, too. The truck is registered to—"

Karl Styebeck's military records, a set not available to the public, plopped on Brent's desk.

"It's his brother, Mike!" Esko said. "He's got a brother. Orion Styebeck. He's a trucker! I don't know how we missed it." Esko placed her hands on her hips and paced. "Something about a doubled letter in the spelling in Karl Styebeck's name and one number on his SSN being off. I bet Karl did that, but it's all there in his military records. No mention of Orion in his Ascension Park file. He's been protecting his freaking brother!"

"Hello?" Stanton said. "You still there, Mike?"

"Go ahead, Walt."

"The truck is registered to a numbered company, which is registered to Orion Styebeck in Texas. Lufkin, Texas."

68

After packing, Gannon took a cab to the airport.

At the counter, he asked the airline-ticket clerk to get him on the next flight to Houston.

"I need to be there now."

"Certainly, sir." The clerk launched into swift keyboard tapping. "We may have something."

Gannon's cell phone rang. It was Adell Clark.

"Jack, where are you?"

"At the airport. I thought you were out of town."

"I just got back. Things are happening. Big things."

"I know," Gannon said. "What've you got?"

"They've found another victim. White female."

"Another one? Where?"

"California. In a remote part of the Sierra Nevada. I've got friends at the San Francisco Field Office. They're moving fast on this one. They checked ViCAP then called Wichita. It's fresh, brazen display, same pattern. A hiker found her."

"They ID the victim? Is it Jolene?"

"I don't know, but there's more. They moved on Styebeck but lost him."

"Lost him?"

"He's gone. They'd sent Tactical to his home with a warrant."

"He's been charged?"

"With accessory in the Hogan and Fulton cases. But when they went to get him, he wasn't home. Wife says he disappeared over a day ago."

"Where?"

"No one knows. He's going to make the FBI's Most Wanted."

"He may be headed to Texas."

"What'd you find?"

"Remember, Styebeck's from Texas. He's got family in Texas."

"What's the connection?"

"He's got a brother there. The story's in Texas and I'm trying to get there as fast as I can."

"Excuse me, sir," the clerk interrupted Gannon. "I can get you on a flight that goes to Chicago with a very tight connection time for a flight to Houston. It's boarding now. No time to check in bags."

"I heard that, Jack," Clark said. "Get going and call me if I can help you with anything."

"Thanks. Yes, I'll take that flight. I've only got carry-on."

"You've got fifteen minutes."

The clerk reached for the phone and alerted the crew, then worked full bore to get Gannon his boarding pass. He rushed from the desk, excused his way through the lines and cleared security in minutes.

69

Some thirteen hundred miles away, on a back road south of Oklahoma City, Polly Lang warmed the coffee of her customer who sat alone, hunched over his map in the far booth of Tony's Home-style Diner.

Her steak, fries, Coke and coffee order.

He was unshaven, wore a paint-stained ball cap and the haggard countenance of a man not to be messed with.

But Polly was the diner's youngest, most outgoing waitress. She liked to flirt and always worked extra hard to earn a smile and a large tip—especially from strangers. At seventeen, Polly thought herself worldly.

"Can I get you anything else?" She picked up the man's empty plate. "We've got some fresh homemade pies. They are so good. I'm talking dyin'-and-goin'-to-heaven good."

Karl Styebeck looked her over.

She was young. Lovely skin, nice white teeth, hair in a loosened working-girl ponytail. And those hoop earrings, those innocent eyes. He considered her potential and released the beginnings of a smile.

"I love pie," he said.

"Me, too."

"What kind are you offering?"

"Pecan and peach."

"How about a slice of pecan to go?"

"Coming right up."

Styebeck watched her disappear into the kitchen, then shoved his dark desires out of his mind. Disgusted by his own sickness, he sought refuge in the cold fact that whatever he was, he was not like his family.

Not like Deke. Not like Orly.

Every day he'd carried the secret of knowing what he'd come from and what his family had done. Every day he'd lived in the desperate hope that the steps he'd taken to sever himself from his past would keep it from finding him.

He'd worked so hard to build his life with Alice and Taylor.

The right kind of life.

And he'd do anything to protect it.

He turned to the window and his thoughts glided over the Texas plains back to what had happened....

After he'd read all of his father's hidden letters, after he'd considered the earring he'd found in the woods, the terrified woman in the chair, he confronted Deke late one night in the barn.

Metal clinked against metal as his father worked on the large generator.

"There's something wrong with our family," Karl said.

Deke didn't acknowledge him until he set the secret papers on the ground next to him and placed the earring on top.

The clinking stopped. Deke stared at them.

"I read all these papers you had hidden and found the earring in the woods. I know everything. You've got to stop."

Deke's shadow fell over him as he stood.

In one swift motion Deke seized him by the shirt. With one powerful hand he lifted him off his feet, inserted him in the chair, fastened the straps and harness.

"No, Daddy, please!"

Deke's big rough hand slapped his face.

"Tell me who you told?"

"No one, sir."

"You stole my papers! Stealing's a sin!"

"I'm sorry."

"You know what I did to sinners in The Walls."

"Yes, sir."

"No, you don't!" Deke groaned and held his head as if in agony. "You know nothing! Your mother and Orly don't know. Nobody knows. OH JESUS, WHY DID YOU HAVE TO GO AND DO THIS? WHY? WHY? WHY?"

Deke stared into the darkness as if something terrifying awaited him.

"You don't know what I had to do because of what we are."

"I'm sorry, sir."

"We are the cursed spawn of Clydell Rudd," Deke shouted to the ceiling, spittle spraying from his mouth. "I am an inbred bastard! A monster! I lied to myself my whole life saying it's not me. I tried to end it. With every execution I tried to erase his evil but I couldn't wash it away, couldn't undo what's done! His poison runs through our blood!"

Deke grabbed the papers and earring, walked out of Karl's sight toward the electric-control box.

He paused there.

After a moment, he left the building. He returned minutes later. Karl heard the pump, a shotgun blast, and his father's corpse hit the ground at the side of the barn.

The time after Deke's funeral was a blur to Karl.

Although Belva and Orly ached to know what had happened, all Karl revealed was how Deke had flown into a rage, put him in the chair and started shouting about losing his job.

As soon as he was old enough, Karl Styebeck left Texas,

never went back, and never contacted his family again. He disappeared into military service, and after his discharge, whenever he filled out forms and applications, he adjusted a digit in his social security number, or the spelling of his name, knowing that it would hamper any records search. That was all that was needed, and for years he'd succeeded in burying his past.

He thought Deke's suicide had ended it.

But they found him, several months ago, when he got the letter from Texas.

Now, Styebeck lifted his map from the diner table and looked at it.

Addressed to him care of the Ascension Park police. It came with photocopies of Buffalo news clippings on him rescuing children from the fire, and a profile on his outreach group's work to help troubled women who were abused, runaways, addicts and hookers.

The letter was written in his mother's hand.

> At last we've found you, Karl. With me so ill and close to death. When Orion found these articles and the pictures and showed me, it tore at my heart. I will never recover from the wound you caused when you abandoned your blood, me, your brother and your father's honor. Now, we find you're helping harlots, helping feed the evil that your father battled to his dying day!!!
>
> YOU SHAME US!!!
>
> You've left ORLY to honor your daddy's legacy to pass judgment on the guilty all by himself.
>
> YOU'RE A WHOREMONGER WHO MUST BE CLEANSED IN THE HOLY WATERS OF RIGHTEOUS JUDGMENT!!!
>
> Karl, as your mother I order you to change your

ways, to get down home now so we can DELIVER YOU TO THE RIGHTEOUS LIGHT WHILE THERE IS TIME!!!

If you disobey me, I'll have ORLY unleash HIS WRATH and USE THE SWIFT SWORD OF JUDGMENT ON YOU!!!!

I PRAY FOR YOUR SOUL AND THE DAY I CAN CALL YOU MY SON AGAIN.

Belva

Styebeck took a breath and considered the truth about Clydell Rudd and his bloodline.

The evil thrived in Orly.

Styebeck had to put it all to rest.

Exhausted, Karl Styebeck removed his cap, ran his hands through his dyed hair, replaced it and stared out at the highway. He could not turn Orly in because Orly had implicated him with those recordings. Styebeck contemplated and calculated the distance between him and what had to be done.

He should have acted on this long ago.

He reviewed the map again. He could be there today.

The waitress returned and put a white box on his table along with the bill.

"I gave you a little extra piece. On the house." She winked.

Styebeck nodded his appreciation, left a ten and two ones, collected his map, and side-stepped two troopers with the Oklahoma Highway Patrol entering the diner as he exited.

That was close.

He walked to the far edge of the diner's lot, which led to a small picnic area. His car was parked on the other side of the outdoor restrooms under a shade tree, unseen from the diner and the patrol cars.

No other people were around.

Styebeck's car, an older Ford Taurus, was in good shape and ran well. It had clean Ohio plates. He'd gotten the car through a connection to one of his informants, on a kind of unofficial rental basis.

All cash. No questions. Nobody knows.

He tossed his map and papers into the front seat. Then, as was his habit on this trip, he unlocked the trunk to double-check its contents. His bag was there, and under a blanket he inventoried: the Mark 4 assault rifle, the Remington 870 shotgun, the rounds and shells.

All there. Good.

Ready to go, he touched the Glock 22 pistol that he wore in his ankle holster, then checked the Glock's magazines. Four in the trunk. Check. And one in each front pocket of his jeans.

Styebeck froze.

Only one magazine.

He thrust his hands deeper into his pockets but nothing changed.

He'd lost a fifteen-round magazine. Must have happened when he went to the washroom.

Damn.

He shot a glance back to the diner. What should he do? Go back and look for it, or keep going?

There were two Oklahoma troopers in there.

His prints were all over the magazine.

Styebeck looked around.

Go, he told himself. Just go.

He got behind the wheel, started the engine and drove away, expecting at any second to see flashing red lights in his rearview mirror.

70

After the flight to Chicago landed, Gannon had forty-five minutes to make his connection to Houston.

Hurrying through O'Hare, he checked his phone for messages.

Nothing.

Not one of the editors he'd queried on a freelance story had shown any interest. Maybe he'd try to sell it to a Texas magazine. But he couldn't deal with that now.

He had things to do.

He arrived at his gate half an hour before his plane was to board. He switched on his laptop, charged Internet service to his credit card. He made an online reservation to rent a small car at Bush Intercontinental.

He checked his files and reconfirmed his route to Orion Styebeck's address near Lufkin. If Karl Styebeck was a fugitive, his brother's home in Lufkin had to be the first place police would look.

It had to be.

Gannon studied the Internet map and driving directions. It would take some three hours on 59 north, out of Houston.

Done.

Gannon then checked the secondary address in the older records. It was a rural property on Dead Tree Road; the farm where Karl and Orion had grown up. But the records showed it was sold long ago. Gannon could go there for color later, get a sense of the place.

"This is a general boarding call for flight..."

As Gannon switched off his computer and prepared to board, his cell phone rang. The call was coming from New York City.

"Gannon."

"Hi, Jack. It's Melody Lyon."

"Hello, Melody."

"Have you got time to talk?"

"I'm about to get on a plane."

Lyon took about two seconds to assess the situation.

"Is your trip in pursuit of the Styebeck story?"

"Yes."

"Where are you headed?"

"I'm not tipping the WPA, Melody, I'm sure you'll understand."

"I'll give it to you straight, Jack. I have a full-time opening and you're my choice."

Gannon's spirits lifted.

"But," Lyon added, "and I'm going to be blunt—there are complications. Because of your history, people here don't want you considered for the WPA."

"I understand."

To buy time, Gannon went to the end of the long line that was boarding.

"I'm alone in supporting you," she said, "because I believe Nate Fowler somehow screwed you over and that in fact you're onto something solid with this Styebeck story."

"Thanks, but what does that get me?"

"Let me propose something to you."

"I've got about two minutes here, Melody."

"The WPA is hot on this Styebeck story. And, from

what I'm picking up, so are the Associated Press, CNN, the *New York Times,* and the *Chicago Tribune.* We've learned that the number of victims could now be three, in Buffalo, Wichita and California. We've just learned that Detective Karl Styebeck is tied to the case, as you'd first reported, and will soon be announced as one of the FBI's most-wanted fugitives in the country. I think a huge story is going to break at any moment, but don't know where the next development will be."

"What do you want from me?"

"Jack, I believe you're a few steps ahead of everyone, but they're gaining on you."

Gannon got his ID and boarding pass ready as the line moved.

"What's your proposal?"

"Tell the WPA everything you know."

"What?"

"If your information is good, I give you my word you'll get full credit, freelance pay, and it will strengthen my case for your hire."

"And if my information is wrong? What happens, Melody?"

"We're done and the WPA hires somebody else."

Gannon was about ten people away from the desk.

He stepped out of earshot and lowered his voice.

"I'm going to Lufkin, Texas, to the address for Orion Styebeck, an independent trucker operating Swift Sword Trucking. He's Karl Styebeck's brother. I believe Orion Styebeck is involved in the cross-country murders, and that Karl is on his way there now."

Lyon was writing notes.

"Thank you," she said. "Keep your phone on when you land. Our Houston and Dallas people will work with you."

71

Nearly three hours later, Gannon's jet landed in Texas.

"Ladies and gentlemen, welcome to Houston. On behalf of Captain..."

The attendant listed connection information as the plane taxied to the gate. When it stopped, seat belts clicked, passengers rose, collected their belongings and began disembarking.

Coming through the jet bridge to the terminal, Gannon's attention went to the bank of overhead television monitors tuned to CNN, Fox and a CBS affiliate.

His jaw dropped.

They showed the dramatic red bars advising, "LIVE: BREAKING NEWS: LUFKIN, TEXAS," with aerial images of a heavily treed property, dotted with run down outbuildings, eviscerated cars, trucks and trailers.

The news crawlers at the bottom of the screens flowed with: "The World Press Alliance citing unconfirmed sources reports the FBI, along with Texas state and local authorities, have converged on the property of a truck driver suspected in the cross-country murders of three women. Ritualistic slayings in New York, Kansas and California are linked. FBI launches manhunt for fugitive New York detective implicated in the case..."

This was his story and he'd lost it.

He was too late.

It was over.

Hang on.

He sat down, eyes fixed to the TVs, and took a few deep breaths.

Think.

Just keep going. Keep going.

He started walking fast to the rental desk, going over his plan as if it were a prayer. Get the car. Get to Lufkin. Hook up with the WPA. Maybe something can be salvaged. His computer bag bumped against him, reminding him he still had exclusive material on the Styebecks from Canada.

The car-rental company was quick.

On the shuttle to his car, Gannon checked his phone and laptop for messages.

None.

It was hot and humid as he headed to the car. Once he was behind the wheel of his Ford Focus, he cranked on the air conditioner, adjusted the mirrors and seat. Then he entered the Lufkin data into the car's GPS navigation system, grateful the airport was on the north side of the sprawling metropolis.

As a precaution, he studied his folding map. He was north of The Loop and Beltway 8 and needed 59. Lufkin was a two-hour drive. He rolled from the airport and in minutes was working his way north on one of the country's busiest freeways.

He turned on the radio for any news on Lufkin but nothing new came up. As he neared Livingston, his phone rang. He pulled over near an on-ramp, stopped on the shoulder and took the call.

"Gannon."

"Jack Gannon, from Buffalo?"

"Yes, who've I got?"

"Wes Coleman, World Press Alliance, Houston. New York told me to call. Where are you?"

"On 59, on my way to Lufkin. What's happening?"

"I'm in Lufkin at the property with a photographer. We've been here for hours. Police are tight-lipped. They set up, went in and are still searching the property. But we're getting the feeling that this is a huge goose egg. At least there's nothing here in Lufkin."

Gannon could hear impatience in Coleman's voice.

"Jack, do you have any other information to pass to us?"

"I've got exclusive background. Can we talk when I get there?"

"Nothing to pass to us now that we could get started on?"

Gannon hesitated, watching traffic stream by.

"Anything at all that we can act on, Jack?"

He'd worked too hard, sacrificed too much to give up everything.

"No," he said. "Nothing."

"Well, when you get to Lufkin, just ask at the perimeter to be directed to the command post. We'll hook up with you there."

After the call, Gannon entered new coordinates into the GPS.

He'd take a detour.

On his way to Lufkin, he would first visit the old Styebeck place near Huntsville, see if he could learn more from anyone who could remember the family. But his GPS beeped a refusal to accept Dead Tree Road, the address he'd taken from the old Texas property records.

GPS didn't recognize it.

The system would get him seven miles north of Huntsville to Pine Mill. All right, he'd go there then proceed the old-fashioned way by asking for directions.

At Livingston, he took 190 West, cutting through dense sections of East Texas forest for nearly an hour before he came to the outskirts northeast of Huntsville and Pine Mill.

Other than an old church, a boarded-up depression-era school and a few buildings scattered on either side of the empty road, there was no sign of life until he saw the TS Convenience Store & Gas Station.

Gannon stopped there.

The temperature was in the high nineties when he stepped from the rental. The porch creaked as he entered the store. Transom bells rang; the dog resting on the floor made the effort to lift its eyebrows. The old woman in a rocking chair behind the counter smiled with as much energy as the dog. The store's big windows were open. Wooden venetian blinds, with some slats missing, kept out most of the sun while letting in the weak breezes. Gannon got a bottle of Coke from the cooler, used the opener tied to the string to pry off the cap.

"How much?"

"That'll be one dollar, young fella. Where y'all from?"

"Buffalo, New York."

Gannon paid and took a long drink. The dog yawned, then yipped and the woman hushed it.

"A long way to come to buy a Coke."

"It is." He touched the sweating bottle to his forehead. "Could you help me out with some directions?"

"If it's within my means."

"I'm looking for the old Styebeck place on Dead Tree Road."

"Well you won't find Dead Tree Road on any map. Farm Road 299 is what you want. Keep going west another mile to the creek. Don't cross it. Turn right, and at the creek, that's Stevens Lane. Take it a mile, you'll see 299, go right again. It's the first place on your right. Almost like you was going in a box."

"Thanks." Gannon set his drink down to take notes.

"What's your interest?"

"I'm a reporter."

"A reporter?"

"I'm doing some historical research on the property and the Styebecks. Do you recall anything about them by chance?"

"I lived all my life around here, and as I remember it, the Styebecks were not much for mixing with people. Deke, the father, was a guard at The Walls, then lost his job some time after Kennedy was shot up in Dallas. The boys moved on. I think Karl went north and Orly moved to Nacogdoches, or Lufkin somewhere."

"What about the mother?"

"Belva? I don't know, heard she went into a home."

"And the property?"

"Got sold, but nobody did anything with it. A few years ago Orly started coming around here, to manage it, rent it or something, is what I heard. The Styebeck place has been for sale for ages. Nobody lives on it or goes there. Back in the 1800s they used to call it Vengeance Road."

"Why's that?"

"Story was a coldhearted banker moved out there after foreclosing on the farmer who'd owned it. Then one night, the farmer came out and burned the place to the ground while the banker and his family slept."

"Terrible."

After noting the history, Gannon took stock of the store. He didn't see a TV or hear a radio. He needed to know if other reporters had been by.

"One last thing. If anyone else were headed to the old farm, they'd have to pass by you here, right?"

"They would if they were coming from Huntsville, but there's been nobody. Now, if they were coming from the other way, say, south from Dallas, Midway or Cobb Creek, or west from College Park way, then no, I wouldn't see them."

"Thank you, you've been very helpful."

Gannon raised his empty bottle to her and set it on the counter. The old woman nodded.

Outside on the porch, he checked his phone, finding the signal was surprisingly strong. Still no messages. He looked around. Eerily quiet on all fronts. As he got in the car he wondered if he was missing the big story in Lufkin.

A mile from the store, he turned off the paved road onto Stevens Lane and soon came to Farm Road 299. Otherwise known as Vengeance Road. He shook his head at the name.

No wonder it hadn't sold.

He proceeded down the desolate stretch of gravel road. It cut through a dense forest for nearly a mile before he came to a weather-beaten For Sale sign. The contact phone number had faded away. Nailed to a tree was a warning: NO TRESPASSING, hand scrawled in letters that bled down the grayed wooden board.

No fence or gate secured the property.

The entrance was less of a road and more of an overgrown grassy pathway, almost invisible. It appeared to be freshly flattened, as if a vehicle had recently passed over it.

He cursed.

Had other reporters come in the other way and beat him on this part of the story, too?

He saw nothing. After parking at the side, under a tree, he started walking down the property. Tall grass and undergrowth slapped at his jeans. Birdsong and breezes rode the air, cooled by the natural canopy of the trees arching above.

As the lane ahead curved, a section of building emerged in the distance and he saw a ramshackle house bereft of life. Beyond it, there was a barn nearly consumed by the dense growth of shrubs that fingered their way through the aged gaping walls.

The sun flashed.

A tractor-trailer was half concealed in a thicket, its door turned enough to show him Swift Sword Trucking.

His pulse quickened.

The trailer's narrow side door was open.

Reflexively, he crouched and stepped to the side of the truck in the brush, moving forward alongside the trailer. He heard and saw nothing as he crept forward to the trailer's side inspection door.

Take it easy.

He glanced inside at the darkness.

It reeked.

Holding his breath, he found a step and pulled himself inside.

After several moments, his eyes adjusted to the lack of light and he surveyed the foul mattresses, buckets of human waste, stinking food wrappers, used and balled duct tape.

Something brownish-red was smeared on the floors and walls.

Was that blood?

A scream startled him.

He thrust his back to the wall of the truck. It sounded like a woman calling for help. It came from the house.

No, the barn!

He eyed the buildings and property for any movement but saw nothing.

It was the barn.

Something was going on in that barn.

He had to get to it so he could see inside.

Carefully he jumped from the truck and crawled under it to the woods, then gauged the perimeter of the property and the thick forest that would give him enough cover to make it to the barn unseen.

He took a deep breath and ran into the forest as fast as he could around the trees, crashing through the branches. After several minutes, he arrived at the edge of the barn. Breathless. He leaned against it, chest heaving, face sweating, nose running as he tried to calm himself to steal a glance through the window.

Just as he turned, his front pocket began ringing.

He'd forgotten to switch off his cell phone!

Seizing it, clasping his hand around it to choke the noise that had shattered the quiet, he rushed into the woods to take the call.

"Jack, this is Adell. Are you in Texas?"

"Adell! Listen!"

"They found nothing in Luf—"

"Adell, I know. Call the FBI now!"

"What?"

"I found him! I'm in Texas northeast of Huntsville. Write this down now! Northeast of Huntsville, Farm Road 299, the old Styebeck place."

"Are you safe?"

"Listen to me! Send somebody now—"

Gannon's cell phone flew from his hand as the back of his head exploded, hurling him into darkness.

"Jack? Jack…"

A snakeskin boot crushed Gannon's phone.

72

Jack Gannon could not move.

As he came to, he could not see.

The base of his skull pulsated with pain. An unyielding pressure encased his wrists, forearms, head, chest, legs and ankles.

Where was he? The broiling air was stale, smothering.... What happened? Go back...flying to Texas...missing the story in Lufkin...the old Styebeck place...the Swift Sword rig... a scream...

Gannon was restrained in a hard wooden high-backed chair.

His eyes flickered open to filmy, underwater vision. Spears of light penetrated the gaps of rickety walls.

He was in the barn where he'd heard the scream.

A large figure stood before him silhouetted against the dim light. Gannon's eyes adjusted first to snakeskin boots, jeans, a khaki western shirt that wrapped a muscular upper body and powerful arms.

Gannon's blood turned to ice.

This was Orly Styebeck. Karl's brother.

The air whipped and the back of a hand cracked across Gannon's jaw.

"I will ask you questions and you will answer with the truth."

The man's voice was deep.

He held up Gannon's wallet.

"You're that reporter, from Buffalo?"

"Yes."

The man spit.

"How did you find this place?"

"Researching the Styebeck family. Let me go. I'll leave. I'm sorry I trespass—"

The hand cracked again. Harder. Fireworks shot through Gannon's head and he tasted salty blood.

"Who were you talking to on your phone?"

"My friend in Buffalo."

"Who?"

"Her name's Adell. We're friends, that's all."

He held up Gannon's keys.

"Where'd you park your rental?"

"Back on the road near the sign."

Keys jingled. The man strode off, and now Gannon saw a woman staring at him less than ten feet away. Like him, she was bound to the same type of chair. Her face was gaunt, bruised.

Her eyes overflowed with terror.

He recognized her.

"Jolene Peller?"

She released a frail cry. "Yes."

Gannon inventoried their surroundings: a loft, a rusted old vehicle, some livestock stalls, a workbench with rusted tools, a large tarpaulin draped over stored objects.

Then he noticed new electric cables running from Jolene's chair to a metal box with a lever switch. He saw additional wiring running to his chair, and wiring going to what looked like a new, industrial-size generator. It was big, with several large fuel cans next to it.

Realization dawned on him.

They were strapped into electric chairs. The kind used for executing convicts. Deke Styebeck had been on the execution team. It all fit. Gannon battled in vain against his restraints.

"He's going to kill us," Jolene said.

At that point, Gannon saw the letters and read the words.

"It says GUILTY on your forehead," he said.

She released a keening cry then caught herself.

"It's how he marks the people he's going to kill," she said. "He marked you, too."

"We've got to get out of here."

Gannon's chair was older. Age had weakened the wood in some areas. He continued struggling, tried to lean forward, to stand. If he took steps to the wall, mashed the chair against it, he could fracture it or break it.

But the contraption was heavy.

He summoned all of his strength, but after several strained attempts he'd only succeeded in standing for an instant. The weight of the restraints and harness cut into him and forced him down. Besides, the chair was tethered by the cables.

It was hopeless.

The light diffused.

Orly Styebeck had returned and backhanded Gannon again.

"You and the whore have been judged!"

At that moment the air tensed with the hitch of a shotgun being pumped at a far doorway.

"It's over, Orly."

A man moved slowly from the light toward them.

"Karl?"

Orly Styebeck began to smile then dragged the back of his hand across his mouth.

"Is it really you?"

"Let them go and let me talk to Belva."

Orly stared long and hard at his brother, memories flooded back, but he damned them up.

"There's nothing you can say to her now, Karl. Nothing can make up for what you did to us."

"You have to know what Deke was. What we are. We've got to put an end to this, to everything!"

"Shut up!"

"We're cursed, Orly."

"You don't know what the hell you're sayin'! You left us. You ran and hid. And for what? To support whores like that one! To undo everything Deke ever done! Everything he fought his whole life for!"

"Let me talk to Belva. It all ends here. It's over."

"No! We can carry on together, Karl. You put a stop to your whoremongering and we can carry on with Deke's righteous work! It would make Belva happy."

"Let me talk to her."

Orly swallowed. Any hint of his misguided hope vanished in the chill of a decision he'd made.

"Fine, Karl." He walked to the tarpaulin and pulled it down. "Seein' you come all this way, you might as well talk to them both."

Jolene screamed.

Two upright coffins faced them. Their lids had been removed and replaced with a clear plastic top. Human remains pressed against them.

"Belva died last year after she wrote to you. First Daddy, then you left us. Then her. I was alone. It hurt me so bad I checked myself into Ranger. But know what, Karl? Belva called to me. Visited me in my room, told me to come get her, to resurrect her from the cold ground. So I got her. Then I got Deke, too. Brought them both back home here, where I come here to listen to them. They told me to get you to stop what you were doing and help me to carry on."

"You need help, Orly."

Karl turned to his brother, who had moved to the lever. He pressed a button and the big generator grumbled to life.

"Orly, no!"

"I HAVE SEEN THE GLORY!"

The shotgun blasted; buckshot ripped through Orly's shoulder before he could push the lever down to fully release the current. It tore through the switch box shredding the cables connecting the chairs to the generator, shutting it down. Sparks exploded throughout the tinder-dry barn, igniting scores of small fires, some near the chairs.

Jolene cried out.

Karl went to her chair as the fires spread.

Orly pulled himself bleeding from the floor and tried in vain to throw the damaged switch. It was futile, the connection was severed. The fires grew rapidly into larger ones, sucking oxygen from the barn as it filled with black choking smoke.

The temperature soared.

The unbearable heat was on the verge of blistering skin.

Coughing and gagging, Gannon tried to warn Karl Styebeck who was working to free Jolene, when Orly seized a shovel, raised it high then brought it down hard on Karl's head, sending him to the ground. Orly crawled, reaching for the gun, but collapsed.

Jolene screamed as the flames rose around them.

Gannon battled against his restraints until he lost consciousness.

73

Jolene Peller's screams blended with the sirens of the two patrol cars arriving at the building from the County Sheriff's Department.

Deputies Tim Crewson and Eddy Huck, both big former linemen, rushed into the burning barn. Guided by Jolene's cries, they found the chairs and dragged them, shredded cables and all, clear of the inferno.

"I think there are more people inside, Eddy!"

As Crewson and Huck started back, the fuel cans exploded. No way to enter. The building was gone. Fire trucks and emergency crews arrived, in response to the radio call Huck had made when he and Crewson had first spotted the smoke on their approach.

Paramedics treated Jolene and Gannon, then transported them to Huntsville Memorial. Their vital signs were good. They'd suffered trauma and some smoke inhalation but no burns.

Within hours, teams of FBI agents, local and state authorities, news vans and satellite trucks had converged on the neglected tract of land.

Helicopters and small planes roared overhead.

Yellow crime-scene tape went up around the property as live coverage and the Internet carried images of it to the world.

Two bodies were retrieved from the smoldering aftermath. While their identities had not been confirmed, police said the victims were thought to be Karl and Orion Styebeck.

However, investigators were puzzled by two sets of older, charred, skeletal remains found at the site. A fuller picture emerged after the FBI took statements from Gannon and Jolene Peller at Huntsville Memorial.

When they'd finished giving their statements, the staff let Gannon and Jolene have a private moment in Jolene's room.

"Thank you," she said from her bed when the door closed, "for finding me."

"Thank your mother. She's the one who asked me to help."

"Yes." Jolene smiled. "She just called and told me about that. And she put Cody on the line. I thought I'd never hear their voices again."

Jolene covered her face with her hands to catch her breath.

Then Jolene said that the Florida company that had hired her had arranged to pay all her expenses and fly her home to Buffalo to recover, before she started her job in Orlando.

"Excuse me, Mr. Gannon?"

A nurse at the door said he had a call that he could take at her desk.

"Jack! I've been trying to get through to the hospital," Adell Clark said. "Thank God! You're all right?"

"I'm all right," he said.

"I called the police. They patched me through to the sheriff."

"Your call saved Jolene Peller's life, and mine, too. Thank you."

"Want me to fly to Texas and come home with you?"

"No, I should be back tomorrow, or the next day."

Not long after Adell's call, Melody Lyon got through to Gannon at the hospital.

"You do get close to the story, Jack."

"Too close."

"I think I can make a case for hiring you, if you're interested?"

"I happen to be available."

"Good, but first we've got some things to take care of," she said.

Gannon gave the World Press Alliance his exclusive story. He spoke to a WPA feature writer in New York. He also sent them all of his notes and got a byline in an exclusive WPA multipart series called "Marked for Death," which would play across the U.S. and around the world.

In the days that followed, investigators found the buried remains of ten victims on the old Styebeck property. All were homicides arising from the cases of women missing from across the country.

In Buffalo, Alice Styebeck issued a statement that said her husband, Karl, was a good man who gave his life trying to stop his sick brother from hurting more people.

"And in the end that's what he did," she wrote. "He stopped a killer. I know my husband had some problems, but I hope people will remember him for the good man, good father and good husband he was."

After clearing the case, Michael Brent submitted his formal request to retire from the New York State Police. Then he sent an e-mail to Jack Gannon.

Bottom line, you're a helluva news reporter. Just keep chasing the truth, it's the best guide to doing the right thing. P.S. A friend with a federal agency says your former boss, Nate Fowler, will be indicted. Something to do with swindling and fraud. I thought you'd like to know.

In the time since he'd returned to Buffalo, Gannon took care of unfinished business. After visiting Adell Clark to thank her, he stopped by Mary Peller's apartment.

Jolene came to the door with Cody clinging to her leg, like he'd never let go. Some of her bruises had started to fade, but he wondered about the scars she'd carry for the rest of her days.

"Just wanted to see how you're doing," he said.

Boxes covered the floor; they were packing for Florida.

"We're going to be fine." Jolene smiled. "I'll take it one day at a time. How about you?"

He shrugged. "The same."

Gannon noticed her locket, the one he'd seen in the Wichita crime scene pictures.

"May I see?"

She opened it and showed it to him.

"Candace Rose, the detective in Kansas, arranged for the FBI to hand deliver it to me."

"Mr. Gannon!"

Mary Peller came down the hall, opened her arms and hugged him.

"You're my hero, Jack Gannon. I knew something about you was different the morning I met you in your newsroom. I saw it in your eyes. I said, if anybody's going to help me, this man will. Thank you!"

Gannon left, warmed by the sight of a small family reunited.

Then he glanced at the gift in the backseat of his Pontiac Vibe and drove downtown west of Main. He parked near the back of a small two-story frame house that was in need of paint. He knocked and heard movement inside. While he waited, he looked at the flower garden.

Bernice Hogan's foster mother, Catherine Field, answered the door, a question rising in her face until she recognized Gannon.

"Hello, Catherine."

"I saw it all on the news. I never expected to see you again."

Gannon passed her an envelope. She looked inside. It was a check for several hundred dollars. She looked at him.

"Bernice shouldn't be forgotten in all this," he said. "I was thinking maybe you could start a small scholarship in her memory at the school."

Catherine's eyes glistened.

"And I have this for you."

Gannon reached down for a planter with a sapling.

"It's an elm. For you to plant here." He nodded to her yard. "Or where Bernice is resting. It's sort of a symbol of hope."

She stared at him for several moments then her face crumpled. She covered it with a wrinkled hand.

"Thank you," she said.

A few days later, in Cheektowaga, in the neighbourhood of Cleveland Hill near where he grew up, Gannon carried one of the last boxes from his apartment to his Pontiac.

His cell phone rang.

"Jack, Ward Wallace at the *Sentinel.*"

"Congratulations on your promotion to managing editor, Ward. I'm betting not many people are grieving Nate's departure."

"Not many. Listen, I'm calling to offer you a job at the *Sentinel,* with a raise, and to let you know we'll make a formal front-page apology to you."

"Ward, I appreciate where this is coming from, but…"

"I know. I know you've accepted the WPA's offer. I talked to Melody. I was impressed that they were generous, paid all your bills on the story, gave you the big check for the exclusive series and the bonus. But we need a guy like you here and, well, I thought I'd give it a shot."

"It's not about the money, Ward, you know that."

"I do. This paper always got more from you than it gave."

Not long after Wallace's call, Gannon set the last box in the passenger seat. Before he turned the ignition he opened it to look at the contents and reached in for one item.

His father, mother, sister and a younger version of himself all smiled back from an old framed photograph.

The ghosts of his life.

He stared at Cora and heard her voice.

You're going to be a great writer someday. Lots of people are going to read your stories, Jackie. Wanna know how I know? Because you're so smart. I see it in your eyes. You don't let go. You don't give up.

Would he ever see her again? *Don't think about that now,* he told himself, dropping the picture onto the passenger seat.

He drove off, realizing that at last, at long last, he'd achieved everything he'd wanted his whole life. He was going to be working in Manhattan, reporting for a global wire service.

The world would be his beat.

His dream had come true.

But man, it came at such a terrible price, he thought, glancing at the photograph as Buffalo blurred in his rearview mirror.

* * * * *

ACKNOWLEDGMENTS

Thank you, Amy Moore-Benson

My thanks to the New York State Police.

Thank you to Valerie Gray, Dianne Moggy, Catherine Burke and the excellent editorial, marketing, sales and PR teams at MIRA Books. As always, I am indebted to Wendy Dudley. I also thank my friends in the news business for their help and support; in particular, Sheldon Alberts, Washington Bureau Chief for CanWest News Service, Glen Miller, Metro, Juliet Williams, Associated Press, Sacramento, California, Bruce DeSilva and Vinnee Tong, Associated Press, New York. Also Lou Clancy, Eric Dawson, Jamie Portman, Mike Gillespie, colleagues past and present with the *Calgary Herald, Ottawa Citizen,* CanWest News, Canadian Press, Reuters, the *Toronto Star, Globe and Mail* and so many others.

You know who you are.

Thanks to Ginnie Roeglin, Tod Jones, David Fuller, Steve Fisher, Lorelle Gilpin, Sue Knowles, David Wright and everyone at The C.C. I am grateful to Pennie Clark Ianniciello, Shana Rawers, Wendi Wambolt and Melissa McMeekin.

Very special thanks to Laura and Michael.

Again, I am indebted to sales representatives, booksellers and librarians for putting my work in your hands. Which brings me to you, the reader—the most critical part of the entire enterprise.

Thank you very much for your time, for without you, a book remains an untold tale. I hope you enjoyed the ride and will check out my earlier books while watching for my next one. I welcome your feedback. Drop by at www.rickmofina.com, subscribe to my newsletter and send me a note.

AUTHOR'S NOTE

I aimed to set this story against the backdrop of the real world. The family massacre on the prairie was loosely drawn from two actual tragedies that go back nearly half a century. Unrelated to those cases, I also drew upon my time as a reporter and memories of interviews with murderers. And there was the time I was taken through the execution protocol, step by step. But in crafting this story, I have taken great fictional liberties with geography, police jurisdiction, procedure and other aspects. I hope my creative mix of fact and fiction does not diminish your enjoyment of the tale.

Turn the page for an excerpt from
The Panic Zone,
the next novel in the Jack Gannon series by Rick Mofina.
Coming soon.

Big Cloud, Wyoming

Emma was about to tell Joe that she loved him, but the words never left her mouth. A sharp blast of their horn jolted her. Joe's expression switched to a surprised scowl.

"What! I don't believe this guy!"

An oncoming car had veered suddenly onto their side of the road, leaving them no escape from a head-on crash.

"Hang on, Em!"

Joe twisted the wheel, swerving to miss the collision.

"Joe!"

The SUV was airborne. With the world churning, glass breaking, metal crunching, sparks flew as it rolled and rolled before everything went black.

When Emma came to she was outside, beside their vehicle, facedown on the ground amid surreal chaos. Their horn was blaring. Tyler was screaming somewhere, but Emma couldn't see him.

She saw Joe.

He'd gone halfway through the windshield. His face was webbed with blood. Emma crawled to him, reached for him and took his hand.

"Stay with me, Joe. Don't leave me."

Emma could smell gas, burning rubber, could hear something hissing—she heard car doors, people shouting.

"Anyone got a cell phone! It's going to go up! Go get help!"

An engine raced.

"My baby, find my baby!"

Emma felt Joe's pulse slowing as people carried her away.

"Oh God, get my husband out! Find my baby!"

The air around them spasmed as if hammered by a huge invisible fist that brought the heat flash and fireball as the SUV ignited.

Joe was swallowed by the flames.

Tyler was not screaming anymore.

Emma was.

BL_203_TDH

A LONELY HIGHWAY. A MISSING GIRL. AND THE BIGGEST STORY OF HIS CAREER.

When Karen Harding ends up driving into one of the worst storms in years, she finds herself stranded on a desolate stretch of highway.

The next morning the police find her car, but Karen has vanished. For rookie reporter Jason Wade, it's the story he's been waiting for and he won't rest until he finds Karen – dead or alive…

www.mirabooks.co.uk